W9-ALM-158

ANN ARBOR DISTRICT LIBRARY

31621014503532

WITHDRAWN

THE FIRST ASSISTANT

Also by Clare Naylor & Mimi Hare

The Second Assistant

THE FIRST ASSISTANT

A Continuing Tale from
Behind the Hollywood Curtain

CLARE NAYLOR

&

MIMI HARE

Viking

VIKING
Published by the Penguin Group
Penguin Group (USA) Inc., 375 Hudson Street, New York, New York 10014, U.S.A.
Penguin Group (Canada), 90 Eglinton Avenue East, Suite 700, Toronto, Ontario, Canada
M4P 2Y3 (a division of Pearson Penguin Canada Inc.)
Penguin Books Ltd, 80 Strand, London WC2R 0RL, England
Penguin Ireland, 25 St. Stephen's Green, Dublin 2, Ireland (a division of Penguin Books Ltd)
Penguin Books Australia Ltd, 250 Camberwell Road, Camberwell, Victoria 3124, Australia
(a division of Pearson Australia Group Pty Ltd)
Penguin Books India Pvt Ltd, 11 Community Centre, Panchsheel Park, New Delhi – 110 017, India
Penguin Group (NZ), Cnr Airborne and Rosedale Roads, Albany, Auckland 1310, New Zealand
(a division of Pearson New Zealand Ltd)
Penguin Books (South Africa) (Pty) Ltd, 24 Sturdee Avenue, Rosebank, Johannesburg 2196,
South Africa

Penguin Books Ltd, Registered Offices:
80 Strand, London WC2R 0RL, England

First published in 2006 by Viking Penguin,
a member of Penguin Group (USA) Inc.

10 9 8 7 6 5 4 3 2 1

Copyright © Clare Naylor and Mimi Hare, 2006
All rights reserved

Publisher's Note
This is a work of fiction. Names, characters, places, and incidents either are the product of the
authors' imagination or are used fictitiously, and any resemblance to actual persons, living or
dead, business establishments, events, or locales is entirely coincidental.

ISBN 0-670-03497-5

Printed in the United States of America
Set in Fairfield Light
Designed by Spring Hoteling

Without limiting the rights under copyright reserved above, no part of this publication may be
reproduced, stored in, or introduced into a retrieval system, or transmitted, in any form or by any
means (electronic, mechanical, photocopying, recording, or otherwise), without the prior written
permission of both the copyright owner and the above publisher of this book.

The scanning, uploading, and distribution of this book via the Internet or via any other means
without the permission of the publisher is illegal and punishable by law. Please purchase only
authorized electronic editions and do not participate in or encourage electronic piracy of copy-
rightable materials. Your support of the authors' rights is appreciated.

THE FIRST ASSISTANT

PROLOGUE

I have just stepped out of the limo to my boyfriend's movie premiere and I'm the happiest girl in Los Angeles. I am an impeccable fifteen minutes late and have arranged to meet him inside the theater. He has been on location in Prague. We haven't seen each other for a month. I am wearing a black Azzaro cocktail dress. It's the first time in my life I know what it means to feel like a million dollars. I manage my vehicular exit without a face-plant and when the driver closes the door behind me I see only the dazzling flashbulbs of the paparazzi ahead.

"Hey, Lizzie, over here!" I hear someone cry out. It doesn't sound like Luke. I look around and within seconds the call has escalated to a chorus of "Lizzie"'s. It is the first time that the paparazzi, who always huddle by the door on these occasions, have known who I am. I wonder *how* they know who I am, too. Strangely it never crosses my mind to ask myself that one truly critical question, "Who am I, anyway?" If I had I would have remembered that I am Lizzie Miller, efficient, but not to the point of fame, first assistant to the head of a Hollywood agency. I have never won a talent show on national television. I am not famed for my inimitable way with Balenciaga and I was never the fiancée of Jude Law. There is no other conceivable reason why anyone would want to gaze at me in *US Weekly* as they wait for a fat transfer injection in their dermatologist's office.

Unfortunately when fame beckons my ego picks up the hem of its evening dress and runs headlong to meet it like a long-lost lover way before my brain can pitch in and warn me what a hiding to nothing even minor, piffling celebrity is.

"Give us a smile, Lizzie!" they call out again. So I take a deep breath and saunter up to the sidewalk in front of the metal railings that they use to separate the hunters from their prey. Now let me tell you something, if you've never seen an actress stand on the carpet and pose for the paparazzi you haven't lived. The whole thing is hysterical. The glossy photos we get to see are no happy accident. They are the result of a ludicrous and humiliating process that no sane person would be party to. The first time I ever saw an actress posing for the cameras at a premiere I was morbidly horrified. She was a beautiful, English rose of a starlet one minute and the next she looked as if she'd caught sight of Medusa and been turned to stone. Either that or her Botox had just kicked in. She was petrified into such a ridiculous pout for such an appallingly long time that it looked as if she might not blink again before the movie, or perhaps the millennium, was over. It was the first time in my life that I was glad I didn't have skin the color of morning milk and a twelve-million-dollar paycheck.

Only now, for the first time ever, it's my turn. I resolve to just give a couple of discreet smiles, possibly verging on the coquettish if I can bring myself to abandon my inhibitions to such a degree, then be on my way. I pull my dress out of my undies where it has lodged on the car ride and launch myself toward the waiting photographers.

"Come on, baby, give us a smile!" they call out. So I do. I stand on the sidewalk in front of them and begin to pose. And actually I might even trade places with the morning-milk skin chick after all because it is all terribly easy. I just pretend that I'm home in front of the mirror and replicate some *InStyle* favorite poses: the Happy Hostess on Prozac look; the Bored Ingénue after a big night; the Nymph in Raptures. I am actually quite enjoying myself until I am roused from the haze of my narcissism by one of the photographers yelling, "Hey you!" I open my eyes and see, not a hoard of adoring males, but a pack of irritated wolves who've just had their supper snatched away.

"Yes, you! Move out of the way!" I am confused for a fraction of a second until I hear a woman's voice behind me.

"How do you want me, boys?" she coos. I turn around and am confronted by the laudable cleavage of Lindsay Lohan.

"Lindsay, you're a doll!" yells the same photographer who'd just told me to stop ruining his picture. They hadn't been calling for Lizzie. They'd been calling for Lindsay.

I quickly scuttle inside the entrance to the theater and out of the way of a pro in action. The flashbulbs explode and Lindsay (who, along with everyone else, is wearing jeans and flip-flops; I appear to be the only person in a crystal-encrusted, floor-length evening gown) does her thing while I skulk in the doorway and contemplate my humiliation. I pause as my blush subsides and reassure myself that the foyer looks blessedly empty so at least the other two thousand people who've been invited to the premiere haven't witnessed my crazed ego getting the better of me.

Or so I delude myself until I walk into the buzzing theater in search of my seat and boyfriend. As I step through the double doors the whole place goes quiet. Heads turn in my direction and, thinking myself sensible in the extreme, I obligingly step out of the way, sure in the knowledge that Ms. Lohan can only be a few paces behind me again and everyone wants to check her out. But this time there's no Lindsay behind me. Then I understand why—on the giant screen ahead, magnified to Olympian proportions, is Lindsay Lohan, still pouting and giggling for the photographers outside. As is traditional at premieres, they film the arrivals on the red carpet and show them on-screen to the waiting audience. It takes me approximately four seconds to understand that every last person in this theater has just witnessed my big "moment" on the red carpet.

ONE

In Hollywood the women are
all peaches. It makes you long
for an apple occasionally.

—Rex Reed

This morning my boyfriend, Luke Lloyd, called from location in Prague and told me that he loved me because I was normal. By this I know he means simply that I'm what he's dreamed of since he arrived in Hollywood fifteen years ago. I'm the kind of girl who can read the newspapers on a Sunday morning without throwing a hissy fit if I'm not *in* them; I do not have a "relationship with food"; I know the difference between G8 and a G4; and while that may not be asking too much of the rest of the world's population, in this town it makes me as scarce as hen's teeth.

However there are many, more disturbing, reasons why I am *not* normal that I do not wish my boyfriend to find out about. They are:

> 1. In my wallet I have a platinum Amex card that does not belong to me. By that I mean it was given to me by my boyfriend to use as profligately as I choose. But despite spending my entire life dreaming of such a thing, thus far I haven't even bought a tank of gas on it.

> 2. I could have given up my meaningless job as First Assistant (aka slave who enables her boss in his forays into drink, drugs, pornography, and cheating on his wife, who happens to be one of my best friends) and gone to Prague for three months to keep my freckly,

doormat-haired producer boyfriend company (aka out of the foul clutches of his ex-girlfriend Emanuelle, who is playing the lead in his latest epic *Dracula's Daughter*). But I didn't. I pretended to him that I was contractually bound by The Agency to stay.

3. I cannot afford toilet paper for the house I live in so I have to steal it from the bathrooms at The Agency and various restaurants across town. This is because I have spent the equivalent of three paychecks on one dress.

4. I have enrolled with a tennis coach who helps you to come to terms with the shadows of your personality. If you can master your backhand you can conquer your emotional demons. Tennis skills and mental health are one. And I happen to believe this to be true.

5. I am addicted to a Japanese number puzzle called Su Doku. I have an entire book of these puzzles and hide them beneath the *Hollywood Reporter* on my desk. Last week I destroyed a month's worth of filing that I'd neglected to do because of said addiction. It can only be a matter of time before I am found out.

And while Luke was away in Prague, freezing his ass off on some god-forsaken, formerly Communist street corner, I was safe. He could harbor his delusions with me as the normal girl he loved back in Los Angeles— keeping his bed warm and his dreams intact. But since he touched down at LAX three hours ago for the premiere, it's become increasingly likely that my whole house of cards is going to come crashing down.

"I can't believe you didn't tell me," I said to Luke as I glared furiously out the car window on the way home.

"I'm sorry, but I didn't know she was coming until the last minute." His exasperation was palpable; he nearly drove us over the side of a canyon as we took a curve. The evening had gone from bad to worse when, post red-carpet humiliation, I finally climbed over an entire row of seated, unhelpful people to reach my beloved boyfriend, only to discover that his ex-girlfriend Emanuelle Saix (pronounced Sex in some parts of France, apparently) was sitting in my seat. She then insisted on giving me three kisses and commiserated with me about my on-screen humiliation. Did I mention that she'd been the face of Lancôme since she was thirteen years old? Why he had finally dumped her for me was a matter for Luke and his psychotherapist.

"And she was supercilious," I informed him.

"She felt bad for you."

"Then, at the party. Your business partner mistook me for a Russian prostitute and offered to pay me two hundred dollars cash."

"That's because you looked so gorgeous." Luke's attempts at appeasement were less convincing than they had first been half an hour ago when we left the post-premiere party. I rolled down the window for some air as we drove up the hill toward home. The car filled with the scent of sagebrush and distant skunk. I tried to calm down because I knew that if we had a massive fight tonight when he was leaving for Prague again tomorrow I'd spend every minute of the next six weeks till I saw him again regretting it. But the humiliation was too raw to bury just yet.

"You could have told me that the dress code was casual, though."

"I had no clue. Didn't my assistant send you an invite?" He scowled.

"I told her to save the trees. Those things come with so much cardboard." I lamented my respect for the environment almost as much as I regretted being the only woman there who was dressed like an Eastern European hooker. "Did I look completely ridiculous walking down the red carpet in a floor-length black dress?" I grinned.

"You didn't walk, baby, you sashayed." A slow grin spread across Luke's face.

"I did *not*. I wouldn't know how to sashay if I tried." His amusement was contagious. I began to see the funny side.

"Did I look completely ridiculous in front of the cameras?" I ventured.

"You looked like you'd been practicing."

"Oh God."

"But it wasn't so much the dress. Or the paparazzi. It was more, well it was more the limo."

"Ah yes, the limo." Everyone else had arrived in a vast, black SUV. I had unwittingly gone retro apparently.

"It was very classy."

"It cost me a fortune. Well, it cost Scott a fortune. I expensed it."

"Oh shit." Luke laughed as the gravel of our driveway crunched under the wheels, signaling home. "Well, it's good to be back."

"Good to have you home." I leaned over and kissed him. Though it'd been six months since I moved out of my one-room apartment in Santa Monica, I still hadn't really lived with him for more nights than I would if we'd been having a torrid affair. Which made it all the more exciting as we shrugged off our seat belts and hastened toward the house.

"How come the security lights aren't on?" Luke asked as he stubbed his toe on a surprise step.

"Brownout?" I guessed, grabbing the back of his sweater so I wouldn't stumble in the dark.

"Can't be. Every house in the canyon's lit up like a Christmas tree."

"Hmmm." At this stage it hadn't even occurred to me that I might have something to feel guilty about. So I remained blithely curious.

"Maybe it's a burglar. Do you have that Mace I bought for you on your key ring?" Luke asked.

"No. I kept having bad dreams about it accidentally going off in Ralphs in the checkout girl's face. So I left it by the bed."

"It's probably a burglar armed with your Mace, then." Luke stopped abruptly. "I'll go in first."

"But what if he escapes and kills me on the way out?" I asked nervously. "I'll come in with you. Here, let's take a brick." I picked up a stone from the rockery and handed it to Luke.

"I have a gun in the car. Wait here."

"You have a gun?" I was stunned. What was my boyfriend doing with a gun? "Are you a member of the NRA?"

"Honey, I'm from the South. I've always carried a gun. Now will you just quiet down and let me deal with this?" Luke marched back to the car while I sat down on the garden steps and tried to come to terms with the fact that I may be dating a Republican. He returned from the car, presumably with the weapon concealed about his person.

"Have we never discussed my issues with bearing arms?" I asked, like the impassioned student of politics that I used to be before I arrived in the moral vortex that is Tinseltown.

"Would you stop being so goddamn earnest and help me out here? We may have a burglar, okay? So just let me deal with it."

Now despite my fears for the future of my mixed-politics relationship, I recognized that maybe I should do just that. So I followed Luke's shadow closely as he stole toward the house with his hand on his gun. But no sooner had it dawned on me that we really could be facing a life-threatening situation, vis-à-vis the burglar, than I realized what I'd done.

"Luke." I stopped still as his shadow tiptoed on without me.

"Sssshhhh," he whispered. "I think I heard something."

"You didn't, actually." I grimaced apologetically, still in an habitual whisper.

"What?" he asked distractedly as he slowly moved his face toward the kitchen window to see if he could glimpse our intruder.

"We haven't got a burglar. I forgot to pay the electricity bill," I confessed at normal volume. Luke turned to me with a look of relief, rapidly replaced by one of bewilderment.

"Oh honey, you didn't?" He wanted to be pissed off, but he knew he couldn't be. He laughed as he put his arm around me. "So I guess we have to check into the Four Seasons, then. Or was that your plan all along?"

Yes, I know, this kind of talk would be manna to the soul of most girls, but since I'd started dating a rich man it had become somewhat of an issue for me. Like every other woman on the planet, I'd always assumed that it would be great to be with a rich man, and even more fabulous to be with a man you were madly in love with who also happened to be able to afford to check into the Four Seasons every time you had a power outage. But to my irritation I found it didn't work like that.

When I met Luke I was on the bottom-most rung of the Hollywood ladder. Some sort of single-celled algae in the pond. My boyfriend was a dolphin, a high-flying, AAA producer. But even though my life was a torment down there with the sea cucumbers, I had clawed my way to a promotion. I was now First Assistant to Scott Wagner, who had miraculously pulled off a coup that only Beelzebub could have shed light upon, and become president of The Agency, the town's most illustrious percentery. And I was actually proud of what I had achieved. I mean, I was well aware that the world wasn't a better place because of my endeavors, but I was just biding my time until I made interesting, entertaining, or important movies that would delight the world. I wanted to produce movies, to prove myself.

What I didn't want, which would be so easy right now, with Luke and his beautiful house and expense account on hand to rescue me like the Julia Roberts character in *Pretty Woman,* was to give up my career and spend the rest of my life having lunch and taking Pilates classes. Because as divine as that may sound when you've spilled coffee all over the letters you just printed up and scalded yourself because your boss crept up and screamed in your ear that you'd forgotten to book him a hotel room in Cannes and now he'll have to sleep on Leo's floor at the du Cap, in your heart you know that being a kept woman is never going to make you happy.

"No, Luke, that wasn't my plan. In fact it's the opposite. Do you know why I haven't paid the electricity bill?" I suddenly felt the damp night air grip me.

"Because you've been busy and you forgot?" Luke asked, clearly a bit pissed that the idea of fluffy robes and breakfast in bed at the Four Seasons hadn't propelled me into paroxysms of ecstacy.

"No, because I didn't have any money."

"But you had my credit card. Why didn't you just—"

"I couldn't. I'm sorry. It just felt too weird using someone else's card. Especially when you don't really know me very well and—"

"Honey, what the fuck are you talking about?" Luke was now totally pissed.

"I like my job. I know to you it might seem pointless and menial, but it's a stepping stone." I sat down on the porch. I'd been needing to say this for a while and now that I'd turned on the tap there was no stopping me. Luke's face began to twitch. He'd just gotten off a twelve-hour flight and here I was, unleashing six months' worth of neuroses on him.

"Right. Well, I'm glad you like your job," he said in a tone that suggested he couldn't give a rat's ass right now. "But I fail to see what that has to do with getting into a hot bath together at the Four Seasons."

"I won't be a trophy girlfriend, Luke. I just won't." And the way he looked at me I knew he was thinking that I shouldn't worry because even in a four-thousand-dollar dress I was unlikely to make the grade. Or maybe I was just being paranoid. Maybe he was just thinking that if he wanted "normal," he should have gone out with Courtney Love.

"Right," he said matter of factly. "Well, why don't I go to the Four Seasons, you can sleep in your car with a newspaper for a blanket, and when I get back to Prague tomorrow afternoon, you can write and tell me how cheap and degraded it makes you feel when I pay my own electricity bill."

"That's not what I mean." I looked at him and wondered if I'd successfully alienated him yet or whether I'd have to strangle a pet before I convinced him of my burgeoning insanity.

"I just want to make it on my own. I don't want people to think that I'm going out with a powerful man to further my career. Or even worse"—my eyes must have been wide with the horror of my fate at this point because Luke took a step backward as if in fear—"that I'm with you because I don't *want* a career. I don't want to be like the shoe-buying fembots in Saks. I don't want to have lips like a fish. I want to be successful in my own right. Even if I only ever make it to a junior agent. I just want to prove myself."

"Oh, honey, you've more than proved yourself," Luke said ambiguously. And I held my breath, wondering if subconsciously I wanted to end this relationship because I didn't feel worthy of his love or something. I'd have to ask Zac, my soon-to-be tennis coach when I could afford a lesson. I couldn't read his look.

"You don't think I'm normal anymore, do you?" I asked, which translated meant, "You don't love me anymore, do you?"

"No. I don't," Luke said, and tossed his car keys thoughtfully in his hand.

"You think I'm a hellish freak and you're afraid that you ever gave me keys to your house let alone your credit card and you're wishing that you could shoot me and bury me under the patio and go out with Emanuelle again. Aren't you?" I said.

"No." Luke shook his head. "No, I'm not."

"Well, I wouldn't blame you." I paused for thought. "What then? What are you thinking?" I stood up as a challenge to him to tell me the terrible truth, now that I'd shattered his illusions and proved that I wasn't the nice, girl-next-door type he'd imagined me to be. Now that my cover was blown.

"I was just wondering what fish lips are. And I was thinking that they might be kind of interesting. . . ." He shrugged. "You know what I mean?"

I looked at him.

"I'm having a dark night of the soul and you're wondering what it would be like to get a blow job from a woman with trout pout?" I shouted loudly enough to entertain the whole Canyon.

"Yeah, I guess," Luke said, and headed for the car. "So do you want to be a kept woman for one more night, before I cut up your credit card, make sure never to slip up and pay for dinner again, and take back the diamond ring I bought you from Harry Winston?" He didn't look back.

"I'm so sorry, Luke, I didn't mean it to come out like that, but I just had to tell you how I feel, and if you still want to pay for dinner then that's great, but sometimes you have to come to Koo Koo Roo on me. And . . ." I stopped. "You were kidding about Harry Winston, right?" I double-checked. Having a boyfriend with a sense of humor was usually something you'd give eye teeth for in this town, but right now it just exacerbated my dilemma.

"Maybe," Luke said as he held open the car door for me. I ducked under his arm and got in.

"You were?"

"Like I said, maybe." He shut the door and strolled around to the driver's side.

"You were joking," I decided.

"Honey, I'm completely in love with you so as far as I'm concerned, whatever you want you get. And if you don't want diamonds and fancy schmancy stuff then I respect that."

"Why do you keep talking about diamonds?" I asked.

"Because, like I said, I have one in my pocket. But you don't want to be a trophy girlfriend, so I'm taking it back."

"You do not." I laughed nervously.

"Do too," he sung as we drove down the hill toward the Four Seasons.

"Show me then," I challenged him.

"No point now." He smiled with equanimous aplomb.

"Of course there's a point." I laughed sweetly, better to trap him with honey. "Were you really going to?"

"Yup," Luke said, as if nothing could matter less now. "I was going to propose to you with it. In the garden tonight. But your electricity protest kind of made that impossible. So I thought, aha, Four Seasons. Then you said you didn't want to be a kept woman. So I thought, okay, we'll drive down to the ocean. And then you hit me with your fear of having fancy stuff bought for you . . . so I guess I'll have to take it back." Luke shrugged, not moderating his usual, easy-going manner.

"You wanted to marry me?"

"Yeah, I did." He kept on driving, nodding at the road.

"But . . ."

"You probably have moral objections to diamonds, too. I should have thought of that. And you were right. I was only thinking about what was conventionally romantic and not what you, Lizzie Miller, might like. So why don't we wait awhile and I'll think a little harder about it . . . you know? I'll return the diamond, buy an American Indian–friendly aquamarine ring or something. Propose at Souplantation. If you can forgive me for being such a selfish pig, of course." Obviously nobody had ever told him that sarcasm was the lowest form of wit. Because he thought he was being hilarious.

I decided that this was simply a brilliantly twisted fabrication designed to punish. But I was smarter than that. I would not rise. I would not give him the satisfaction of watching me humiliate myself by begging for a ring that didn't exist. Instead I took the high road. I let it go, acting like even if he had the Hope diamond in his pocket, I wouldn't be interested. And I obviously did a very good job because he dropped the subject immediately and turned up the radio.

Later, at the Four Seasons, while Luke was brushing his teeth, I just happened to pick his jeans up from the floor and just happened to notice an unnaturally large lump in the pocket.

"Are you coming to bed, sweetheart?" I called out, just to make sure he was still foaming at the mouth in there.

"Shhhure," he spluttered. Which I knew gave me at least enough time to delve into his pockets. Which I did shamelessly. And what did I find? The biggest, most sparkling, perfect ring I'd ever seen in my life.

Well, it wasn't the biggest I'd ever seen, really, but it was the most perfect. For me. Because I'm not the amazing, moral, unmaterialistic, sweet girl that Luke took me for tonight when he vowed to return my ring to Harry Winston. And as I gazed at it I didn't think it was vulgar or immoral or anything of the kind. And as it twinkled at me from its navy blue velvet box, I knew that I wanted that ring on my finger so badly I could have cried. Which I suppose proves one thing, anyway—that, as girlfriends go—I am completely normal.

TWO

It's somehow symbolic of
Hollywood that Tara was
just a façade with no rooms inside.

—David Selznick

"Hi there. Do you want to take off my undies?" I arrived at work the next morning in no mood to hear Scott being propositioned by an actress through the office walls. By eight o'clock this morning when I left the Four Seasons, Luke still hadn't proposed to me, and now he'd gone back to Prague for another six-week spell. Naturally I had managed to convince myself that the "Harry," as I'd come to know the diamond, was now destined for the more delicate, less agriculturally-capable-looking third finger of Emanuelle's left hand.

"Who's Scott got in his office?" I asked Amber as I took off my jacket.

"I don't know. But I've been here since seven and he hasn't emerged," she said smugly, just to let me know how much earlier than me she'd gotten in.

I rolled my eyes. Amber was Scott's new Second Assistant, whom I'd painstakingly hired to be fabulous at all the things I was no good at, so that between us we might be a perfect team and best serve our mutual boss. However, what I hadn't realized was that the word "team" was not in Amber's vocabulary. In fact, her job advertisement should have read:

> WANTED
> Self-involved, scheming, malevolent Judas for junior position at talent agency. No morals needed. Must have an unhealthy interest in rich and powerful men and a desire to succeed at any cost.

Lara, Scott's former First Assistant and now his Second Wife, had pleaded with me not to hire anyone truly beautiful to work alongside her weak-willed husband. Because although she and I both knew that he loved her and their new baby, Lachlan, to the ends of the earth, when something was offered to Scott on a plate, he invariably wanted a nibble.

So I'd assumed that Amber Bingham-Fox was a safe bet. She had a history degree from Cambridge, was fluent in French, and was as plain as it is possible to be. In fact when Lara quizzed me about her looks after I'd interviewed her, I could hardly remember.

"I don't know. Her hair was brown, she had eyes, a nose, lips, I assume, but whether they were thin or luscious I have no clue."

"Does she have a good body?" Lara had asked with the desperation of a woman who has gained sixty pounds with the birth of her baby and now did little but bob in the pool all day in order to avoid contact with the cookie jar.

"I don't know. She just is . . ."

"Is what?" Lara persisted.

"Is. She just is. She's plain. What can I say? She wears okay clothes. She may have some freckles. But if she does that's as interesting as it gets," I reassured Lara.

"You promise?"

"I swear to God." And I was telling the truth to Lara. Amber seemed to be the most innocuous girl I'd ever met. With all that modesty and reserve and self-deprecation that Jane Austen led us to expect from English chicks. But neither I nor Lara nor Jane Austen could have anticipated what a complete piece of work Amber Bingham-Fox would turn out to be. Her plainness made her unthreatening to women in power, whom she befriended as if they were going out of fashion; it made her tantalizing to men in some perverse way.

Lara's theory was that if a girl as plain as Amber acted in the overtly sexual way she did—i.e., forever discussing her threesomes and bikini waxes with them—then she had to be a rocket in the sack. And everyone but everyone mistook her English accent for class. Except Lara, who thought it just sounded like she was continually sucking someone's cock. Either way Amber was not the girl you want sitting six feet away from you all day long, gasping to get her hands on your job, your best friend's husband, and your previously well-hidden Su Doku secret.

"Where's the letter from Tom Cruise's attorney of the fifteenth of May?" she asked as I turned on my computer.

"In the file," I said confidently, wondering whether I'd burned it last week when the filing had all become too much for me. The choice had not been hard—either trip over the pile of filing every time I leave my desk for the rest of eternity or burn it all on a small office pyre and instead enjoy a Fiendish Su Doku before I left the office for the day.

"No it's not," she said briskly, as if she were on to me but just biding her time before she worked out how she could best ruin my career with the information. Thankfully we were interrupted by the woman in Scott's office again.

"How would you like me, baby?" she asked.

"Poor Lara." Amber sighed without a hint of sincerity, as she continued to hunt through the files for the probably-charred letter.

"Poor Lara's fine." I felt compelled to defend my friend. "He loves her madly. He just has a problem with addiction. That woman in there's no more to him than a game of blackjack or a line of coke."

"It wouldn't work for me, that's all I'm saying," Amber snapped.

I was dying to ask what *did* work for Amber. Lara and I had become obsessed by the girl's sex life after hearing that she was simultaneously dating the heads of two major studios and a married actor. She had also been written about on Defamer after a naked-in-a-hot-tub-at-Sundance escapade with an unidentified TV actress and a producer so antiquated he had passed from "legendary" to "immortal" in the Hollywood lexicon. Clearly Amber was prepared to do whatever it took to pole-vault her way up the echelons. But in true snake-in-the-grass tradition she played her cards very close to her chest. She had also befriended Katherine Watson, the copresident of The Agency, by asking her to mentor her. They now had a regular Wednesday-afternoon-in-Barney's-shoe-department date. Their friendship was a thorn in my side—with Amber knowing exactly when to play the fawning acolyte and admire Katherine's "extraordinary figure for Hermes" and when to drop in some tale from the Cambridge debating society to remind Katherine that she was also a viable companion for an intellectual woman of power. God, I was envious. Why didn't I have the nerve or the nous to foster such a friendship? But before I could ponder that question I was dealt a swift, brutal reminder.

"That was Emerald Everhart on the phone." Scott emerged from his office with ruffled hair and the unslept look that I knew so well, and that invariably preceded the arrival of a furious and half-dressed Lara in the office demanding to know where he'd spent the night. Usually Lachlan was slung under one arm and a brown bag from McDonald's under the other. Lara's reaction to motherhood was to eat all the food she'd deprived herself of since she was eighteen years old and first begun dieting. Sometimes she tried to eat it all in one afternoon. But Scott seemed to like her curves, and she'd forgotten how much she liked French fries. So for the time being everyone was happy. Fortunately neither Lara nor the actress from his office had made an appearance yet. They were probably waiting for the same moment.

"And?" I said to Scott. Emerald Everhart called an average of eight times a day. It didn't usually warrant Scott having to leave his desk.

"She wants to borrow you." He shrugged.

"Me?" I didn't think that Emerald Everhart was aware of my existence, though I had patched her through to Scott more times than I'd had hot coffees since she joined The Agency a few months ago in one of Scott's first big signings as copresident.

Emerald was the new teen starlet in town. You know her: she's the cheesy little comet on the cover of *US Weekly* every week while she's orbiting the celestial galaxy at the speed of light until she loses her baby fat, develops a relationship with food, and her star burns up and she vanishes, leaving room for another Tara or Lindsay or Britney. She's gum-chewing, mentally unstable, and has the unerring ability to make all the haute couture garments she borrows look like Juicy Couture. She was born with her dark roots showing. Men love her because she looks like she'd fuck you in the bathroom right after she's met you, and she has such an impact on the dance routines and vocabulary of eight-year-old girls that their parents want to move to Pennsylvania and become Amish.

Then I remembered my only other encounter with Emerald. Last week she'd dropped by to see Scott and was fretting over a text message she was writing to a guy she was dating.

"How do you spell 'absolutely'?" she'd asked me as she passed my desk.

"A.B.S.—" I had barely begun when her hot pink cell phone was thrust into my hand.

"Here, you do it," she said. So I began to repair her "asbolutely." "It's to this guy. He's been really mean to me but I really don't care because he has such a great look and I really want to fuck him so badly that—"

"Then you asbolutely can't write this." I smiled at her.

"What?" she had asked, alarmed that I had an opinion, let alone that I had the courage/stupidity to express it to her.

"You can't tell him that you want to do all these things. You'll never see him again." I scowled. I wasn't usually so frank, but I'd just gotten back from lunch with Lara and her plain-speaking was infectious.

"I can't?" Emerald had transformed from a knowing starlet into an ingenuous teenager.

"Let's try this," I said as I tapped a much more curt, ambiguous message to the mean date. And sure enough, before she'd left the building Emerald had a text back inviting her to the Solomon Islands for the weekend.

"What do you mean, borrow me?" I was always civil to Scott, but our relationship had long since progressed beyond the needlessly polite. I was friends with his wife—he ignored me when I was visiting and he came home and found me crying in his sitting room or playing with his baby in his swimming pool—I was part of the furniture, and if I was too nice to him he would simply be suspicious. I did my job, he took me for granted. It was a functional relationship.

"She wants to take you to Thailand with her on location," he informed me as he flipped through his call sheet on Amber's desk. "Nice call sheet, Amber. Why can't your call sheets look like this, Lizzie?"

"And you told her no. Right?"

"No, I told her I'd think about it." Scott gave Amber one of his winning smiles; she flashed one back. It was like watching a dental floss commercial. "We could manage without you for three months, couldn't we, Amber?"

"Yeah, I think we could." Amber grinned. "We'd get by."

"Well, you won't have to, I'm not going," I said charmlessly and returned to my e-mailing.

"Emerald Everhart usually gets what she wants, you know," Amber reminded me midafternoon when I was busy looking up naked photos of Emanuelle Saix online so I could further torture myself after my bitter night with Luke.

"Well, Emerald Everhart hasn't crossed swords with *me* yet," I said unconvincingly. Amber didn't dignify my comment with a response. She simply clacked away on her keyboard eagerly. I was convinced that nobody could work as hard as Amber seemed to and sometimes sent myself on false missions to the bathroom or mailroom only to return a minute later in a bid to catch her slacking off and calling a friend: maybe telling them about the fabulous blow job she'd given Studio Head #1 last night. But so far the worst I'd caught her doing was sitting on the corner of Scott's desk telling him that he would never need Rogaine because he was blessed with a full head of hair. She was such a kiss-ass I wanted to kill her.

"Oh, hi Emerald, I'll put you through. I know. But have you tried bribing him? You know, offering him something that he wants?" Amber was saying when I came back from a legitimate trip to the bathroom. "It's worth a try." She laughed. "Okay, I'll just put you through."

"What was that?" I asked when Amber hung up with Emerald.

"Oh, just Emerald," she said and snapped shut like the clamshell she was.

"You were telling her to bribe him." I stood defiantly looking down on her desk. Damn it, did being First Assistant count for nothing these days?

"Just making a friendly suggestion to one of our more important clients." She managed to maintain her psychotic typing speed.

"I'm not going to Thailand," I said petulantly.

"I hear the brothels are great." She smiled enigmatically.

I returned to my desk and decided that I had to book a lesson with Zac the tennis coach/shrink no matter whether I could afford it or not. Perhaps I'd even book a package of six and put them on Luke's credit card. After all, I wasn't exactly getting bonus points for being a selfless, unmaterialistic, self-supporting martyr, was I? I was just becoming more churlish, heading for singledom, and was probably about to be re-placed in my job by someone I'd hired. There had to be a better way. And if Zac could help me with my backhand, I'd be sure to find that higher path.

"Fucking fantastic. Fan-fucking-tastic." Scott swung out of his office like an enthusiastic Tarzan-o-gram.

"Score a deal?" I asked in my new unchurlish way.

"Did I fucking ever!" Scott came and high-fived me. "What a juicy score, baby!"

"Five-picture deal?" I smiled.

"1955 Mercedes-Benz 300SL Gullwing in fire-engine red."

"A car?"

"With red leather seats." Scott was apoplectic. He kept punching pieces of furniture and the air. Amber remained beatific.

"For Emerald?" I squinted at him.

"For me." He grinned.

"Great. Lucky you." I was about to return to my work. Doubtless Lara would put paid to the dream car when she heard about it.

"And I have you to thank." Scott spilled his upper body over my desk and gave me a clumsy hug.

"Me?" I mumbled through a mouthful of yesterday's shirt.

"Em loves you. She thinks you're indispensable to her life, so I'm swapping you for the Gullwing." He beamed.

"You're what?" I pushed Scott away so that I could make sense of his bounding Labrador behavior.

"You're going to Thailand with Em and I get her Gullwing. Jesus, Lizzy-baby, have you ever seen a Gullwing?"

"It's not legal, Scott."

"Don't give me legal, baby, I'm your boss." Scott gave me a boyish grin. "Here, I'll show you a picture." He grabbed my hand and dragged me into his office, where his printer was demently spilling out page after page with a red car on it.

"Isn't she a beauty? Can't you see me growling into the garage at the Peninsula for lunch in this baby? I get a boner just thinking about it."

"It's a lovely car. Well, it's not, actually, it's kind of weird looking. But either way, you can't swap me for it." I was pleading now. I knew that

Scott could in fact do anything he wanted. This town did not seem to recognize the labor laws that governed the rest of the United States. If your Hollywood boss didn't like you, your Hollywood boss didn't keep you. As it is with wrinkles and double chins and fat thighs and ugly noses in this town, so it is with employees. Erase them. Forget them. Pay to have them removed and ensure you never see them again.

"It's only for three months. You'll hardly notice you're gone." Scott dismissed my fears, then me. "Get me a latte, would you Lizzie-o?"

"Don't worry. I'm sure you won't have to stay in Thailand for three months, anyway," Amber informed me when I walked out of Scott's office in a daze.

"Why?" I asked, realizing that the bitch had well and truly screwed me when she'd suggested Emerald should bribe Scott.

"Because nobody can stand her for more than a couple of weeks. Either she works them into a nervous breakdown with her petty demands or she sexually harasses them and they sue her."

"Well, I'm used to hard work and I'm a woman." I picked up my purse to do the coffee run. At least the people in the Coffee Bean were friendlier than in my office.

"That you're a woman won't bother her one tiny bit," Amber nonchalantly informed me. For someone who appeared to work so hard, she clearly spent more than her fair share of time reading the V Pages on *Variety*'s Web site.

"She's a lesbian?" I scowled.

"She's what *my* generation call bicurious." Amber smiled. "Though the girls she's slept with have always been really beautiful, so I wouldn't worry."

And the pathetic thing is that it wasn't until I was halfway across Beverly that I realized Amber had just insulted me.

Naturally I stayed in the Coffee Bean for twenty minutes longer than it took to froth a latte, because I had to call Lara to complain. Not only about her insensitive husband who wanted to trade me for a car, but also about Amber, who had alarmingly become our most-oft-discussed topic. Something we were both aware was pathetic and made us feel like bitter, ageing crones, but nonetheless it was a habit we couldn't seem to shake while the girl insisted on being such a prize bitch.

"You'll never believe what she's done this time," I spluttered at Lara as quietly as possible, because the place is full of, if not secret agents then certainly agents—short ones, tall ones, ones squeezed into their Zegna suits, ones yelling into cell phones about Brad—so I had to be careful because agents, like walls, have ears.

"Tell me, tell me," Lara demanded, and I figured at least this was more stimulating for her mushy mommy brain than repeats of the OC.

"She's trying to get Scott to send me to Thailand on location with Emerald. Do you think she's after my job?"

"Your job and my husband," Lara said tersely.

"Are we just being paranoid?" I asked, suddenly a little embarrassed by the fact that I was huddling in a corner telling tales on a twenty-two-year-old.

"No, we're just being realistic," Lara said. "I'm coming over there. Now." These were all the words I needed to propel me back to the office and ensure that Scott wasn't in any sort of compromising position that might alarm Lara.

It wasn't as if Lara wasn't used to Scott's appetites—in fact, not only had she been witness to them in her four years as his assistant, she'd also facilitated many of them—she'd picked up his Ritalin prescriptions, she'd kept his ex-wife, Mia, at bay when he was having "meetings" with cute young actresses that lasted considerably longer than it took to discuss a five-year plan; in fact, she'd often been the girl in tow on his "business trips" to Napa, so she knew the deceptions and excuses and was determined that they'd never happen again. Lara had pretty much turned Scott around—he hadn't touched any substance more potent than espresso since their honeymoon at the Meadows Clinic in Arizona and even fooling around had been off his radar (until the last few days with the mysterious actress in his office). Lara was a formidable woman and having a baby and getting her man may have meant her figure had softened, but it had taken none of the angles off her character; she was still as arch and tough as they came, and I didn't envy Amber at this moment in time as Lara eased herself behind the wheel of her SLK and hot-tailed it over from the Palisades.

"I can't find the paperwork for Russell's new movie," Amber informed me immediately when I walked in the door.

"Have you checked the file?" I dumped my purse and went to knock on Scott's door to deliver his coffee.

"Of course, do you think I'm completely thick?" Amber said in her cut glass accent, and rolled her eyes. "Oh, and I wouldn't go in there. I think the actress is back. She just asked if he wanted to put his head between her legs."

"Really?" I withdrew my hand before it could make contact with Scott's door.

"She sounds as if she's fifteen." Amber smiled in a self-satisfied way.

"We have to get her out of there." I grimaced.

"Rather you than me."

"Lara's on her way over." I tried to peer through Scott's wooden blinds, but they were firmly down. Amber's face lit up.

"Well, she is his wife. I suppose she has a right to know if he's being unfaithful." She smiled.

"Help me get her out or I'll tell Scott you used a company courier to have your macrobiotic lunch biked over from Silver Lake," I threatened.

"And I'll tell him that you burned six months' worth of irreplaceable paperwork on a bonfire in your wastebasket because you were too lazy to file it."

"What are you talking about?" I said, taken aback. I couldn't believe she'd bust me. I blinked in horror.

"There's a burn mark on the carpet by your desk."

"Do and I'll kill you," I spat, but she didn't seem too convinced by my threat because she just carried on typing,

"Hmmm, I wonder where the paperwork is for the seventeen-million-dollar contract we've just done for Nic. I suppose I should ask Scott if he's seen it." But before I could snarl anything back at her, my phone rang. The single ring of an internal call.

"Hello," I answered.

"Lara Wagner's on her way up," the receptionist sang.

"Shit." I put down the phone and ran back to Scott's office door. I glued my ear to it.

"Would you like me standing up?" the girl asked. And she did sound fifteen, Amber hadn't been lying. Jesus, they were taking their time. Was she introducing Scott to Tantric Sex?

"Scott." I knocked loudly. "I've got your coffee. And Lara's here!" I yelled so that he'd hear me through the heavy door of a powerful man's office.

"Wassup?" he shouted.

"Lara's on her way up!" I repeated urgently.

"Shit!" I heard Scott shout, as something crashed to the ground. I closed my eyes and prayed that the girl would make it out of his office with a passable amount of clothes on before the elevator pinged at the end of our hallway. At least we were in the movie industry where there's nothing too suspicious about a girl wandering around in a skirt and bra—that's all actresses wear all the time, anyway.

"Lizzie?" Lara stood in the doorway looking circumspectly at me. "What's going on?"

"Oh, nothing. Nothing at all," I said without moving from in front of Scott's door. It wasn't as if I was trying to protect Scott, more that I was trying to protect Lara.

"Then why don't I go in and say hello to my husband?" she challenged calmly. I must have looked like a deer caught in headlights.

"Sure," I said and reluctantly stepped aside as slowly as possible. But just as I did, Scott flung open his office door with a big grin on his face.

"Honey," he said. "Come in." Lara narrowed her eyes as she walked by me into his office. It was no use even attempting to hide anything from her. "Where's Lachlan?" he asked.

"With the nanny. We need to talk," she said and closed his door behind her. I waited an ultracautious thirty seconds for either Lara or the pantyless teenager to come flying out the door, but nothing happened. Eventually I walked back to my desk, still holding my breath for some flotsam to come hurtling at me. Scott's office was on the top floor; there was no way the girl could have left without passing us. No convenient fire escape, even. She must be stashed under his desk or behind his plasma. Still, it appeared he'd gotten away with whatever it was he was up to, which was a temporary relief.

Half an hour later Lara and Scott emerged from his office. There was an easy way about them that suggested they'd made up.

"We're going for a cocktail, ladies," Scott said. "I'm in a meeting with Ang Lee. Okay?"

"Sure," Amber and I piped in together. Lara winked at me; clearly she'd gotten her own way.

"Baby, I'll catch up with you, I just have to give Lizzie my boxing teacher's number," she told her husband.

"Okeydokey." Scott did a detour into Katherine Watson's office.

When Katherine wasn't busy mentoring the butter-wouldn't-melt vampire slut on the desk next to me, she was the brains behind The Agency. It was Katherine who'd encouraged Scott to join her in a hostile takeover last year to oust the then-president Daniel Rosen from power. She was his polar opposite, a smart, neat-freak mother-of-four—with a devastatingly attractive photographer–husband—who managed to be that most oxymoronic of things, an ethical businesswoman. "Kathy, got any juice for me?" we heard Scott ask.

"So, you're not going to Vietnam," Lara said loudly enough for Amber to hear.

"Thailand," I said. "Are you sure?" I couldn't believe that Scott would relinquish his new toy-to-be so readily.

"Positive." She smiled. "And I didn't even have to raise my voice. Come to lunch on Saturday?"

"Great," I said as she hugged me good-bye. "And thanks for sorting that Thailand thing out. I'm not sure that Luke and I would have sur-vived the two of us being on location at the same time."

"Bye, Lizzie. Bye, Amber." She smiled pointedly at our archenemy, who ignored her.

"It must be hard getting old in this town," Amber said as she watched Lara get into the elevator with Scott. "But to be old *and* fat? I'd rather be dead." Luckily the phone rang, because I didn't have a nasty retort ready to fire back at Amber at that precise second.

"The Agency," I answered.

"It's me." It was Scott, presumably from the elevator. "I didn't bring my call sheet."

"I'll run it down," I said and hung up. I went into his office and couldn't resist a swift check under his desk for the pantyless one. She wasn't behind his Space Invaders machine either. I even looked up to see if she might be hiding Spidey-style on the ceiling. I grabbed the doodled-on call sheet from his desk and raced down to the parking garage with it.

"Here you are." Scott was chatting with a very familiar-looking and very handsome actor by the valet booth as José, one of my two beloved valets, both of whom were named José, went to get his car.

"Great." Scott took the call sheet and seamlessly continued telling the actor how stellar he'd been in the screening of his new movie. This was why the stars loved Scott—he was the most effortlessly charming guy in town. "So we need to get you a really big fucking movie next. You know, triple-A. You reminded me of a young Joaquin Phoenix. Y'know?" The actor nodded and believed every word of it.

Lara was on her cell phone nearby, talking to the nanny. She smiled at me and I was about to disappear back upstairs when there was an almighty screech of tires at the entrance to the garage. Suddenly a fire-engine red car drew up beside us and it's horn exploded into an excited cacophony—as if its driver had just won the Grand Prix and was doing a lap of honor. José, who had just brought around Scott's car, aged about five years in an instant. Lara glared and held her phone aloft in a fury and I took a step back.

"What the fuck?" Scott, who had been standing with his back to the car as it entered, turned around. But the look on his face turned from one of serious irritation to that of a five-year-old on Christmas morning as he saw where the noise came from.

Now, I hadn't studied Scott's printouts of the Gullwing Mercedes too closely, but I was in no doubt that this was she. This was the piece of tin that I was going to be exchanged for before my heroic Lara had intervened. I was in even less doubt about this fact when the sides of the car raised up like, well, like the wings of a gull, and Emerald Everhart stepped out in what appeared to be a white nightie and black over-the-knee boots with an indecent glimpse of brown thigh on display in between.

"Scottie, sweetie. Just the man I was looking for. What do you think?" She squealed even louder than the tires and rushed toward him for her hug.

"Holy Shit." Scott stood and stared at the car as Emerald barreled into him. He whistled loudly and took six awed steps nearer to the object of his desire. "Un-fucking-believable."

"Scott?" Lara called out as she surveyed the scene. But he didn't hear her. He didn't hear anything except the low growl of the Gullwing's engine as Emerald sat back in the driver's seat and played footsie with the pedal.

"Wanna have a drive, sweetie?" Emerald purred, her new nylon blond hair tumbling around her shoulders like a pornographic Medusa's.

"You bet I do," Scott said and graciously shot his wife an apologetic look as he clambered in. Lara stood by, openmouthed, as Emerald hopped over the gear stick, flashed her lacy panties, and let Scott take the wheel. The next thing we knew the doors were closed and the car spun around on the asphalt and headed for the streets of Los Angeles with a jubilant honk of its horn.

"I think you might be going to Vietnam after all," Lara said as I stood by speechlessly and my life as assistant to Emerald Everhart flashed before me—the cigarette runs, the tantrums, the inevitable retrieval of plastic hair from shower drains and men's zippers. Not to mention that I'd be thousands of miles away from my boyfriend and Dracula's daughter herself, Emanuelle Saix.

"Thailand," I corrected Lara. "I'm going to Thailand."

THREE

An associate producer is the only guy in Hollywood who will associate with the producer.

—Fred Allen

It was a rare treat to see Jason Blum these days. Since he'd written, directed, and produced *Sex Addicts in Love,* he'd been too hot to be in touch. But now his film had wrapped and he had time between edits and rewriting the ending and buying himself a house in Santa Barbara to call me.

"Hi, doll," he said when I picked up the phone. Jason had gone overnight from being one of the most intense film geeks UCLA had ever produced to a guy who wore his pants lower than his underwear and had a regular table at the Chateau. It was Sunday morning and I was trying to do a million chores around the house. Luke's long-term cleaning woman, Mrs. Mendes, was coming in on Monday and for some bizarre reason I deemed it necessary to tidy up *before* she came in case she reported my slovenly domestic habits to him. I didn't really want to delve into the reasons why I felt my boyfriend might be compelled to take his maid's side over his girlfriend's and what that said about our relationship, so I scrubbed the bathtub instead.

"Jason Blum," I panted into the phone as I stood up and stretched my aching back.

"Were you having sex?" he asked. The old Jason didn't look as if he knew what frottage was, but the new Jason probably made love sixteen hours a day with a chocolate box of beauties.

"No, Luke's in Prague," I said. "You do know who Luke is, don't you? I mean I've been dating him for a year now, but I'm not sure we've spoken for a while."

"You're such a wit, sweetheart. Of course I know who he is. The old guy went out with that hot French chick. Right?"

"He's not old. He's thirty-five," I said and wrung out my sponge as if it were Jason's neck. I ignored the reference to Emanuelle altogether.

"Maybe he just seems older because he's no fun," Jason ventured.

"Probably seems older because he's so powerful," I shot back.

Jason used to be my closest friend in Hollywood in the days when I didn't know anyone except Lara and I thought *she* was a semipro because she was secretly dating Scott and always had new shoes. He'd worked in the Coffee Bean across the street from The Agency and I'd helped him get an agent for *Sex Addicts in Love,* the screenplay he'd written. I'd long since forgiven him for how foully he'd screwed me over when his big moment came and my promised coproducer credit never materialized. But our friendship was still laced with a pretence of amicable hatred. After all, Jason and I had spent every evening for the better part of a year eating takeout and doing our laundry together. And if he hadn't been so off-puttingly earnest in those days, we may even have got together. That said, I would certainly have been dumped by now for something altogether cuter with a more impressive chest measurement than my own. It was actually really good to hear his voice.

"Touché." Jason laughed. "Now when can I see you, sweetie?"

"Well, how about Monday? Or Tuesday? Or, hey, maybe Wednesday. I'm free on Thursday," I said.

"That's tragic."

"I know, but I date an important man. That's the price I pay," I said, suddenly realizing that it actually *was* tragic. I hadn't been to dinner with anyone other than Lara and my yoga-teacher friend, Alexa, since Luke left for Prague. I'd had a cocktail with Katherine Watson's assistant, Georgia, because she was having a nervous breakdown, but that was the sum of my social life. It really was a bummer having the person I most wanted to spend time with halfway around the world.

"Well, then, you can come with me to the screening of my movie tomorrow evening," Jason offered.

"Oh, really. You've made a movie? That's great. What's it about?" I asked sarcastically. Then laughed.

"Not funny." Jason sounded bruised. "You know how bad I still feel about that and how I still have nightmares about the day Daniel Rosen gave me a contract to sign and your name wasn't on it."

"I know, but the three-million-dollar deal made it an easier blow to bear," I reminded him. "Don't worry, I understand." And I really did. Jason had been under enormous pressure from one of the most devious men in the world to sign that contract and there was no way Daniel would have wanted me tagging along in any way whatsoever. I was an assistant at his agency; he'd much rather save the producer credits to hand out like Halloween candy to his own people.

"It's at Universal City Walk at four P.M. I'll meet you outside Theater 3," he said.

"Can't wait," I said as I hung up and resumed my tub-scrubbing. I thought about calling Luke and telling him that I missed him, but he'd doubtless be out to dinner somewhere candlelit, eating suckling pig on a Sunday night in Prague, so I desisted.

"Great, great. I thought you'd be late." Jason looked pale and was dragging hard on a cigarette as I approached him at the Universal City Walk the next afternoon.

"Not in a million years." I smiled breezily. At least being left out of the movie hierarchy meant that I didn't have to be nervous right now. If the movie was a dog, I wasn't going to be laughed out of town. "Is this the first time you've seen it with an audience?" I asked as I looked around us at the milling people who were clearly a test audience—a huddle of students who'd probably come in the hope of free popcorn; some vagrants who'd been rustled up from the pier in Santa Monica; and single mothers who wanted a break from their six tonsil-flashing kids. They were a motley bunch to say the least, and I wasn't sure I'd want the fate of my movie in their hands. Since this was a test screening, these people got to give their views on everything from the lead character's outfits to the ending of the story. And the studio would listen to them. I shuddered for Jason.

Out of the hordes a man in a suit sailed toward us.

"Jason." He had the shaven head so beloved of receding men, which gave him a thuglike quality even in Armani.

"Hey." He and Jason hugged each other in a macho way.

"Nervous?"

"Excited."

"Perfect."

"Yup."

"Enjoy."

"Sure."

"Wow," I said as Jason and I made our way into the movie theater, "that was a scintillating conversation."

"I can live without the pithy comments, thanks, Lizzie." Jason shot me a warning look.

"Sorry, I was trying to relax you," I said, chastened. I stroked his arm reassuringly instead. "Who was he, anyway?"

"He's the senior VP in charge of the project." Jason looked around the room in terror. "Fuck, the head of Marketing's here, too."

"That's great. It means they're really into it, right?" I said, but Jason just grunted.

We took our seats in the middle row and I sunk excitedly into the red velveteen chair. The last I'd seen of *Sex Addicts in Love* had been just before Jason signed the deal. I'd worked on at least thirty-eight drafts of the script with him but imagined that a lot of it had changed since then. I didn't even know who the actors were, as Jason had diplomatically not really mentioned anything about the project to me again, except when he called from the outdoor hot tub at the Post Ranch Inn with one of his prettier cast members and told me how tough the shoot was.

"It's going to be great, Jase. I know it is." I patted his hand.

"I feel like a whore," he said.

"Don't be silly."

"It's like I'm naked and everyone's staring and wants a piece of me." His face was screwed up in anguish. "I didn't know it'd be like this. I wish I still worked at the Coffee Bean."

"Shhh. It's starting. It's gonna be great," I whispered. "Look, here are the credits—oh my God, it's you; they're going to have your name up there."

But Jason was too stone-faced to be excited with me. I suppose this was his life's work, his reputation, his bread and butter, and his entire future. Not to mention that if this was a flop and he had to go back to the Coffee Bean, his love life might go up in froth, too. There was a lot at stake. Still, I did squeeze his hand very tightly when

JASON H. BLUM

came on-screen in big black letters on the vast screen before us. It gave me goose bumps. Jason just looked as if he might throw up. In fact, it came on three times: directed by, written by, and produced by. I have to confess that I did hold my breath through the producers credit in case

ELIZABETH B. MILLER

had somehow been slipped in there in a moment of sloppiness, but alas, it hadn't.

Sex Addicts in Love was every bit as incredible a movie as I'd hoped it would be. And as I sat and watched the brilliant performances, the incredible eye of the director, the lighting, the moving story lines, I forgot that I'd ever been involved with it and became carried away with what was quite simply a wonderful movie. I laughed, cried, and from time to time thought to myself, "Dammit, I'd be a great producer." The only sour note in the proceedings, apart from the perfume of the woman in front of me, was the balding studio executive Jason had met beforehand, who spent the entire screening playing with his BlackBerry.

He was sitting right in front of us, and by the middle of the second act I was ready to kill him with my bare hands.

"Some people are so rude," I hissed, but some people were obviously deaf as well because he didn't flinch. He just kept on drilling away with his little stick on his screen, doubtless telling some other writer/director/producer how "fucking phenomenal" he thought they were and how he wanted to buy their latest movie, utterly oblivious to the fact that another phenomenal writer/director/producer whom he'd raved at and about for months was having his big moment behind him. And if this was how bored and fickle these men were when it came to work, imagine how horrifying their behavior was when it came to women. I shuddered and tried to ignore his demented tapping and the eerie glow from his screen.

When the movie finished Jason still stared numbly ahead. There was a shuffle in the audience as people stood up, found their jackets, kicked over their empty Coke cups, and made their exit. I had expected rapturous applause and standing ovations. In fact, I'd begun to clap myself when the end credits rolled, but it sounded so lame that I hastily turned it into a winter's day–type hand rub.

"Let's go and talk about it outside," I said cheerily to Jason.

"I need a cigarette," he said without moving his lips. I looked around for the BlackBerry-bearing studio executive whose cue it was to come racing toward us with promises of unprecedented marketing spends and Academy Award nominations, but he was pacing by the fire exit on his cell. I tugged Jason to his feet, hoping he wouldn't notice how resoundingly he was being ignored by the powers-that-be and marched him through the audience, for whom normal life had resumed already. *Sex Addicts in Love* hadn't seemed to alter their lives in any way whatsoever.

Once we were safely secreted away in Ben and Jerry's on the City Walk, I gave Jason an unreciprocated hug.

"I can't even begin to tell you how much I loved it," I said truthfully. "It was so beautiful, so inspiring, absolutely everything that I always knew it would be."

"Diet Coke," Jason said to the girl behind the counter without even scanning the list. "Grande."

"I'll have a raspberry ripple smoothie," I said, ordering the first thing I saw on the board. "And the casting was genius."

"They hated it," he said flatly.

"They aren't the people who matter."

"Everyone was supposed to love it."

"They will. But you can't expect people who come to test screenings to love a movie about a dysfunctional kid from New Jersey who has an affair with his stepmother," I told him.

"I need fresh air," Jason said as he pulled his Marlboro Reds from his pocket and headed outside. I scurried after him with our drinks and followed him back toward the movie theater, where he took up residence by a concrete pillar.

"You've got to believe me, Jase, it was an incredible movie." And for the first time since the movie began, Jason looked as if he'd heard what

I said. He turned his head halfway toward me and examined me out of the corner of his eye,

"Really?" he asked quietly.

"I promise." I leaped overenthusiastically at the breakthrough. I couldn't bear him being depressed like this, especially as his film wasn't bad. It was brilliant. "I really thought that it was . . ." I was about to launch into superlatives when a guy walked in the door.

"Did you just see that movie about sex addicts?" he asked, as though he recognized us from the milling throng.

"Yes," Jason said and stood to attention, animated for the first time all day.

"Me too," the guy said as he lit his own cigarette and took a painfully long inhale, during which time empires must have risen and fallen for Jason.

"What did you think?" Jason asked eventually, in what he clearly thought was a measured way but in reality made him sound a little like a psychopath.

"I thought it was a piece of shit," the guy said plainly. Jason and I stared at him, unable to comprehend the magnitude of what he'd just said. I wanted to tear his cigarette from his fingers and stub it out on his tongue. Jason just blinked.

Later, after our sixth whiskey each at St. Nicks, a dark dive bar on Third, Jason's eyes began to focus again. Until now they'd been glazed and stared longingly ahead at the innumerable bottles of hard liquor behind the bar.

"The thing is, you can't expect a guy like him to know what he's talking about. This is an Academy Award–winning movie, Jason. I know it."

"No, it's not; it's a piece of shit. That's what it'll say on the posters if it ever gets released. Which it won't, but it would if it did. From the director of that piece of shit, *Sex Addicts in Love.*"

"Every genius is misunderstood," I said flatly as I waved my arm in the air to indicate to the bartender that he should bring us another round.

"Not driving are you, honey?" the campy guy asked as if he was my mother.

"Oooh no, I'm not driving. I can't even find my legs, let alone my car,"

I reassured him. "Will you just call us a cab when the time comes?" I slurred.

"Right. I'll call one now, then." He nodded pertly and promptly went over to his phone.

"Asssshhhhole," I told Jason. "If I want to get blind drunk, then I will. My best friend is in trouble." And as I said this, Jason turned to me and looked at me as if for the first time in his life.

"Oh my God, Lizzie. That's it," he said.

"What's it?"

"You're my best friend. I'm yours. You're the most loyal girl in the world. And you're beautiful. And . . ."

"Whoa there, Jase the Ace. I have a boyfriend," I reminded him primly.

"No, I don't wanna fuck you," he said as an appalled look flashed across his face.

"Oh." I deflated.

"I wanna make you a producer on my movie." His eyes shone in the seedy darkness.

"Again?" I asked.

"Yes. Again. And again and again," he said as the bartender arrived with our check and looked quite jealous at what Jason was planning to do to me. Four times.

"Your cab's waiting," the bartender said curtly as Jason handed over a wedge of cash.

"The Agency, please," Jason said to the driver as we clambered into the waiting cab. "On Beverly."

"What are you talking about?" I said. "I don't have to be at work until tomorrow morning."

"What time does Katherine Watson finish work?" he asked me as we closed the cab doors and sped along Third.

"Late." I shrugged vaguely.

"Exactly."

"Lizzie, I should have known all along that you were my champion and that to capriciously kick you off this movie would be bad karma for the project."

"Oh come on, Jason, I don't mind one bit," I said as we arrived outside The Agency and Jason threw yet more cash at the driver and pulled me through the front doors of the building. It felt very weird arriving at my place of work, not just at nine P.M. but also smashed. And it wasn't until the elevator doors opened on my very floor that I suddenly started to panic.

"I can't get out," I said as Jason tugged at my arm.

"I have business to do," he barked.

"Jason. No." I dug my feet into the ground like a mule, so in the end he had to drag me bodily along the carpet.

"Come on, baby."

"It's okay for you. You're a director, you can get away with being hammered and behaving weirdly. I'm an assistant here."

"Not anymore, darling girl. You're a producer," Jason said triumphantly as we careered through the door of Katherine's office.

"Jason. Elizabeth. Come in." Katherine rose from her seat, resplendent in a DVF wrap dress, smiled and shook our hands as if she'd invited us to tea and we'd arrived with cream cakes and a bunch of sweetpeas. That was the thing about Katherine Watson—she was so unflappable that I couldn't bear to be in her presence. It made me feel so ruffled and useless and unpoised that I wanted to shoot myself. Being drunk in her presence was unimaginably horrible. Even Jason was shamed into sobering up somewhat and hitching his jeans above his butt crack.

"Katherine, we just stopped by because I'd like to make an amendment to the credits of *Sex Addicts* if that's okay?" he said.

"Well, let's see, shall we? Why don't you both take a seat?" Katherine went to her computer and began to look things up. I took the farthest seat from her in case she caught a whiff of my whiskey breath, not that my bloodshot eyes and mangled hair weren't a giveaway that I was plastered. "It'll depend on the studio somewhat, and the nature of the deal, but since you have sole producer credit, I think we'll be able to arrange that for you. Who's your lawyer?" she asked.

"Karl Austen." Jason was now sitting upright like an obedient schoolboy.

"Good, I'll get him on the phone. Hold on," Katherine said. How she managed to make it to the end of the day with her hair still attached to her head, let alone wearing a dash of lipstick and immaculate mascara,

I had no clue. Having Scott as my business partner would certainly have made me tear my hair out.

As Katherine talked business with Jason's lawyer, I made the mistake of closing my eyes for a moment. Seconds later I was spinning ever faster, around and around in my head. I opened my eyes and saw the room was still in the same place.

"I've got the spins," I whispered to Jason, who now seemed to be engaged in a serious discussion with Katherine about back-ends and ceilings and bonuses. Or they could have been discussing what their grannies gave them for their birthdays, for all I could tell.

"I'm sorry, Elizabeth, what was that?" Katherine looked at me expectantly, as if I were about to announce the reinvention of the wheel.

"So we're all agreed that this is not a financial amendment?" she asked.

"Oh, that all sounds just fine to me," I improvised. She looked relieved.

"Okay. And Jason. You're happy with all this? I'll call the studio in the morning to okay it, and we can get the paperwork to you tomorrow, if so. Karl said he'd expedite it. Obviously with screenings going on at the moment, you'll want to get Elizabeth's name in lights sooner rather than later." She began to stand up, her charming way of ushering us like dust balls from her office so she could get on with some real work for clients who weren't drunken retards. "Then Elizabeth can share all the glory." She smiled sweetly. God, could it really be that she didn't have a bad bone in her perfect body?

"Exactly," Jason said, with a tone in his voice that I began to recognize as my haze of alcohol burned off with the heat of shame.

Jason was being devious. I knew how he acted when he was doing something sly—after all, I'd witnessed it many times as his erstwhile—and now it seemed, reinstated—producing partner. I'd seen him use and abuse a few people along the way. And now it dawned on me what he was doing: He didn't want to share the glory with me, he wanted to share the blame. He wanted someone to be by his side and suffer, too. "Thanks for your time, Katherine. We gotta have that lunch sometime soon," Jason said, kissing her on both cheeks.

"We will. And Elizabeth, see you in the morning."

"Yesshhhh," I said as I tried to slide away unnoticed down the hallway. This was the last time I was getting drunk with Jason Blum—bad things always happened.

The next morning, I woke up and found Jason in bed next to me. I hastily closed my eyes again and replayed the evening. But before I could scream or remember details of our lurid sex games, there was a loud yawn next to me,

"It's okay, sweetie, nothing happened. You got a little vomitty, so I brought you home, tucked you in, and fell asleep myself."

"Yuck, I'm sorry," I said as I felt my body to see what I was wearing and found I still had on every bit of clothing I'd set out for work in yesterday—even my pantyhose. I grimaced.

"Least I could do. You were there in my hour of need," Jason began.

"Oh yeah, about that credit for producer," I said with a sheet over my mouth in case I smelled as toxic as I felt.

"Don't mention it," Jason said as he stretched out in Luke's place.

"No, really, I mean, I'm flattered but I wouldn't feel comfortable. I really didn't do much more than develop it for you. I was just a second-rate, unqualified D-girl."

"It's okay, you're not getting paid or anything. You probably don't remember, but we agreed on a nominal credit only."

"Oh, I see." I nodded. Jason really had covered himself. He could tell the world that it was my producing that was lousy, and I didn't even get paid to be blamed—sounded like a great deal. Though I still adhered to the view that it was a great film, so I wasn't going to protest too much.

As it was I didn't get to protest at all, because when I looked out over the sheet I saw the thunderous face of Mrs. Mendes staring down on me. She was the maid who used to darn Luke's socks before I came along and threw the holey ones away and replaced them with new ones from Neiman Marcus.

"Oh, Mrs. Mendes. Good morning," I said as I visualized the scene from where she was standing—me, the slatternly new girlfriend who'd replaced her beloved Emanuelle in Mr. Luke's bed, in bed with someone who wasn't Mr. Luke. "This is my friend Jason," I said, as if it might make the whole thing better.

"It's none of my business who he is." She spun on her heels on the shiny parquet floor and marched out of the room with her nose in the air.

"That's okay, baby," Jason said as I jumped up from my bed after her to explain. "She'll never tell him. She'll just shrink your cashmere and burn holes in your favorite skirts," Jason said with surprising perspicacity.

"Really?" I stopped in my tracks and slid halfway across the room in my stocking feet.

"Sure. You'll just have to do your own laundry from now on. It's a small price to pay not to get found out."

"But I haven't done anything," I protested.

"We could if it would make you feel better." Jason winked at me. Had he always been such a flirt or was this a by-product of success, I wondered? He got out of bed and stood in front of the bedroom window stark naked. But before I could warn him that Mrs. Mendes was now noisily sweeping the veranda outside the bedroom window, it was too late. She'd seen all she didn't need to see.

"Shit," Jason said as she dropped her broom in horror and vanished from sight.

"You might want to cut off the phone lines, though, so she can't call Luke and share the good news."

FOUR

Hollywood is like life. You face it with
the sum total of your equipment.

—Joan Crawford

"May I speak to Luke Lloyd, please?" I asked the woman who'd answered my boyfriend's cell phone.

"Hold a moment, please," she said. I thought the whole point of cell phones was that when you called your boyfriend at midnight his time and three P.M. your time, he'd answer it. It seemed that I was wrong. There was an interminable crackle and some thudding noises.

"Hello?"

"Hello, I was holding for Luke Lloyd," I said, trying not to sound impatient lest a rumor get spread on set that poor Luke had a pissy girlfriend.

"Who's speaking, please?" I wasn't sure if it was the same woman who'd answered it the first time.

"It's Elizabeth Miller," I said. Then couldn't restrain myself. "His girlfriend."

"Okay. Hold on." When I could have been the head of the studio, she'd been nicer to me.

When I'd dialed Luke's number, I'd been in a loving frame of mind. I'd just caught sight of a little sandstone elephant he'd bought me on our vacation in India last year and remembered how much I loved him. When Prague and his codependent housekeeper and his huge job weren't getting in the way. I'd snatched the moment when Scott's office door had been shut for long enough to assume that he was napping and

Amber had been in a staff meeting taking minutes. But any minute now I knew she'd be back and overhear every sweet nothing I shared with my boyfriend.

Finally Luke came to the phone. "Hello."

"It's me," I said, melting on impact.

"Honey." He sounded surprisingly mellow considering he was clearly surrounded by aggressive harpies. "Hold on a minute, I'm taking this outside." There was more rustling and lots of people in the background.

"Where are you?" I asked, trying not to sound too curious or neurotic.

"Oh, we're at someone's place. Just all having supper. Some of the crew, y'know."

"I miss you," I said. "The cat misses you. Mrs. Mendes misses you. We all miss you."

"Darlin'," he said in his irresistible Southern drawl, "I miss you, too. I don't know how I'm getting through the days without you. Why don't you come out?"

"I've told you. I can't. I have to work," I explained gently. For the fourteenth time.

"Oh yeah, sorry, I know better than to mess with an independent woman." He laughed.

I wrapped the phone cord around my wrist longingly. "So what have you been doing?" I almost licked the phone. I never knew how much I missed him until he was on the other end of the line.

"Oh, great news, actually, you know that my deal was up for renewal at the studio?"

"Yup," I said, though I only knew because I'd read it a few days ago in *Variety;* we hadn't actually managed to have a real conversation since he'd gone back.

"Well, I got all that I wanted and so much more." He sounded like an excited child, not a jaded powerbroker. Which was another reason why I loved him, I remembered. "I got all these people working for me and the deal's more money than I could have dreamed of. But you know what's best of all?" he prompted.

"No, I don't, sweetheart."

"I get a golf cart." I could practically hear him grinning.

"A golf cart?" I repeated.

"Yup." He waited in silence for me to share his excitement.

"In what sense?" I asked cautiously.

"I get a golf cart with Lloyd Pictures on it, and I can drive it around the lot. It's part of my deal."

"Wow, that's really amazing." I smiled. Only my boyfriend would find the golf cart to drive around the lot in the best part of what was inevitably a multimillion-dollar deal with a major motion picture studio. But I guess it was the boy equivalent of getting a free lipstick in a goody bag after a party. It didn't matter that you could afford to buy hundreds of lipsticks with the money you'd spent on the party ticket and that the color didn't suit you. It was free!

"I'll come pick you up from your car next time you visit me at the office," he promised.

"I can't wait," I said.

"So, honey, how about you?" he asked.

"Me? Well, I've been busy being me, y'know?" I said, not knowing whether to begin with my new role as executive producer on Jason's movie or to broach the subject of me going to Thailand, which didn't seem to be going away. Especially since Scott had made me spend the entire morning finding a special sort of turtle wax for the "Gully" as he called Emerald's Gullwing Mercedes. Admittedly he hadn't talked to me about the idea again, but then I wasn't necessarily intrinsic to the deal, anyway. Just a pawn whose permission didn't need to be sought.

He interrupted my train of thought. "It's actually kinda cold out here, honey. Can you hang on while I go back inside?"

"Sure." I waited and wasn't exactly thrilled to hear a distinctly French accent in the background.

"Darling, would you close the door? The snow's getting in," the voice said. I couldn't hear Luke's response.

"Right," Luke said a few seconds later, "I'm back. It's minus twenty degrees here, by the way."

"I see," I said, suddenly registering somewhere around the same temperature myself. "Where exactly are you, Luke?" I asked, trying to hide the chill in my voice.

"I told you. Having dinner at someone's place." He sounded defensive.

"Whose?" I knew this was not the route to take, but my inner psychopath was getting the better of me.

"Emanuelle's," he said with a guilty cough so he might blur the news.

"So, why didn't you tell me that before?" I tried not to sound too demonic. Especially not since Amber had just walked back into the room—mysteriously without a trace of the ink that always covered my hands and cheeks after I'd taken minutes at the staff meeting. It crossed my mind that she was a witch. "Hmmm," I said, but as I didn't want to make too much of a scene I reverted to passive-aggression. "I might be going to Thailand for three months," I said remorselessly.

"What was that, baby?" he asked distractedly. I wondered if Emanuelle was sucking his toes.

"Don't worry, you're probably too busy to listen. We can talk another time," I suggested.

"No, really. I was just getting comfortable."

"I may be going on location to Thailand for a while," I repeated.

"You're not serious?" Luke said with the desired note of shock in his voice.

"I know, I don't really want to, but Scott wants to swap me for a car," I said.

"Honey, my line's crackling. I can hardly hear you. Are you really thinking of going to Thailand?"

"No, but I might have to," I said.

"When?" He sounded concerned.

"In a week or so," I replied. If I were going, that's when it would be.

"But I'm home in two weeks for your birthday. We'll miss each other and who the hell knows when we'll be together next?" He did seem genuinely upset. That is, until I heard the dulcet tones of Emanuelle again.

"Darling, I've poured you some more wine. Who is that, anyway?" she asked peevishly.

"Oh, nobody," Luke said.

"Nobody!" I yelled with enough force to knock the earth off its axis. Amber looked as happy as I'd ever seen her. Discord in other people's lives was manna to her black heart.

"Oh Jesus, Lizzie, grow up won't you?" Luke snapped. "She's my leading lady; I've got to keep her happy."

"I beg your pardon?" I said, feeling as if I'd been kicked.

"If she thinks I'm being all cozy with you, she'll get upset," he said. "You know how these actresses are."

"Is she still in love with you?" I asked, fear gripping my throat. Now I really did have something to worry about; I no longer had to invent it. And it made me feel nauseous.

"No. Yes. No. Maybe." Luke wrapped his tongue around the lies. "Yes," he finally admitted.

"Are you in love with her?" I asked, slowly enunciating every word.

"Of course not," he said. Which wasn't the "no" I wanted.

"Why 'of course not'? She's very beautiful."

"I know but . . ." he began. God, he was getting this all very, very wrong. He was supposed to say, "So are you." Or, "No she's not. She's ugly inside." He wasn't supposed to say, "I know."

"I have to go," I said as I realized I'd need some time to digest what may or may not be happening on the set of *Dracula's Daughter*.

"No wait, honey," he pleaded. But it was too late. If I held on any longer I'd cry in front of the real-life Dracula's Daughter who was sitting beside me, and I couldn't afford to do that.

Instead I hastily closed down my computer and went to knock on Scott's door. Only a few weeks ago, Scott had employed an open-door policy, mostly because he had such chronic ADD that he got completely bored if his door was closed and he didn't have a full view of "cubicle life." Even though his office was filled with every executive toy on the market and a few nonexecutive, five-year-olds' games like Twister and a basketball hoop, he still got twitchy if he didn't have a visitor or someone on a call. Most agents have an assistant listening in on their calls so that they can write down numbers and make notes of what scripts have to be sent and so on, but Scott actually needed coverage on three-minute phone conversations because after a minute he would get distracted and not remember a thing that had been said. Thankfully this was Amber's job now that I was First Assistant, because if being Scott was boring even for him, having to listen to his inane flattery and "don't fuck with me I'm the king of the world" negotiating tactics was a guaranteed narcotic.

But recently Scott's door had been wedged shut. Even Amber, who pretended to be above such things, had had her interest piqued by the mysterious occurrences behind the PRESIDENT plaque, which had re-placed the old Lakers sticker on his door. For days we'd eavesdropped on the filthiest talk, which, no matter how noisily I typed to drown it out (admittedly not *that* noisily because I considered the dirty-nothings quite educational in their way), could still be heard all the way out into the hallway. Whatever was going on in Scott's office, the chick had lungs and was getting some seriously good action. I'd contemplated telling Lara a million times, but as we never saw the adulteress in ques-tion, there wasn't anything tangible to report just yet.

"Yeah?" Scott yelled.

"I'm going to see a screening of Tara's new movie!" I shouted, nam-ing a B-list actress whom he'd probably struck off his Christmas card list and wouldn't know whether she had a movie out or had moved to Tulsa.

"Then go!" he shouted back. And I swear the panting and little pussy-cat noises continued. Jeez, where was he getting his stamina? Surely it wouldn't be long before Lara noticed his diminished sexual appetite. Then there'd be hell to pay.

"I heard in the meeting that *Dracula's Daughter*'s going to run over. Is that true?" Amber asked with a sadistic smile as I gathered up my gym bag and ran from the room before I dissolved in tears.

"Right, let's see you serve," was the first thing that Zac said to me when I shuffled onto the tennis court for my first coaching session with the renowned guru who was going to change my life, not to mention my strokes.

"My serve?" I asked worriedly.

"Sure." Zac stood with his arms folded and waited. I'd expected him to be younger. But then again he was also a zen master so I guess that had taken a few years of sitting around and trying to imagine nothing. His eyes were a terrifying blue and were a little too close together for him to look kind, as I'd imagined he would be. His leathery wallet of skin belied the fact that he was obviously as fit as a fiddle, even though he must have been seventy.

"Oh, I think there's been a mistake," I said. "I can't really play tennis. In fact, I haven't served a ball since 1989."

"Then why are you here?" He looked in slight bewilderment at my new white tennis skirt, pristine sneakers, and the über-racket I'd borrowed from Talitha, my old cube-mate and newly high-flying PR for everyone from Fendi to Puma. I was glad that when we'd worked together I'd never complained about the fact that she never seemed to do a stroke of work and instead spent all her days on Match.com. Now she was dating the head of worldwide distribution for Prada so she was so ecstatic with her lot in life she'd be happy to lend you her stunning body for an evening out if she could.

"I'm here because I don't know where I'm going," I said as I twirled my tennis racket head on the concrete. "I was told that you changed people's lives."

"I teach them tennis," Zac said impatiently as he grabbed my racket from ruination.

"But you helped my friend Jason become a successful director," I reminded him. When Jason had been about to make *Sex Addicts in Love* he'd had such a crisis of confidence that he spent the first three days of the shoot wandering the aisles of Ralphs. Eventually some bright spark at the studio hired Zac to go and pluck him from the canned goods section and focus him on the task at hand.

"Jason who?"

"Jason Blum," I said, suddenly hoping that Jason hadn't ended up seducing Zac's daughter or some such.

"Jason. Okay. Well yeah, we did figure some stuff out for him. But his backhand showed promise from the get-go," Zac said as he looked at me like the disaster with a ball that I was. It was as if he was X-raying me for skills and saw the bones of a not even halfway decent player.

I resorted to pleading. "I've been booked in for three months." It was true. In fact, I'd rather stupidly put almost every decision in my life on hold until I got my appointment with Zac. He was supposed to help me find career direction, reassure me that someone as successful as Luke could love a mere nitwit of an assistant like myself, and help me find a way to reconcile my desire to be a good human being with working in an industry where behind every good deed there's an ulterior motive.

"Well, let's see what you can do," Zac said without optimism. "I'll hit you a few balls."

With that Zac retreated behind the net and began to serve in my direction. I ran headlong toward the first ball.

"Oops," I said as it skimmed past my ear and my racket plummeted down. I proceeded to miss the next seven shots and ran around like a spastic Don Quixote tilting at imaginary windmills with my arms aloft for ten minutes.

"Okay, enough," Zac said with exasperation as he leaped over the net, his creased brown legs vaulting with the energy of a teenager.

"I'm sorry." I hung my head and prepared to head for the dressing room. I guessed I was going to have to handle my problems myself, without the help of the legendary Zac.

"First rule of life. Don't apologize for who you are." Zac flashed me a lizardy smile.

"I'm sorry," I said before I could help myself, then laughed. "Oops."

"You're the worst tennis player I've seen in years." Zac shook his head.

"Am I really?" I looked around to see if the people on the next court, who'd been gaping in disbelief as I flailed around after the balls, were listening in. "I'm sorry," I reiterated.

Zac grabbed hold of my hand and shook it in congratulations. "I haven't been so excited to help somebody in a long time. It'll be a challenge for me. Not only are you pathetically bad at tennis but your self-esteem is in the toilet."

"I can really stay?" I asked.

"Yes," Zac said, "so let's start with the serve." He stood next to me with his racket and what seemed like hundreds of balls stuffed disconcertingly in his shorts, and showed me how to reach and throw. I copied him again and again. And I stopped apologizing, even when my arm swooped around and bashed his kneecap.

"If you're calm inside, your serve will reflect that," Zac explained as I bashed away ball after ball.

"I'm not very calm," I told him. "I think my boyfriend's cheating on me."

"And if he is, is that his problem or your problem?" Zac asked in his wizened croak.

"Well, it's kind of mine because . . ." I began as I sent a ball sailing over the fifty-foot-high perimeter fence.

"Wrong," Zac barked, and I wasn't sure whether he meant my serve or my answer. Then I realized that it was both. The inner game *was* the outer game.

"If your boyfriend wants to live his life as a cheating bastard, that's his problem. Tell me this, Elizabeth, if someone gives you a gift and you choose not to accept it, to whom does that gift belong?"

"To . . . uhm . . ." I was never any good at the sound of one-hand-clapping stuff even when I was sitting in the lotus position with my yogi-friend, Alexa; now that I was all out of breath in the evening sunshine, I found it impossible. So I took a guess. "To the person who gave me the gift?"

"Cor-rect," Zac said as he took my arm and described a large circle with my racket. "If you don't accept his shit, it's still his shit and not yours."

"You're so right," I said, and as the words came out of my mouth, I executed the most impeccable serve of my life.

"See?" Zac stood back and grinned at me. It was like the parable of the prodigal son—there is more joy for Zac at the successful serve of a tennis-spaz than ninety-nine naturals who win all their league games— or something like that.

"Thank you." I wanted to hug Zac but I was dripping with sweat by now. "Can we talk about my job, too? I really need to work out whether I should leave to pursue my own projects or stay and climb the ladder."

"We'll do a few minutes of backhand," Zac promised as he turned on the ball machine at the other end of the court.

"Now go," he instructed as the balls came gaily pinging toward me.

"Too fast!" I yelled as he adjusted the machine.

"Is it now?" he asked. "Or is it just you who are too slow?"

"A bit of both?" I smiled as he made his way back toward me.

"Now sweep and follow through. Don't let the ball leave your racket until you're ready for it to leave," he said as I tried to obey his orders but ended up being brutalized by a trinity of stray balls that came at me while I was nurturing the last ball and sending it off to college with a hug.

"You're holding on too long," Zac said. "Let go sooner."

"Are you telling me to leave my job?" I asked.

"No, I'm telling you to let the ball leave your racket at the precise moment it's ready. Now feel for that moment. Okay? Go. Feel for the moment. There it is, you feel it?"

"Yes. I do." I smiled. And I did. I turned off my whirring and thinking and deliberating and fretting and focused on the ball and how it felt against the strings. I paid attention to when it was ready to go.

"I'm not leaving yet," I told Zac as I guided a second ball lovingly over the net.

"Exactly." Zac stood back and watched as I fired shot after shot across the court until I was a crimson-faced Bride of Shrek. "Enough, enough," he finally said and silenced the machine.

"Thanks, Zac." I shook his hand, even though I secretly wanted to marry him. "You've been such a help."

"The bliss is within, you know." He patted me and sent me on my way. "Same time next week."

"I'll be here," I promised as I made a mental list of all the things we could work on next time.

As I drove home I knew that Zac was right, the bliss was within and it was all up to me. I'd decided in the zen moment of my backhand that I would stay at The Agency until I found a project that really appealed to me, that would be worth pursuing. I'd signed the contract for *Sex Addicts in Love* this morning and whatever happened I had a producer credit to my name now, which was incredibly valuable, no matter how the movie fared at the box office. I'd just wait until I found another project that I was passionate about and then maybe I'd quit The Agency to produce it properly this time, rather than doing it during coffee breaks as I had with *Sex Addicts*. I also decided that I'd give Luke a break. Even though he may be pandering to Emanuelle's every whim, I knew in my heart that it was me whom he loved, and that sometimes a producer had to bend his own rules a little to keep his movie together. If that meant lying to Emanuelle about who he was on the phone with, then so be it. My backhand and I were bigger than that. We understood. So it was with a smile on my face and a very sore right arm that I got in my car and drove home to call Luke and tell him I loved him.

FIVE

Hollywood gives a young girl the aura of a giant, self-contained orgy farm, its inhabitants dedicated to crawling into every pair of pants they can find.

—Veronica Lake

It must have been a blue moon because Lara and I were having a night out. Not just Lachlan's leftover macaroni and cheese and a bottle of red wine at her kitchen table, which was our usual, but a party for which we were required to wear something other than Nuala yoga pants. Nathalie Cook was a former president of the Lit Department at The Agency and she'd left her enormous job to launch her own line.

"What is it that she makes again?" Lara asked as we sped up the PCH. Lara had spent the afternoon wrapped in seaweed in Santa Monica in a bid to lose weight for tonight's party. But the undesirable pounds still clung mercilessly to her hips, so she had simply draped herself in her trademark black pants. I did understand what a drag it must be for her facing a bunch of women who were so educated about good fats, bad fats, trans fats, and fat asses that they could have advised the World Health Organization on any dietetic matter on the face of the planet. Poor Lara, there was no way she was leaving this party without at least seventeen phone numbers for personal trainers and four new diets that she "had to try."

"I can't remember what they're launching." I rummaged in my purse for the invitation. "Is it handbags? Jewelry?"

"She was always pretty stylish. It's bound to be some line of fabulous clothes," I said, and Lara and I looked at each other and groaned. "Here it is." I fished a piece of cardboard out of my bag. "She's launching LovelyLab."

"Is it a spa?"

"I have no clue," I said as we veered off the street to park alongside at least forty Porsche Cayennes and twenty Mercedes.

"Do you know that this party alone has probably guzzled more gas than the Chinese use in a year?"

"You might want to keep your thoughts on that to yourself," Lara said as we climbed down from her SUV. "These are the most powerful divorcées in Hollywood. You don't want to alienate them."

Lara was right. If their cars alone could eradicate the need for the Kyoto summit, their combined divorce settlements could run an entire Third World country for several decades. And this was no exaggeration. Their influence was like an invisible web that wove its way through the lives of almost anyone you cared to think of in this town. They were the young and beautiful ex-wives of the studio presidents, the producers, and the most powerful agents. A few had been married to Talent—actors or directors—but only those divorced from the AAA list were permitted here. And even more intimidatingly, most of them lived here, in this ludicriously chic Malibu apartment building. They counseled one another on all matters alimonious, their nannies competed over their charges, and they passed as friends in a world where to copy the same dinner table arrangement was to be frozen out of the set.

"Are you sure they won't mind me coming?" I asked.

"Not at all," Lara whispered as we walked up the path toward the floodlit white façade of the building. "Anyway, you're one of them now."

"What do you mean?" I scowled. I couldn't see how I was like them in any way.

"You're with Luke," she informed me. "They know you're safe, now."

"Good God in heaven."

"I know. Don't take it so seriously. They're not ogres." She smiled as the elevator doors closed behind us. "Just really intelligent women with too much time and money on their hands."

The door was opened by an efficient blond with a clipboard.

"Welcome. And you are?"

"Lara Wagner and Elizabeth Miller," Lara said.

"Right," she said and stared at me a moment too long before checking me off the list. "Go on through. Have fun!" she said in a jaunty way that didn't sit easily with her.

"Lara." A woman whom I assumed was Nathalie stepped forward. She was like the prettiest movie star you've ever seen—petite and fine-boned and exquisitely dressed. "So glad you could make it."

"This is Elizabeth," Lara said as she unwrapped herself from what must have been an unevenly matched hug—Nathalie couldn't weigh much more now than she had as a fourteen-year-old cheerleader.

"Elizabeth Miller?" I swear she scrutinized me. Maybe they were going to ask me to join some sort of Masonic fellowship and get me to marry and divorce Luke very quickly before I joined. Fat chance, I thought—even our conversation last night, when I'd only called to be nice to him and not nag about the Emanuelle dinner party, had ended with a frost worthy of Eastern Europe when he'd told me that he could only talk for five minutes because he had to play chess with the director. "Great to meet you."

"So, I can't wait to see your new line," Lara said vaguely.

"Oh, you're going to love it." Nathalie touched her arm conspiratorially. "Now come on through and we'll get you girls some cocktails."

The room was teeming with women dressed in the kind of clothes you had to preorder straight from the designer at the beginning of each season. The waiting-list boots by Stella McCartney, the only-fifty-in-existence handbags by Alexander McQueen. I looked down at my party outfit and it suddenly felt very tired. If only I was less proud, I would take Luke's credit card and exercise it a little in Chanel, but I'm not sure that I could ever justify five thousand dollars of anyone's money on a blouse.

"Champagne, ladies?" a waitress offered. Lara and I each took a glass and, as we sipped away, took in our surroundings. The apartment was a tasteful blend of olive greens and ice-cream pinks; the saccharine edge had been taken off with the shelves and shelves of books—most of them vast books with Arabic on their spines. The artwork, too, had a Middle Eastern feel.

A woman appeared at our side. "Doesn't Nathalie have great taste?"

"She certainly does," Lara said. "Didn't she do some art history course or something after she left The Agency?"

"She did a master's in Oriental Studies," the woman told us as we looked out over the white sand of the beach, which glowed ghostly in the dark, and listened to the foaming waves breaking a mere fifty feet from the balcony. "I'm Jessica, by the way," she said, and smiled.

"Lara Wagner."

"Hi, Lara."

"I'm Elizabeth Miller."

"Good. To. Meet. You," Jessica said, and looked at me for a moment too long. Only the third person to do that tonight. Or maybe I was being paranoid? Maybe this was just the way of the Malibu divorcée.

"So what do you do, Jessica?" I smiled and relaxed into my new role as, if not "one of them," at least a person with a name. It was the first time I'd ever been at a soiree like this and not had to serve drinks or make sure the party magician didn't get Emerald Everhart pregnant. Her reputation for having sex with strangers in bathroom stalls was not merely the invention of the tabloid press, I'd discovered at the last Agency party. But here I was a fully fledged guest for once.

"What do I do?" Jessica took half a step backward and looked at me as if my mental illness hadn't quite been diagnosed accurately yet, but she was determined to figure out what it was. I sensed I'd made a faux pas but couldn't tell what.

"Oh, sorry," I said, suddenly realizing my mistake. "So how old are your children?"

"I don't have children," Jessica said warily, as if she'd suddenly diagnosed my illness and had decided that it might be contagious.

"Oh, I see." I smiled.

"How's the charity work going?" Lara chimed in casually.

"Charity?" Jessica finally dragged her uncomprehending eyes off me and turned her focus on Lara. "Great, really well in fact. I'm going to have a lunch for land mine victims at Ivy on the Shore next month. You have to come."

"I'd love to." Lara nodded and as Jessica went on about the popcorn shrimp she was going to serve, Lara winked at me. She had my back, thank God. Well, how was I to know that even the women without children didn't have jobs? I thought the days of the housewife had gone out with the ark. Especially if you didn't have a husband. Clearly I had a lot to learn about the Malibu divorcée.

As Lara valiantly received the details of the first miracle diet of the evening, I slid off to check out LovelyLab. There was an entire table in the corner covered with little white bottles and potions and shiny packets. And there was a woman standing behind the table looking very professional.

"Hello, madam, would you like to sample LovelyLab?" She smiled.

"Sure," I said as she handed me a small bottle. I squirted a bit on the back of my hand and sniffed.

"We're not very big on fragrance in our line, madam," she told me. "We believe ladies should smell as nature intended."

"Great." I nodded and picked up a packet of wipes. "And these?"

"These are for use after a long day in the office. Before that special date."

"Okay." I stared at the label. There was a small triangle-shaped logo.

"I love your range," I said to Nathalie as she came up beside me clutching her glass of water.

"I'm so glad," she said. "I really think there's such a gap in the market. Don't you?" But before I could answer she had moved on. "I'm going to make my speech now."

"Good luck," I said, and stood back a few paces as she took the stage.

"Okay, listen up, girls." Nathalie was suddenly addressing what must have been at least a hundred of her closest friends and the occasional imposter, like myself. I saw Katherine Watson at the back, looking riveted. "Tonight is the launch of my new range of products."

"Go, Nathalie!" one of the other cheerleaders chirped from the back.

"LovelyLab is my pride and joy." She smiled. I tried to move out of the way but couldn't get by without making a commotion and stepping on the goody bags that littered the floor beside me. Shit. I wanted to exit stage left but was trapped. "I've been working on it for the last year and I can honestly say that no purse is complete without my beautiful pink crocodile wallet of LovelyLab products." There was the *pop pop* of flashbulbs at the back as the reporters and photographers from *InStyle* got to work. I secretly pouted and hung my head demurely so that I wouldn't ruin the photos entirely.

"I want one!" Another trusty friend of Nathalie's piped up at the back.

"Well, Daphne, you can have one." Nathalie smiled. "As you know,

LovelyLab is for the intimate part of your anatomy, that gateway to heaven, your very own cutebox." I heard a cough and looked up.

It was Lara who was on the verge of turning puce with surprise. "Ladies, we love our labia and we want to keep them as soft and pampered and sweet-smelling as possible. But soap and water won't do. . . ." I suddenly tuned in and couldn't believe what I was hearing. I blushed to the roots of my hair as I thought about a roomful of women who possessed "cuteboxes." I looked at Lara who was at the back and practically bent over double trying to stifle her giggles. Oh shit, I had to get out of here.

"If we don't love our lovely labs then we can't really expect anyone else to, now, can we?"

I picked my way between the lurid pink goody bags—the color alone was enough to give me Freudian nightmares swirling full of intimate bits—and wove my way to the bathroom door. Lara had gotten there before me. We hurled ourselves into the bathroom and locked the door behind us.

"No wonder they're all fucking divorced," she said in a ten-decibel whisper. "They have cuteboxes!"

"No way. Oh my God, Lara, did you see me? I turned the same color as the goody bags—labia pink."

"Can you believe the woman has a master's in Oriental Studies? She's fluent in Mandarin and used to run the Lit Department of the biggest agency in the world and she's devoted herself to making the gateway to heaven smell sweet."

"It'll probably sell really well," I had to admit.

"But she has money. Imagine her poor kids. Would your son want to be the heir to the LovelyLab fortune?" Lara sat on the side of the bath and lit a cigarette. "They're really nice, though," I said. "I mean in a creepy Bree Van De Kamp way."

"I know. But I think we have to go."

"Do we have to take a goody bag? If Mrs. Mendes finds mine, I'm in trouble," I said.

"Hell, I'm taking three. I'm going to give them to my sisters for Christmas." Lara dragged on her cigarette and exhaled into the toilet bowl in case of smoke detectors. "Okay, we have to go out again. We'll wait till the end of the cutebox congratulations and then make our escape."

"Cool," I said as Lara wafted the door a few times to ventilate after her cigarette.

Thankfully when we went back into the room the speech was over and a hundred women were handling little bottles and spraying Lovely-Lab's signature fragrance, LoLa, everywhere. Lara and I coughed and spluttered a bit and made our way toward Nathalie to thank her for a great evening. But on our way we were accosted by Amber.

"Oh my God, Elizabeth. I can't believe you're here," she said. I couldn't believe *she* was there. When I was a Second Assistant the only thing I got invited to do was to go fuck myself by Scott. But as Katherine Watson was hovering behind her, I assumed that she'd come with her mentor.

"I'm Lara's guest," I said, in case everyone thought I was a gate-crasher. And thanks to Amber's glass-shattering English accent, everyone was suddenly eavesdropping.

"No silly, I don't mean that." She reached into her handbag. "I just thought that with everything that had happened . . ."

"What are you talking about?" Lara asked suspiciously.

"Oh don't get me wrong, I think you're really brave," she said and I felt as if I was being drowned in molasses. Amber didn't suit sweetness any more than I suited a size two pair of Marc Jacobs hotpants. The next moment Nathalie appeared beside me and handed me another glass of champagne as if she were handing over the Nobel Prize.

"Oh honey, we heard what happened, and we want you to know that we all understand."

"I'm not sure what you think . . ." I said, suddenly worrying that they were mistaking me for someone who had recently given birth to triplets without pain relief. Admittedly I looked tired and a little thick-waisted. "But I think you've got the wrong person."

"You mean you haven't seen *People*?" Amber asked as she fished the magazine from her purse. I squinted at it as she handed it over.

"Oh my God. She doesn't know!" Nathalie said as I blindly turned the pages of *People,* looking for who knows what.

"What the hell are you talking about?" Lara suddenly stepped forward and grabbed the magazine from my shaking hands. "Amber?"

"It's Luke Lloyd," Amber confided with barely concealed delight. "He's cheating on her with Emanuelle Saix."

"What?" Lara snapped the magazine open.

"It's on the front cover," Amber helpfully pointed out.

"What the fuck?" Lara glared at the picture, that I now know so well—of Luke and Emanuelle on the broodingly romantic Charles Bridge, hand in hand and mouth to mouth. She in a long Cossack-style coat, her hair perfectly tousled, he in the sweater I bought him last Christmas. The headline read, HOLLYWOOD COUPLE SEAL REKINDLED LOVE WITH A KISS. There was no denying it, though I wondered for an optimistic moment whether the Eastern European light might cast weird, unfaithful shadows.

"Honey, I totally understand. My husband left me for a two-bit-slut-of-an-actress, too." Nathalie was consoling me as if she were my mother and new best friend rolled into one lifesaving package.

"All actresses are sluts," another woman said from somewhere in the gathering, emoting crowd.

"Thanks ladies, it's been a great evening, but I'm sure you'll understand if Lizzie and I head home now." Lara took the magazine from my numb grip and led me away.

"I'll call you," Nathalie said when we reached the door. "We'll do lunch." I didn't have any words to answer her with, so I just blinked. "Oh, and don't forget your goody bags," she said, thrusting two in my direction. "You'll need LovelyLab when you're back on the market."

"Okay, what's his number?" Lara said as we climbed into her car and sat with the engine off until I learned to breathe again.

"I don't . . . I mean, I can't . . . I just . . ." was all the speech I could muster.

"Pass me your purse," Lara said as she rifled at my feet, then managed to retrieve my cell phone. She turned on the light and began to run through my speed dial until she came across Luke. "Is this it?" she asked. I didn't look. "I'm calling him, okay? Can you speak to him?"

"No." I didn't have the will to even shake my head.

"Sweetheart, you really need to hear his side of this before we go any farther. I mean, this photo"—she shook the copy of *People* that was still clenched in her fist—"it could be anything. We're not going to believe it till we've spoken to Luke, okay?"

"Not okay," I said as I stared blindly at the entry phone on the front of Nathalie's building. "Let me see that picture."

"I'm not saying he isn't an asshole of the highest order, I'm just saying there's a possibility that he has an explanation for this. And as we know Luke's a good guy at heart, we're not going to hang him just yet."

"There is an explanation. He's having an affair with Emanuelle," I said.

"You don't know that." Lara took off her jacket and put it over my shoulders.

"I know there's something going on. The other night he was with her and he pretended that he was speaking to someone else. And he's still being nice but . . . well, you know he had the engagement ring. He must just have given it to her."

"Honey, this isn't Luke's style. Just because he's thousands of miles away, you can't erase what he's like from your memory."

"I don't know what his style is anymore. I've hardly seen him in months," I said. Still, I hadn't shed a single tear. I didn't even feel pain; it was as if someone had taken an ice-cream scoop to my insides and re-moved everything.

"You should definitely call him." Lara had her finger poised to dial Luke, but I couldn't conceive of what I'd say to him. No words would come out.

"Will you call Scott for me?"

"Scott?" Lara looked quizzically at me.

"Please?" I said as I took the phone from her hand.

"Why?"

"Hold on." I had the phone in my hand and it was ringing. I knew that what I was about to do was not rational. It wasn't emotionally healthy, either. But I've always been an ostrich when it comes to con-frontation and I'd rather not face up to what I knew would be the heart-breaking truth from Luke, so I stuck my head into the sand and began to burrow.

"I thought you were with my wife?" Scott answered. He was clearly in a "bar" somewhere and I couldn't exactly hear the sound of panties falling but I sensed they were.

"I am. She's right here," I said.

"Wassup, then?" Scott asked, probably losing his hard-on for the pretty stripper who was settling her G-string on his lap.

"You really want that car, don't you?"

"What car?"

"The Gullwing."

"Sure I fucking do," Scott replied, not grasping for a moment where this was all going.

"No way." Lara tried to make a grab for the phone but I held on to it determinedly.

"Scott"—I shot her a warning look—"I want you to exchange me for the car. I want to go to Thailand and be Emerald's assistant." I said this with my eyes closed because I knew that what I was doing was wrong and that Lara would be furious with me.

"You cannot run away from this, Lizzie," she said under her breath.

"Can't I?" I challenged her, then continued. "So what do you say, Scott?"

"She's going tomorrow. You know that?" Scott's voice was laced with suspicion.

"I know," I said.

"Well, what about the car? I mean, I'm not losing out on a day without you *and* the car. I want a straight exchange. You for Gully." Typical agent.

"I'll go to the office now and call Emerald. I'll arrange for a temp to cover me and I'll have the car in the garage at The Agency tomorrow morning at nine A.M. I won't leave the country until you have the keys," I promised.

"Shit, Lizzie," Scott said with admiration. Clearly the lapdancer had gotten pissed and was now sitting sulking with her friend. "Have you always been this efficient?"

"Yes," I lied.

"Well, what the fuck am I doing letting you go?" he asked. "In fact, you know I'm not even sure that I want to."

"You've got Amber," I reminded him hastily.

"Oh, yeah. So I do."

"And you'll have a temp," I told him. Lara was now practically doing voodoo on me to my left. I could hear her snorting with rage, but she couldn't stop me because I wasn't in control of my right mind, and she knew that. I was dangerously unpredictable and might bite her if she made a move to stop me.

"So I will. She'd better be cute." Scott was no doubt smiling now, wondering whether one of the girls making out with the pole in front of him might be hot at typing as well as writhing. Lara had every right to hate me.

"Of course," I said, hoping Lara hadn't overheard.

"Okay, then it's a deal, I guess," he eventually conceded.

"Great. Well, see you in a couple of months then," I told him, as the impact of my words crashed over me like a tsunami. Was I really going to do this? Was I really going to skip the country and go to Thailand without telling Luke where I was? Without calling and asking for his version of events? Without a word?

Too damn right I was.

SIX

Every now and then when your life gets complicated and the weasels start closing in, the only cure is to load up on heinous chemicals and then drive like a bastard from Hollywood . . . with the music at top volume and at least a pint of ether.

—Hunter S. Thompson

I stood in my underwear, fixated on the duffel bag by the front door. It was perfectly packed. It had taken me all night to get it just right. Unfortunately, as I waited for SuperShuttle to pick me up, I couldn't resist ruining a good thing. But then when could I ever?

I don't know, but there's just something about going away for three months to work for a teenage starlet you've only met once in your life that makes a girl need the comforts of home. So I made the fatal error and unzipped my suitcase. Then the frenzy began. I knew there was something in the closet I had forgotten. And as usual, I was right—my sheepskin slippers. Perfect for a subtropical climate. Then I clocked Luke's "only on special occasions" silk bathrobe. I buried my nose in it. It smelled like him. And though I hated him, it had to come. Then of course every body cream I'd never used and the six works of fiction by Salman Rushdie that I'd been meaning to read for ten years. At least if Luke and I ever did speak again I'd have jumped to another intellectual plane. But the most vital discovery was the snakebite extractor kit. I found it in the back of the guest bathroom medicine cabinet. There must be deadly snakes in Thailand. And what kind of assistant would I be if Emerald got bitten and I was unprepared? I was so caught up with extraneous objects that I didn't even register the persistent honking coming from the driveway.

I glanced out the window. Shit. It was here, the bright blue chariot that would transport me to my new life—aka, a van that would spend the next hour picking up strangers around LA, making a half-hour journey extend to two hours. But before I could even contemplate departure or the fact that my suitcase looked like the result of a controlled explosion, the phone started to ring. And suddenly I realized how much I wanted it to be Luke on the other end of the line. Calling with a perfectly reasonable explanation for the photo, like he'd met his long-lost identical twin in Prague. I raced to answer but as usual the cordless wasn't in its cradle. I could hear the ring but couldn't locate the source. Then the knocking started. In a panic I ran back to the door to tell the driver to hold his horses, but I was still in my underwear. I'm not an exhibitionist by nature, but Lara had reluctantly laid out the perfect outfit for international travel with a superstar when she'd dropped me at home last night and I'd had no intention of ruining it before I'd even stepped out of the house.

"I'm coming!" I yelled, hoping he could hear through the four inches of oak. Where was that damn phone? I had to find it before it stopped ringing and I lost my boyfriend forever.

I got down on all fours and stuck my head halfway under the sofa and stretched my arm into the mystery beneath. I'd just gotten my fingers around the handset when something sharp hit me in the face. I screamed and jumped back in stunned agony clutching my wound. I was bleeding. Then I saw Chucky fly past me and disappear into the bedroom. No. I wasn't on any meds and it wasn't a creepy red-haired doll wielding an ax. But not far off. Chucky was the name I'd given to Charles, Luke's evil orange tabby after he'd taken his first pound of flesh the day I'd moved in with Luke. It was now clear that Chucky and I had never really recovered from that first encounter.

The cat had been a gift from Emanuelle when she and Luke had played house for a few months. And she'd happily told me at the premiere all about how they'd gone to the pound and saved the life of this *très petite chat* and how they'd fed him with a dropper. Apparently Charles had totally adored her. He had been their test child. I chose not to point out that she'd abandoned the cat. But since then I'd had an irrational hatred for Chucky spurred on by Luke's absolute devotion to him. Every time Luke stroked him and made him purr, Chucky would suddenly become a dead ringer for Emanuelle, and I had to bite my lip as her juicy French pout nuzzled into my boyfriend's lap.

As I felt around the scratch to see if he'd hit any main arteries, I realized that the phone had stopped ringing. Emanuelle had triumphed again. I got up, dropped the phone in the charger, and went to the mirror to examine the damage. I heard a last honk of the horn and resigned myself to paying the extra sixty dollars for a taxi. I didn't have much choice as now I'd have to drop Chucky off at the kitty spa. I looked at my scratch and realized it was really a blessing in disguise. I'd completely forgotten Chucky existed. And would have been happily sipping Mai Tais in my five-star hotel in Thailand while Chucky died of starvation. Though it was a pleasant fantasy, I knew that a dead cat would be the proverbial nail-in-the-coffin of my relationship. Though I was running away, something deep inside of me was still waiting for that last-minute reprieve. Proof that Luke wasn't a lying rat but the lovely dreamboat that I still believed in my heart he was.

The phone rang again and I looked to the sky certain there was a God.

"Hello," I answered in my sexiest voice possible

"Is Elizabeth Miller there, please?" I hated when he had the PA put through the calls. The least he could do was dial the number himself.

"It's me. You can put him through."

"Put who through?" asked a perplexed voice on the other line.

"Luke! Listen, I'm in a bit of a rush."

"This is Music Express." Now it was my turn to be confused.

"Who?"

"Your car service to take you to the airport. Our driver is running ten minutes late and we just wanted to apologize for the delay." Though I wasn't getting what I wanted, I was certainly getting what I needed. And I wasn't going to look a gift horse in the mouth.

"No problem. But since you're late, would you mind terribly making a quick stop on the way?"

"Ms. Miller, it's your car. You can stop as many times as you like." Wow. I made a little mental note to see if The Agency could switch their car service.

"Oh. Okay. Well thanks. See you soon"—I was about to hang up—"wait! Sorry. Would you mind telling me who ordered the car?"

There wasn't even a moment of hesitation. "Emerald's Third Assistant." I didn't even know she had a second assistant, let alone a third. I wondered where I fell in the ranks? I'd just assumed I was the one and only, but obviously there was an entourage. I would have been thrilled if my current experience with assistant's assistants wasn't proving to be such an unpleasant one. But I didn't have time to think of my future, and if I'd taken the time I would have been launched into a deep, un-recoverable depression. So, best not to go there.

With a ten-minute reprieve, I pulled on the mushroom-colored Juicies and a cashmere hoodie and went in search of Chucky. I donned a thick plastic apron and rubber gloves—my armor—and laid out the baby blue Hermes kitty carrier, which had definitely been an Emanuelle hangover.

I discovered Chucky in my half-open stocking drawer maliciously shredding every pair of Wolfords and fishnet stockings I'd been careful enough not to run. I swear he even smiled when we made eye contact. Luckily when I dove to catch him he got his paw caught in a bit of fish-net that was hooked to the drawer handle. I successfully managed to shove him and my favorite twenty-dollar Agent Provocateur thigh-highs into the carrier.

As I slid onto the cool leather seat of the car, I let out an enormous sigh of relief. The driver and I both had to sit on my bag to get it zipped, but we'd triumphed, and all my belongings, including Chucky in his cat carrier, were safely stowed in the trunk. I'd never been so happy in my life to lock up a house and escape. There had been no call from Luke and every minute in that place without him made me feel more inse-cure. Maybe this little hiatus from my life was exactly what I needed. It wasn't just my romantic prospects that I needed to revaluate but my pro-fessional ones as well. And though I wasn't riding in the latest stretch Hummer or even a Mercedes Vito, it *was* a town car and as we all know the *only* town car is a Lincoln. Black with tinted windows and cushy black leather seats. And for once it felt . . . I don't know, appropriate. What I failed to realize was how many different ways I was going to have to pay for all the little perks that were about to come with my new life. My reverie was interrupted by the driver.

"Excuse me, miss. I don't know much about cats, but is that sound coming from the trunk natural?" I tuned in and heard what sounded like a strangled wail coming from the trunk.

"Yup," I replied. "He's probably smelled some girl kitty in the hundred-mile radius." Chucky wasn't going to ruin my brief moment of relaxation before I was plunged into my new job.

"It sure is a noisy one," the driver said.

"You should try sleeping through it. Sheer murder. Just turn up the radio. That's what I usually do." The driver smiled and did just that as we cruised down Sunset.

I was thankful that as we pulled up in front of the Beverly Hills Pet and Day Spa, Chucky had gone quiet. The last thing I needed was some braying cat that the nice receptionist would refuse to accept. If I got in and out of there in three minutes, I could still manage to get to the airport before Emerald. I knew how very important it was not to disappoint my new boss. So I dashed from the car, grabbed the cat carrier out of the back, and sprinted into the kennel.

"Hi. Elizabeth Miller. Dropping off Chucky." The woman looked perplexed. "Sorry. Charles Lloyd," I said. Her face lit up. Well, as much as her Botox would allow.

"Oh. You must be Emanuelle's assistant." She obviously didn't see me blanch as she pressed on. "We haven't seen Charles in ages. We're just such big fans of Emanuelle's. She's so down-to-earth and so gorgeous. How is she, anyway?"

"Oh, you didn't hear?" I said. The girl shook her head in anticipation. She was practically salivating. "It's very sad. If she makes it through I know she's planning on suing the plastic surgeon." I sighed convincingly.

The girl practically squealed. "Plastic surgeon?"

"We're just hoping she won't be disfigured for life. But since the collagen implants moved from her lips into her cheek, it does look a bit like elephantitis. You know, really uneven." I screwed up my face in a way that made it abundantly clear how poor Emanuelle was looking.

"Oh my God." The girl put her hands to her face in horror. "And I thought her lips were real."

I leaned toward her in a stage whisper. "Just between you and me, okay? You know since I am her assistant and I did sign a confidentiality agreement."

The girl put her hand to her heart. "I promise I won't say a word."

"Everything is fake!"

"Everything?" Her jaw was practically on the floor.

"Think Cher. Now I have to run. But take good care of Chu . . . Charles." I gave her a wave and dashed off. I know I shouldn't have, but it just felt so good. Anyway, it served Emanuelle right for lumbering me with her evil feline and stealing my boyfriend.

As we pulled into the terminal I looked at my ticket for the first time. "First class!" I yelped. I didn't mean to brag but I was so shocked I had to say it out loud. The driver glanced into his rearview mirror and gave me a smile. I took this as an opening and shoved my ticket toward the front seat.

"Would you mind taking a look at my ticket? I know it sounds strange, but I think it says first class." The driver grabbed the ticket with one hand.

"I can confirm that you're flying first class, Ms. Miller."

I took a deep breath and a grin spread from ear to ear. I had never flown first class on my own merit before, only as the guest of someone else. This was a momentous moment and thankfully I'd given some thought to my outfit as a T-shirt and my most comfortable pair of sweats definitely wouldn't have done in first class.

I practically bounded from the car when we arrived. I was just so excited to walk up to that lone, empty desk. I knew the check-in lady would look at me like I was on drugs, certain that a girl my age would never be flying first class. I was relishing that moment of satisfaction when I handed her my ticket and she went from rude to deferential. This was going to be fun, after all, a real adventure. I knew now that I'd made the right decision. Well, the right decision had been made for me, but what difference did that make? I was here. My lovely driver carried my bags to the first class desk and I followed him like an eager puppy. I waved good-bye and thanked him profusely for his patience, and then I handed over my ticket and passport. To my great disappointment the woman didn't even bat an eyelid. She smiled politely as she looked at my picture. Either I wasn't looking as young as I thought I did or Lara had dressed me so artfully that I looked like I belonged. I was more inclined to go with the latter. When she saw my name on the passport, she breathed an audible sigh of relief.

"Miss Miller. Thank God you're here." I broke into an instant sweat as anxiety flooded my body.

"Did something happen to my family? Is Luke okay? Did I forget to turn off the gas at the house?" I just knew this wasn't going to be a smooth ride. The check-in lady looked baffled for a brief second.

"As far as I know your family is alive and well. You're Emerald Everhart's assistant, right?" she asked.

I nodded dumbly.

"Well she's waiting for you in the first class lounge. She's been rather . . ." The woman trailed off nervously. "Let me just check you in *quickly.*" Now that didn't sound good. My anxiety worsened when she tapped a colleague on the shoulder and they did one of those whisper-stare-whisper things. I felt like I had a wart on the tip of my nose.

Her colleague took my ticket and passport.

"Just come with me, Miss Miller. I'll escort you to Miss Everhart. It'll be quicker." He picked up my carry-on and began sprinting toward the gate. I had no choice but to follow since he had my passport, wallet, and laptop.

"Excuse me, is there a problem with Emerald?" I called out as I jogged after him.

He stopped briefly and looked at me closely. "You're not her usual assistant, are you?"

"No. I'm new," I puffed.

He let out a nervous laugh, then carried on with his jog, practically knocking people out of the way like a prize running back. He'd hurry up to whomever he was trying to circumvent and I'd hear Emerald's name and then like a flash I was through. We made it to the American Airlines lounge, when I suddenly got very cold feet. He opened the door and held it open expectantly. But I was rooted to the ground. This was my very last chance to escape.

"Ms. Miller, you really *have* to go in." He looked as if he was on the verge of tears. And before I could turn tail and flee, I was grabbed by another concerned representative and dragged through the door. I thought to myself then and there that I really needed to be a bit more proactive with my life. I was in this situation because I'd allowed myself to be traded for a car.

The AA representative who was pulling me by the arm was dressed in an official flame-retardant suit. "Miss Miller. Thank God you've arrived. I'm Carol Powers, head of AA customer relations. This is a potential PR nightmare. We do everything in our power to guarantee the privacy of our customers, but there is just no way of being absolutely certain that a member of the press isn't in our midst." All the while she was dragging me closer to what sounded like an injured hyena.

"What is that noise?" I asked nervously. But as I rounded the corner, I discovered the answer for myself.

Emerald was standing on the bar in her Manolos and micro mini in the middle of performing a strip tease for twenty or so transfixed businessmen.

"Is she drunk?" I stammered. Hoping—actually praying—that this was the case, because if this was her sober, God forbid she cracked a Corona.

Carol Powers swallowed hard as Emerald launched into a rather off-key rendition of "It's Raining Men." I hoped for all of our sakes that she didn't have any repressed rock star dreams.

"Yes. I believe she had a few drinks. And I know she's only nineteen. And we do have a strict twenty-one-only policy at the airline. And I've already reprimanded our bartender. But you see she was quite insistent and he was very starstruck and . . ."

"Duck!" I yelled and hit the ground as a shoe came sailing across the room in our direction. Unfortunately or fortunately, depending on how you looked at it, Carol had clearly never been a Hollywood assistant. I knew this because the poor girl's reflexes weren't up to snuff. The six-inch snakeskin stiletto hit her smack in the forehead with such force it knocked her to the ground.

I heard a cackle from the direction of the bar.

"Ooops. Sorry!" Emerald squealed, and then continued on to the next verse of "It's Raining Men."

There was a slight moan from Carol and then an odd snuffling sound. I looked to make sure she was breathing and then scrambled over to help her stand up when the second high heel whizzed past my face.

"Carol, I think it's best we just sit here on the floor. Let me look at your head." I did a quick examination. There was already a bruise and a little blood but nothing hospital-worthy.

"Am I bleeding?" She sounded oddly hopeful.

"Not really. There's just a small spot of blood from impact."

"But there'll be a bruise, right? A visible one? You know, one that you can see in a picture?"

I helped her up and had a good look at her pupils. They weren't remotely dilated, so she wasn't concussed. Then I saw it clear as day, the green in her eyes. And did I mention they were actually brown?

"I could sue her for this, you know," she said, barely able to contain her excitement. I had to think quickly as a lawsuit on my first day of work wasn't exactly going to endear me to my new boss.

I smiled and leaned in close to Carol as a sweater landed by my feet. I gently turned her in the direction of the disrobing starlet. "And Emerald could sue your airline for serving alcohol to a minor, resulting in potentially career-ending behavior." I had no idea if this was true or not, but it sounded good. "Anyway, it was clearly an accident and there are all these witnesses here to give their statements." I glanced at her again and I could see the dollar signs starting to fade. I pressed on. "I'm sure Emerald is terribly sorry. She'd love to send you an apology present. Why don't I get your address?"

Carol looked from me to Emerald. "I always did want a pair of Manolo Blahniks," she said hesitantly.

"How about this season's entire collection?" I responded magnanimously. She was practically salivating. I had her hook, line, and sinker.

"I'm a size nine. And you have to agree not to sue the airline," she said quickly.

"We wouldn't dream of it. Now let me go and fetch Emerald before she gets that last hook on her bra undone and they shut down your lounge under the Indecency Act," I said. I knew studying politics would come in handy some day.

But the real dilemma was how to remove a drunk nineteen-year-old from the top of the bar when she seemed to be having the time of her life. It occurred to me that she really should be traveling with a publicist, but as I neared the bar Emerald and I made eye contact for the first time that day. Her face lit up and she let out an ear-splitting screech and jumped from the bar practically into my arms. Luckily a kind man standing behind us braced me at exactly the right moment, allowing me to absorb Emerald's hug without us both landing on our rear ends.

"Lizzie! I'm so glad you made it. I was really worried you wouldn't want to come. I mean, I know Scott probably didn't give you much choice. And I know you probably think it's strange considering we've only met once, but that e-mail you wrote for me was so smart and you look so much like my cousin who used to babysit me in Missouri. And I really loved her. She used to braid my hair. She was killed by a drunk driver when she was seventeen. But, anyway, I'm so glad you came. We're going to have so much fun together. We're going to be best friends. Right?" she screeched, barely taking a breath. The entire bar was gripped by her verbal incontinence, including me. But my heart went out to her. She was obviously sweet and well-meaning, just a little wild and a lot young. It was a hard town to grow up in and it seemed there was no one to look after her. She was a baby after all, adrift in a sea of sharks.

My maternal instincts were too busy bubbling to the surface to notice a rather shifty-looking man enter the lounge. But he got my attention quickly enough when a bright flash went off in our faces. Then another. And another. However, before I could pounce to protect my ward, Carol flew from left field and tackled the man to the ground. I think she was gunning for a few new handbags. The security guards were there in seconds, and the man was pinned to the floor.

"I'm flying first class! You have no right to eject me from this lounge!" he was screaming as he waved his ticket in the air. Someone had obviously tipped him off and he'd gone and purchased a ticket knowing he'd be able to sell the photos for a lot more than the cost of the flight. The paparazzi were a whole new experience for me and I just stared dumbfounded as Emerald burst into tears.

"Oh my God. My publicist is going to get so mad at me. She'll probably fire me!" she wailed. Luckily Carol took control because I was certainly incapable of doing so.

"Get that piece of scum out of here, please," she said to the overeager airport security guards. "And though you may have permission to be here, we have the right by law to eject anyone we please from the premises. Please read the sign at the door on the way out. It says STRICTLY NO PHOTOGRAPHS." And with that she scooped the camera out of his pinned-down hand and opened the back, yanking the finished roll of film out and handing it to me.

"This is a violation of my Fifth Amendment rights! I'll sue you!" the paparazzo yelled. Carol smiled, unperturbed. She closed the camera and handed it back empty to the photographer. She gave a head motion to the guards and they pushed the man out the door.

"Thank you for flying American Airlines. It was a pleasure to serve you," she said with a professional smile. Then she turned to Emerald and me, flashing her pearly whites again. "I was a flight attendant for thirteen years before I joined the corporate group."

Emerald turned to look at Carol for the first time. I noticed that Emerald's eyes were beginning to close and she was swaying on her feet a bit. She grabbed my arm for balance. "Lizzie, I don't feel very well," she said, slurring her words. But before I could steer her toward the bathroom, Emerald gagged and then projectile-vomited all over Carol's well-pressed suit. Carol turned to me with that same enormous grin. "I've always wanted to own some Prada."

"And you will," I said with a pained smile.

SEVEN

Hollywood is a place where they
place you under contract instead
of under observation.

—Walter Winchell

"Wakey, wakey, Lizzie."

I closed my eyes tightly, hoping that I was still in the middle of a nightmare. But no matter how deeply I buried my head into the delicious down pillow, the slightly midwestern twang of my nineteen-year-old persecutor just wouldn't fade to black. Instead the voice seemed to get closer. And then I was rudely forced to consciousness by a pair of slightly smelly feet jumping up and down inches from my nose.

"Lizzie! We're in Bangkok!" Emerald screamed at the top of her lungs followed by a few sharp, well-placed bounces that sent me flying out of my enormous bed onto the hotel room floor.

"I was really hoping that wasn't the case, Emerald. But I see it is," I grumbled with my face pressed to the carpet. This seemed to take the wind out of Emerald's sails momentarily. She collapsed onto my bed dramatically.

"We're only in Bangkok for one night and you're sleeping!" she stated peevishly.

I pulled myself hesitantly off the floor and grabbed one of those luxuriously thick white robes that only the best hotels know how to provide and wrapped myself in it, longing for some sort of protection. I looked around my sumptuous room and knew I wasn't going to get a chance to admire the beautifully painted mural on the ceiling or take advantage of the decadent marble bathroom suite. I could even see one of those mirrors I loved that amplifies everything by a million.

I tried once more. "Emerald, we've been on a flight for twenty hours."

"I know and I slept the entire way," she replied happily.

And in truth she had. I, on the other hand, hadn't slept a wink on the plane. It had nothing to do with being fifty thousand feet up in the air or discomfort—the seat was enormous and went completely flat. It had more to do with sheer terror. Terror that if I took my eye off my charge for one second, Emerald would be into the stash of champagne. And more likely than not the six-foot-ten-inch man across the aisle would be into her. They had recognized each other immediately. Don't get me wrong, not a word passed between them, but there was that "I'm a celebrity and so are you" kind of nod-thing that had happened when they both took their seats. I'd tried to ask Emerald quietly who he was but she had barely known her own name at that point and refused to cooperate. A real shame since I was certain that he had to be a basketball player. I don't like to buy into stereotypes, but no one that unnaturally tall traveling first class could be anything else. And though I didn't care an ounce about the sport, Luke was a die-hard Lakers fan. He turned into an adolescent when the topic came up, and he had a collection of signed shirts in his office that were his pride and joy. And though I'd sworn to never speak to Luke again, if he did have a good excuse it wouldn't be a bad idea to have a little kiss and makeup present. So all I could think of as Emerald flopped around in her seat, stinking of booze, was how to ask the tall man for an autograph without breaking the "we're all so cool and famous in first class that we pretend not to recognize one another" unwritten rule.

I'd only turned my head for a brief second but when I looked back Emerald was clutching a glass of champagne. I gave up any hope of impressing my estranged boyfriend by way of reflected basketball glory and focused all my attention on my charge. The stewardess just stood there with a bottle of icy Tattinger like Eve in the Garden of Eden. She obviously hadn't heard about the debacle in the lounge. I realized then and there that danger lurked everywhere. Though Emerald could barely speak and she still smelled like puke from her little misadventure at the airport, she'd managed to artfully get that glass to her lips without being spotted. I tried to wrest it away, but Emerald had a firm grip and our tug-of-war resulted in the glass emptying itself down my cashmere hoodie. That sweet smell of sick and alcohol mixed with a faint stench of wet sheep gave me a distinctive odor similar to the homeless woman who lived outside of Barneys on Wiltshire. But anything was better than an international incident over the Pacific. Which I'm sure would have resulted in front-page news and the loss of my job with Emerald and The Agency as well. I was still technically on their payroll, though I had managed to force Scott into wangling me an obscene five-thousand-dollars-a-week as a bonus for agreeing to this lunacy. And though my agency job was no great shakes, I was attached to it in an unhealthy sort of a way, so the idea of getting fired filled me with absolute dread. I had never been fired before. Laid off? Yes. Fired? No. And I had no intention of bucking the trend. So while Emerald slept for twenty hours straight I sat up, my eyes shriveling into little piss holes in the snow, watching every movie available to guarantee that my little teen dream stayed put.

When we finally arrived at the Mandarin Oriental in Bangkok I was so exhausted I could barely put one foot in front of the other. The idea of my own room, a hot bath, and a little space from Emerald was like a fantasy come true. But that wasn't to be. Emerald needed a playmate and I was getting paid to be just that person.

"Emerald, how did you get into my room?" I wanted to make sure that she didn't have some special skeleton key and that I wasn't going to be spending the next three months having to barricade my door every time I went to bed.

"Oh. I told the concierge you had a drug problem. I said you weren't answering your phone and I was very worried that you'd overdosed. Aren't I just brilliant?" she yelled as she started to bounce on the bed again.

Brilliant wasn't at the top of my list. Effective. Pathological. Juvenile. Spoiled, maybe. All I could do was hope that the concierge wasn't reporting to the production. I had yet to meet the producers of *The War Fields,* and I didn't relish their first report being one of an addled junkie. I looked at the clock as Emerald made a mess of my bed, and I realized she'd let me sleep for all of forty-five minutes. I was filled with an intense hatred that only extreme exhaustion can engender. I literally had to take a few of those deep om breaths that Alexa had taught me. And for the moment it worked. I felt my shoulders dropping from around my ears and I was able to put things into perspective.

"Come on, Lizzie, get dressed. Bangkok is famous for sex and I want a taste," Emerald said with giddy excitement. A smile started to creep across my face. I had to look at this in a more positive light. She certainly had a unique enthusiasm for life. Emerald bounded from the bed like a Labrador puppy and headed straight for the bar. Before I could edit myself, the words just tumbled from my lips.

"Emerald! If you so much as crack open that minibar I am shoving you and the bottle of whatever you've got out the door and I'm putting on the chain. And I won't care if you get abducted into white slavery or screw the entire hotel staff!" I yelled. Emerald stopped in her tracks and looked at me in total shock. Then her big blue eyes narrowed and she looked a lot like Mike Tyson before he bit that guy's ear off. Obviously they were both used to getting their way. And who was I to be the stumbling block? She was my boss, after all. We stood in silence as I contemplated the twenty-hour flight back to LA. Then, as quickly as it appeared, the storm cloud faded. Emerald batted her eyelashes and gave me an Oscar-winning pout.

"But we're in Thailand. There is no drinking age," she whined.

I breathed a sigh of relief. Obviously she kind of liked being told what to do. Still, it was an experiment I reminded myself not to repeat too often. I'd seen something in her eyes for a brief second that had made my blood run a little bit colder than usual. I decided to soften my approach.

"That's not the point, Emerald. I can't deal with a repeat of the airport. I only brought so many clothes and I don't like the smell of puke," I told her.

She didn't seem to get the irony as she opened the minibar and started routing around. "Oh is that all? I'll buy you a whole new wardrobe. Yours was looking a bit boring, anyway."

I walked to the minibar and slammed it shut. Practically taking her perfect little nose with it. "I like my wardrobe. And if we're going to go out in Bangkok together I need you to have just one of your wits intact. Okay? Listen, I'm not your mother, but . . ."

"That's obvious," she interrupted with a guffaw. "Mom was the one who gave me my first cocktail when I was ten. She said it kept me quiet. You're not one of those Christian Right kind of people, are you?"

I was having a moment of empathy for Emerald's mother when this latest insult knocked me sideways.

"Fuck no!" I had to put in the fuck to emphasize my heathen morals. "You can have a drink when we get to the club. Okay? I just don't want to have to carry you there."

This seemed to make sense to Emerald. "Oh. Okay. Why didn't you just say so?" she said as she opened the fridge again. I was certain I'd lost the battle until she pulled out a Diet Coke and gave me a mischievous wink. "I think we're going to have a really good time, Lizzie." Her smile was contagious and for a brief second I almost believed her. She did have a point. We were only in Bangkok for a night and though I felt like an old lady compared to Emerald, I was under thirty and did have a vague recollection of how to have a good time without a boyfriend.

"Okay, Emerald. Why don't I meet you in the lobby in fifteen minutes and we'll hit the town," I said, and glanced at my tightly zipped suitcase. "If I can find anything in my bag, that is."

Emerald was halfway to the door when her eyes lit up like a birthday cake. She spun around with a big grin. "You so don't want to unzip that bag. I can just tell that it'll take you hours to get it packed again," she warned, and she wasn't wrong. I really didn't relish the idea of getting up an hour early tomorrow to repack my bag, only to unpack it again an hour later when we reached Phuket.

"Oh my God! I have the best idea in the world! I'll dress you tonight!" Emerald squealed with delight. My face must have registered shock and horror as I examined her micro mini and sequined top. Don't get me wrong, she could carry it off, but either my boobs weren't as young or hers weren't as real. I think I gave an audible gag.

"Please, Lizzie, it'll be so much fun. And the good thing is you won't run into anyone you know!" She wasn't as dumb as she looked. "It'll be so much easier. Then you won't have to open your bag and you'll get to sleep an extra hour in the morning." She was reading my mind and I was teetering dangerously.

Part of being a star is having absolute confidence in what you put on your body. If you have the attitude, you can get away with almost any-thing. Hence dresses that make a woman's career: Liz Hurley and her Versace safety pins. Jennifer Lopez and her handkerchief outfit. Lizzie Miller and her split minidress?

I stood there on the street corner looking like a prostitute. A very ex-pensive one, as the piece of fabric I was wearing was worth three thou-sand dollars. Though I was certain someone somewhere must be rolling with laughter, because the black piece of jersey that barely skimmed my behind must have cost all of ten cents to make. It wasn't the length that made me self-conscious, though I've always hated my knees, but the fact that there was no material from my neck right down to my belly button and a repeat down the back. The entire thing was actually strung together at my shoulders by a fat-link silver chain. My boobs were stuck in with some tape and every time I moved, the draped bits swung in a way that suggested a game of peekaboo wasn't far off. Thankfully Emerald and I had different shoe sizes so I got to wear my combat boots, which gave the whole thing a slightly rocker vibe that I preferred to the Peninsula hooker look.

Not only had Emerald dressed me, but she'd done my makeup as well. All the while assuring me that she'd gone to school to be a makeup artist before she'd started acting. When I looked in the mirror and asked a few more questions, I realized that "school" was the beauty counter at Bloomingdales. Hence the overabundance of slightly orange foundation and the plethora of green eye shadow.

But as we climbed into the tuk-tuk, a form of cart on the back of a moped and the only mode of transportation in Bangkok, I was filled with a sudden rush of excitement. Though Luke and I still hadn't spo-ken and he had no idea where I was, in my head we'd already broken up. So as far as I was concerned I was single, I was young, and I had the world at my feet. It was time to enjoy and experience life. Who knew what would happen with Luke in the future, but for now I was free and it was time I took full advantage of it. Instead of looking at this trip merely as a means of escape, I was going to look at it as a way of broad-ening my horizons. I had to think of this as a get-out-of-jail-free card. If

Luke was off canoodling with Emanuelle, I'd be a total fool to just sit here in Thailand pining over someone I'd never had in the first place. Zac's tennis instruction had been even more helpful than I'd thought. I was going to approach this trip like I'd just emerged from the womb. I could be whoever I wanted, forget the past. And tonight I was going to be Lizzie Miller, friend and playmate to Emerald Everhart. Hell, I looked the part, I might as well act it.

Riding side by side in the tuk-tuk we were speechless. It was eleven o'clock at night and the sheer multitude of people on the street was overwhelming. The cars were backed up, honking, and the tuk-tuks were swerving treacherously in and out of the stand-still traffic. Our driver's name was Klahan, which he happily informed us meant "brave" in Thai. And by the way he was driving, I didn't doubt it. When he'd picked us up outside the hotel, he'd looked us up and down and had smiled knowingly. "*Patpong. Patpong.* Ladies want good time."

I wasn't sure if he was suggesting we buy a good time or sell a good time, but I decided to go with it.

"You famous, right?" Klahan smiled his toothy grin as he drove along. Emerald preened. There was nothing that a movie star liked more than being recognized, especially in a foreign country.

"I didn't know my movies played in Thailand. I guess it's probably no surprise, though, since I have been in twelve films. I know. I know it's hard to believe as I am only nineteen. But—"

Klahan interrupted Emerald in midgush. "You in movies, too?" He looked at Emerald briefly and then turned to me. "You with the split dress," he said, staring down at my crotch while almost steering us into a parked truck. "You in that movie where naughty girl show your nono on camera."

Emerald, who'd been looking rather irritated at not being recognized, let out a guffaw.

"No. I'm sorry to disappoint, but I'm not an actress of any kind. Would you mind just keeping your eye on the road, please?" My newly found enthusiasm vanished. I just wanted to go home and put on some clothes. I waited a moment and then turned to Emerald.

"Emerald. Maybe I'll just go back to the hotel and pull on a pair of jeans," I said, trying not to sound like being mistaken for a porn star by a Thai tuk-tuk driver meant anything to my obviously fragile self-image. But Emerald was thrilled and had bonded with Klahan as a result.

"Don't be silly, Lizzie. We've got the best driver in Bangkok and I bet he'll show us around if we ask nicely. Right, Klahan?"

Klahan was now completely uninterested in me and only had eyes for Emerald, which was better for all concerned. Emerald dug a hundred-dollar bill out of her purse and waved it in Klahan's face. He grabbed it, smelled it, and fell in love for life.

"Sure, little missy. I be your guide and bodyguard as long as you in Bangkok."

Great, I thought grumpily, as I tried to pull down my skirt and take in the sights at the same time.

Klahan kept his word and was the best tourguide two scantily-clad Americans could have. I even asked him about the history of the area, and he happily launched into a bit of local lore, much to Emerald's disdain. I was fascinated and I couldn't believe the entire area was owned by one family. It had once been a plantation and now the four acres was the center of the biggest sex industry in the world. There were over a hundred clubs and the family who owned it made over ten million baht monthly on rent alone.

"The Patpongpanichs are a very wealthy family," said Klahan reverently. "They bought Patpong from bank of Indochina for sixty thousand baht. Very smart."

Emerald started to giggle as he parked his tuk-tuk on a main street. "Patpong*arich*? You've got to be kidding me!"

I started to laugh, too, as did Klahan, after he finally caught on.

"Yes. Patpongarich. I get it."

We stepped out onto the street and were immediately sucked into the flow of people. There were so many neon lights, it felt like Vegas. I was holding on to Klahan's arm hoping not to lose him when I realized Emerald had disappeared.

"Lizzie! Over here!" I saw her standing in front of a window, waving me over. I hurried toward her and we both stared in confusion. In the window were twenty girls sitting on stools in various stages of undress.

Each one had a number hanging around her neck. They were chatting and generally looking bored.

"Why are they sitting in there?" I asked naively.

Klahan smiled widely. "They hooker. You order up the number inside. See?" He pointed around the alley to the door.

"You mean it's like takeout?" Emerald asked baffled.

"Exactly! Saves time picking girl and hopefully the girls so cute it pulls you in." He gave us a sly look. "If you interested I know much better place. Much prettier girls."

"Don't be ridiculous. They're girls. Let's go!" I said. The scene was unbelieveable. It was four acres of sex. So overwhelming that the human body began to lose its appeal. Well, certainly its novelty. On sale right next to the sex was an enormous outdoor market hawking every imaginable designer rip-off. Now this was something I could get excited about.

"Emerald, look at these!" I held up a perfect copy of this season's Chloe handbag.

"Amazing!" Emerald said as she bought a dozen in every color. "I'll send them to all my cousins back home. They'll never know the difference," she said, thrilled with the deal. To be honest I couldn't tell the difference, either. And I was looking closely. The leather was soft and the label in the right place. Even the big chunky gold lock was deadly heavy.

"Are these fakes?" I asked stupidly. The woman at the stall shook her head convincingly.

"Nah, fake. Real leather." I decided I was fighting a losing battle and handed over my twenty dollars. Then I emptied my scruffy Coach bag and tossed it into the trash. It was oddly liberating.

But then I saw the Rolexes and my heart plummeted. There in the pile of imitations was the same watch that Luke wore. The green bezeled anniversary edition that he'd so proudly shown me when he'd first bought it.

"How much?" I asked on impulse. Just then Emerald walked over. She looked at me oddly as I negotiated for the man's watch.

"Why the long face?" she asked perceptively. I had no intention of pouring my heartache out on my boss, but at that particular moment she felt like a girlfriend and I needed to tell someone. The man handed me the watch and I slid it onto my wrist.

"My boyfriend had one just like this. We broke up two days ago, though I haven't told him yet. No big deal." I looked at the watch and burst into tears. I hadn't cried since seeing the picture of Luke and Emanuelle and it felt really good to let it all out. And before I could see it coming, Emerald threw her arms around my neck and gave me an enormous bear hug.

"I'm so sorry, sweetie," she said genuinely, as she embraced me like a little child, burying my face into her ample bosom. I had promised myself that I wouldn't discuss my private life on the job and here I was on our first night out already sobbing in my boss's arms. I really had to get a handle on things. I gently pulled away, swallowing my tears.

"Thanks for the support, Emerald. I'm sure I'll be fine," I said bravely as Emerald gave a big sigh.

"Of course you will. Fuck him. There are plenty of fish in the sea. I bet he wasn't worth the ground you walk on."

I wished for a second that that was the case. "I don't know. He was pretty great. I think it was probably my fault. . . ." And the problem was I believed every word I was saying. I'd practically driven him into Emanuelle's arms. He had wanted me and somehow I'd made him want her.

"Come on. Let's go get wasted." Emerald grabbed my hand and gave it a tug.

"Sure. Why not?" In for a penny in for a pound, I decided. Alcohol was probably the only way to soothe my broken heart, and at that very moment I really didn't care how much my head hurt in the morning.

EIGHT

You can't find any true closeness in
Hollywood because everyone does
the fake closeness so well.

—Carrie Fisher

"A Slow Screw, please!" Emerald bellowed to the bartender with a flick
of her flaxen locks. The bartender looked perplexed and just stood
there staring at her blankly. I usually wouldn't have intervened, but I
knew that Emerald had no idea what a Slow Screw was. She'd only
ever had the fast variety in club bathrooms. The order had been placed
solely for optimum shock value. And shocking this bartender was not
going to be an easy feat. First, we were standing in a bar called Screw
Boy Go-Go and up and down the streets were establishments with
names like Super Pussy's and Pou Pee. And second, there were ladies
removing their panties while circling their legs like windmills at his eye
level. And not even this distraction made the bartender overpour a single shot. So nothing Emerald Everhart could do or say would surprise
anyone tonight. It was this realization that set me free. And I needed a
night of forgetting—to be anonymous and drown my sorrows without
having to worry that it would be posted on the message board at The
Agency the next day by Amber and her little team of spies and back-
stabbers. Or that I'd turn a corner and see another picture on the
newsstand of the perfect and sexy Emanuelle with her fangs in the
neck of the man I loved. Well, at least thought I'd loved until he'd
turned into a rat.

   "Do you have Absolute Citron?" I ventured, determined to get some
sort of numbing agent down my throat as quickly as possible. I had
nothing against the female anatomy, but I was no Eve Ensler. I'd just

never been the kind of girl who had any interest in looking at my private parts up close with my dressing-table mirror. I think it was the first time in my life that I'd cursed my twenty-twenty vision.

The bartender waved an Absolute bottle in front of my face and I practically grabbed the whole thing.

"Shots, please. Two." I turned to Emerald. "Em, let's just do these shots and get out of here. There's supposed to be some great cigar bar on the other main drag." But Emerald wasn't listening to me. She was busy craning her neck toward the other side of the bar. My testosterone alert had obviously rusted into oblivion, because there, standing ten feet above everyone else, was the basketball player from the plane. And who was smiling at his side looking as handsome as ever but Jake Hudson.

"Make it *four* shots, please!" I yelped. At that moment I needed alcohol more than Betty Ford could have ever imagined. I managed to get two of the shots down before Emerald even turned around.

"Oh my God! That's Freddie Murray!" She noticed my blank stare. "The center for the Lakers?" Then suddenly she started to flip her hair in a manner that looked almost painful. I made a mental note to book a massage for her on our arrival in Phuket. And "Oh my God. That's Jake Hudson!" she said excitedly. She mistook my look of repulsion for lack of recognition and I had no intention of correcting her. "Lizzie. He's like the head of the studio that's doing my movie! And he's fucking *hot.*"

Before I could pick her up, throw her over my shoulder, and run from the bar, she was tapping Jake on the shoulder. I tugged on my dress self-consciously, but every time I gave the skirt a yank, the top came dangerously close to disappearing.

I couldn't exactly hear what she was saying, but she was doing a lot of pointing in my direction and gesticulating. Though the world is a big place, Hollywood is a very small one. Jake looked up and our eyes met. He gave me a respectful little nod. But then his eyes drifted quickly to my right, and when he looked back, he gave me the naughtiest wink imaginable. I turned, perplexed, and there, hovering a mere three inches away from me, was a very beautiful Thai woman wearing only her underpants. She placed her hand on my arm.

"You want to go outside for walk?" she said with a remarkably innocent smile for a girl with no clothes on. I was about to pull my arm away, but she looked so young and sweet I didn't want to hurt her feelings.

"No thank you. I'm just here with a friend."

"We can go and you just pay bar fine five hundred baht. We discuss hanky panky later."

I glanced over at Jake, but he was gone. Great, now everyone in Los Angeles was going to think I had a penchant for Thai strippers. It would probably do wonders for my image, I thought ruefully. I turned back to the girl.

"Girls aren't my thing. I'm sorry," I explained, but the hostess seemed to take offense. She began to jabber inanely, waving her arms around and drawing lots of unwanted attention in my direction.

"It's not that I don't *like* girls," I said in a panic. "I *am* one, of course. And you're very nice and everything. But I like boys. Do you understand? You know, men. I like to kiss men—"

"Yes. I remember," a deep voice whispered in my ear as a rather possessive arm slipped around my shoulder. Though my romantic interest in Jake was null and void, there was something so comforting about having that six-foot-two-inch frame supporting me. I unconsciously leaned into him and could smell the hotel soap and his faintly damp hair. I couldn't help but think how nice it would be to curl up in those big arms and forget anyone else existed. But then the memories came flooding back, and though the two vodkas were dulling the pain, they hadn't actually erased my memory.

The last time I'd gone out with Jake Hudson, he'd ended up getting some action in the darkened movie theater from the publicist sitting to his left, while I, his unsuspecting date, sat to his right getting my hand crushed to some mysterious rhythm.

"I remember, too, Jake," I said ruefully, as I pulled away and tried to gather my wits. But the hostess was still there standing stubbornly inches from my face. Thankfully Jake took charge of the situation in a way only a seasoned professional could do. And his credentials had nothing to do with movies.

"She's with me. But we'd love to buy you a drink," he said to her, casually handing over a few bills. She finally scurried off and I breathed a sigh of relief. I looked up into those perfect clear blue eyes and those

Chiclets teeth and felt absolutely . . . nothing. Though my hopes of anonymity were dashed, there was something oddly intimate about being in a foreign country with people you didn't know very well. There was an automatic familiarity that would never happen in your own country or city. And I realized that I was glad to see Jake.

"Elizabeth. Why aren't you my girlfriend?" He was obviously having the same experience.

"Because, Jake, you don't do girlfriends. Or if you do, you do a lot of them at one time." I punched him in the arm trying to establish the "we're just buddies, let's have a beer" kind of rapport and grabbed for the remaining two shots. I handed one to him while he gave me his best Boy Scout look. We clinked glasses and downed the vodka.

"But you could change me, Elizabeth."

"Yeah. And I've heard if I buy a ticket I can win the lottery, too." I turned to the bartender. "Two more of these, please."

"So how's Luke?" Jake said as he looked me squarely in the eye.

I was taken aback by the question. I couldn't believe he actually knew we were together. And I was even more shocked that he didn't know we'd split up. The public nature of Luke's infidelity was bound to be headline news to those in the know.

"Luke is . . . away! Away filming *Dracula's Seventh Sister*. Or something Oscar-worthy like that," I said vaguely.

"Luke's one of the good guys, you know," he said with sincerity.

I choked on my own tongue as Jake pressed on. "But that said. *I'm* better."

I started to laugh. It might have been verging on the hysterical, but I don't think Jake would have been able to differentiate.

"I think you're not wrong, Mr. Hudson. I'd say you're about equal in the quality department and you just might be edging ahead slightly."

Thankfully Emerald bounded over before I was stuck explaining myself. She had the gentle giant by the hand and occasionally she'd turn and give his stomach a big hug.

"Lizzie. Oh my God! You know Jake! He's here for our first day of shooting. We're all going to fly on the studio jet to Phuket tomorrow. Isn't that great?"

"That's great news, Em," I said. All I could think of was the possibility of an extra few hours in the yummy Frette sheets at the Oriental.

"And if you girls stay out and party with us tonight, I promise to have the plane leave in the evening after a day at the spa on me. Apparently they have coed massages. Either of you game?" Jake looked directly at me. But thankfully Emerald didn't notice his pointed stare and jumped up and down with glee.

"I am. I am! But first we all have to go upstairs. You won't believe what Freddie and I discovered. It's so *cool*."

I had almost forgotten that Freddie was there. He hadn't said a word and as his face was so far above mine it was almost too easy to treat him like a tree trunk. But instead of leaning against him, I stuck out my hand.

"Lizzie Miller," I volunteered.

"Freddie Murray," he said, smiling down at me.

"I hear you play some basketball?" I was getting a crick in my neck just looking at him.

"That's what they tell me. But Jake here's trying to persuade me to be in movies," he drawled in a slightly Southern twang.

The alcohol was really starting to hit me now.

"Are you famous? Like someone my boyfriend . . . well, ex-boyfriend, would die to have an autograph from?" I asked.

Luckily Emerald intervened this time, as my ability for subtlety was waning at an alarming rate. She handed shots all around. "Okay. Alabama Slammers. Then we're going upstairs." The four of us grabbed the shot glasses, clinked, and down they went. Then upstairs we went.

Emerald had arranged four seats right on the edge of the stage. We couldn't have been any closer unless we'd joined the act. I looked around, thrilled, because no one seemed to have better seats. This job certainly had its perks and the best of everything was one of them. I scouted the room and noticed that there was a drastic change in décor from downstairs. Every possible surface was mirrored harking back to 1983 with a slightly dated 9½ *Weeks* feel. And lo and behold a woman suddenly appeared onstage in a bowler hat and tuxedo jacket. I stifled a yawn at the idea of a protracted striptease. She started to take off her clothes to the music as I focused on the colorful balloons attached to the pillar right by my ear.

"Do you think she's hot?" Jake leaned over and whispered in my ear. I leaned in close and whispered back.

"I know it's *hard*." I patted his leg amicably. "But you really should try and mask your puerile fantasies just a little bit. A less obvious approach would probably be much more effective." I was getting ruder by the minute and the odd thing was it seemed to be turning him on. He just laughed.

"If I were any more effective, I wouldn't have time to work." Jake winked as he waved down the waitress and ordered a bottle of vodka. I would have liked to write this comment off to a grossly inflated ego, but I knew he was just stating the facts. If you had the right job in LA, you could get almost anyone to sleep with you.

I rolled my eyes and shifted my gaze back to the stage just as a Ping-Pong ball went sailing by my right ear. The woman in the bowler hat had shed her clothing with remarkable speed and was now naked facing me on all fours in a crablike position. She let out an enormous grunt and another object came shooting by my left ear this time. I blinked, unable to comprehend exactly what was happening, when the performer started to insert a bamboo tube between her legs. The crowd was cheering as I just sat there in shocked horror. Emerald was practically rolling on the stage in fits of hysterical giggles between make-out sessions with Freddie. Obviously somebody found it erotic. But we all went silent as the stripper proceeded to hold up a dart. Then she gave another grunt and there was a loud pop. For a second I was sure she'd punctured her innards, until I realized that it was simply the balloon above my head. The dart dropped onto the table, right in front of me. Emerald made a dive, grabbing it like a baseball at the World Series.

"I've got it! I've got it!" she screamed as she held the dart up in the air like a trophy. I grabbed the vodka bottle and doused Emerald's hand.

"What are you doing?" she squealed, annoyed, as I accidentally covered half her arm and most of her front in the process.

"It's a *dart*, Emerald, and it has been up a Thai hooker's pussy," I whispered.

Emerald displayed a tiny bit of sense and quickly dropped the offending dart and proceeded to cover her own hand in the remaining vodka. But my whisper had obviously not been quiet enough because I heard a grunt and then felt a sharp sting in my left arm. I glanced down at my bare shoulder and sticking straight out of my flesh was the dart. While I was still blinking in horror, the human cannon sashayed over, ripped the dart from my arm, and said angrily for all to hear, "I no hooker. I actress!"

I was shocked speechless, torn between two emotions. I felt terrible that I'd insulted this poor girl who was now busy shoving a string of razor blades inside herself, and completely freaked out that I'd possibly just contracted HIV. What was I doing in a place like this, anyway? The poor girl had probably been sold into slavery as a child and made to perform like a trained monkey to provide a roof over her head. My sister's face kept flashing in front of me. I knew she'd be sick with horror that I was contributing to the unregulated sex trade and essentially giving money to perpetuate the enslavement of women. I deserved to get AIDS and die.

Emerald took the opportunity to get some payback and started pouring the vodka all over my arm and dress. I think the alcohol was making me a bit melodramatic or perhaps it was the lack of sleep, but suddenly my bottom lip started to quiver and I could feel tears sting my eyes.

Jake and Freddie looked at me in horror, and I couldn't help but sniff and laugh at the same time. Here were two grown men who could watch a woman fire razor blades out of her private parts and not be fazed, yet when a tiny tear welled in a girl's eye they turned white. It made me adore them both instantly. Emerald was still busy pouring vodka on me, totally unaware of the change in tone, until Freddie yanked the bottle out of her hand.

"Leave her alone. She's upset," he ordered.

Emerald looked at me closely and then at the boys who were hanging on my every hiccup. Jake was holding my arm, examining the wound, and Freddie was wiping the vodka off of me with his shirt. She was not a girl who enjoyed being outdone by a mere assistant.

"It barely pierced the flesh, Lizzie. I wouldn't worry," Jake said.

"Yeah, and if you watched closely, the dart goes in the bamboo tube. So really it doesn't have any contact with her pussy," Freddie said reassuringly. Then out of nowhere there was an animal keening and a wail. The three of us turned around in concern as Emerald was bent over with a dart protruding from her left thigh.

"Oh my God. I've been shot. Call an ambulance," she screamed as only an actress could. Freddie dropped me in a second and turned to

Emerald. She collapsed in his arms, and he stroked her hair, whispering soothing sweet nothings.

Jake leaned in to my ear and said under his breath, "You've got to give her credit for being such a good method actor. It must have really hurt to stab that thing into your own leg."

I started to laugh and then noticed a man join the girl onstage.

"If those people start having sex on this stage I'm going to be sick and then the night will be over," I said as Emerald glanced at the couple walking toward each other.

"Then let's get out of here," Jake said.

Emerald was less than pleased and Jake clocked it immediately. He gave me a quick wink before turning his full attention toward Emerald. With what sounded like genuine concern he patted her thigh where the dart had been. "Are you okay, baby? Poor little you. I'm going to tell the hostess downstairs that they better send that one back to target practice." I stifled a laugh. But Jake continued. "Now we better get you out of here before anything else happens. I have to protect the studio's investment, you know. Do you have any idea how much the insurance is on you? Lordy."

Emerald preened at the attention and of course the allusion to her vast six-million-dollar-a-movie price tag. Jake took one of her arms as Freddie took the other. They supported her as she dramatically limped away from the stage and down the stairs. I gathered our bags and followed behind as I watched Emerald quickly forget her limp.

"Let's go to the cigar bar. Lizzie, you won't mind that, right?" she called out to me. "You come from Washington, D.C. I bet they don't do anything at this place that Monica Lewinsky hasn't tried," Emerald said with a guffaw.

She was obviously fully recovered by the time we made it down to the bottom of the stairs, because she pulled away from the boys and headed toward the bar.

"But before we go, how about we all have one more drink? All that drama made me thirsty. Anyway, I need it to sterilize the wound." Emerald looked up at Jake and batted her eyelashes, but Jake's attention had shifted to a pretty blond student-type who'd just walked in the door. Emerald didn't seem to care. She was a good sport, after all, and was really just chasing a perennial good time. "You up for a cocktail, Lizzie? You know you need to sterilize your wound, too." I didn't have the heart to mention that it didn't work from the inside out. So I just smiled and took the proffered drink.

When I opened my eyes the next morning, I was completely disoriented. I expected to see Chucky purring by my head and to smell the eucalyptus wafting in through the open window but instead there was the faint smell of last night's cigar smoke and the gentle whirr of the air conditioner. I breathed a sigh of relief as my eyes adjusted to the gloom. There was nothing to worry about. It had been a great night and, though my head felt like a pinball and my mouth tasted like I'd been licking the pavement, I was alone in three-thousand-thread-count sheets, there was not an ounce of light aggravating my headache, and there was a steam room downstairs waiting to cleanse my polluted bloodstream. And as far as I could recall nothing disgraceful had happened. I looked under the covers and was pleased to see that I was still wearing Emerald's little postage stamp of a dress. You never could predict what a little vodka could do to one's judgment.

Oddly, heartbreak was having the opposite effect on me from what I'd expected. I would have thought that I'd have thrown myself in someone like Jake's arms last night, if not for revenge at least for comfort, but I had no interest in romance or sex at the moment. If anything, I wanted to punish the male race. I knew this wasn't the healthiest approach, but since I couldn't take my broken heart out on Luke, I figured that I might as well work out my aggression on another man. And Jake had been the perfect target. He had skin like a rhinoceros and took pleasure in my verbal lashings. The more waspish I had become last night, the more bullish he had been. As I gave it a moment's thought it actually all made sense. No one got to his position in Hollywood without enduring serious abuse on the way up. So in order to get his fix, he either paid some dominatrix in LA to dress him in a diaper and spank his bottom or he pursued whatever impossible challenge was available. And last night it was me. My guess was that Jake indulged in a bit of both.

I picked up the phone and dialed room service. I ordered eggs, pancakes, fruit, hash browns, coffee, orange juice, a smoothie, and a Bloody

Mary. It was enough food to feed a small army. And though it was decadent, at that moment I didn't care. As I hung up the phone and wandered into the bathroom, I tried to understand why I couldn't just do that when I was with Luke. What was the big deal? It wasn't like he paid for anything himself. It was all expensed to the studio. It was all so meaningless to him, and I'd made it into a ridiculous drama. Why did I have such a difficult time taking anything from him? For some reason, I felt I needed to prove my worthiness.

I bent down to fill the enormous bathtub and dumped the delicious-smelling bubble bath in. I looked at the label, JO MALONE. LIME, BASIL AND MANDARIN. I inhaled deeply and reminded myself to steal all available travel products when I left. I unhooked the dress and instead of falling to the floor like a Dove ad, it seemed to just stick to my boobs like a drowning man to a life preserver. I gave the material a hard yank and it came off in my hand, leaving two pieces of double-sided tape on my bosoms. I tired to pick at the tape, but it wasn't budging. I resolved to never let Emerald dress me again as I closed my eyes and gave the most almighty yank, taking half the skin and part of my nipple with me. I almost passed out with the pain and had visions of being called Cyclops for the rest of my life. The other piece would have to wait. I wasn't married yet and there were no longer any prospects in the hopper so I was going to need my one remaining nipple. I shook my head and tried to think positively. At least I'd made it through the night with the head of the biggest studio in LA, a famous basketball player, and the most talked-about teenage movie star of the decade without embarrassing myself. That was a first. Maybe I was learning the Hollywood ropes after all.

As I walked away from the mirror I stopped in my tracks. There was something on my behind. I walked backward toward the mirror. It was writing. What did it say and how had it gotten there? I got as close to the mirror as possible. Whatever it said was written in a black Sharpie. I looked at it closely and read out loud.

"Luke. Wish you were here. All the best, Freddie Murray."

I started hyperventilating and grabbed the bathroom phone dialing Emerald's room. "Hello." A sleepy Emerald answered.

I breathed a sigh of relief. "Em. It's Lizzie. I was just getting into the bath and I seem to have Freddie's autograph on my ass."

Emerald started to laugh and then to cough. "You were so cool last night, Lizzie. I just love you. Hold on for a second." I could hear her talking to someone in the background. "Freddie, will you be a doll and order me some breakfast on the other phone?"

"Emerald, how did I get the autograph?" I demanded.

"You don't remember? I can't believe that. You hold your booze really well. I'd never have known. Well, after the orgy we—" she began as I started choking. Emerald quickly put me out of my misery. "Jesus, Lizzie, take a breath, I was just kidding! God, you are so not the type. You were banging on about your nasty ex who was engaged to some French tart and how he was a huge fan of Freddie's and would have died for an autograph."

"Oh, Emerald, was I embarrassing?" I hated to ask but it needed to be out in the open.

"No. You were cute," she assured me. I wasn't sure how the tables had been turned so terribly but I promised myself not to let it happen again. "Anyway. Freddie suggested he autograph your butt and then we'd take a picture so Luke would know what a good time you were having and that you'd moved on with your life. Both Jake and Freddie said that they'd be eating their arm with jealousy if their girlfriend sent a photo like that."

"So we took photos of my naked butt?" I screeched in horror.

"Don't worry, it was only with my cell phone."

"Erase it, Emerald! Now! Please!" I begged.

"Okay, okay. Hold on." She called out again. "Jake, honey, can you bring me my phone?" I did a double take and practically dropped the phone. Jake? But she'd just had Freddie order breakfast. "It's erased. Okay? Now call me when you're heading down to the spa. Bye."

I hung up the phone and climbed into the marble bathtub. It was enormous, easily big enough for two, or three for that matter. As I sunk down into the water, I began to fear that I might be completely out of my depth.

NINE

That's the trouble with directors.
Always biting the hand that
lays the golden egg.

—Samuel Goldwyn

Southern Thailand was one of the most beautiful places I'd ever been
to in my life. The tropical climate made you feel like you were living in
a magical greenhouse. And the balmy humidity left you fantastically
lethargic, though this made life even more challenging as I'd hardly had
a chance to sit down since we'd arrived two weeks ago. Jake had delivered us safely to the set, said his hellos, and then disappeared the next
day on the company jet off to some other film set in an equally glamorous location, leaving us to get on with the work at hand. *The War
Fields* had begun with a bang that very morning, thrusting Emerald and
me into ten-hour days. She barely had a moment to adjust to the jet lag
before she immersed herself into her character, Betsy, an American
nurse during the Vietnam War. My job was to support Emerald in all
things. So I had spent the two weeks getting hyperorganized. I even had
the snake bite extractor kit in the trailer as part of her own first aid kit.
I had every hour of her day tightly scheduled, and everything was running like clockwork.

But now that the flurry of the initial setup was finished, I started to
understand what life was really like for an assistant on location. Boring.
Today I had been assigned a very important task by Emerald. It required
me to sit in her dark air-conditioned trailer all day by myself and pour a
bottle of Evian through a Britta water filter. When the bottle was empty,
I poured the filtered water back into the old bottle. Then I took a red

Sharpie and placed a red check mark over the label. I'd been doing this for two hours and had only managed to complete eighteen bottles. Someone on the set had gotten sick from an amoeba in the water and Emerald was desperately afraid she'd be next. She only drank Evian. And though I tried to reassure her that there were no amoebas in France, she'd said in a tone that clearly stated "no debate" that the water wasn't in France but in Thailand. What if the production, in order to save money, filled the Evian bottles with tap water? There was no arguing with that level of paranoia. I'd tried to palm the job off onto a lowly PA, but Emerald said he might not be clean enough. If she were worried about cleanliness, she shouldn't have gone to bed with Jake Hudson.

There was a knock at the trailer door.

"Come in!" I yelled.

I'd been so busy getting Emerald's life set up that I hadn't had much of a chance to get to know any of my coworkers. And though everyone was friendly, they all seemed to keep their distance. So I was thrilled to see Kathy and Fred, our married producer team, pop their heads in the door. But my joy quickly faded to dread when I saw their anxious faces.

"Hi, Lizzie. We know you're incredibly busy, but do you have a moment?" Kathy asked as I saw her register the Evian bottles and filter. I was midpour and blushed, mortified by my position, or lack thereof. I quickly shoved the Evian bottle to the side and then bustled around like a fifties housewife welcoming her guests.

"Please come in. Can I get you any tea? Coffee?" I plumped some cushions as they shook their heads somberly. Ken let out a big sigh and then collapsed onto the sofa like the weight of the world was on his shoulders. What had Emerald done now? I wracked my brains but for the life of me I couldn't think of anything. She hadn't touched a drink or even a guy since we'd left Bangkok. Emerald was so exhausted after the long days of shooting that she went straight to her bungalow and passed out. And I knew that for a fact because she made me come with her to sweep the house for boogie men each night as she brushed her teeth and climbed into bed. Kathy picked up a bottle of the red-checked Evian and looked at it absentmindedly.

"She's paranoid of amoebas." I felt the need to explain.

"Maybe you should put tap water into those bottles, then," Fred suggested with a wry smile. So did Fred not like Emerald, hence his desire to give her the runs? Things were so complicated on location.

"I thought it was a religious thing," Kathy said with an awkward laugh.

"Nope. So what can I do for you guys?" They were making me nervous and though Emerald's trailer was a two-bed two-bath monstrosity, it was starting to feel claustrophobic.

"Nothing, really," Kathy said as she continued to touch everything. "Just seeing how you're adjusting. If she's happy, that sort of thing?"

"We're great. Tired. That hour commute back and forth to the hotel every day is a bit of a trek. But I think she's fine," I said with a reassuring smile, waiting for the true nature of the visit to rear its undoubtedly ugly head. And then it hit me. It didn't take a rocket scientist to realize the issue when Kathy picked up the empty jar of Nutella on the kitchen counter and gave Fred a meaningful look.

"Oh I get it. You wish Emerald had an amoeba because she's been putting on a little bit of weight?" I said. They looked relieved at not having to mention it themselves and I was relieved that Fred wasn't trying to kill Emerald. We all breathed a collective sigh of relief.

You see, Fred and Kathy Klein were a different breed of producer. No strippers, drug habits, or fetishes in sight. They'd met at Princeton and fallen in love at a lecture given by Germaine Greer. Instead of throwing a bouquet at their wedding, Kathy had tossed her well-worn copy of *The Female Eunuch,* and off they drove to Hollywood in their Volvo wagon to conquer the town. With their principles still intact and a daily morning run with their chocolate Lab, Einstein, they were Hollywood's version of the intellectual. And it could be deemed pretty un-PC at the moment to be seen to encourage anorexic tendencies, especially in a teen starlet. But with a ninety-million-dollar budget and a monsoon prediction in the forecast, the cracks were starting to show.

Fred stood up and walked toward me with the look of a drowning man. "Lizzie. You have to help us here. She's gained fifteen pounds in ten days, and she keeps getting bigger. We're shooting a war film here. She's supposed to be a POW in Vietnam. Have you ever seen a *fat* POW? No. We're supposed to buy that she's been surviving on a bowl of rice and a stray rodent for months, but instead it looks like she's devoured half the Vietcong army. I mean, we could rewrite the script and make it a horror film about cannibalism during wartime . . ." Fred stopped for a second, seriously considering his idea. He looked to Kathy, who shook her head vehemently. It was clear who the brains of the family were. As Fred mulled over his stroke of genius, Kathy took over. She walked toward me and gave me a motherly pat on the hand. She couldn't have been more patronizing, and if I'd been braver I would have mentioned that I'd gone to Georgetown and I wasn't the moron she obviously took me for. But then, she had caught me filtering Evian.

"Listen, Lizzie. Fred and I are very conscious of female body image. Especially in young women of Emerald's age, and we would never want to encourage her to chase after a shape that wasn't her natural state of being. But on the other hand, for the authenticity of the film, a little bulimia wouldn't kill her, now would it? I mean it's fast, effective, and once she's back down to 112 pounds, she can stop," she said matter-of-factly. Was she kidding? But they just stared at me, waiting for an answer. I blinked a few times, unable to fully comprehend.

"So you want me to tell her to stick her fingers down her throat?"

"Yes," Fred and Kathy replied simultaneously.

"Maybe if you just had the craft service guy remove the Snickers and Hershey's Kisses from the table it would help. I mean, I've even gained a few pounds," I said.

"Perfect," Fred interrupted. "You can do it together."

"Great idea," Kathy said, and opened her mouth wide. "If you stick your finger all the way to the back of your throat and kind of press"— she was starting to retch—"the first time is really difficult, but once you get the hang of it you barely even gag. Just comes right up. Takes no time at all." She obviously wasn't as wholesome as she looked.

"Listen, I'm sure she'll lose the weight really soon. I'll tell her to try fruit instead of cookies," I said. I really didn't want to be responsible for encouraging Emerald to develop an eating disorder and wasn't much interested in having one myself.

"Lizzie, we don't have time," Fred said, getting even more agitated. "If you care about your boss, you have to say something. Because if you don't, I'm going to personally serve her some Evian that I've fetched out of Pang Nga Bay." I'd seen sewage being dumped in there when I'd taken a walk the other day, and I was almost certain a limb had floated by. I thought of Emerald hunched over, sick from every orifice. And then I thought about who would have to hold her hand and clean it all up.

"Fine. I'll talk to her," I conceded. They looked relieved. "But if I do, you guys have to do something for me." I was getting the hang of this Hollywood thing.

"Fine! We'll give you six thousand a week. But that's the highest I can go," Kathy said without flinching. I obviously wasn't getting the hang of this at all because instead of saying thanks a million you rich idiots, I said something really stupid.

"I don't want money." Instead of seeing respect light up their eyes, I saw mistrust. But it was too late to turn back now. "I'll get her to go on a diet but only if you go talk to Ken and tell him to go easy on Emerald." Ken was the movie's evil little Hitler of a director. And he treated Emerald like she'd just murdered Eva Braun. "I think the reason she's piling on the pounds is because every time Ken yells at her, she retreats to this trailer and eats a jar of Nutella followed by a chaser of Snickers. Comfort eating. He is almost pathologically cruel to her, you know?" I said, hoping for some insight into Emerald/Ken. But these two gave nothing away.

"Deal. We'll talk to Ken and you talk to Emerald. Today. Okay?" Kathy said quickly. I nodded my agreement, regretting already that I hadn't taken the money. That extra thousand a week would have made a huge difference in the standard of apartment I would be able to rent when I moved out of Luke's once I got back to LA. And I'd need extra cash to pay the security deposit, too. But there was something about Emerald that activated my dormant mothering instinct, and though I was certain she wouldn't sacrifice a fingernail for me, I just couldn't help myself.

"Let's go then," I said, happy to be abandoning my filtering duties.

I grabbed my notebook and we all walked out together. I shut the door and then nervously glanced at Fred. I'd seen him eyeing my Evian stash as we'd left. I dug in my pocket for the keys and then quickly turned back and locked the door. I was certain I'd seen a flash of disappointment cross his face, but I could have imagined it.

The production had spent three months re-creating a Vietnamese village at the base of a lush Thai hillside. Whenever I walked onto the set it felt like I'd stepped into a time machine and been transported to another world. They'd actually built rice paddies and authentic grass huts. The oddest thing was that the production had hired hundreds of Vietnamese extras that had been living in temporary settlements on the borders and brought them onto the set. And instead of staying at the local hotel, the extras had asked if they could move into the village as it felt so much like home. The picture had been delayed by three months due to weather, and the extras had literally moved in. There were chickens, water buffalo, and even a stray dog or two. It was incredibly surreal and absolutely magical. You could smell the cooking as you traveled down the dirt road.

As I bounced down the path in the back of Fred and Kathy's golf cart, I tried to think up subtle ways of telling Emerald to go on a diet. I desperately wanted to make everyone happy, especially Fred and Kathy. My dream was still to produce and I was certain there was a lot I could learn from them. Maybe they could fly a nutritionist in? The girl did eat her broccoli fried. But though that might help her in the long run, only some sort of crash diet would help right now. I wasn't going to suggest bulimia, but maybe a bit of subtle anorexia. I held a pile of Emerald's mail in my lap and seized the new copy of *Glamour*. I started to flip through the pages and lo and behold there was an article about Julia's diet after the twins were born. I skimmed the recipes and they looked healthy enough. After all, the diet was designed by a leading Los Angeles nutrition guru. It was a green diet. She could eat anything green. It was genius as nothing could be simpler to follow. There was only one hitch that would certainly take some convincing. The first two weeks were all about cleansing, and Brussels sprouts were the only thing on the menu. That and green tea. I wondered if they had Brussels sprouts in Thailand? I'd approach it gently and maybe suggest we do it together.

But I didn't get the chance to try subtlety. We all arrived on the set at a very tense moment. Ken Holmes, the director, was in the middle of directing a torture scene. Emerald and the other female lead, Carmen Cash, were tied to a tree, muddied and bloodied, and there were twenty extras dressed as Vietcong ripping their fingernails off. They were fake fingernails, but it still looked like it hurt.

"Who is trying to rescue you? What are their names?" the Vietcong general yelled. As Emerald went to say her lines, but one of the soldiers stuffed a rag in her mouth and Carmen spoke instead.

"We're American nurses and we gave an oath to save lives. And nothing you can do to us will make us tell you where our soldiers are hiding. You can rip every fingernail from my hand, but I won't give them up. I just won't!"

I was flummoxed. That had been Emerald's monologue. She and I had been practicing her lines every day in the car ride back and forth to the Amanpuri Resort and I knew her scenes backwards and forwards. This was actually one of the few enjoyable parts of my job, as I got to indulge my inner actress. And once again remind myself that a good actor makes it look easy. And I wasn't a good actor, but, then, neither was Carmen. I grabbed a script off the chair with Em's name on it and quickly read her highlighted scene. I wasn't wrong. Carmen was supposed to be unconscious and the only line she was supposed to have in the entire scene was "Betsy, you're so brave."

I glanced at Emerald, who was desperately trying to get her hands untied in order to get the rag out of her mouth as the scene continued without her. A handsome, quite burly member of the crew appeared out of nowhere and walked right into the middle of Ken's shot. No one said a word as he went to Emerald and pulled the rag from her mouth. I hadn't noticed him before.

"Cut. Cut. Cut. Jesus Christ, what the fuck do you think you're doing? Who the fuck do you think you are? Get the fuck off my set!" Ken screeched at the top of his lungs. Ken Holmes was maybe five-foot-seven on a good day and he had a textbook Napoleon complex. His shiny bald pate was turning a grotesque shade of purple as his flavor savor bobbed up and down on his lower lip. Ken was one of those men who got lucky. A mediocre commercial director, he had once been brought in at the last minute to direct a brilliant script and the movie had made a fortune. His ego grew exponentially with every million the film grossed. But during his next film, the producers kicked him off the set halfway through the shoot because the actors were threatening to quit and the footage looked like it had been shot by the producer's five-year-old. The rumor was that the studio executive had to direct the reshoots and edit the film. But once again, it had been a huge grosser and thanks to an ironclad contract, he'd received "directed by" credit. So here he was directing *The War Fields* and torturing everybody, but most of all, Emerald.

Emerald gasped for breath as the handsome crew member untied her hands. Ken was still screaming that the guy was fired, so once Emerald was freed, he walked right over to Ken and just stood there, his six-foot-something frame silently dominating the smaller man. Ken spluttered a bit but became mute.

"You want to fire me? Fine. Then I and all this equipment here— which, by the way, I own—like the dolly your camera is on, will get on the next plane and go back to LA."

Fred and Kathy immediately jumped into action, and not a second too soon. Kathy went directly to Emerald as Fred stepped in between the two men.

"Listen, Chris, he didn't mean that. You're not fired. Right Ken? But you shouldn't have stepped into the middle of his shot. What were you thinking?" Fred said. So his name was Chris. And he was all man. I couldn't believe I hadn't noticed him before.

"Fred, the girl obviously wasn't expecting it and she clearly wasn't happy." Chris gave one last menacing look at Ken, who stepped behind Fred for protection, and then walked off. Ken made sure Chris was out of sight and then started yelling.

"Emerald, if you knew your fucking lines, we wouldn't have a problem here!" Emerald turned around and slapped Carmen, who was still tied to the tree.

"I knew my fucking lines. That bitch stole them." She turned to the Vietcong soldier and grabbed his hand in hers. Then she took his finger with the same pliers they had been using to pull her fingernails off.

"Who told you to put that rag in my mouth? If you don't tell me, I'll tear your fingernail off, and I know yours aren't press-ons. Who?"

The soldier howled in terror and caved quickly under the pressure.

"Carmen! She kissed me and told me she'd make me a star!" he yelled. Carmen just shrugged her shoulders and smiled innocently.

"I knew it!" screamed Emerald. "She's out to get me. And Ken, you let her!"

Ken looked slightly sheepish and then walked over and untied Carmen.

"You're supposed to be a POW, Emerald, and it looks like you're storing nuts in your cheeks for winter. You're fat and you're ruining my film."

The set went silent as poor Emerald looked stunned. She burst into tears and took off with the golf cart before anyone could stop her.

Emerald had fled to the safety of her trailer nearly two hours ago and no one had heard a peep from her since.

"Emerald. Please open the door," I pleaded as I shifted uncomfortably on the metal steps, baking in the unbearable sunshine. I was dehydrated, exhausted, and really had to go to the bathroom. But I couldn't leave my post. I was responsible for delivering her to the set every day and I was terrified that if I left that step for one second she'd give me the slip. Then the entire production would grind to a halt and everyone would hold me responsible. I could just see it now, a million dollars a day being flushed down the toilet as the cast and crew played tennis because Lizzie Miller couldn't keep track of one teenager. My hopes of being a producer would be dashed forever. I knocked harder.

"Come on, Emerald. Let me in. I have to pee." I thought I'd appeal to her baser instincts. Though that hadn't worked for Kathy and Fred, who had spent an hour on the step reasoning, explaining, begging, and eventually offering her a bribe if she came out. They'd even forced Ken to come and apologize through the mail slot. But Emerald was worryingly silent.

"Fine. Don't come out. I've had enough. I'm going back to the hotel." If honesty didn't work I'd try a little manipulation. I'd noticed that the only time she fell into line was when I threatened departure. It was probably horrible to take advantage of the information, but she'd told me that her father had left when she was seven and she was terrified of being deserted. So I'd used a little bit of my Psych 101 and whenever she put me in an untenable situation, I threatened to leave. I knew my trump card could only be played so many times, but this situation seemed pretty dire.

I made loud rustling motions and stomped down the two metal stairs. I started walking really slowly and was about to turn around and tell her I was just kidding when the door opened a crack. I quickly turned my back and pretended to be marching away. A plaintive little voice called out to me between sniffles, "Lizzie. You can come in. But only if it's just you." I turned around and she was gone. But the door was open a crack and I practically sprinted to it before she could change her mind.

It took my eyes a few moments to adjust to the gloom. But when they did I saw Emerald quietly sitting alone on the sofa with her feet on the coffee table. I looked around expecting the place to be torn to shreds, but it wasn't. If anything, it was tidier than when I'd left. Her scripts were in neat piles and the stack of dvd's by the television were perfectly organized.

"The bathroom is free if you're desperate," she said.

So she had been listening, after all. I dashed to the restroom, shut the door behind me, and quickly searched the medicine cabinet for those Ambien I'd seen her take the night before her first day of shooting. I'd had a momentary panic outside her door, imagining her in the trailer having overdosed, so I felt it best to preempt any such disaster. I saw the nail scissors and wondered if it was possible to remove all sharp objects from the trailer.

"Coming!" I yelled as I stuffed the pill bottle in my fanny pack.

When I came out Emerald hadn't moved an inch. I couldn't tell if she was performing or if she was truly upset. But I guessed that it was probably one and the same for her. She'd been acting since she was seven years old, and I don't think she actually knew the difference anymore. What I was certain of was that she'd been crying. And not those fake crocodile tears I'd seen her produce on command. So I went and sat next to her and patted her gently on the arm. I didn't know what to do. If it were my sister or a good friend I'd wrap my arms around her and give her a big hug, but she was my employer, after all, and I didn't want to invade her personal space. But my friendly pat just seemed to make her cry harder.

"It's just so tough, Lizzie. You don't understand. I'm alone here."

"You've got me," I ventured. That was clearly what she needed to hear because she threw herself violently into my arms and started sobbing like her heart was breaking. I smoothed down her hair like I would a child's.

"Just let it out," I said in a maternal tone. I sounded like a bad self-help book, but I remember my mother saying that to me when I was kid and it just seemed appropriate. However, when she put her head in my lap, I realized just how inappropriate it all was. The boundaries were all gone and I knew that I'd live to regret this.

"You see, Ken is just so hard on me. Even when I nail a scene he never says 'good job.' He just yells 'cut' and storms off like I did something wrong."

On the first day of shooting, when Emerald complained that Ken was unnecessarily critical of her performance, I'd just assumed she was being a neurotic, oversensitive actress. But by day three I realized that Emerald was actually being generous in her assessment of Ken. He didn't not like her; he hated her. When he'd accused Emerald of being a pampered brat when she asked for a break on his thirtieth take of her hoeing a rice paddy in the noonday sun, it occurred to me that maybe he wanted to bump her off. And I think I was second on his list. Ken and I had had a run-in when Em was fifteen minutes late for makeup one evening. What I quickly learned was that *no one* yelled at the star. They just yelled at the assistant.

"I never should have taken this movie," Emerald moaned. "But the character of Betsy was such a great role. And it was such a departure from all those teen movies I've been doing. A real chance to prove my acting chops."

"Emerald, of course you should have taken the part. I've been watching your performance and it's fabulous. You can do this." And for once I wasn't lying. She was surprisingly talented. Emerald pulled herself up to sitting and wiped away her tears. She seemed to literally shrug off the soft, vulnerable girl who'd just had her head in my lap. And the mantle she slipped on had more sharp edges than a carving knife. She stood up and started pacing the trailer.

"Oh I know I can do it. That's not my problem. My problem is with that cuntface Cash," she snarled. I involuntarily flinched as all my maternal instincts went out the trailer window. "She's fucking Ken. And that smart cow obviously was screwing him before we started filming."

Carmen had risen from *Baywatch* fame to Brigitte Bardot–status in a matter of a few short years. She was the curvaceous siren in an age of string beans and she played her cards like an ace. Though she'd yet to prove her acting chops, every director wanted to cast her. Well, bed her at least. But Ken had clearly fallen hard and Carmen was to get second billing behind Emerald, which had been a contractual sticking point during the negotiations. But one of the producers had made the mistake of telling one of the PA's who told one of the parking attendants who told his wife who did laser hair removal at the salon Emerald went to that Ken had wanted Carmen to play Betsy, Emerald's role, in *The War Fields*. But apparently the studio had put their foot down and told Ken that unless Emerald was the lead there was no film. It was all about bankability. And Emerald was bankable. Carmen, though possessing a cult following, was not. Ken had stormed out quitting the project but quickly returned the next day and hired Emerald. It was a huge studio movie and even he wasn't immune to his seven-figure salary. "So I heard this all word for word when I was in the middle of getting my art wax," Emerald told me.

"What's an art wax?" I made the mistake of asking.

"Oh, it's fab!" She yanked down her shorts and underpants and displayed a Gucci symbol cut into her pubic hair. It was apparently all the rage. "See? I had to do Gucci because I have a modeling contract with them. But next time I think I may do a Mercedes emblem." She pulled her pants back up and continued. "So after my wax I called Scott and told him to get me out of the part. I knew Ken would be a shit if he'd been forced to hire me. But I'd already signed a pay-or-play deal and Scott said there was no way out of it."

I cast my mind back and I did remember Emerald's contract sitting on my desk and Scott walking out of his office after he'd gotten off the phone and asking me to hand deliver the contract to the business affairs office at the studio ASAP. If Emerald only knew what that damn Gull-wing had done to her life she would have set it on fire. "Scott promised to try to get me out of the contract, but in the end the studio wouldn't budge." Yes. Scott had tried really hard. He'd gone back into his office after I'd dispatched Amber on the errand and, instead of calling Jake at the studio, he'd called Quentin and told him all about his new car.

So the die was cast early on for a deep-seated hatred between Emerald and Carmen with nasty Ken pulling the strings. And once fully informed, it was obvious that the situation was a pressure cooker; the explosion was inevitable. You would think it would be Ken that Emerald hated, but oddly he seemed to escape relatively unscathed as she tore Carmen into pieces, blaming her for all her feelings of insecurity and general misery on set. But I'd noticed a theme in Hollywood. People with power were like Teflon. None of their bad deeds stuck. They just seemed to slide off and land on their underlings, who then spent their time covered in grease. But as I mulled over my bad analogy, I realized that maybe the little nineteen-year-old was a lot wiser than I was about this business. She couldn't afford to hate Ken. He was going to imprint her image on celluloid that would hopefully be seen by millions of people around the world for generations to come.

"And to make matters worse, Lizzie, I'm fat. And every time Ken yells at me, I get fatter. Because the only thing that makes me feel better is chocolate."

I tuned back in to Emerald's rant as the word "fat" reminded me of why we were sitting in her trailer in the first place.

"Well, that's easy to solve, Em," I said excitedly. "You put the weight on in two weeks; you can lose it in less. I've read about this great green diet. I've gained a ton of weight, too. We can do it together."

"Yeah. I noticed your thighs were looking really chunky. So who's done this diet?" she asked. I gave her the finger behind her back as she walked to the fridge and grabbed a Diet Coke.

"Oh, Julia. She lost all her pregnancy weight in, like, a month," I told her. Emerald turned back around, totally unimpressed. I had to think on my feet. "Oh, and the Olsen twins." She was looking more interested. "And Paris. Apparently that's how she keeps that catwalk figure." I grabbed the copy of *Glamour* off the sofa and stuffed it in my bag when she wasn't looking.

"Great. That sounds perfect. We'll start today. And I want a trainer. And he needs to be flown in from LA. And you have to train with me." It was more of an order than a request.

"Great," I said with as much enthusiasm I could muster. "Well then, I'd better go talk to Fred and Kathy." I was already halfway out the door.

"Oh, and Lizzie?" she called out. I should have known. It was all feeling a bit too easy. "Tell them they have to fire Carmen Cash or I'm not coming out of my trailer ever again." And with that she slammed the door.

TEN

Hollywood is where they shoot
too many films and not enough actors.

—Walter Winchell

When I'd first walked into the lobby of the Amanpuri Resort in Phuket, I knew I'd returned to my spiritual home. That is if I were a Thai princess in my last life. There was a sense of harmony to the open-air lobby with shining golden Buddhas discreetly tucked away in all the right places. And when I walked to the other side of the hundred-foot-high thatched bungalow, the view took my breath away. The hotel was built into the side of a lush green hill and at the bottom of a hundred winding granite steps shone the white beach and the magnificent Andaman Sea. My own bungalow was right at the bottom, just a stone's throw from the soft sand. Every night I'd drift off to the sounds of the waves lapping against the shore and wake to the cawing of parrots more beautiful than any I'd ever seen at the zoo. Well, that's how it should have been at least, but unfortunately we'd been shooting nights for the last couple of weeks. I knew the sea was there, but I'd only managed to go swimming once since I'd arrived. And the parrots' noise was happily drowned out by a pair of fantastic earplugs I'd borrowed from the props guy in charge of firearms. I recognized ruefully that my sense of déjà vu was probably completely valid, but I'd gotten it a bit wrong as usual; in my last life I wasn't the Thai princess after all; I was the Thai slave. And I was obviously still smack in the middle of my karmic circle.

Though we were in paradise, the last couple of weeks had been a living hell.

"I don't mean to be picky, but Emerald needs the sprouts blanched.

Not boiled. Understand?" I explained as politely as I could. Thailand's equivalent to a Michelin star chef looked at me with such hatred I was certain I'd be served up a special dish of the Avian flu for dinner. But at the moment, a hospital bed and raging fever sounded like a much needed respite. I'd just managed to crawl into bed three hours before when the panicked hotel manager came knocking on my bungalow door. He'd just had a plate of Brussels sprouts hurled at him by Emerald at speeds worthy of an Olympic discus thrower and was terrified to return with the dish if it wasn't perfect. So he'd dragged me from my bed and down into the depths of the kitchen on my day off to oversee Emerald's sprouts preparation. Not only were sprouts not native to Thailand they were impossible to locate, and I'd had to get permission from three different producers to fly them in at great cost to the production.

The good news was that both Emerald and I had lost ten pounds. The bad news was that we both had such bad indigestion that we were too embarrassed to talk to anyone else on the production. And we were starting to get very sick of each other's company. Emerald had returned to the set without the head of Carmen Cash on a platter thanks to the Kleins' expert classes in negotiation at Princeton University. Peace had resumed, and for the moment Ken was behaving himself with a little help from the powers that be. Namely, Jake Hudson.

When we'd gotten back to her bungalow that night, I'd put a call through to Jake for Emerald. For some odd reason she'd asked me to stay on the phone with the pretence that we were going to roll calls. But as I'd suspected Jake was her one and only phone call that evening. Emerald was just showing off, or perhaps giving me a bit of free education in the ways to get ahead in Hollywood. Though she was sitting in the other room, her pout could be heard all the way to LA, and Jake was surprisingly responsive. There was an unspoken camaraderie between the two that hadn't existed at their last meeting. Well, at least not when I had been in the room. Oddly he seemed to treat her with more respect, which is what confused me the most. I'd learned years before in high school that the girls who slept around were treated with little or no regard. But obviously I was on a very different playground. Maybe it was because Jake and Emerald were both powerful in their own right so no one had the upper hand. Maybe it was because Emerald had slept with him like a man: sex with no emotion or expectation. But whatever reason, there was obviously some swingers' conduct manual that I wasn't privy to. And though it would be nice to call the president of a studio and get him to do your bidding, I was in no hurry to learn the secret handshake.

I'd heard the next day from Kathy and Fred that Jake had called Ken that night for a little chat. What was actually said on the call, we'll never know, but Ken seemed to have an enormous attitude adjustment. He kept mentioning throughout the day how much Jake admired Emerald's talent. I couldn't help but snicker as I was sure Emerald's talents were extensive. But Emerald was well pleased with the groveling director, and it did seem to bring back some perspective to the entire thing as Ken only had eyes for Emerald.

I left the kitchen pinching my nose shut with one hand and holding the offending sprouts as far from my body as possible with the other. I walked down the winding path to Em's bungalow and wondered what condition I'd find her in this morning. But if the quaking manager was any indication, it was going to be a long day. The first two weeks of the Julia diet were sprouts only. This was meant to have a unique cleansing effect, which I can now vouch for. But for Emerald the diet seemed to cleanse her body as well as expel any sense of humor or goodwill that she possessed. Hence the temper tantrums and almost unbearable mood swings, which seemed to be getting worse with every bite of cabbage.

With night shoots dominating the last ten days, I was averaging about three hours of sleep a day. I'd developed a twitch in my left eye that seemed to start every time the next day's call sheet was slipped under my door. Shooting nights meant that Emerald's call time was seven in the evening, hence mine was six, leaving me just enough time to get Emerald out of her massive four-bedroom villa and into her car to arrive on set in a timely manner. But by the time we returned home at three in the morning and I'd tucked Emerald into bed, dealt with all the e-mails and phone messages, and organized my to-do list for the next day, it was eight in the morning. I'd collapse into bed comatose only to be woken at eleven by Emerald or, more often than not, someone who wanted something from Emerald. The demands seemed to keep coming and I was supposed to be her Great Wall of China. It was endless:

another magazine cover, publicity for her last movie, endorsements, fan mail. It seemed everyone wanted a piece of Emerald Everhart.

I was starting to understand why celebrities lost touch with reality. The sifters, like me, were necessary to allow a star to have any kind of normal life, but that was the catch-22. By sifting out all the humdrum annoyances and realities of real life, it was nearly impossible to remain grounded no matter how hard I imagined they tried. And even worse were the sycophants. They seemed to spring up in every nook and cranny wanting to be friends with Emerald in hopes that some of her celebrity would rub off on them. And not a single one of these new *friends* would tell Emerald a word of truth. If she asked the wardrobe assistant, Kelly, a new friend, what she thought of a pair of shoes she owned, Kelly would first gauge how Emerald felt about them and then just confirm Emerald's opinion. So when Emerald asked my opinion and my answer wasn't what she wanted to hear, she'd canvass the syco-phants and use them to prove me wrong. Which was incredibly infuri-ating as the ass kissing was rampant from Kathy and Fred all the way down to the PA at the production office.

I'd always thought it was pathetic that all the stars seemed to be best friends with their assistants, but the longer I worked for Emerald the more sense it made. Before you took a job for a star, you had to sign a confidentiality agreement, so no selling their story to *Star Magazine*. The assistant was a safe haven in potentially shark-infested waters. I mean, even family members couldn't be counted on. Another reason Emerald was in a bad mood this week, besides the plethora of greens, was because she'd received bad news from her lawyers. Her mother had been trying to publish a book called, *My Precious Gem: Emerald Ever-hart's Most Embarrassing Moments*. Emerald had managed to get a tem-porary injunction halting the publication, but the court upheld her mother's right to publish and the book was coming out next month. Needless to say they no longer spoke. So it made sense to befriend your assistant if you were in Em's position; as you were already paying them, they were legally prohibited from spilling your deepest darkest secrets, and they were with you at all times, since, as a busy actor, you spend half your life away from home. But it was certainly no walk in the park trying to navigate the minefield of being the hired best friend.

I walked into Emerald's villa, grabbed a plate from the kitchen, and divied up the sprouts between us both, then wandered out to the pool. I found her lying in the sun on a chaise.

"'Morning, Emerald!" I tried to sound cheery, though the look on her face was anything but. She didn't respond, just glanced up at me holding the two plates of sprouts and turned back to her copy of *People*. "I've got your sprouts, cooked just how you like them." I put one plate next to her right hand and stood there like a drug dealer at an elementary school. "Don't you want to even try one? You must be hungry. Look, I'm eating mine. Yum." I stuck one in my mouth and struggled not to gag.

I should have just dropped off the sprouts and left the building, but I wanted to see her eat at least a few of them. I hadn't seen a sprout cross her lips in twenty-four hours. I was getting concerned that I had forced her to join the Rexy files as she was losing weight at an enormously rapid rate.

"Come on, Emerald, you have to eat if you're going to have the strength to perform."

She turned to me in defiance, picked up the plate, and sent it flying like a Frisbee right into the pool. Great, I thought. I got out of bed for nothing. I watched the sprouts bob up and down in her private plunge pool and all I could think of was how they were going to get stuck in the filter.

"I'm supposed to be a POW, Lizzie. Imagine what my character Betsy ate? Probably zilch. I'm method acting. Can you order me some green tea ice cream from Nobu in LA and have them send it over? That's part of the green diet, right?" She looked at me challengingly as I absentmindedly stuffed another sprout in my mouth. But somehow I couldn't chew it. It just sat there whole, polluting my tongue as I stared blankly at Emerald.

I'd lost all ability to react. She could shrivel up and die at my feet and all I'd be able to produce was the vacant expression that was on my face now. I had been surviving on no sleep and Brussels sprouts for ten days, and this was supposed to be my day off. It was Sunday and I had been dragged out of bed to force sprouts down the throat of this horror. A strange noise escaped from my mouth, a mix between a snort and a sneeze, and out popped the Brussels sprout, hitting Emerald right between the eyes. It wasn't intentional, but I certainly found it funny. I tried desperately to hold in my laughter, but I just couldn't control myself. I was far too exhausted. I picked up my plate of Brussels sprouts and dumped them in the pool with hers, all the while hysterically laughing. Emerald watched me like I was an escapee from the loony bin, and if there'd been a qualified professional around that's probably where I would have ended up.

"Emerald," I choked out between bouts of hysterical giggles, "you're right. This diet is foul. It's my day off." I was now just plain snorting like some bizarre pig on speed. "And I'm going to the beach." Then I turned around and left the villa.

My stomach hurt from my bout of hysteria, but I felt an enormous weight lifted from my shoulders at the thought of spending an Emerald-free twenty-four hours. I walked into my gorgeous grass hut and slipped into one of my fabulous bikinis. I'd spent a week's pay on three to-die-for bits of cloth under the delusion that I'd be spending half my time getting native. But the only action they'd seen was when I ran out of clean bras and wore one under my clothes to the set one evening. And thanks to Emerald's diet, I was looking pretty good in my bikini and I didn't even mind that my pasty white legs were covered in their usual mysterious bruises. I'd lost ten pounds and they happened to be the ten pounds I'd been trying to lose since I hit puberty. I packed a little bag, slipped on a sarong and my favorite fruit-covered flip-flops, and off I went to explore. I'd grab a ride into Phuket and maybe catch a boat to PhiPhi Island. I remembered seeing *The Man With the Golden Gun* as a kid and dreaming of going to that tropical paradise. And here I was on my day off just a boat ride away. Maybe if I talked to enough backpackers, they could tell me where the mythical "beach" was.

I managed to get about ten feet from my front door when a very helpful man in a lovely pressed-white outfit approached me and offered me the most comfortable looking sun lounger I'd ever seen. It beckoned me like a temptress and I followed him dumbly toward the lone chair. It was perfectly positioned all by itself in the shade under a palm tree. I settled myself onto the clean white towel and kicked off my flip-flops. Then I made the fatal error of ordering myself a large rum cocktail. It arrived innocuously enough dressed in fruit and umbrellas and went down so smoothly I felt the need to order another. But by the time the second arrived, I was off with the fairies. I hadn't had anything to drink in a month, and losing ten pounds and missing two weeks' sleep had made me an official lightweight.

I woke to someone unlatching my bikini top and rubbing lotion into the skin on my back. I was still in a daze and it felt so good I just couldn't possibly resist. Still technically in a dream state, I imagined that it was Luke who gently caressed my shoulders and that I wasn't really taking care of a teen monster in Thailand. I rewound the clock to the moment in the car when he'd been about to propose. And instead of being the slightly neurotic girl that I am, I was normal and secure in his love and adoration for me. And now we were in Thailand on our honeymoon and we were blissfully in love. We were going to live happily every after and have the six kids we'd both always wanted. Well, I'd wanted three and he'd wanted six, but for the sake of my fantasy I gave him everything *he'd* dreamed of. I'd almost succeeded in deluding myself and was making embarrassingly pleasurable little moans under the masculine hands of Luke when the person hooked my bikini top back up and literally snapped the strap with a painful crack against my skin. I sat up and turned around furious, confused and wide awake, only to be faced with Chris, the guy from the set who had saved Emerald. I'd seen him zip by running his crew almost every day since, but he'd made no effort to speak to me and I'd generally assumed that he had no idea who I was. He was the key grip, the guy in charge of every piece of machinery on the set from a sandbag to the scaffolding and happened to own it all as well. He had a team of about fifteen men that physically would set up every shot Ken wanted to make. I was about to yell at him, but all my ferocity drained from my body as he just stood there smiling at me with an annoyingly sexy little grin.

"What are you doing?" was all I brilliantly managed to get out.

"Obviously something right since you were clearly enjoying it."

"I thought . . . I thought . . ." What had I thought? That it was Luke? I certainly couldn't say *that*. Chris did the gallant thing and saved me.

"Lizzie, I was only teasing. I tried to wake you but you weren't budging." He nodded his head at my empty cocktail glass and the second full one sitting there wilted in the sun.

"It's my day off," I said defensively, still completely disoriented.

"Listen, I wasn't passing judgment. If I had to do your job, I'd have a flask of whiskey on me at all times. Actually, I do anyway." He smiled again, putting me at ease.

I took a deep breath and turned over, but as I leaned back against the chair I screamed in pain.

"Jesus. Owww!" I howled.

"That's why I was trying to wake you. Your back is the color of a lobster and not when they're nice and happy floating in the tank."

"But I was under the palm tree in the shade," I said dumbly, noticing that the shadow of the palm tree was now a good five feet to my right. "Ah yes. The earth moves," I said. Trying not to seem like a complete idiot.

"Oh, so you felt that, too?" Chris said with an absolutely straight face.

Whatever wits I was starting to recover went out the window.

"Your face is even redder than your back now," he said calmly.

Unable to come up with a response I jumped up from the chaise. "I'm going for a swim." I marched into the water with such purpose and speed that I stepped on a shell. I tried to ignore it, but my limp was obvious as I hobbled farther out. Though my foot was throbbing, the cool sea was relieving my singed skin. I closed my eyes and disappeared under the water, holding my breath, letting the cool saltiness wash away my mortification. I hoped if I stayed under long enough I'd reemerge and Chris would be gone and I could continue with my day of solitary pleasure. I could no longer hold my breath, so I launched up to the sky above. I was gasping for air and couldn't help but smile at the exhilaration. And happily when I looked to the beach, there was no Chris in sight.

"If it's bleeding you should probably let me look at it," I heard a voice from behind me say. I swung around and there was Chris watching me from a few feet deeper in the water. I had no idea how he got past me without me seeing, but he certainly looked good with that messy thatch of wavy black hair glistening around his brown face. And once again he seemed to take the words right out of my mouth.

"Before you think I'm stalking you, I just want to explain that I was concerned for your well-being. You have a sunburn, you've been drinking, you haven't slept, and I'll bet that was a pretty sharp shell you stepped on when you were running away from me. Though you did handle the pain remarkably gracefully."

At that I started to laugh.

"Well, I'm used to it. I spend my days taking pain gracefully. I had to have dinner with Ken and Emerald last night." The ice was broken and we both just stood there bobbing in the water.

"I'm Chris Hanson," he said as we shook hands.

"I know who you are. You own all the equipment and are willing to take it all and get back on a plane to LA." I quoted his outburst to Ken. For once it was Chris's turn to be at a loss for words. And it felt much better to have the shoe on the other foot, as it were.

"Well, I don't usually lose my temper like that. But that guy was behaving like a real fucking ass and I'd had enough."

"So you're into saving damsels in distress?" Oh I *was* warming up.

"I like distress but I like the damsels even more when I have an excuse to remove their bikini tops in their sleep."

I hit the water, intentionally splashing him in the face.

"Think you need to cool off there, mister." I laughed.

"I wasn't the one moaning," he said. I couldn't believe this guy. He was outrageous. I hadn't had this much fun flirting in ages. I'd forgotten how thrilling it was.

"Be careful, if your ego inflates any more you might not be able to dive under the water. Anyway, I was dreaming and it wasn't about you."

"I'll just have to change that then," he said as he picked me out of the water like a feather and tossed me over his shoulder.

"What are you doing?" I screamed as my bikini started to do a persistent crawl up my backside. "Put me down!" But he was already stomping out of the water.

"No. You're injured and you need to get out of the sun. You don't want that bleeding foot to attract sharks now, do you?"

I wasn't sure if he was serious or not, but I had a pathological fear of sharks ever since watching *Jaws* with a babysitter one night when I was nine. So instead of fighting to get down I literally lifted every bit of my body out of the water in horror.

"There aren't really sharks here, are there?" We'd just made it to dry land.

"Yeah, but I'd have saved you."

How can you not fall in love instantly with a man who just wants to save you all the time? I know it's a cliché, but I so desperately needed to be saved. From what, I don't know, but I'd been so obsessed with taking care of Emerald for the last month I'd barely thought of myself for a second. And here was this sexy man holding me in his arms, carrying me across the hot sand, and all I could think of was how much I'd like to roll around in it with him.

I squealed with delight as he started walking away from the Amanpuri. "Where are you taking me?"

"You don't think us lowly members of the crew get to stay at the Aman, do you?" I hadn't even thought about it actually. I was whisked to and from the set every morning and evening with Emerald so I didn't see the rest of the crew coming and going each day. I hadn't noticed anyone other than Ken, Carmen, Kathy, Fred, and Emerald and me at the Amanpuri. I'd just assumed everyone else hung out somewhere fun that I simply wasn't invited to. That was usually how it went.

"I'm going to show you a bit of the island. Though the Aman is incredible, judging from the color of your skin you haven't tasted much local flavor since you've been in Thailand."

"But you're not local." I couldn't believe I'd just said that, but Chris was bringing something out in me that I'd thought was dead and buried—my sense of fun!

The crew's hotel was just down the beach from the Aman. In no way did it compare in beauty or luxury but it had the casual comforts of a well-lived-in home. The crew had taken over the entire hotel for the three months of the shoot, and many of them had been there for seven weeks of preproduction prior to the start date, building the sets, scouting, casting, etc. Chris and I went to his room first, where he sweetly applied aloe to my back without once letting his hand wander anywhere that wasn't in need. He then lent me an oxford to cover my burn and I slipped into my shorts that I thankfully had tossed into my beach bag at the last minute earlier, and off we went. We walked down to the pool and I saw lots of familiar faces from the set. There was an easy camaraderie, like at a family Thanksgiving party. Chris introduced me to everyone and I made a real effort to try to remember their names. They all seemed to know exactly who I was, and I realized that I was really missing out. No one here was lonely. It was like a twenty-four-hour party with some work in the middle. I obviously had the wrong job. I wondered if I could make a request to be moved to this hotel. A little trot down the beach would be just the space I needed from Emerald to make our relationship that much healthier. But who was I kidding? This was the first day we'd spent apart in a month. She wasn't going to let me go anywhere, but at least I could enjoy the fantasy.

And I did enjoy it. It was like oxygen to a drowning man. Chris took me to a little local fish restaurant on a rocky beach up the coast and we talked endlessly about our lives. We drank enormous ice-cold Singha beers and sampled all the things on the menu we couldn't translate. He was so easy to talk to, and though I'd only just met him, I felt like I'd known him all my life. I told him all about my job at The Agency, my confusion about what to do next in my career, my breakup with Luke, and he told me about where he grew up, his father's death, and how he had started his company. He even confided in me his insecurities about being a grip. It was a predominately physical job and he felt people discounted his intelligence. I realized as I sat there playing with my chopsticks that we had shared more intimate details about our lives than I had with Luke in the whole year we'd been together. I couldn't quite figure out if it was a flaw in my relationship with Luke or a false intimacy that forms from being in very close quarters away from your friends and family. Chris seemed to take the words right out of my mouth.

"Sorry. Probably too many personal details. It tends to happen on location. People are away from their usual support network so they form new ones out of human necessity, I guess," he said, smiling easily.

"Yeah. This is my first time on location, but I think it's nice. The new friends thing." And it was. He was so straightforward and didn't have a career that required everyone to kiss his derriere. He was just a normal guy who did a normal guy's job. Yet he was intelligent, kind, and obviously had a strong sense of moral justice, which I hadn't encountered very often since I'd been in Hollywood. Chris was seriously crushable.

After dinner we walked down the beach back to my resort. It was a perfectly clear night and the stars seemed to be hovering just inches from the sand. A body-temperature breeze blew through the oxford shirt, cooling my sunburned body. I walked closer to the sea letting the cool water wash over my feet. Chris walked silently beside me, neither of us feeling the need to fill the space with conversation. He reached out and took my hand in his. His hand was dry and warm and our fingers just seemed to knit together organically. It suddenly occurred to me that maybe this was how love was supposed to be. Maybe in any other town besides Hollywood or New York this is how it happened. Two people meet, have a connection, hold hands, and then live happily every after. Isn't that what it said in all the fairy tales you were warped by as a little girl? I looked up into Chris's handsome, open face and felt for a second that maybe there was still good in the world. It felt like a salve on my bruised heart, and though my skin was burning, the hot knot in my stomach seemed to ease just a little.

We arrived at my bungalow and there wasn't even that awkward beat that comes with a first kiss. He just pulled me to him and kissed me in the most deliciously passionate way. It erased my memory, my reason, and possibly my good sense. Though my mind was a bit addled from the sheer force of my attraction, I couldn't really come up with any grounds for why I shouldn't be kissing this yummy man on this beautiful beach. Luke obviously didn't care, and anyway he was kissing his own "perfect" woman. We kissed for a few more minutes against a palm tree.

"Think maybe we should take it inside?" Chris said casually. I couldn't have agreed more.

"Hold on one second. I just have to check something." I'd run out of the bungalow in such a daze this morning, I wanted to make sure that I hadn't left dirty underpants sitting around or other equally girlie things that were bound to kill the mood. I kissed him and dashed inside.

I didn't even bother turning on the lights as I grabbed piles of dirty clothes off the floor and shoved them into the closet. I quickly unwrapped the scented candle that sat by the bed. I couldn't believe how fragrant it was. I hadn't even lit it yet and the room smelled like a rose garden. I dug around for matches with no success, so I switched on the light to have a better look. And there on every available surface were beautiful bouquets of roses. They covered the entire spectrum of the rainbow: yellow, red, purple, coral, white. I couldn't quite figure out how Emerald had managed to order flowers all by herself. She couldn't even order room service without calling me first. Obviously she was feeling bad about her earlier behavior and wanted to make sure we were still friends. I found the matches, lit the candle, and turned off the light. The flowers were so amazing and so over the top, I had to give it to Emerald for impressive gestures. I quickly squirted my perfume in all the important spots, yanked the card off the red roses, and opened it just as I was about to step out of my beautiful and now romantically candlelit bungalow. But I stopped dead in my tracks with one foot out the door as the little envelope dropped to the ground. The card read:

> You're a hard girl to track down, but then rare things
> always are. I miss you. Please can we talk. Love, Luke

I looked up in panic at Chris leaning against the palm tree and every ounce of romantic feeling drained from my body. Confusion reigned supreme. He looked up and must have caught the expression on my face. He motioned to the card in my hand.

"Bad news?" he asked gently.

I shook my head. "I don't know. Listen, do you mind if we take a rain check? I . . ." I didn't know what to say. Thankfully, Chris did. He walked over to me and kissed me chastely on the forehead.

"Lizzie, there's absolutely no rush. You and I will have plenty of time to get to know each other. I don't doubt that. I'll see you tomorrow, okay? Get some sleep." I smiled and gave him a little wave as his big frame turned and loped down the beach toward his hotel.

I walked back into my room, blew out the candle, and turned on the lights. I held the card in my hands and studied it. It wasn't his writing, but it didn't matter; I felt like he was in the room and I missed him more than I ever had before. I wanted to pick up the phone and hear his voice. I wanted to tell him all about Emerald and the crazy time I was having in Thailand. But then I remembered the picture of him kissing Emanuelle and then the silence. I slipped out of my clothes and climbed right into bed. I tried hard to think of Chris and the evening of anxiety-free pleasure we'd just spent. But images of Luke kept sneaking in from my subconscious. I squeezed my eyes tightly shut, trying to erase Luke's face from my memory, but the smell of the roses just kept assaulting my senses, making it impossible for him not to dominate my dreams.

ELEVEN

Good-bye, Mr. Zanuck. It certainly
has been a pleasure working
at 16th Century Fox.

—Jean Renoir

I woke the next morning feeling rejuvenated. I'd decided, in the hour of tossing and turning I'd done before I'd finally drifted off to sleep, that I didn't need to deal with the Luke situation just yet. I wanted to revel in the pleasure of knowing that Luke still wanted me, yet avoid the inevitable pain and confrontation a discussion would require. A week or two wouldn't make any difference, except hopefully make him suffer, and it was the perfect opportunity to explore things with Chris guilt free. After all, the picture of Luke and Emanuelle pretty much gave me carte blanche as far as I was concerned. I had a spring in my step as I got dressed in my best pair of shorts and favorite tank that Emerald had given me. It managed to create a bosom where not much existed. It was much more fun to drag yourself off to the set in the mornings if you knew you had a handsome boy to flirt with over eggs at the catering trailer.

But when I went to pick up Emerald, I realized I'd made a fatal error at not going back and dealing with her after I'd walked out. Emerald was nowhere in sight. I called her name and quickly did a tour of her villa, but it was empty. I found her maid sitting in the kitchen making freshly squeezed orange juice and drilled her for Emerald's whereabouts. She shrugged and said Emerald had gone to work.

I called the production office in a panic and they said that they had no idea where Emerald was. The smug PA reminded me that keeping track of Emerald was supposed to be my job. I called her cell phone, but it rang once before my call was unceremoniously dumped to voice mail. Then I tried Tensin, her driver, but it went straight to voice mail as well. I left a panicked message with him begging him to call me the second he got the message. I said a quick prayer hoping that all those early-morning cappuccinos I'd charged to room service for him would have bought me a little loyalty. Perhaps it was karma as I was doing a similar thing to Luke, but I was getting the distinct feeling that I was being ignored. I called the production office again and asked them to send a driver as soon as possible and anxiously went to wait in the lobby for the car.

Thankfully on my way to the set, Tensin called in. He whispered into the phone that Emerald had insisted he leave without me and then wouldn't let him take my calls. The situation was worse than expected, but at least she hadn't gone AWOL and was on set, on time, and in one piece. Anxiety started to build in my gut in preparation for the inevitable drama. I knew I had to just take hat in hand and apologize for my outburst, but I had a sneaking suspicion that Emerald wasn't going to make it easy.

When I got to the location, Emerald was already on set. She apparently had wanted to get there early to rehearse the escape from the bamboo prison cell scene, though she hadn't bothered to mention that to me the day before. I called down on my walkie-talkie and asked the assistant director to put me on with Emerald. The AD went silent for approximately one second, then, sounding rather embarrassed, said that Emerald was too busy to talk to me. With urging from someone in the background, the AD proceeded to say that I wasn't needed on set today and should just go wait at the hotel and answer Emerald's fan mail until she got back. Great. The only day I actually wanted to hang out to flirt with Chris, I was being dismissed like some third-rate lackey. I walked over to one of the drivers and asked if someone could give me a lift back to the Amanpuri. Maybe it was better I didn't see Chris until I was a little more certain about what I was doing with Luke. I didn't want him to think I was a tease. I really appreciated his honesty and laid-back approach to being shunned last night. While I waited for a driver to show up, I walked over to the caterers and ordered the Thai version of an Egg McMuffin. It was such a pleasure to be able to abandon the sprouts and eat real food again. One of the key comforts of being on location was that the food was really good. The caterers were exceptional and cooked a variety of meals ranging from Pad Thai to fish and chips right there on set. And being the assistant of the star meant you could beg and plead to satisfy any bizarre food craving you might be having and they'd usually cook it up right then and there for you. But the egg McMuffin was standard and I'd just managed to take an enormously greedy bite into the soft runny yolk, which was now dribbling down my chin, when Chris walked up. He gave me an enormous smile and once again I felt all anxiety and stress drain from my body. How did he manage to do that? He was like Valium but in human form.

"Good to see you eating properly again." I couldn't believe he'd noticed I'd been starving myself. I guess that meant he'd been watching me for a while. I felt a flutter of excitement in my stomach as I wiped the egg off my chin and swallowed my mouthful.

"Trust me, I plan to make up for lost time," I said as I noticed a few of the crew members watching us with silly grins on their faces. Location was like a coed boarding school and no one behaved much beyond adolescence. Chris had given me a run-down yesterday of who exactly was sleeping with whom, which was another reason I was excited to get on set this morning. I hadn't noticed any of it before and was now longing to watch the dramas unfold before my very eyes. Apparently the married DP, director of photography, was having an affair with the makeup girl. The script superviser was in love with Ken so she frequently gave Carmen a hard time about continuity. The Second AD wanted the job of the First AD, but she was sleeping with him anyway to ensure that, if she didn't get the promotion, she'd be brought along on his next film as Second AD. Then there were the two set PA's who were inseparable but apparently not having sex, which baffled the entire crew. And now there were Chris and me. I leaned in and whispered, "Everyone is staring at us."

Chris shrugged his shoulders and laughed casually. "It's because those who didn't see us together at my hotel pool just heard a story from your little bigmouthed boss about how she saw us raping each other by the palm tree."

My jaw must have dropped because Chris literally closed it for me and ran a naughty finger across my lips.

"I can't believe Emerald saw us!" I blabbered.

"Why does it matter? You're a grown woman. You're allowed to kiss whomever you please."

And he was right but I had a sneaking suspicion that the reason I was being dismissed from the set had nothing to do with me hitting Emerald in the face with a Brussels sprout and everything to do with me kissing Chris. I saw one of the drivers pull up in his van and wave to me out the window. I waved back.

"Are you leaving?" Chris asked, confused.

"Yes. Obviously the rumor mill isn't up to speed. I've been dismissed."

"What do you mean?"

"Emerald doesn't want me on set today. She wants me at the hotel opening her fan mail."

Chris gave me a look of complete understanding. We both nodded our heads in unspoken communication. Not bad for knowing each other a mere twenty hours.

"Will I see you tonight at the party?"

"I wasn't invited to a party," I said pathetically. Chris laughed. My insecurity must have been written all over my face.

"We're all invited to the party, Lizzie," he said as he held up the call sheet and pointed to the notes section at the bottom. I took it out of his hand and read it.

Come celebrate a month of hard graft with a little swing music and margaritas.

"Oh. Well then, of course I'll be there. Sounds like fun," I said, trying to sound nonchalant. A call came through on Chris's walkie-talkie and he gave me a peck on the cheek and a wave.

"See you tonight," he said, picking up his radio and launching into a discussion with his second in command about how to set up the next shot.

I was in the van riding back to the hotel and thinking about Emerald's bad behavior. I wondered if maybe she had a crush on Chris. He had saved her from Ken's bullying and she had mentioned him a couple of times in passing. I hoped that wasn't the case because it would make the rest of my time in Thailand a nightmare. A spurned teen actress was not something any normal human should be expected to deal with. But her moods seemed to be as versatile as her wardrobe, and I reasoned that she was sure to get over it by tonight.

Anyway a day back at the ranch sorting through the backlog of paper-work and e-mails was actually not such a bad idea. There was a pile of scripts as high as my beach hut that Emerald had asked me to read and comment on. This was the opportunity I had hoped for to prove myself as more than just a glorified gopher. The scripts had the slick black cover and the silver writing of The Agency stamped across them, but I hadn't had the time to crack a single spine. Emerald usually required twenty-four-seven hand-holding. She'd said it didn't matter, anyway, because she wasn't in the mood to decide on her next part yet. Her agents were chomping at the bit. One of Scott's junior agents had even been leaving messages every day begging, pleading, and demanding that Emerald return her call.

Emerald was a producer on one of her upcoming films and every time we set a conference call with the writers, Emerald decided she needed a nap or wanted to do her nails. I felt a bit responsible for her avoidance tactics since she'd asked me to read the script and I'd com-mented honestly. It was crap. It was based on a novel about a young fe-male madam who set up a prostitution ring to pay for her student loans at Berkeley. The book was brilliant, but the writing team was just mak-ing a mess of the screenplay. They were dumbing down good material and that's what I'd told Emerald. In my short tenure at The Agency I'd noticed that it was a constant problem in Hollywood. Anything slightly different was stripped of its originality and more often than not made to conform into the mold of the last big hit. She hadn't hired the writers and was now doing a silent protest by not returning the producers' calls. That reminded me I had to reschedule the conference call again.

I walked into Emerald's bungalow and went straight to the phone. I was going to order in a masseuse for my lunch break, maybe I'd even have time for a facial. Emerald's punishment wasn't so bad after all. At least I'd look good for the party tonight. I picked up the handset but someone was already on it.

"Hello? Hello? Emerald?" A woman was saying. I immediately recog-nized Amber's voice on the other end of the line. I stayed silent for a second trying to think up some horrible practical joke I could play. But Amber stuck her foot right in it without any help from me. "I'm so glad I finally got you. Scott is so looking forward to talking with you. Lizzie is really useless, isn't she? I mean, you'd think she could at least man-age to put you through to your agent on a regular basis. She's so lucky to have a job with you, Emerald, because I really doubt if she'd have lasted at The Agency."

I couldn't believe what I was hearing. Amber would stop at nothing.

"Hi, Amber. It's Lizzie. Put Scott on the phone." For once I had the upper hand.

"Oh, Lizzie. You know, you shouldn't pretend to be Emerald. It's really—" I took a page out of Emerald's book and cut Amber off mid-sentence.

"Amber, is this a bad line? I told you to put Scott on *now*," I barked. I could almost hear the expression of shocked horror on the other end of the line. It was very satisfying.

"No need to get uppity, Lizzie. Here's Scott," she said in her cut glass English accent. But the blinders were well off and no English accent was going to fool me into believing that Amber had a thimbleful of class.

"Lizzie. Where the fuck have you been? We miss you here," Scott's voice pinged in, and I really hoped Amber was still on the phone.

"Oh? Amber said you wanted to fire me," I said innocently. I heard a distinctly female choking sound on the line. Amber was obviously still on the call. I smiled at my little bit of petty revenge.

"Don't be an idiot. I need you here," he said, and I blushed with pride. He was obviously appreciating my superior assistant skills. Fi-nally! "No one keeps Lara out of my hair as well as you do." I deflated into a dollar-sized pancake. "Anyway, I crashed her stupid car. So feel free to come back anytime. But before you do, be useful and get her to commit to one of those million fucking projects that are sitting on her bedroom floor. Christ, I'm sure she's dumped them on you. So pick the Warners' project. You know, the action one. I owe the head of produc-tion a favor and they're desperate for her. Script sucks so don't bother reading it. Just tell her it's genius and she'll believe you. You've got an Ivy League education, for fuck sake. She should trust you. Okay, got to go. But get me an answer by the end of the week."

"Okay, Scott but—" the line was already dead. I put the phone down and was about to go and try to dig the Warner script out of the pile when the phone started ringing again.

"Hello," I answered professionally, determined not to make the same mistake twice. It was Kathy calling from the set.

"Lizzie, where are you? Emerald is here on set and she's furious." Kathy sounded incensed.

"Kathy, what are you talking about? I just got back to the hotel ten minutes ago. Emerald sent me home from the set," I stammered, completely confused.

"Well, I've just left her side, and she was very angry. She said she needed you to run an errand for her and apparently it's only an errand *you* can run. So you'd better get back here right now."

I shook my head in frustration. I could handle crazy insecure Emerald but bipolar bitchy Emerald was beyond the pale.

"Did she mention what she needed, Kathy? I just want to make sure it's something we have on set because I wouldn't want to come all the way back and then have to send a driver all the way back here again to get whatever it might be."

"Hold on, I'll check." Kathy disappeared for moment as I quickly started shoving my notebook, laptop, and industrial-strength Advil into my bag. "She said it's private and none of my business. There's a driver on his way now from the production office at the other hotel. He'll be with you in five. Hurry! She's picking fights with Ken and we're already a week behind schedule and if she walks off set today I may just slit my wrists. Do you want my blood on your hands, Lizzie?"

If she were dead, at least it would be one more person off my back. All I wanted to do was scream. But primal scream therapy wasn't really my thing. I was much more of the internalize-it-all Waspy mentality that was certain to give me an ulcer and then cancer later in life. I riffled through the pile of scripts I hadn't even taken out of the latest box from LA and found the Warner one, slipped it in my bag, and ran out the door. I needed to make sure I had a job to come home to just in case Emerald decided not to forgive me.

I got to the set in fifty minutes, record time, jumped onto my valiant steed, the dusty baby blue moped I'd been given for the duration of my stay, and zipped down the dirt road to the set. The walk from base camp to the set took twenty minutes and Emerald was constantly sending me back and forth to fetch little bits and pieces, so, instead of having to call for a ride every time, Kathy and Fred had ordered me a Vespa. I loved it, as it provided me with a legitimate escape and a bit of independence. The journey back and forth down the beautiful dirt road was usually rejuvenating, but today nothing looked particularly thrilling. There were ominous clouds hovering low over the set and a strange fog was rolling in. I arrived on set midshot and watched as Emerald worked with Carmen cutting away at a bamboo cage with a makeshift knife. Chris was standing just out of shot and we caught eyes and exchanged smiles. Thank God for him or things would have seemed totally unbearable.

Emerald noticed me just as Chris and I were in the midst of a bit of sign language flirtation. She stopped middelivery and walked off camera. "Ken. Your camera is on Carmen. Don't waste my time to improve your girlfriend's reel." Then she stalked off like a little tornado, flattening everyone in her path. But the eye of the storm was saved for me, and she made sure everyone heard her.

"Lizzie. You're supposed to be my assistant. If you're not on set, you can't assist me now, can you?" she said, putting her hands on her hips.

"Emerald, you told the First AD that I should go home."

"No I didn't. Don't make excuses for your laziness. And when you are on set, I expect you to behave like a professional, not spend your time flirting with the crew." I was blushing with the sheer humiliation of it all as everyone on set was cringing, embarrassed to be witnessing such abuse.

I decided the path of least resistance was the only approach, otherwise this would become a four-alarm battle. I swallowed the fury that was building up in the back of my throat and gritted my teeth. "You're right, Emerald," I said as quietly as possible. "What can I get you?"

"I want a peanut-butter-and-jelly sandwich. I'm wasting away here."

"Okay," I said slowly, "but Kathy said you wanted something special, something you couldn't discuss with the PA?"

"That's what I wanted. It's not up to you or Kathy to decide who gets what for me, now, is it?" And with that she stalked to her director's chair and sat down. "Makeup. I need makeup now!" she yelled.

So off I went on my moped to get the caterer to whip up a sandwich. I was back half an hour later with the most deliciously juicy-looking PB&J a girl could imagine but when she saw it she looked at me with total disdain. "I told you to cut the crusts off, Elizabeth. How hard is it to remember that?" She watched me carefully and seemed well pleased with my look of stupefaction and then the blush that followed, which, in twenty-odd years I still hadn't managed to get under control. I looked around at the thirty or so cast and crew members who were watching her little power-hungry display and wanted to dive into a rice paddy. "I can't eat that," she continued. "Go back and get me another."

First, she'd never mentioned anything about crusts, and second, what nineteen-year-old needed her crusts cut off? But I wasn't there to argue and I guarantee if I'd come down with the crusts cut off she would have sent me back to base camp to get the crusts put back on. So I got back on my Vespa and was five minutes into the drive when the heavens opened. The rain came pouring down in sheets as I drove at breakneck speeds taking my fury, humiliation, and powerlessness out on the road. I hated everything about this business: Amber, Emerald, Scott, and even Luke. Not one of them had an ounce of integrity. Why couldn't more people be like Chris? At this rate I was never going to be a producer. I was going to stay the whipping post for people with the intelligence level of rodents for the rest of my life. Right at that moment a wet chicken came running out into the middle of the road and I instinctually swerved out of the way. I really wasn't trying to end it all, but I think the chicken might have been. My moped hit a wet pothole and over it went, pulling me along through the mud before we both came to a grinding halt. I lay in the mud in the pouring rain and realized that I really needed to reevaluate my life. I pushed the bike off me and tried to stand up but a shooting pain seared through my ankle. I sat back down on the side of the road and checked my limbs to make sure they were intact. Besides a really bad case of road rash up and down my left leg and arm, all seemed to still be attached. I looked at my ankle, which was already starting to swell in my Converse sneaker, and burst into tears. Just then Chris appeared in the pouring rain on his moped. He saw my bike on the side of the road and literally jumped off his moped in midmotion and ran toward me.

"Jesus, Lizzie, are you okay? I was just coming up to make sure you weren't too upset at that bitch's outburst." He was examining the road rash on my leg, as I tried to explain, but my hiccuping sobs seemed to get in the way of polite conversation. "You must have been going damn fast to get that scrape. All for no crusts?"

I started to laugh as the rain continued to drench us both. "My ankle," I said half-laughing and half-crying.

Chris took it gently in his hand and looked at it. "Think you broke it, babes. I'm going to call and get Dr. Pen and a golf cart. I can't take you on my bike. It's too wet and I wouldn't want you to fall again and do more damage." I nodded like a pathetic little girl.

Chris got on his walkie-talkie and within seconds there was a golf cart with Dr. Pen and his black medical bag. Chris lifted me carefully into the back of the golf cart and held me tightly as we bumped along back to base camp.

I wasn't sure if I was more terrified of my broken ankle or Dr. Pen. He was an ongoing joke on the set. He'd been brought on specially by Fred and was a psychiatrist. Apparently they'd been friends since college and they'd done many an acid trip together in the guise of exploring the hidden depths of the psyche. And now Dr. Pen was a favorite among the movie crowd, as he felt perfectly comfortable prescribing everything from Vicodin to Ambien or any other prescription med one felt the need for. At least I was certain I wouldn't be feeling any pain.

TWELVE

Hollywood is loneliness beside the swimming pool.

—Liv Ullman

They'd rushed me to a local Phuket hospital and Kathy kindly came along to hold my hand. We swapped war stories about nightmare Hollywood nut cases while we waited for the results of the X rays. Thank God she was there to distract me as the one-room hospital with its thatched roof and dirt floor wasn't very reassuring. I was pleasantly surprised to see they had electricity and even more shocked when they wheeled me into a room with a brand new X-ray machine. The nurse explained that one of the Hollywood studios had donated it. There had been so many accidents on the set of their last movie they'd decided it was cheaper to donate the machine than to send people back and forth by private jet to Bangkok.

I was pleased to see that Hollywood was bringing something positive to the community after all. There was such gross inequity in the lavish lifestyle Emerald and I were living and the poverty all around us. I made a mental note to convince Emerald, if I ever spoke to her again, to donate some money to the community to put a floor in the hospital, and maybe a door! At least my tenure as assistant to one of the highest-paid actresses in the world wouldn't be a total waste after all.

Two hours later we were still waiting. Though they had the machinery, they apparently didn't have the film. Kathy was on her phone and I was anxiously watching the space where the door should have been for the driver with the X-ray film. I'd counted all the burst blood vessels on my swollen ankle and was moving on to the freckles when Emerald burst into the room in a flurry of guilty excitement. She came toward me at such speed she ran right into my propped-up ankle. I winced in pain as she covered me with kisses and apologies while Kathy hung up the phone and looked on in amusement.

"I'm so sorry, Lizzie. Please forgive me. I'm a terrible person. You're my best friend in the whole world. If you hated me I'd die."

I looked at her face and knew that she genuinely meant every word she'd just said. She was so lost I found it difficult to stay mad at her. Being unable to hold a grudge was a major flaw in my character, but no matter how hard and twisted I felt, I always ended up forgiving everyone in the end. And when she carefully laid a velvet box in my lap I momentarily forgot why I was mad at her in the first place.

"This is just to say sorry and thank you for doing such a good job in the last month. You've been a saint." I didn't even open the box, just stroked the velvet, let out a big sigh and then handed it back.

"Thanks, Em. But no thanks. I can't be bought." Sometimes it was really hard to do the right thing. I couldn't help but remember what had happened the last time I'd refused diamonds.

But Emerald wasn't so easily put off. She opened the box for me and took out the most beautiful art deco diamond bracelet I'd ever seen in my life. I saw Kathy involuntarily step forward. Emerald rolled it around in her hand, letting it catch the sunlight.

"Lizzie, you have to take it. It's a friendship bracelet. And if you don't accept it, I'll think you don't want to be my friend."

Now, this was twisted logic, but I felt myself caving.

"Em, I will definitely not accept it if you try to manipulate me." But she could hear the cracks in my resolve. It was clearly bad luck to reject such generosity.

"Okay," she said with a pout. "Fine. But why do you have to be so cynical? I'm just trying to give you a present. I've already said sorry, and you've already accepted my apology, so this bracelet is just a reward for work well done."

"The girl has a point," Kathy said with a smile as she ripped the bracelet out of Emerald's hand and caressed it once before snapping it onto my wrist.

But I still wasn't sure.

"Look. If you had as much cash as I do, you'd buy people diamonds all the time too," Emerald said with a smile as she played with the bracelet on my wrist. "And if you feel the guilt is too overwhelming or end up hating me, you can give it to charity."

"Okay," I said slowly. "City of Hope does do good work. But before I forgive you and then thank you profusely, you have to give a hundred thousand dollars to the hospital."

Her eyes went wide at the amount, but not as wide as the nurse's. But then Emerald looked around, as if for the first time, at the uncomfortable bed and chicken running by. She shrugged and then started laughing.

"Okay. I guess I can donate my per diem to a good cause. Actually, I'll give them two hundred grand and then they can name the hospital after me." She looked happier than she had in weeks. "Kathy, can you arrange that? Now."

"Sure, Em, after I make sure Elizabeth is all right, okay?"

Emerald turned on Kathy.

"I'm here now. Lizzie doesn't need you," she said with such venom that both Kathy and I paled. Emerald noticed and changed her tone. "I'm a nurse, after all, and I just want to make sure I get a chance to make it up to Lizzie. That's okay with you right, Lizzie?" She turned to me pleadingly. "Just the two of us?"

Kathy raised an eyebrow at me behind Emerald's back and I gave her an "I guess so" nod.

"Well, it looks like you girls have it handled. I'll be getting back to the set and work on your donation." She gave a wave, but Emerald had already forgotten about her. She was too busy trying to convince the nurse to let her give me the shot of painkiller when it was needed.

I had to fight Emerald off for the rest of the afternoon, reminding her again and again that she wasn't a real nurse but was only *playing* a nurse. She waved off my protests, but luckily the brilliant Thai nurse gave me the injection before Em and I finished our discussion on method acting. When the doctor finally came back with my X rays, I was pleased to hear that nothing was broken. Luckily, I'd escaped with a bad sprain. I'd have to wear an Ace bandage and stay off my feet for the next few weeks, but Emerald didn't seem to mind. She said she'd get me my own assistant to make life easier.

As Emerald and Tensin bundled me into the car I felt slightly on edge, which was a surprise considering I'd been dosed with painkillers. Maybe they'd only given me a local anesthetic or the dosage was too low. The Thai people were a lot smaller than I was, after all. As we drove along, I remembered Dr. Pen's promise, and hoped that the extra large bottle of Vicodin would be waiting in my hut. The day's events had left me wound unusually tight, and I still wanted to enjoy the party tonight. I wondered if taking painkillers and then going to a party would be considered recreational drug use. I reminded myself that I was injured and that they were necessary for medical reasons. I'd never tried Vicodin, but Scott swore by it.

"Lizzie, has Chris called you?" Emerald said innocently enough as we bumped along back to the hotel.

Then it hit me. The anxiety wasn't related to my ankle but to Emerald. I knew there had to be more to the 180-degree turn in her behavior than just my injury. She seemed oddly ebullient as she chattered on about tonight's party the entire ride home. Maybe it was simply a case of cabin fever. Emerald had gone from party monster to party pooper. The girl just probably needed a few cocktails and smooch. Obviously, the threesome had sated her overactive libido and now her tanks were empty.

To both Emerald's and my excitement Dr. Pen had dropped off the Vicodin. I made her swear she wouldn't take any, but when I hobbled back from the bathroom, she had "thief" written all over her face. Knowing her penchant for excess, I later counted them to make sure she had only taken one. Three were missing, but that was restraint in Emerald's book. We ordered champagne and got dressed together. She couldn't have been more of a delight. We laughed and danced around the villa to Madonna. She even insisted I tell her about Chris and the kiss. The Vicodin was obviously kicking in, since all my anxiety disappeared along with the sharp throb in my ankle. I even confided in her about Luke's flower delivery. She said that I shouldn't forgive him so quickly but make him earn it. At the time I liked her thinking, and she seemed to have totally gotten over the Chris thing. We were both dressed for the party and I was feeling no pain. The Vicodin was heaven. I felt completely myself but totally free of all pain and anxiety. No wonder Scott had had to go to Arizona to kick the habit. I popped another pill and off we went.

We were both giggling like excited schoolgirls when we arrived at the crew hotel. I felt like the guest of honor as everybody made a big fuss over my bandaged ankle and crutches. The set designers had done a brilliant job creating a Mexican Fiesta in Thailand. The hope, they said, was that we'd feel a bit less homesick. It was working for me, or maybe that was the pills. There were little red pepper fairy lights strung on every available surface and a bar set up with four blenders and the best tequila money could buy. Emerald and I headed straight for the bar and ordered fresh blended strawberry margaritas. Emerald suddenly grabbed my hand in shock and pointed to the other end of the pool.

"Look, Lizzie, they have me hanging from a tree."

And true enough, there was an effigy of Emerald hanging from a branch. The likeness was remarkable. But quickly I realized that she wasn't alone. On various branches and doorframes were life-size dolls of all the lead actors as well as Ken, Kathy, and Fred.

"Emerald, they're piñatas." I started to laugh, then turned to look at her reaction.

There was no way this wasn't going to cause a serious temper tantrum.

"You mean they're going to beat me until candy comes out?" Emerald said, stupefied.

"It looks like it." I was biting my lip so hard, trying to hold back the laughter, that I think I could taste a bit of blood on my tongue.

"Oh. So basically it's just a reenactment of my life," she said drily. Emerald never failed to surprise me. Which was why I was still standing there by her side sipping margaritas and wasn't back in LA sorting out my future.

She turned to me with a wicked glint in her eyes. "I'd love to take a shot at the Carmen piñata. Think anyone would notice if I was the first to have a whack?"

"Nope. But I think if you waited for the girl with the tequila holster and canastas to finish her rounds, you might get some people to join you."

Emerald nodded her head in agreement as we watched the scantily clad Thai girl in hot pants and a shooters holster pour tequila down a gaffer's throat.

We propped up the bar chatting with the wardrobe assistant and the head painter and drained two more cocktails. I probably should have read the warning label on my industrial-strength bottle of Vicodin, but I pretty much knew what it said—*no alcohol*. But it was a party, and Emerald and I both really needed to have a good time.

Emerald took off with the script supervisor to go and try to break Carmen, the piñata that is, and I found myself a chair a bit out of the way. Just as the waiter delivered a fresh drink, Chris appeared by my side. He was clean-shaven and his thick black hair was still wet. His tan was set against a white oxford and he looked the picture of surfer-boy good looks.

"It took you long enough," I said.

"I was waiting for Emerald to leave. I didn't want to cause you any more problems." He nodded toward my foot. "In the end I had to bribe the script supervisor to distract her." He noticed the diamond bracelet on my wrist. "Looks like you guys made up anyway." I blushed, hating Chris to think I was that kind of girl.

"I'm going to donate it to charity when I get home," I explained feebly.

"I wish I could buy you diamonds," he said wistfully. I couldn't quite believe what I was hearing. He was obviously feeling an even stronger connection than I was. A little thrill ran through my body as Chris pulled up a chair next to mine. Thoughts of Luke flitted through my head, but I dismissed them and focused on Emerald beating the shit out of the paper Carmen.

Carmen had just arrived and had taken no time grabbing a bat and was now going after the Emerald piñata. Both girls were sweating and the party had divided into two different camps cheering the girls on. I think I even saw someone taking odds. The poor Thai staff looked terrified. I imagined that beating effigies was probably not something Buddha encouraged. But the substances coursing through my veins were giving me an overall feeling of well-being, so when Chris hooked his foot under my chair and pulled me close, nothing around me seemed to matter much.

"Do you want to tell me where it hurts?" he whispered in my ear.

I touched my lips and he kissed me softly. Then I touched my head and he leaned over and kissed that too. Just as I was about to point to something too obscene to mention, Emerald came waltzing over with an entire armload of candy.

"I split Carmen's ass," she chortled, "and it was really big." She dumped some candy in my lap and turned to Chris.

"So, Chris, where do you live in LA?" she said with a seemingly genuine smile. She grabbed a margarita on the rocks from a passing waiter and sat down next to us.

"Malibu," he said warily. He'd obviously had more practice than I'd had at predicting a change in the weather.

"Where in Malibu?" Emerald persisted. I probably should have intervened, but all I could do was smile and think how nice it was that we were all friends.

"In The Colony," Chris said. And it suddenly occurred to me that for the first time he seemed a bit uncomfortable.

"That's where my house is too. Cool, we'll be neighbors. So is anyone at your house right now?"

"Why?" Chris was starting to squirm in his chair.

"Well the rug fitters are coming by. And I have a key hidden under a rock by the front door." I looked at Emerald, wondering where on earth this was going, and then she dropped the bomb. "The script supervisor mentioned that your girlfriend worked from home. Do you think there's any way she could let them in? Her name is Susie, right? I hope I'm not imposing. I hear she's like some famous romance writer or something. Probably explains the house in The Colony, huh?"

Chris looked from Emerald to me like a snared rabbit. Emerald's tolerance for illegal substances was obviously much higher than mine as her wits seemed to be completely intact. I, on the other hand, was struggling to keep up.

"Emerald, did you just say that Chris has a girlfriend he *lives* with?" I said stupidly.

Chris turned his back on Emerald and looked at me. "Lizzie. I wanted to tell you about her, but it's complicated. We've been together for ten years and . . ."

"You're a liar?" I said, blinking like a mole emerging from its hole.

Chris put up a hand in protest. "I am not a liar. I never told you I *didn't* have a girlfriend."

I couldn't believe what I was hearing.

Emerald looked pretty pleased with herself.

"But you were supposed to have integrity. You were supposed to be different."

"Listen, Lizzie. I was going to break up with her when I got back. I just didn't think it was fair to do it over the phone. You're special. I promise. I really want to get to know you better."

I looked at him and wanted to believe. It wasn't that I really cared about him as a person. I barely knew him, but I really wanted to believe that there was something real and honest and wholesome left in the world. I teetered for a second.

"That is such a load of shit, Chris," Emerald jumped in. "Apparently you fall in love with a new girl every time you go on location and then go back to Susie the second your plane hits the tarmac in LA."

Chris looked at Emerald in fury, but I could see from the look on his face that his game was up.

Thankfully, I was too stunned and stoned to move as it would have been impossible to make a dramatic exit on crutches without looking like a total idiot.

Chris stood up, knocking over the plastic chair he was sitting in. "I don't have to sit here and take these insults." And with that he turned around and stormed off. In disbelief I watched him go.

Emerald picked up his chair and dusted off her hands. "Good riddance to bad rubbish," she said, looking like the cat that ate the canary.

I knew I felt upset, but the painkillers and tequila seemed to send a different message to my brain. I started to laugh and then stood up abruptly, forgetting about my ankle. Pain surged through my body as I put my full weight on it. I almost fell over, but Emerald was there to catch me.

"Lizzie, are you okay?" She looked genuinely worried. I grabbed my crutches.

"Yeah. I'm fine. I just need to get out of here."

"Okay. Let's take a walk on the beach." Emerald grabbed a bottle of tequila. She walked and I hobbled toward the sea.

I only made it a few feet away from the lights of the hotel before I collapsed. Walking in sand on crutches intoxicated was no easy feat.

Emerald sat down next to me and cracked the bottle. We each did a few shots.

"So are you mad at me for telling you about Chris?" she asked nervously.

"No," I said after a few seconds. "I guess I don't really care. Would have been better if you'd told me in private."

"Yeah, I know. I actually heard the rumors on set earlier but needed confirmation before I told you."

I watched her as she practically gulped the bottle of tequila. "Take it easy girl," I said, taking the bottle away from her. "If you pass out I won't be able to carry you back to the hotel."

"Lizzie?" She looked like she was about to say something but stopped.

"Yeah?"

And then it happened; she lunged at me. You know the kind of lunge that happened when you were sixteen and the boy next door, who your mom made you go out with, was dropping you home after a movie. I was so stunned I just sat there as she kissed me on the lips. But when she stuck her tongue in my mouth, I quickly snapped back to reality. I pulled away and shook my head.

"Emerald . . ." I didn't know what to say as she looked like a puppy dog and I didn't quite have the heart to crush its little head.

Emerald was focusing on her hands now, embarrassed.

"But you went to bed with the basketball player and Jake Hudson," I said, stupefied.

"Yeah. So what? Anyway, it never hurts to have a studio head in your back pocket if you need one," she said honestly.

"So you're gay then?" I asked, even more confused.

"Not really. Just bicurious I guess."

"Do you have a crush on me?" I was really struggling to understand what was happening here.

Emerald went silent and thought for a while. "I just really like you. You're the first person who has been honest with me in years. I don't want you to leave me."

"So you thought if we had lesbian sex I'd stay?"

"Yeah, basically," Emerald said, like it was the most logical thing any-one had ever said.

"Emerald. Sex doesn't make people stay." I considered the sentiment for a second. "Well, not for any period of time," I corrected. I could tell Emerald didn't quite believe me.

"So you'll stay with me and be my friend as long as I don't kiss you again?" she said and looked up at me hopefully with her big green eyes.

"Exactly," I said firmly.

But that wasn't true, either. The last twenty-four hours had made me really miss home. I'd run away from everything I'd built in the last two years. And though it had been the distraction I'd needed, being the per-manent playmate for a damaged nineteen-year-old wasn't my goal in life. My face was clearly an open book as Emerald seemed to read my mind. Again.

"I know being my assistant isn't enough for a smarty-pants like you. So why don't you be my producer? Warner Bros. wants to give me a pro-ducing deal and you can have whatever job you want. We'd have so much fun as a team. We'd be like sisters. Come on, Lizzie. What do you say?" Emerald said persuadingly.

What could I say? This was what I'd been dreaming of since I came to Hollywood, but not really.

"You don't need that silly Luke Lloyd," Emerald continued. "Even if you did get back together, you'd always worry that he was kissing some ex-girlfriend behind your back."

As quickly as the fantasy had blossomed, it withered on the vine. Emerald may not want to have sex with me, but she wasn't happy with anything less than ownership. It just made her feel too insecure. I could never work for Emerald and have a life of my own at the same time.

"You can't refuse this offer, Lizzie. I'll give you five minutes to think about it. Don't talk to me until you say yes," she said with that edge in her voice that made the hair on my arms stand on end.

I looked around for a distraction, but it was dark and there was noth-ing to interrupt us but the stars, sand, and swaying palm trees. I couldn't even get up and scurry away. I cursed my crutches. Then it happened. Scott saved me. Emerald's phone rang.

"I'm not answering it." She let it go to voice mail. But then a second later my phone started to ring. Emerald looked at me challengingly as I grabbed it.

"Emerald. It's obviously important. I have to. It's my job." I put the phone to my ear. "Lizzie Miller," I said. Scott's voice boomed through the receiver. I held it away from my ear.

"Lizzie, what the fuck are you doing? We have a crisis here. Pictures of America's teen sweetheart drunk on the bar in the American Airlines lounge doing a striptease have just appeared in *Star*. And it happened on your watch. This is a media nightmare. Disney withdrew their offer for her next film. And I'm guessing Warner is about to do the same. And her cosmetics contract has just been canceled too. Is she with you? Put her on the phone." I handed Emerald the phone in shock.

How did those pictures get out, I wondered. I'd taken the film from the paparazzo's camera and sent it to Scott to destroy properly. I'd have to ask him about it when I got back. Maybe someone else was there photographing the incident. I was clearly in over my head. I looked at Emerald, who had suddenly gone very pale. I'd never heard her so docile. She just kept saying, "Yes. Yes. Yes."

Then she hung up the phone and turned to me. "Lizzie, you're going home. Anyway, it doesn't look like I'll have a job to offer you anymore."

I felt immense relief, but also horror. Did that mean I was fired from The Agency too? How was any of this my fault? I couldn't imagine going back to LA without a job or a home. And if this did mean I was axed, what was I going to do with my life now? Thank God I'd been stashing away that per diem. Maybe I'd just make a clean break, throw in the towel, and move back in with my parents in D.C. I could try to get in touch with some of my old contacts in politics. But the thought of moving back east really depressed me. I'd become addicted to the manic pace and excitement of Hollywood life. I didn't want to leave yet. Anyway, I still had so much to accomplish.

"Scott says he needs you in the office. You're going back home on the first plane tomorrow. He's sending in a professional to do damage control," Emerald said as she picked up a handful of sand and let the grains run through her fingers.

A sigh of relief slipped from my lips.

"I guess it's for the best. Who wants to hear the truth all the time anyway? If I did I wouldn't have become an actress," she said with a little shrug.

I wrapped my arms around her in a big sisterly hug. "Emerald, I'm sorry. But if you ever need a friend, you can always trust me. I promise I'd never sell you out."

Emerald gave a hard laugh as I struggled to get up on my crutches. "No, of course you wouldn't. You signed a confidentiality agreement. I'd sue you." So that was going to be the way it ended. I tried to make eye contact, but she wouldn't look up.

"I should go and pack. Are you okay?" I said.

"I'm fine. See ya." This was a clear dismissal. I stood there for a second, but she still didn't look up. I turned around and was about to walk away when I noticed my bracelet glinting in the moonlight. I took it off, turned around, and held it in front of her face.

"You might want this back," I said.

But Emerald shook her head violently. "No. It was a gift," she said. I could hear the tears in her voice. "Have a safe trip, Lizzie. You better go. You've got a lot of packing to do."

"Well, thanks." I stood there wishing she'd at least come back to the hotel with me. " 'Bye again."

There was nothing left to say, so I turned around and hopped off down the beach on my one good leg. I stopped to catch my breath and looked back over my shoulder at the solitary figure of Emerald sitting in the sand.

Emerald Everhart was one of the most desired woman in the world, yet she was one of the loneliest people I'd ever met in my life.

THIRTEEN

Hollywood is a place where they'll
pay you a thousand dollars for a
kiss and fifty cents for your soul.

—Marilyn Monroe

It was strange being back in Los Angeles. Right after I'd left for Thailand, Lara had gone over to Luke's and piled my belongings into a duffel bag or three and slid the key back through the mail slot. So now, as I sat on the plush double bed in Lara and Scott's guesthouse, where I was staying until I found somewhere new to live, I rummaged through the remnants of my former life as the girlfriend of Luke Lloyd. A life that seemed so far away that I'd almost forgotten who that girl was. The Lizzie Miller sitting here now was a slightly more cynical, much more resourceful and worldly creature than the girl who'd hopped on a plane to Thailand a month ago. Which had its drawbacks—now I was also less sure than I had ever been in my life of just what direction my life and career should take. Which wasn't a state I was given to. So maybe this was the moment—maybe I'd finally grown up enough to know that you can't always know.

Fortunately I wasn't due back at The Agency until Monday—three days away—so I had a little time on my hands to ponder my future. Unfortunately this process was more painful that I could ever have anticipated. Most significant, it was the first time since I'd first laid eyes on "that photograph" in *People* magazine that I'd had to listen to myself think. For the past five weeks I'd endured an unending cacophony of demands from Emerald, so silence had never been an option. Now, though, in the still of the afternoon, it was deafening. Forget facing the music, now I was forced to face the silence.

I pulled out my black Azzaro dress. The night I had worn it I'd gotten my first hint that Luke and I had not been alone in our relationship. Emanuelle had glued herself to Luke's side during the premiere and my insecurities had bubbled to the surface when he'd almost proposed to me. I should have gone with him to Prague, I should have given up my dumb, meaningless job and followed him. I could have read Russian novels all afternoon, learned rudimentary Czech, volunteered at a local school, and looked pretty and ready to take to dinner when he came back from a cold day's shoot. Then all this would never have happened. Luke was a man like any other and he wanted his woman by his side, I thought with the lunacy of heartbreak.

Clearly five weeks in the presence of Tomorrow's Woman, aka Emerald Everhart, had made me wary of emancipation, financial independence, and a woman's right to wear anything other than a burka, I thought with alarm as I pulled a stray sock of Luke's out of a duffel bag. What did my world hold without him, I wondered. I wasn't sure whether I wanted to do my job anymore, playing nursemaid to someone. I wanted to get on with making my own mark. There was no Luke to hide behind now and no excuse. I vowed to keep my eyes open and look for a producing opportunity, but this time I wouldn't let anyone like Daniel Rosen cut me out of the deal. I'd have my eyes open and I'd be in charge. I also didn't have a home anymore, and my only rock of sanity in this whole horrible town, Luke, the man whose mere existence had counteracted every sleazy, cheating, double-dealing man in Los Angeles, had let me down. But before I could even blink out a tear and drown myself in the misery of the past month, there was a knock on the cottage door.

"Come in," I shouted, glad of a distraction.

"Settling in?" It was Lara and she had Lachlan balanced on her lissome hip.

"Yes, thanks. It's great. The bathroom's gorgeous," I said cheerily as she came in, set Lachlan down, and sat in a chintzy armchair under the window.

"I meant, how is it to be back?" Lara asked, while looking pointedly at the navy blue man's sock I was wringing in my hands.

"Horrible." I let out a deep sigh.

"Thought so." Lara scooped Lachlan up before he could insert his tongue into the electrical socket behind the television. "So, Scott's away in New York for a premiere for a couple of days and I've got a babysitter. We can hit the town."

"Oh no, really, it's sweet of you, Lara, but I just can't," I protested. The idea of going out anywhere made me want to crawl inside my unpacked duffel bag from Thailand with all my mildew-scented clothes.

"It's not open for discussion," Lara said. "We're going out, and that's all there is to it."

"But if you had any clue how many clubs and bars and parties I'd been forced to go to recently, you wouldn't be making me do this," I pleaded without optimism as Lara stripped my trip duffel of its contents.

"Don't care," Lara said as she pulled out a jean skirt and a gold and white top that clearly belonged to Emerald and that I didn't remember packing. "Wear these."

"That's not mine. . . ."

"I'll meet you at the house at eight o'clock. I'm going to give this little monkey his bath now," she said as Lachlan nuzzled his face into her neck.

"Where are we going?" I asked as she walked out the door.

"Somewhere fancy," Lara said, and left.

"You're an incredible mother," I said to Lara later on, after I'd rallied, forced my boobs into Emerald's top, and stopped protesting to Lara that I never wanted to go out again. We were sitting in the garden at the Sunset Marquis. We were apparently planning to go to the VIP room at Spider afterward, but I was hoping to dodge that particular annex to the evening.

"Everyone's an incredible mother," Lara told me.

It was weird how our wild night out was tamer than our talks over Chinese takeout used to be.

"It must be amazing, being a mom," I said, gazing over the top of my champagne cocktail into the middle distance.

"It is." She shrugged. "But it's also amazing going on location to Thailand and having the world at your feet, I'm sure." She looked at me meaningfully, but I dodged her inquisitive stare.

"Do you think I'll ever have children?" I sighed.

"No, never. I mean look at you. Why would anyone want to bother impregnating you?" She raised her glass and winked at me.

"Do you and Scott still have sex?" I asked, wondering whether Scott's affair with the actress was an ongoing concern.

"Sure, all the time," she said casually. "That's true, by the way. My husband, as you know, is an addict. So one thing I'm guaranteed until the day I die is lots of sex."

"Do you think you'll be together until the day you die?" I asked.

"Well, most likely until the day *he* dies," she said confidently. Which was probably a fair enough point, that Scott would shuffle off this mortal coil first, given how much he'd abused his body in the past. Unless, of course, all that booze and powder had merely served to preserve him.

"Do you think that Luke and Emanuelle will be together until they die?" I asked, suddenly not able to help myself from bringing up the subject, picking at it like a scab.

"You still don't know if they're together or not Lizzie," she said. "You haven't spoken to him since it happened. To be honest the poor guy must be going out of his mind wondering what's going on with you." Lara had already promised me that she'd obsessively pored over every magazine on the shelf in search of Luke and Emanuelle gossip, but after that one sighting had found none. Though I was taking nothing for granted. I had heard no more from Luke since the flowers in Thailand and still wasn't ready to reach out. In fact I wasn't sure I ever would be.

"Well, he knew where to find me," I said glibly, and bolted back a mouthful of champagne.

"Actually, he didn't," Lara reminded me. "You were in a paddy field. Remember? And didn't he send you a roomful of roses when he did finally track you down?"

"I'd prefer it if we didn't discuss Luke Lloyd," I said firmly.

"Have you cried once since this happened?" Lara suddenly lowered her head and looked me in the eye.

"I can't remember." I turned away.

"Elizabeth?"

"Yes." I sniffed. "I cried almost daily in Thailand. I cried when I crashed on my moped. I cried when I saw how much Emerald's annual clothing budget was. I cried when her personal trainer made me do four hundred lunges in one session. I cried . . ."

"Have you cried about Luke?" Lara demanded.

"No."

"That's not good." She took my hand. "Lizzie, you loved him. You guys were together for a year."

"Yeah, and he didn't love me," I said as I pushed my glass out of the way and stood up. "I'm going to pee."

When I emerged from the refreshingly sterile bathroom, I determined to enjoy myself. I'd taken a hard look at myself in the bathroom mirror and told myself I was not going to waste my time pining for a man who could cheat on me, and if Luke wanted to be with Emanuelle, I wasn't going to be a clingy freak and try to stop him. I would move on with my life without so much as a backward glance. How could I ignore fate then, when it seemed to intervene on my behalf?

"Hi there." A tall man with blond hair and a very sharp suit was standing by the bar with some friends. I half-smiled out of politeness but didn't want to make eye contact. "How are you?" he asked.

Ever well-mannered and not one to cock a snoot at the mores of fate I felt obliged to answer. "I'm fine, thank you," I replied, but didn't really stop walking.

"I'm Anders," the man informed me. I smiled again and hastened back to my table where Lara was in full flow on her cell phone.

"Sorry, honey," Lara said. By the time she got off the phone, I had finished my drink and caught Anders's eye once or twice more. I didn't mean to but I had to look somewhere, and he and his entourage were compellingly handsome. Certainly they weren't American, which was always a pleasant treat. They were like a collection of Norse gods hanging around waiting for their Viking longboat to drift into view across a fjord and take them to war. Though God knows I probably had my cultures all mixed up.

"That was the babysitter," Lara said. "Lachlan won't settle down. But she can cope for now. Let's order another drink and see what happens." But no sooner had the words left her mouth than the three Vikings appeared above us.

"Ladies. We'd like to buy you drinks." Anders was at the helm. The other two were silent. Perhaps they didn't speak English.

"Oh, we're fine, thanks." I smiled. "We're just having a quiet girls' night out."

"I would just like to buy you one drink." He seemed very earnest and he was focusing all his attentions on me. "You will offend me if you don't." He smiled.

"Thanks but no," Lara said firmly. She was always good at getting rid of unwanted attention, unlike me who always hesitated for just long enough to let any nutcase determined enough into my life.

As Anders was refusing to take his eyes off me, a young couple approached our table and tapped Lara on the shoulder.

"Oh my God, hi." Lara stood up and began an excitable conversation with her long-lost friends, leaving me at the mercy of the Vikings, like many an innocent maiden before me, I thought giddily.

"We shall keep you company while your friend is talking," Anders said quietly. "What's your name?"

"Elizabeth," I replied, not really wanting to get involved but, well, what else was I going to do? Play beer mats by myself while Lara chatted?

"Elizabeth," Anders repeated in what was clearly a Scandinavian accent. "Would you mind if we joined you for a moment?"

"Well, I suppose for a moment." I shrugged as Anders et al. sat down on the sofa next to me. "But when my friend comes back, we'd like to be alone. We have some catching up to do," I explained.

"Surely," Anders said as one of his friends motioned for the waiter. "But first you'll have a glass of champagne?"

"I already have a drink, thanks." I shook my head and cast a look at Lara over my shoulder, but she was clearly still filling whoever it was in on the past three years of surviving Scott and motherhood.

"Ah but my champagne is so good," Anders said as his long, dark gray–clad leg brushed faintly against my knee.

"It's fine, thank you," I reiterated. I knew that once I accepted a drink I was complicit and there would be no getting rid of the Vikings. Which would result in Lara getting brusque with them and me getting embarrassed. Besides, while it was nice to have a little clean-cut attention, I really did want to spend my evening with Lara. We had a lot of work-shopping to do tonight that was sorely needed for my general sanity and reintegration back into my life.

"But there's something very special about my champagne." Anders nodded and leaned close to me, his blond curls skimming his shirt collar sexily.

"Is there really?" I asked, transfixed by his locks and his voice. I mean, who could resist that gentle accent so redolent of emancipated men, recycling, and the most liberal laws in the world? Everyone knew that Scandinavian men were perfect in every way. They were everything that chauvinistic, backward-thinking American men weren't. My sister, Melissa, and I had often longed for a Lars or a Björn. Even before we knew about the child-care policies of their homelands.

"Oh yes, I'll show you."

The next thing I knew one of the entourage had stepped forward, dropped to his knees beside Anders, and began to roll up Anders's trouser leg. I kid you not. I looked over my shoulder to see where Lara was, but she'd gone over to the couple's table and was now busy saying hi to at least another eight long-lost friends, who were being delighted by the photos of Lachlan she was showing them on her cell phone.

I watched as Viking #1 removed a small velvet bag that was strapped to Anders's ankle. Then he handed it to Anders. This was a very unexpected turn of events, even for someone who had walked the meandering path of unpredictability that was Emerald for the past four weeks.

"Here," Anders said as he unrolled the piece of velvet onto the table before me, and a cluster of uncut diamonds fell out and arranged themselves into a dazzling constellation. I looked on with a mixture of wonder and bewilderment. But before I could respond, Anders had picked up the biggest of the stones and was holding it between his fingers, subjecting it to an impartial gaze.

"Oh, you're working on a movie." I laughed. "You brought the props home with you. It's not the remake of *Raiders of the Lost Ark,* is it? I heard the script was great."

"I'm not in the movies," Anders said, suddenly looking extremely intense, even for a Viking. "These are real." He seemed affronted at my suggestion. And I suspected that he wasn't lying. But then they couldn't be real. What would a sane, Scandinavian man be doing with a bunch of diamonds up his pant leg?

"I see." I smiled. "Very nice."

"Now you will drink the champagne, see?" he said as he dropped the gem that he'd been holding into a glass of Cristal that was fizzing with a million tiny bubbles.

"Now I definitely *won't* drink it." I laughed.

"But you must." Anders put his hand on my knee momentarily.

"Where are you from, Anders?" I asked, trying to detract his attention from the fact that I was going to do no such thing. If only because I was terrified that Lara would be furious that I'd blown our girls' night out on a bunch of pretty boys. Not that she had any right to talk at the moment when it came to blowing our evening. Couldn't she come back now?

I looked around to see if she'd returned, but she was perched on the edge of a woman's chair and chatting to someone on the other side of the couple's table. Anyone would think *she'd* been out of town for the past month and not me.

"I'm from Denmark," he said patiently. "Copenhagen. Now if you drink the champagne, you can keep the diamond," he said with a twinkle.

"Oh, really, that's funny, but . . ." I began. But he silenced me with a shake of his head.

"For me," he told me. What he could possibly want out of this trans- action I had no idea. But he was oddly determined and compellingly glamorous.

"I really have to go and make sure my friend's okay. It was nice meet- ing you," I said, tearing my eyes off the shimmering gem at the bottom of the glass that seemed to be fizzing with excitement.

"You only have to drink the champagne," Anders said calmly. "And the diamond is yours."

"No, really, I have to—"

"You've nothing to lose." He spoke to me as though I was making a big mistake.

I looked around and took stock of the situation. Only a few tables away were Lara and a host of her laughing friends; in the corner with the plants was Courtney Love, engrossed in a cozy conversation with some guy; and all around us were couples nursing cocktails and chatting.

Surely nothing too awful could happen if I drank one small glass of chilled, bubbling Cristal. I would only have a sip. Enough to satisfy Anders and then I could go and hang with Lara, who was rapidly falling out of favor with me. What use were Vikings and diamonds if you had no friend to laugh about it all with?

"Please," Anders said, not taking his blue eyes off me.

"Okay then." I took a breath and reached for the drink. "But then I have to go and sit with my friend."

"Of course," Anders said, showing a small flicker of excitement. I looked for Lara one last time but to no avail.

"Here goes nothing," I said and took a sip, as the Vikings looked on with curiosity. Anders nodded his approval. I narrowed my eyes suspiciously at him as I took another sip. I glanced down at the diamond in the bottom of my glass and saw it momentarily shift. I blinked as it shuffled again. Maybe it was the bubbles that were creating an optical illusion, I concluded as I looked up at Anders and the men again.

"Delicious, isn't it?" Anders took a swig from his glass and clinked mine.

"It is, but—" I began, but before I could finish my sentence I was overcome with a raging thirst and reached again for my drink.

The next thing I knew all I could feel was the cold glass beneath my fingers as I gripped it. My head began to swim as I concentrated hard on moving the glass toward my lips. I took a deep mouthful of the steely-apple liquid and tipped it down my throat. For that moment nothing else mattered, though I was still parched. Then it was as if there was interference on the television and everything began to flicker with static.

"You drank the diamond?" I heard Anders say from the far reaches of my world. I couldn't see straight and began to panic.

"Excuse me. Elizabeth Miller?" I heard someone else say before I could open my lungs and call for Lara.

"Yes."

"Miss Miller, we have a phone call for you in the office. Would you mind coming with me?" I had a moment of lucidity and saw a man in a black suit standing above me. He was clearly a member of the staff, I deduced from the pulsing gold name tag that was flashing before me.

"She's with me," I heard Anders say.

"It's an important phone call, sir," the man said reasonably as I attempted to pull myself together and stand up. "This way please."

I put one foot in front of the other and made my way carefully across the room behind the strange man.

"I'm seeing stars," I said, and I really was. "And I don't mean Courtney Love." The man turned around and looked seriously at me.

"This way please, miss," he said.

"Coming." I wasn't in any mood to rebel and I could only hope that I was doing the right thing. I turned around and looked for Anders, who was scowling at me. I attempted an easy smile in his direction; after all, I did have his valuable diamond plummeting down my gullet at this moment in time. Anders nodded, as if granting me momentary permission to take my phone call.

"Miss Miller." I was escorted into a room behind the reception desk, where a fax machine was spilling out pages and a plump girl was engrossed in preparing bills for the hotel guests.

"Yes?" I asked, still feeling very peculiar and not at all well.

"We saw what happened out there." The man who'd come to collect me for my "phone call" suddenly looked very grave indeed.

"You did?" I wondered whether there was a law against drinking diamonds. Was it like taking X or something?

"We know who those men are and they're incredibly dangerous."

"I see," I said, but I didn't really. "Who, Anders?"

"There's a car waiting outside the back entrance. We're going to put you in it and the driver will take you home. We'll inform your friend and have her sent home separately. But you have to leave now."

"But the phone call?" I was very confused.

"There was no phone call. They spiked your drink. Then we saw you swallow their diamond and we needed to get you away from them immediately. Now get in the car. We have your purse," he said as he handed me my purse, which I'd assumed was still underneath the table.

"But . . . what?"

"Just leave," he said. "Before they realize what's going on."

"How did you know my name?" I asked as they forced my purse on me and almost pushed me out the back door.

"We had your credit card. We've put it back in your wallet. Now please go."

"Thank you, I erm . . . I don't really . . . I . . ." I began to splutter as I fitted together the whole bizarre jigsaw puzzle with me lurching around somewhere in the middle.

The next thing I knew I was sitting in the back of a town car with a very sweet, concerned driver who kept checking his rearview mirror. Presumably for the Danish mafia who might be in hot pursuit. Though how one would identify them I wasn't entirely sure.

"Don't worry, miss, we'll have you home in no time," he reassured me. I merely groaned and leaned my pounding head against the cool leather on the inside of the car door. I experimented with closing and opening my eyes, but either way I still had unbearable, hundred-mile-per-hour spins. After what felt like hours later, we pulled into a driveway.

"Here you are, miss," the man said and the car stopped. "I'll see you to the door."

"Oh no, it's fine. Thanks," I said as I smiled at him and tried to extract my wallet.

"Oh, this is on the house, miss," he informed me kindly.

"Thanks so much." I tried to sound more sober than I felt and made a supreme effort to walk in a straight line toward the house. In fact I was trying so hard to compose myself that it was only after the taillights of the car had vanished into the distance that I realized what a terrible thing had happened.

"No!" I wailed at no one in particular as I threw myself onto the doorstep. I was at the wrong house. I looked up and saw, not the shiny black door of Lara and Scott's house with the silver elephant's head door knocker, but the marble doorstep and white minimalist gleam of Luke's front door.

I immediately tried to run away, but my legs were weak and I felt nauseous. I looked to see whether there were any lights on in the house, but thankfully it was plunged into the kind of blackness that suggests nobody's been home for a while. Probably five weeks to be precise. I took a deep breath and rested my cheek on the marble. At least I was safe in the knowledge that though I might die here tonight, I wouldn't be discovered just yet. After the short break in my mortification, I made an executive decision in my still woozy head to call Lara. I pulled out my phone and held it in my hand for what felt like a long lifetime before it began to vibrate of its own accord.

"Hello?" I answered.

"Holy shit, babe, are you okay?" It was Lara.

"No," I managed to respond. "I'm at Luke's."

"You're where?"

"Driver's license." I guessed.

"Oh shit. But, babe, they told me what went on with that guy, and I guess you're lucky that the hotel got you out of there. I mean, after all, you still have a diamond inside you."

"Really?" I said, suddenly feeling panic-stricken. I'd completely forgotten about the eleven carats in my stomach. I wondered whether it might catch in a vital organ and injure me. "Oh my God, hang on a minute," I said, and as I did I moved my phone away from my mouth and threw up all over Luke's doorstep.

"Lizzie, you okay?" I heard faintly from my cell.

"Ugh," I croaked as I was overcome with another wave of nausea.

"Okay, I'm coming over. Wait there," Lara said. "Don't move a muscle. Just keep warm, okay? And if you need me, just call me back. All right honey?" she said. I nodded and hung up the phone.

I had no idea how much later it was, but when I opened my eyes what I did know was that I'd thrown up at least five more times since Lara called and I was only just beginning to really see straight. Well, straight enough for me to realize that if I had a diamond inside me at any point, it was more than likely that it was outside me now. On Luke's step, to be precise. I had been inert up until this point, but as the fog cleared, I remembered that if you waved your hand in the air, Luke's security lights came on. So I did just that.

"Yay," I said to myself as the porch was suddenly bathed in light. I looked down and in my delirium saw not the nasty champagne puke but instead the possibility of owning something to pawn so I could make a down payment on an apartment. There was a diamond somewhere here and I was suddenly compelled to find it. I crawled closer to the vomit and began to stare into it as though it were a crystal ball. I even picked up a stick and began to shift small bits of undigested food around to try to spy the little critter that was going to put a couple more zeros on my bank statement. I was still somewhat delirious though, and as I absorbed myself in the task at hand was vaguely aware that this was not normal behavior. When Lara got here I'd stop, I decided. But it was a curiously engrossing activity, especially because the nasty Rohypnol shock was now fading to a pleasant druggy buzz.

"Oh my God, what's going on?" was the next thing I heard as I intently moved a small morsel of my lunch to one side because I'd seen something twinkle beneath it. Unfortunately it turned out to be a fleck of silver in the marble. "What on earth?" I heard a man say next, and I suddenly came to my senses. I sat bolt upright, hoping Lara hadn't brought Scott with her. That would be too humiliating.

However, it wasn't Scott. Neither had Lara come to my rescue yet. And as I sat with my little stick in my hand staring up into the blinding security light I didn't need to hear another single thing to realize how horrendously unlivable my life was about to become.

"Lizzie?" the man said.

"Luke?" I asked, knowing full well it was him. I was petrified on the spot. As if Pompeii had washed over my moment of shame and preserved me here in lava for all eternity.

"What's going on?" He immediately crouched down and put his hand on my shoulder. "What are you doing here?"

"The diamond," I slurred. "It's here somewhere."

"Honey, how long have you been here?" Luke looked pale and concerned. I shrugged. It was definitely too much for me. The threat of death from the Danish Mafia, a diamond lodged in my windpipe, my boyfriend whom I hadn't seen for nearly two months, and the fact that I was lounging in my own vomit. "Okay, well, let's get you inside and figure this out, shall we?" Luke stood up and valiantly took my hand. I say valiantly because I can't have been a pretty or even hygienic sight sitting there. "Come on, baby, it'll be okay."

I can't honestly imagine what Luke thought I was doing there. Whether perhaps I'd been there since the day he'd returned to Prague with my ring; or perhaps since the day I saw the *People* spread. Clearly all was not well with me.

"Right," he said as he undressed me and eased me into a steaming shower. "You get warm and clean in there. I've got to get my suitcase in from the car and then you can tell me what's going on."

"Okay," I said meekly as I clutched a washcloth to hide my modesty from the man who'd betrayed me. It hadn't even occurred to me to be angry yet, I was so shell-shocked from my weird evening in outer space.

Less than an hour later I was wrapped in his robe on the sofa, the fire was blazing, and Luke had fed me chicken noodle soup from Greenblatts. I'd been mute since he carried me in the door, but now I was slowly coming to understand where I was and what was going on. I'd already told him the whole I-swallowed-a-diamond-fed-to-me-by-the-Danish-Mafia story and he'd boringly suggested that I say bye-bye to that particular gem forever. Apparently, Lara had been duly called and told to turn back as we had "things" to discuss. Being kind of kidnapped twice in one night must be some sort of record, I decided.

"So what the fuck's going on with us, sweetheart?" Luke finally sat down on the edge of the sofa and looked at me with his soft brown eyes, which always made me want to cry; even in happy times they had a melancholic effect on me. I wanted to pretend nothing had happened but knew that he needed me to explain why I'd vanished from his home and life without a word. I tried to be reasonable but clearly I was channeling Bette Davis, because I was incapable.

"Well, this really weird thing happened," I began disingenuously. "I was at a party and suddenly there's this sort of intervention whereby all these women crowd around me and inform me that my boyfriend's a cheating asshole." I smiled laconically. Luke didn't attempt to interject so I continued, "Of course I don't believe them because I live with the sweetest, most un-Hollywood, straight-shooting man I've ever met. He's also caring and considerate. So I assume they're lying. Until I remember that he hasn't exactly been that nice to me lately, he's impossible to reach on the phone, and when we speak he pretends to the star of his movie, his ex-girlfriend by the way, that he's talking to his dentist or someone."

"Lizzie—" Scott began, but I was a ship in full sail and I'd made this speech at least five hundred thousand times since that day, so I had every pitiful-yet-dignified bat of my eyelids down to perfection.

"Anyhow, I still don't really believe them because only a week or two before, this lovely man had proposed marriage to me, sort of. So clearly there hadn't been enough time for him to fall in love with another woman or anything, so these women must be wrong. Right?" I looked at him with such burgeoning menace and vile sarcasm that I even scared myself. "Wrong. You see, these women had my best interests at heart and weren't remotely smug about my plight, and even Amber the vengeful witch of a Second Assistant only wanted to see me happy. Which was why she pulled out a copy of this magazine called *People*. And much as I missed my sweet boyfriend, it didn't really matter, because, guess what?"

"Please . . ." Luke had the bottom half of his face covered with his hands. He momentarily closed his eyes. I had wondered earlier when he was behaving so normally toward me (well, as normal as it gets when your girlfriend vanishes for a month then turns up on your doorstep throwing up and reenacting her own twisted version of *Tomb Raider* in the hunt for hidden treasure) whether he really hoped that I just hadn't seen that copy of *People*. Or if maybe even *he* hadn't seen it. But when I saw the look of unmitigated misery on his face, I knew that he was fully up-to-date with his reading.

"I got to see his face. His handsome, familiar face." I did sound slightly demented, but then who cared, I'd been drugged. "Only the funny thing was, my sweet, loyal boyfriend was kissing someone else. His ex-girlfriend, to be precise. So, I thought, oh well, if he doesn't love me then I'll just run away to Thailand so that I never have to see him again. Only the goddamn taxi driver got my address wrong and here I am." I gestured around me in bewilderment.

"Lizzie, you've got to understand. I've been trying to reach you since the day it happened," he began with an agonized look in his eyes.

"Since the day it happened, Luke? Or the day that you realized the paparazzi had caught you and you were going to make the front pages of every sleazy gossip rag in America?" I asked.

"I've been going out of my mind."

"You seem very sane to me."

"I love you, Lizzie."

"That's okay. I'm sure it's perfectly normal to love two women." I shrugged, then shouted, "in Utah!"

"Can I explain?"

"So it's true? You were kissing her? It wasn't just a trick of the light?" I asked helplessly.

"I didn't know where I stood with you after that whole proposal debacle. Emanuelle was in love with me and she was familiar. It didn't even feel as if I was cheating on you because it was only a few kisses. It wasn't as if she was someone new I'd fallen in love with. It was too easy."

"Are you engaged?" I asked, my chest as tight as a drum over my pounding heart.

"Of course I'm not engaged. What on earth gave you that idea?" He looked genuinely amused.

"I just thought that you had the ring . . ." I stammered.

"Lizzie, I wanted to marry you. I still do." He reached out and took my hand for the first time as if he were my boyfriend and not a paramedic.

"Really?" I asked, suddenly very confused. He *had* cheated *but* he wanted to marry me.

"Yes," he said. "What's really changed?"

"What's changed?" I thought about this very hard for a while before I replied.

"Yes?" he whispered as he moved closer to me, still holding my hand. Was Rohypnol a truth drug, I wondered, as I began to say some things I'd very likely regret later. I should have melted into his embrace, etc., and kept quiet. But foolishly I didn't.

"Well, nothing. Which is probably the problem." I took a deep breath. "When I was living with you I never felt that I could be myself. This whole thing," I waved my arm carelessly at the cold, white-washed perfection of his contemporary art gallery of a house, "none of it was me. I wasn't Lizzie anymore. People didn't come up to me at parties and talk to Lizzie Miller. They came and asked questions about you. I was your girlfriend, and that was amazing for a while, until I realized that no matter what fabulous things I did on my own, I'd never be anything else because you were so successful, so hot, so important. And then when Emanuelle came back on the scene things got even worse. I was haunted by this dazzling couple you and she used to be, and I knew that everyone was disappointed by me."

"No, sweetheart, please stop," Luke said with anguish and tried to

catch hold of my arm, which was hitting my knee in a painful bid to illustrate my point.

"Oh, I don't mean poor little me," I quickly corrected him. "I don't
mind being me. I don't mind that I have a job that I'm not remarkable
at and that I don't look like Emanuelle. Because I really think I'm fine
and I know that you love me. It's just that I want to earn my own money
and do remarkable things, and I want people to ask me about them, and
with you I'm not sure I'd ever get that," I finished.

"But people love you," Luke protested.

"Luke, people love me because they want to impress *you*. Really, they
couldn't give a rat's ass about me because I'm not in the power one
hundred."

"But who gives a shit what those people think?" he asked angrily.

"I don't know," I said. I'd begun with such conviction and now he was
making me feel lame. Who did care? Me? My fragile ego?

"I love you. We love each other. What the fuck else matters?" Luke
was now pacing crossly in front of the sofa.

"But you kissed another woman," I tossed into the fray.

"I didn't love her. You weren't ready to settle down, Lizzie. I was hurt.
Pissed off with you."

"Then why didn't you tell me?" I shouted.

"Why didn't you tell me that you felt like you were living in my
shadow? In a prison?"

"I'm sorry," I said.

"Me too." Luke came and sat next to me. "I'm sorry I kissed
Emanuelle and that I didn't notice what was going on with you. And I
promise that I'll think about that stuff you've just told me." Luke leaned
over and kissed me on the cheek. "I really will."

"Okay," I said weakly. Suddenly all my remaining strength evaporated
and my eyes began to close with the relief of having finally said what I'd
needed to say for so long. "Can I go to sleep now, please?"

FOURTEEN

I'm a Hollywood trainwreck.

—Christine Anderson

When I opened my eyes the next morning, the sense of happiness I felt was overwhelming. Even before I'd computed what had happened the previous night, I knew that I was in a safe place. The pillows were airy and light, the way Luke's pillows always were. The blinds were closed but the sunlight was forcing its way through the cracks, and the sheets smelled of my boyfriend. I hadn't felt so complete in a very long time. I could hear him singing "California Here We Come" in his terrible tuneless way in the kitchen as the clatter of dishes chimed in occasionally. I knew that there was still stuff to sort out between us and we had to address some unpleasant truths, but as I lay there none of that felt daunting. Just easy. What would we do today, I wondered. It was Saturday and I hadn't had him home on a Saturday for a very long time.

First of all we'd make out, that was for sure. I noticed that I was still wearing his robe from last night so he certainly hadn't taken advantage of the date-rape drug whizzing around my bloodstream. I stretched and sighed loudly.

"Luke?" I shouted out.

"You awake, Elizabeth?" he called out and the dishes stopped chiming. I loved it when he called me "Elizabeth." It made my stomach lurch with anticipation.

"I am!" I replied as I sat up in bed and adjusted the pillows behind my head.

"Hey." Luke appeared at the bedroom door in his shorts and an old surfing T-shirt. He was barefoot and holding a tray with my breakfast on it.

"You look like you've been up for hours." I smiled.

"Oh, only since five o'clock." He raised his eyebrows. "The joys of jet lag."

"Of course." I nodded happily.

"I made you some breakfast." He raised the tray an inch or so in the air as if proof might be needed.

"Thanks," I said as he walked across the dark wood floor toward me. I liked the gloss of formality that seemed to exist between us right now, it made me feel as if we were excited strangers who'd just spent our first night together.

"Yeah, it's a good time to think, five in the morning." He placed the slightly surgical-looking tray onto my lap.

"So what were you thinking?" I asked flirtatiously as I put the cup of bitter espresso to my lips.

"Plenty."

"Oh good." I smiled and bit into a strawberry. "Lovely breakfast, by the way."

"You're welcome," Luke said as he settled at the foot of the bed, on the other side. I offered him a piece of pineapple but he just shook his head and bit his lip. "So the thing is, I have been thinking. And I think you're right."

"You do?" I said in a satisfied way. I wasn't sure what exactly I'd been right about, but I always liked being right.

"We rushed into this without thinking about the practicalities." He wasn't looking at me but I was watching him intently, suddenly a little unsure where this was leading. "We met, we fell in love, we moved in together. I thought that was the way it was supposed to be, but clearly I'd been too simplistic about it. I thought that love conquered all, but I was being inconsiderate to you. I didn't stop to think how it might be for you, just coming into my world—my house, my parties, my friends. You're right, you're young and you want to climb the ladder for yourself. I got to do that and so should you."

"No, that's not exactly what I meant," I interrupted before this could go any further down a road that I did not like the look of.

"But it's true. You should experience those thrills for yourself. It's the greatest time of your life doing all this stuff, finding your way, struggling. I did it. I loved it. And I think that because you seemed so smart, I never noticed the age gap or the lifestyle gap. But it's there. And there's nothing I can do about that. It breaks my heart, but you really have a valid point."

I picked up another strawberry and held on to it for dear life.

"But I am old enough," I protested like a true fourteen-year-old. Did this mean that Emanuelle, who was all of thirty, though she only admitted to twenty-eight, was more his age? I panicked.

"Of course you're old enough. But I'm holding you back, Lizzie. That's why we were fighting so much. You resent me for not allowing you to grow and make your own mistakes. And for overshadowing you with my career. Though Christ knows I don't give as much of a fuck about what I do as everybody else does," he said with a note of bewilderment in his voice. And it was true—he didn't—which had always been the reason I felt as if he were the only man in Hollywood for me. The only man in the world for me, in fact. He had his priorities in place, he didn't drive a dick-on-wheels of a car, he lived in an art gallery because he liked paintings not so he could show off, he loved me when my ass was fatter than usual, he preferred staying in to schmoozing at parties. He was a real person. And I was beginning to feel as if I might have made some irrevocable, horrific mistake. He was dumping me and I was to blame.

"I know you don't," I said regretfully. "But that's not what I meant really. I love living with you, I'm as proud of your career as you are of the fact that I have a master's in political science." God, I remembered, that was another of his amazing traits, someone at the Golden Globes could be sitting next to him, droning on about how great they thought his last movie was, and he'd be telling them about me. About how much I knew about Middle Eastern politics and then he'd call me over from the other side of the table to get me to explain the Intifada to some guy who thought it was a new high-end furniture shop on Melrose.

"I've been thinking about it for a while. And I guess I knew it when I came back last time. Which is probably why I did what I did with Emanuelle." He looked confused. I wasn't. He'd done what he'd done with Emanuelle because she was a fang-toothed vampire with lips like pillows and breasts like a bouncy castle.

"But that's okay. We can forget all that and move on together," I promised desperately. "You'll be back from Prague for good in a couple of months, won't you?"

"Actually, I'm back now," Luke informed me. "I came back last night so that I could come and find you. I started wrapping things up there weeks ago when I couldn't get ahold of you. I left Randy in charge and came back to be with you."

"Then let's be together," I said as I cast my breakfast tray clumsily to one side and tried to extricate my feet from the sheets. "I had no idea."

"I hated what you said last night. I wanted to put that ring on your finger in your sleep and have you as my wife when you woke up. But in the cold light of day it was true. If you love somebody, set them free, right?" he said.

"No," I protested as I finally made it to Luke's side and lay my head on his broad, familiar shoulder. "We should be together."

"It won't work, Lizzie." Luke gently took my face in his hands and looked at me. "It was too difficult. We'd lost the joy. *You* know that."

"But we could get it back," I pleaded.

"Sweetheart, I love you. But this is the right decision. And you'll thank me one day."

"But—" I protested. Luke kissed me on the lips and stood up.

"I'm going into the office to catch up on some paperwork. Don't worry about double-locking the door, I won't be out for too long," he said as he grabbed a sweater from the back of a chair and walked out the door.

If I thought that my life couldn't get any worse after breaking up with Luke, I arrived back at The Agency on Monday morning and found the police waiting to interview me.

"Miss Miller?" demanded the rather mean-spirited looking member of the LAPD.

"Yes?" I replied. Thank God I still seemed to know my own name. I'd spent the better part of the past two days crying so hard into Lara's guesthouse pillows that it was a miracle I hadn't washed my brain away in the deluge.

"We'd like to ask you some questions," he said, tapping his notebook menacingly.

"What about?" I scowled as I looked around my office for the first time since I'd left for Thailand. At least it *used* to be my office; it wasn't exactly the familiar place I used to call work anymore. For starters, Amber was comfortably ensconced in *my* cubicle, watching me unsmilingly from behind my computer.

"We've had a burglary," she informed me gravely.

"When?" I asked, looking for upturned filing cabinets and any other textbook signs of a break-in.

"We don't know, miss," said the cop, who seemed to be looking very suspiciously at me. "We suspect it's an insider job."

"Oh, I see." I felt a small surge of relief, because even though I knew that the burglary had nothing to do with me, I had the sort of built-in guilt mechanism that always kicked in when a store alarm was activated and I began to suspect myself of walking out of Victoria's Secret with a six pack of thongs without paying. "Well, you probably don't need to talk to me, officer, because I've been away over a month."

"We don't base our work on facile assumptions, Miss Miller," he said condescendingly. "And besides, we believe that this theft predates your departure from the country."

"Oh, I see," I said, slightly alarmed. "Well, where would you like to speak to me?"

"We have an incident room. If you'd like to follow me," he said, and led me out of the office and along the hallway toward the elevator.

"Elizabeth, good to have you back." Katherine Watson was coming out of the elevator as we passed.

"Good to be back," I lied, wishing for happier days in Thailand, like the time I'd tried to bribe Emerald out of her trailer with Krispy Kremes I'd had couriered into the country at triple the cost of my weekly salary.

"What was the purpose of your trip to Thailand?" A second cop, an even meaner-looking female officer, stared at me over her coffee. They'd taken up residence in a glass-walled corner office on the second floor, and everyone who walked by stared shamelessly in on my interrogation. It must have been some burglary to warrant them setting up an incident room, I thought uneasily, especially if they'd been here for a month.

"Business," I said working on the premise that the less information I gave them the quicker I'd be out of here.

"Business?" the woman officer asked. I nodded in affirmation. "Have you ever used drugs, Ms. Miller?"

"I'm sorry?" I replied.

"Are we to take that as an admission that you have?" she asked. Good God, this was completely surreal. I hadn't even gotten to my desk yet.

"No," I said ambiguously.

"No you've never taken drugs or no that wasn't an admission?"

"Oh for God's sake," I suddenly said. I'd had enough of Tweedle Dum and Tweedle Dee. I suddenly found myself with my Washington head on—from the days when I was a smart intern with a job for a senator, in the days when I had a brain that I got to use. Not when I was a risible Hollywood assistant who got drugged by gangsters and wound up accidentally breaking up with the man she loved most in the world.

"It's not an admission. And I fail to see what that question has to do with the burglary in question." I pulled myself up in my seat and prepared to get myself out of this hell, even though it was at least taking my mind off the fact that Luke was probably having a Monday morning of languid sex with Emanuelle in the tasteful house in Malibu I'd read about in *InStyle*. I brushed the thought aside for the purposes of self-preservation.

"Now, unless I'm a suspect in your investigation, I suggest you furnish me with the details of what was stolen so that I might actually be of some help to you with your enquiry," I said, managing to impress even myself with my snittiness. The cops looked at each other briefly.

"Sometime after the twenty-first of November, several highly confidential documents went missing from the office of Mr. Wagner," the woman officer informed me. "We're treating this as a case of either industrial espionage or a serious breach of privacy laws."

"What?" I choked.

"The files were highly confidential. They also contained copies of some photographs of a sensitive nature that have since been used to blackmail several high-profile clients of The Agency." The man sat back with his arms folded as though he'd already decided I was guilty and he just wanted to figure out how tight he'd have to make the thumbscrews before I confessed. But sweet Jesus, I *was* guilty, I suddenly realized. Well, not of blackmail, of course, but of burning the damned paperwork. And then I considered the photographs with a heavy heart.

"These photographs?" I asked cautiously. "Were they of Emerald Everhart dancing on a bar?"

"How did you know?" The woman narrowed her eyes at me.

"I sent the film to my boss, Scott Wagner, to keep safe. They could have ruined Emerald's career if the press had printed them. It's standard practice when dealing with stars."

"Those particular photographs were sold to the press. Others are missing and being used to extort money from clients," she said haughtily.

"God, I wish I'd thought of that." I smiled. Something about these two po-faced bullies made me want to behave badly. They couldn't arrest me for smiling could they?

"Are you saying that you might have done such a thing?" Columbo was obviously keen to hasten along his finest hour.

"Of course not, or I wouldn't have sent the photos of Emerald to Scott, would I?" I said.

"Unless you were trying to cover your tracks. Even a fool could work out that little smokescreen," he said. And I had to admit he had a point. That coupled with the fact that I had been the one to "steal," aka burn, the paperwork definitely gave me the hue of guilt. Even if I wasn't. Or wasn't technically guilty, anyway. Unless burning paper was a crime.

"It's our belief that whoever took the files is likely to be the blackmailer, or in league with the person who is blackmailing clients. We were alerted to the theft by an employee of Mr. Wagner's," the woman told me. I took this piece of information on board and then attempted to look as innocent as possible.

"I'll try to recollect events in November and let you know if I recall anything suspicious," I said and made to leave my chair before they could arrest me on a technicality. "Perhaps you have a card you could give me." I held out my hand and the male officer fished in his pockets reluctantly.

"As you and Ms. Bingham-Fox were the only two keyholders for the filing cabinet in question, and owing to the fact that we've eliminated her from our enquiries, we will be interviewing you further," they informed me as I straightened my black pants that I hadn't even had the will to iron this morning, I had been so suicidal.

"You know where to find me," I said as I left the office. Doubtless they'd be calling me back, if only because I'd been such a snooty bitch that they'd want to make me suffer. But I didn't care, I could hardly suffer any more if I was locked up in the state penitentiary than I was over the breakup with my boyfriend.

Fortunately Scott was still away on location in New York because I wouldn't have wanted him to slip in the blood that was going to be on the carpet after I'd finished with Amber, I thought, as I steamed down the hallway toward my office, not even stopping to smile at people who were ambling around the building.

"I think you'll find that's *my* desk." I shoved my way through the door and stood above her as she flipped through the trades.

"Oh, you're back. I thought they'd have plenty of evidence by now to incarcerate you." She sighed without looking up.

"Get out of my seat," I snarled.

"Oh, there've been some changes around here," Amber said as she continued to look at V Page, doubtless to see if she'd made the cut at last night's big premiere.

"Scott's completely okayed the move. I told him I was sure you wouldn't have a problem with me sitting here."

"Well, I do. So move before I have you fired." I was in no mood to be messed with, having already lost almost everything that mattered to me in the world.

"Oh, you don't want to piss me off, do you, Elizabeth?" She broke off from her reading. "Not when your very freedom's on the line," she said pointedly. She was so insidiously poisonous that I couldn't help but have my curiosity piqued.

"What are you talking about?" I sniffed.

"Well, I'd say that burning files is a very suspicious thing to do." She shrugged and smiled at me.

"Who called the police?" I snapped, getting unpleasantly close to her face. She didn't even flinch, she was so unnatural.

"The police came after yet another one of Scott's clients had been blackmailed over photographs from our 'private' archives." She smiled and then picked up *Entertainment Weekly*. It was true that Scott's clients more than most seemed to be the most likely to be photographed in compromising and indiscreet situations and that our file of naughty snaps was bulging more than most at The Agency. And it was true that only Amber and myself had access to those files.

I resigned myself to having to sit in her chair. At least until Scott got back from the set and I could sort this whole mess out. Though come to think of it, I wasn't sure how I could tell him that there hadn't been a burglary at all, just a big, flaming bonfire of documents pertaining to the biggest names in the business. And simply because I'd been too lazy to do anything meaningful with them. Nobody in this entire building ever went into their filing cabinets to look up old documents, there simply wasn't enough time in the day, and if you wanted a figure or a contract you just called the client's lawyer. And Scott was even less likely to dirty his hands with yesterday's documents. I'd taken a very calculated, safe risk when I made my small bonfire. Clearly, though, it hadn't paid off. I shrank into Amber's seat reluctantly. I'd get her back, I vowed to myself. I just wasn't sure exactly how I'd do it yet. And so far her English slyness was most resoundingly outwitting my American sassiness. But I would even the score. Even if it killed me.

That night, as Lachlan splashed in his bath, oblivious to my woes, Lara and I sat on her baby's bathroom floor and wondered how we could best rid our lives of Amber without further risk of imprisonment, on my part at least.

"I think we should hire a man. I met this guy at J.Lo's birthday party who gave me his number. He was a total thug," Lara volunteered as she soaped up her mewing son's hair.

"Too obvious, especially because the police are on to us. I think we need to marry her off instead. Let's have a dinner party with some rich old director and invite her," I said as I pulled at the leg of one of Lachlan's rubber bath-time toy animals.

"Then we'd never get rid of her. She'd be lurking at every premiere, wearing a better outfit than us and making passes at our husbands," Lara said dismissively.

"I don't have one," I reminded her. The only good thing about this whole burglary business was that it was a great displacement activity for curling up in a ball and sobbing in the corner of my room with Luke's stray sock.

"Well, my husband, then." She scowled. "I swear to God she wants you out of that office so that she can get her hands on Scott once and for all."

"Do you think she'd let something as petty as me stop her from doing that?" I asked. "Because if you do, I think you're underestimating her. She'd glory in the fact that she was doing my best friend's husband. She'd probably have sex with him on *my* desk while she did her typing."

"Please." Lara glared at me and pointed to Lachlan who was such a prodigy in his mother's eyes that even at thirteen months he'd understand not just what I was saying but it would serve to reinforce negative female stereotypes to her spongelike son.

"Maybe I have to tell Scott what happened with those papers," I said eventually. "I mean, he does understand the nature of addiction. And I was seriously, probably clinically, addicted to Su Doku."

"Not in other people." Lara shook her head and lifted Lachlan into a towel with a hood and bunny ears. "You can't confess. We have to somehow prove that Amber set a trap for you and was trying to frame you. It has to be her blackmailing everyone, right? I mean only you and she have access?"

"Maybe there was a burglary as well," I posited. "I mean, it's not impossible."

"I'm convinced it was her, and when we find out it is, she'll definitely be out on her ass in the cold."

"Don't forget she has Katherine as her champion," I reminded Lara.

"Once we show her up for the blackmailing harridan that she is, it won't matter."

"Okay," I said, unconvinced. "But this isn't *Cruel Intentions,* Lara, it's my life. Try to remember that, will you?" But Lara wasn't listening. She was clearly enthralled by some noir fantasy where she got to wear a Roland Mouret femme fatale dress and wreak vengeance with her snakeskin purse.

As Lara read a story to Lachlan and I was mooching around the kitchen, my phone began to vibrate on the counter. I dashed toward it, as I had every time it had rung since Saturday morning, and thought I must be hallucinating when I saw Luke's name appear on the screen. I wanted to answer it but I was rendered motionless as it bounced up and down, oblivious to the earth-shattering significance of its mission. I moved my hand to answer it and then snatched it back, lost in a vortex of indecision and fear. Was I angry? Forgiving? Contrite? Excited to hear from him? Or on a date with someone else already? I was at a loss to know what to do so waited impatiently for him to leave a message. Though after five minutes of waiting for the message light to flash, I realized that he wasn't actually pouring his heart out but that he'd hung up without saying anything. Which only exacerbated my dilemma. To call back or not to call back?

After an hour or so in which Lara and I exhausted my fears, anxieties, regrets, and hopes for the future, including rather shamefully that Emanuelle get hit by a truck, it was finally decided that I would call Luke back and accept his apology.

"Okay, just do it," Lara said, looking with heavy-lidded eyes at her watch. "It's almost eleven. You can't call him after that."

"He stays up late," I told her.

"You can only call someone after eleven if you're fucking them," she said firmly.

"Okay, I'll call him in a minute," I promised. "But just remind me, what's he doing now?" I asked, craving reassurance.

"He's realized that he made a huge mistake because he was so jet-lagged and tired and now his house is all empty and he doesn't like having takeout alone and there's nobody there to tell how his day was and he's regretting it and wants you back," Lara repeated by rote.

"Are you sure?"

"Of course," Lara said confidently as she cleared away our wine-glasses. "What else would he be doing?"

Sadly, Luke was doing something *very* else when I finally plucked up the courage to call him.

"Hold on, I'm going outside," he said as I held the phone away from my ear so as not to be deafened by the blare of Franz Ferdinand.

"Where are you?" I asked, as though I were genuinely, casually curious and not still his suspicious girlfriend.

"Some place called Avalon!" he yelled. Oh, so only the hottest club in town on a Monday night, I thought with a mounting sense of concern. Already this was not going as Lara had promised.

"Sounds fun," I said, then moved on swiftly so as not to overplay the inherent difference between a broken man and one on the town with Paris Hilton et al. "Well, I was just returning your call."

"Oh, yeah," Luke said and suddenly the background noise vanished from his end of the phone and all I could hear was my beating heart. "I just wanted to know what the fuck you thought you were doing?" he said unceremoniously.

"What I thought *what?*" I scowled as Lara plumped up the cushions on her sofa before heading for bed and gave me a confused glance.

"So today I went to the pet spa and what do I find?" he asked aggressively.

"I have no idea," I replied, feeling sure, for the second time today, that whatever it was he found, I was in the clear and this was some ridiculous misunderstanding. "I find," he said, having clearly left Avalon and found some deserted wasteland near a Dumpster, it was so ominously quiet now, "that you have killed my fucking cat."

"I've what?" I asked, mystified.

"When you took Charles into the pet spa, you delivered him dead."

"Don't be so crazy," I said, wondering happily if being apart from me had already driven him to the very edge of sanity.

"I am not being crazy," he iterated every word menacingly. "Because not only had Charles been strangled by a nylon stocking before you dropped him off, you then proceeded to tell the people at the spa that you're Emanuelle's assistant and that she'd been maimed by a plastic surgeon!" He was yelling now.

"Charles died?" I said, trying to get a handle on the drama that was unfolding here.

"He was murdered!" Luke shouted.

Lara had stopped her domestic fussing and was now sitting on the arm of the sofa in rapt attention. I shrugged my shoulders at her to denote that I had no clue what was going on, either.

"Look, Luke, I'm really sorry that you think someone killed the cat, but I'm sure they're really professional people at the spa and . . ."

"He arrived dead! Okay?" Luke yelled, and now I held the phone between Lara and myself so that she could hear his burgeoning insanity. "You strangled him with hosiery before dropping him off."

"Really, Luke, I think you're a little upset," I said in what could have been construed by an upset person to be a patronizing tone. I mean, this really wasn't my fault, was it? I thought back to the morning of my departure for Thailand, the hunt for Chucky, who'd insisted on hiding from me, the chaos . . . and . . . oh God, my underwear drawer, I'd found him in my underwear drawer and he'd been chewing a stocking. "Oh God," I suddenly said involuntarily. "I think Chucky committed suicide."

"What?" Luke asked.

"Chucky. He must have wrapped the stocking around his neck on the way to the spa."

"Chucky?" Luke said. "You called my cat Chucky?"

"It was a term of endearment." I tried to get out of it while banging my forehead on the door at my own stupidity. "It's a cute name."

"And was it cute to tell them that Emanuelle had been disfigured under the surgeon's knife?"

"Probably not," I admitted meekly.

"Well, I'm unimpressed, Lizzie," Luke said as Lara put her arm around me to comfort me. "I guess I'll see you around."

"But wait, Luke?" I pounced desperately, "Maybe we can . . . ?"

"I don't think so, Lizzie. Good-bye," he said and the phone went dead in my hand. I looked at it like the harbinger of doom it was, then tossed it onto the sofa in despair.

Dear God, I will never again say bad things about cats or actresses, I vowed.

FIFTEEN

In Hollywood if you don't have
happiness you send out for it.

—Rex Reed

I wasn't sure if I was the first person in the history of Universal Studios
to do what I did but you'd have thought so from the crowd that gathered
around my car as if I were the launch of Beyonce's new fragrance. I had
somehow managed to drive onto the studio lot through the wrong gate
and had dramatically impaled my tires on the alligator teeth that are designed to stop terrorists and deranged fans of The Rock from breaking
and entering. Much to the incredulity of the studio heads and D-girls
heading out to lunch.

"Stop right there, ma'am." A security guard came flying toward me
with his hand fingering his holster rather too enthusiastically for my
liking. When he saw that I was a mousy-haired girl with no cartoon-
terrorist mustache, he thrust his head through my passenger window
and barked at me. "This is not the entrance. This is the exit."

"I noticed," I said as I opened my door a crack to see my brand new
Pirelli tires slowly deflating on the spikes like unsuccessful soufflés.

"I'm sorry. I didn't mean to do it," I said helplessly. "I'm tired and my
mind just went blank." Really I'd been listening to Coldplay in a daze,
thinking about Luke. Nothing new there.

"Well, you can't stay here forever. You're causing a backup." The security guard seemed more afraid of the burgeoning lunch hour line behind
the barrier than the fact that I might have explosives strapped to my body.

"It's okay, I really have no intention of doing that if I can help it." I
grimaced and shut my door again hastily. A man in a suit got out of the

car in front of, or rather behind me, I couldn't tell which it was as it wasn't clear whether I was now coming or going. He made his way over.

"Have you been drinking, lady?" he asked.

"No I haven't," I hissed.

"Well, it's a pretty fucking dumb thing to do and I have a lunch with Spielberg at Orsino in fifteen minutes so you'd better get your sorry ass out of my way."

"Okay, okay." I fretted. "I didn't do this on purpose, you know."

"Stupid bitch," he mumbled as he strutted back to his car to abuse the other security guard. I leaned half my body out the window and yelled, "Oh and by the way, I'm sure that Mr. Spielberg wouldn't have wanted to do business with you, anyway; he seems like a nice man and you're clearly an asshole! It would've been a bad match!"

I sat back in my car and resisted the urge to stick my finger in the cigarette lighter hole and electrocute myself. I'd come over to the Universal lot to have lunch with Jason, who now had a deal here and a bungalow that I'd yet to visit. We'd planned our get-together as part of his effort to cheer me up after my brush with the law and brutal treatment at the hands of Luke and as a way of celebrating the release of *Sex Addicts in Love* at twenty-three movie theaters nationwide.

"What should I do? Call Triple A?" I asked the security guard who was still staring at me as if I'd landed from the moon.

"We can't allow them onto the lot without prior permission from a member of staff and security clearance." He shook his head gravely.

"Okay, then, I'll just call a friend," I said as I dialed Jason's office number and ducked down behind my steering wheel in case anyone identified me and sold the story of the mentally ailing assistant to *Variety*.

Thankfully Jason came to my rescue only a few minutes later in inimitable Blum style.

"Honey, just forget it," he said as he levered me from the driver's seat and told me that this was the most exciting thing that had happened at the gate since one of the town's most desperado actresses had handcuffed herself to Sam Mendes's golf cart.

"I'm sorry," I said to the security guard for the umpteenth time. Thankfully there had been one nice security guard on duty who had been to West Point and he was taking great delight in the traffic filter system he'd constructed out of six traffic cones and a fluorescent jacket, so Jason and I were able to eat our lunch without being honked at anymore.

"Never apologize," Jason whispered as he kissed me hello. "I've brought some lunch for us to eat while we wait for Triple A," he said, dumping a brown bag of Cinnabons and Cokes onto the hood of my car.

"Zac told me that, too," I remembered.

"Zac's where it's at, baby," Jason said and offered me a taste of his icing. I bit in and smiled. "That's better. No tears allowed this lunchtime because I have some good news for you."

"Really?" I looked at him in disbelief; I was hardly on a lucky streak at the moment.

"We're on the radar," he said triumphantly.

"What radar?" I resisted the urge to turn around and look for it.

"The studio's radar," he said, as if I was supposed to know exactly what he was talking about. "*Sex Addicts,* baby. You know, that little movie that I wrote and directed that you're producer on?"

"Oh my God," I instantly perked up at the memory of something that wasn't Luke or The Agency. "Really?"

"Well," he said and leaned in conspiratorially. "I've heard that they're discussing the marketing plans for the awards season and guess which movie they're doing a major campaign for?"

"No!" I stared at him openmouthed. The last time I'd thought about *Sex Addicts in Love* it was with a sense of loss that a movie I considered to be wonderful could be so carelessly dismissed. And now the studios were in love with it, too. It seemed that they were going to promote it as one of their Academy Award contenders. For Jason things couldn't get much better.

"Oh my God, why are we even sitting here on my hood?" I squealed. "Let's go to the Ivy."

"I'm so over the Ivy." Jason shuddered. "If I see another one of their fishcakes I'll hurl. I think I've been there every day for the last month."

"I feel the same way about Starbucks' ham-and-mozzarella panini." I sympathized.

"I have a better idea." Jason suddenly leaped off my car and got on his cell. "Let's go and see this house I want to buy on Bluebird. We can celebrate by making an offer if you like it."

"You're buying a house?" I asked. "Have you found yourself a sugar mommy?" It was common knowledge that you couldn't buy a walk-in closet in Los Angeles for under four million right now.

"Zac said I need to grow up," Jason informed me as we started to make our way to his office to pick up his car. "I figure I need to stop renting a duplex on Sweetzer now. I'm going to throw dinner parties."

"Great idea. But are you sure he didn't just mean that you need to grow up figuratively? I mean he may have meant that sleeping with a different girl every night isn't very grown up," I ventured. "Not that there's anything wrong with it. But it's not exactly Zen."

"You could be right. I'll ask him next time I see him. So come on, honey, what are we waiting for?" Jason asked.

"Is my car going to be okay there until Triple A comes, do you think?" I took a backward glance at the tires that had cost me dearly.

"I have an assistant," Jason said with the phone to his ear. "Tallulah, it's me. Can you come to the front gate, please? And could you also book an appointment to view the house on Bluebird at one-thirty? Thanks."

While it was true that Jason had an assistant and a bungalow on the lot, it was clear, as we made our way toward it, that he hadn't had a real hit movie yet because his bungalow was a full twenty-minute walk from the Dreamworks building and when we got there we had to duck behind some bushes to get through the entrance.

"It's great, isn't it?" Jason said as we walked up the three rotting wood steps into what was effectively a beat-up trailer.

"And it's all yours," I said proudly.

"Well, actually, I share it with the guys who did *Rasputin Returns*," he admitted quietly.

"They did what?" I asked, following suit and whispering in case they overheard.

"Well, *exactly.*" He gave me a look. "It cost seventy-five million and made about six million back. But they've still got a year left on their deal."

"So they've been sent to bungalow Siberia?" I guessed.

"Correct." Jason smiled as we walked into his office.

It was just like his house—you could learn all there was to know about cinema just by looking at his posters and books. Every movement in film history was represented and documented, every frame ever shot was written about on his shelves. Jason, despite his new director-about-town image was at heart still an intense film geek and that was clearly why *Sex Addicts in Love* was being so well received by people who knew about cinema. There wasn't a shot in that movie that he hadn't lovingly planned and imagined a thousand times in his head over the last five years.

"So this is where it all happens?" I asked as I sat in his office chair and banged my fists on the desk, in an imitation of power.

"Damn straight," Jason said and lay back on his sofa. Then he leaned forward and hesitantly asked, "Lizzie, do you think we might win something? An award, I mean?"

"I have no idea," I said as I looked at his desk, which was heaving with at least a hundred scripts. "But I know it's a great movie and it deserves to. What are all these, by the way?"

"Projects I'm being offered," he said with surprising modesty.

"You're really on your way, aren't you?" I asked, suddenly realizing that for all the overexcitable behavior he'd been indulging in for the past year, since he'd inked a very fine deal, he really was on his way to the big time.

"I hope so." He shrugged. "So should we go and buy me a big-ass house so that if I get nominated I can have a party by my infinity pool?"

"In your pants, more like," I said as we headed for his car.

"Those days are over," he informed me. "I swear, Lizzie, the chicks in this town are overrated. Seen one you've seen them all."

"That's so insulting." I shoved him in the ribs with my elbow as we strapped ourselves into his new Porsche Carrera, which was waiting outside in his very own parking space.

"Lizzie, do you have any idea how boring it is going on dates with women whose idea of a simple restaurant is Nobu Malibu because it doesn't have tablecloths?" he implored.

"No, but I'm sure they're worth the blackened cod."

"They're not. I went on a date with this actress the other night. You know, she was somebody's girlfriend from 'Nip/Tuck'? Well we're driving along the PCH to Nobu."

"Naturally." I nodded.

"I told you—she wanted simple." He sounded pained. "And I hear this cracking noise. First I think it's the rocks by the ocean cause it sounds like an avalanche. Then I realize it's *in* the car. So I assume that there's something wrong with the bodywork," Jason tells me as we're leaving the lot and I cast a last, backward glance at my sorry Honda, which is being heaved by AAA onto their tow truck. Until I hear the actress making whimpering noises and I look over and she's desperately clutching her head."

"Why?" I asked, noting the difference between the life of a First Assistant and that of a newly celebrated director. And to think we used to share the same sofa every night of the week and I cooked chicken dinners for him and we were, to all intents and purposes, each other's other halves without the sex.

"Her hairspray was cracking in the wind." Jason laughed so hard he almost forgot to turn off onto the freeway. I was glad that success had made him loosen up a bit. He used to be so earnest it hurt. These days, now that he was fulfilling his creative urges (not to mention his carnal ones) instead of frothing milk at the Coffee Bean, he was altogether more fun.

"No way." I laughed. "So what happened?"

"I had to take her home 'cause she was in tears."

"Okay, well then maybe I can see why you would be fed up with actresses," I agreed.

The "bird streets" are a bunch of winding roads that are vertiginously perched above Sunset Strip with views from the Los Angeles Basin to Downtown to Malibu. They have names like Swallow, Flicker, and Nightingale. Everyone lives here. By everyone I mean Tobey Maguire, Courteney Cox, Keanu Reeves, Leonardo DiCaprio. And now of course, Jason Blum. They were pretty houses, surprisingly close together for privacy-hungry stars, and the most expensive real estate in the city.

Jason and I climbed effortlessly up the streets in his Porsche and talked about his next project. He asked me if I'd like to produce for him again and of course I agreed. He was thinking of something on a larger scale, more epic, possibly about war. I couldn't argue with that. It seemed to be what male directors who were shown a glimpse of an award did—made movies about war and disaffected heroes.

When we arrived at the house the real estate agent was waiting in the driveway in a bigger, shinier car than even Jason's. He got out and shook our hands in a bone-crunching fashion that I assumed had died out in the nineties. He had parked across the driveway to stop the electronic gates from closing.

"Hey guys," he said with cheery casualness. "I'm Ivan."

"Jason. And this is my friend and business partner, Elizabeth," Jason said as he looked up at the house. The ultimate in Los Angeles real estate with its white front and imposing black doorway.

"You're loving it already, right?" Ivan laughed at the look on Jason's face. "Well just you wait until you see inside."

"So how long has it been on the market?" Jason asked as we were let in by a pretty maid: No Mrs. Mendes for this house with her nanny goat's beard and furrowed brow, I noticed, only the most aesthetically pleasing décor.

"It was bought by a couple six months ago, but they made the renovations, changed their minds, and never moved in." Ivan shrugged. Then, as if by way of explanation, whispered, "Internet software."

"I see," Jason said as we walked through the stark white hallway into the living room. There wasn't a stick of furniture in sight, just acres of glaring white space. Ivan led us up some stairs to a landing from which we could see corridors leading off to the master suite, the never-ending kitchen, and outside to the pool, and then the part I guessed you'd be paying your millions for—the view. Jason and I stood transfixed and I thought back to the day, almost two years ago, when I'd just moved to town, and my new friend Jason, whom I wasn't sure if I had the hots for or not, decided to take me hiking in the Canyons. I guess this was one of the houses we'd have seen that day. One of those that Jason had looked down on and pointed out as a future home. I had, of course, no such ambitions then, I was very happy with my studio apartment in Venice, which was probably the reason I wasn't buying a place for several million dollars today. As Somerset Maugham famously said, "It's a funny thing about life, if you refuse to accept anything but the best, you very often get it." I guess that was the difference between me and Jason. Not that I was complaining.

"Do you really think you might buy it?" I whispered, although it was impossible to whisper in here without it carrying around like an echo chamber.

"Yeah, I think I will," Jason said as we wandered around the master suite with its bathtub that you could see for miles from.

"Imagine bathing in that every day," I said to Jason.

"It'd be great for the soul," Jason agreed. I was sure that it was possible to do good things for the soul without having to spend a trillion dollars, but I guess a leg up the ladder to a higher plane wouldn't hurt.

"Maybe that's why the Dalai Lama comes from the mountains of Tibet," I said.

"Could be." Jason wasn't really looking at the view anymore, though. I noticed that as I'd been touching marble work surfaces and staring off at the horizon, he'd begun to look at me. His eyes were following me around the room. In fact, if I thought about it, he'd been looking at me more intently today then ever before. Perhaps it was the dark circles under my eyes that made me look as if I were suffering and consequently poetic. It certainly wasn't my sundress, which I'd worn a million times before with him.

"That dress reminds me of that day we went to Neptune's Net in Malibu and we ate cheap lobster and got drunk on the beach," he said wistfully. I almost jumped out the window. Could Jason be psychic? Or was it the inspiring view?

"Really?" I squeaked. Oh God, Jason didn't get a crush on me, did he? Of course he didn't. Jason liked girls over five-foot-ten who could wear a bikini in public without the need for a sarong. Perfect girls.

"Yeah. Do you remember that night?" he asked when the realtor was asking the maid all sorts of questions about the AC and the pool pump and what her telephone number was.

"Yeah, I do," I said. "I can cast my mind back to Neptune's Net. No pun intended." At which Jason gave his new, wonderfully free laugh. In fact his laugh was so infectious and natural that even I, oh cynical one, was momentarily won over.

"God, Lizzie, do you know how long it's been since a girl made me laugh?" He shook his head.

"Actually, Jason, it wasn't really very funny." I was faintly embarrassed.

Thankfully we were saved from certain mortification when Ivan came back in the room.

"Well, guys, how are you finding everything?" he asked, fiddling with his cell phone. Clearly our time was almost up.

"Great!" Jason said.

"Good, because if you don't mind I have to make an appointment in the Colony, but Lucia will let you out when you're done." Ivan twitched.

"Oh, okay." Jason stood up to shake Ivan's hand.

"I'll call you later to see what your feelings are," Ivan said, backing away toward the main hallway. He threw me a hasty wave and I smiled back and shrugged my shoulders.

"Bye, Ivan. Thanks!" I called out as he disappeared down the stairs.

"What would we do if we lived here, Lizzie?" Jason asked as we heard the front door close and the supernatural haze of the afternoon sun poured over the valley.

Wow, I thought carefully for a moment, what would I do if I lived here? "Well, I guess I'd swim in the morning as soon as the sun came up; I'd have an office overlooking Sunset and I'd make a few calls for work, for my production company." I laughed. "I'd drink delicious coffee and read the papers."

"What about children?" Jason asked as he came and sat beside me on the side of the bathtub, which was the best view I could find.

"Children?" I repeated. I looked at Jason for signs of irony, but he was on his own fantasy so I went along with him. "Well, they'd be named Grace and Frodo."

"Frodo?" Jason sat back with surprise.

"I like Frodo. It's sweet."

"It's a hobbit."

"Are you going to argue with me?" I asked, with a grin. "When I've gone to all that trouble to give birth and lose my figure?"

"I guess it would be pretty harsh." Jason laughed.

"Right, so then in the afternoon I'd take Grace and Frodo for a walk in the Canyon with Lara and then we'd come home and make dinner for Daddy."

"Daddy?" Jason pointed a finger at himself questioningly. I nodded.

"Well, it is *your* house, and you asked about *our* lives, so I guess you'd be the daddy," I consented with a giggle.

"And then what?" Jason asked, riveted by our game.

"Then it'd be bath time so we'd come up here and everyone would get in the bath and we'd have big towels and put on pyjamas and when Grace and Frodo were finally asleep Mommy and Daddy would go downstairs and have a glass of wine, a bowl of pasta, and a talk about the fascinating movies we were making." I finished. Jason didn't reply. "Right?" I turned to him and smiled, but Jason was just looking at me now.

"That's so cool, Lizzie," he said with a glazed look in his eyes. "That's the life I want."

"That's the life we all want," I said pragmatically, getting up from the side of the bath but losing my balance when my foot slipped on the mat.

The next thing I knew I had fallen backward into the deepest bathtub ever made and was as stuck as a beached whale.

"Help," I demanded. Jason was watching me, laughing that laugh again. I stopped struggling to get out and looked at him for a second. He was cute with the afternoon sun burnishing his hair and giving him a halo of light. And as he reached out and took my hand I had a feeling I'd never experienced in his company before. I understood why all those women fell for him. He was natural and charismatic and smart. And we loved each other like brother and sister, right? I asked myself.

Well, it seems we used to, but in that instant when he reached down and pulled me up it was as if all our friendship and shared memories and nights collapsing drunk into bed together were ignited by the conversation we'd just had. By the idea that Jason and I were as natural together and as right as anyone I'd ever met. I felt safe with Jason as he pulled me out of the tub, as if he wouldn't let me fall and would never do anything to hurt me.

"Thanks," I said quietly as I found myself inches from his face.

"You're welcome." Jason didn't take his gaze away from mine. And the next thing I knew, we were kissing.

I don't know who made the first move, for all I know it was both of us. At the exact same second. All I know was that a few minutes later I was kissing Jason. My lips were on his and I could feel his cheeks, his hair, and his body in a way that I'd never felt them before. This was such a new experience, to be doing this with Jason, that it sort of blew my mind. Well, it must have tripped some switch in my brain, because twenty minutes later I was in my underwear, in the empty bath, having the most athletic, fun sex I'd ever had in my life.

With Jason Blum.

SIXTEEN

Half the people in Hollywood are
dying to be discovered and the
other half are afraid they will be.

—Lionel Barrymore

"Scott Wagner's office," I said with as much enthusiasm as I could muster. Maybe it was the weather, but as I jotted down the details from the mechanic on all the things that needed to be repaired on Lara's new Porsche Cayenne, I realized I was feeling slightly depressed. As I looked out the window at the sheets of rain beating against the glass it occurred to me that it wasn't the steady deluge that was getting me down but the climate shift in my office. Since my return from Thailand, fall had taken hold of my desk and the color was pure Amber.

The police hadn't reappeared and no one had mentioned blackmail or missing photos, but something just wasn't right. The Agency was now rife with gossip and speculation about the missing files and every day it was rumored that another star was being threatened with having his/her ass/breasts or gay/adulterous incriminating shots posted to the press if he/she didn't come up with several million dollars. I'd been meaning to talk to Scott about it, but every time I tried he shrugged me off with irritation. And to make matters worse, I'd been unofficially demoted by Amber, who had Scott eating out of the palm of her hand, and I had no idea how to get my old job back.

The situation was impossible because no matter how hard I plotted and schemed, I couldn't find a single concrete reason why Amber should be fired. Besides being a slippery reptile, which certainly didn't qualify as grounds for dismissal in this town, she hadn't done anything wrong. To all intents and purposes, she'd done everything right. She

was much more organized than I'd ever been, hence my feeling of alien-
ation when I returned and couldn't find a single thing in my office.
She'd devised some new filing system that was clearly only decipher-
able to English girls with classics degrees. Or more likely she'd devised
some enigma code for the filing system that would take the offspring of
Steven Hawking to figure out, in order to move me one step farther
away from steady employment.

The long and short of it being that every time Scott asked me to get
something from the files, I couldn't find it and had to ask Amber, who
then happily bypassed me and pranced into Scott's office telling me to
relax and put my feet up. As a result Scott didn't bother to ask me anymore. He just went directly to her. But as my salary was still the same
and my job title intact I couldn't really complain to Scott or Human Re-
sources. I realized as the lightning struck dangerously close to the
building that the only way to tackle the situation was head-on. That
meant I needed to confront Amber directly, taking the power back that
I had involuntarily surrendered during my foray to the Far East.

But there was a slight problem with this brilliant plan. I just wasn't
born with a confrontational bone in my body. Lara had sweetly, or perhaps in dire self-interest, tried to talk to Scott about Amber, but Scott
just waved her off, attributing her comments to too much time spent
alone with the baby. Lara had quickly retreated, terrified of alienating
him lest she end up driving him into the arms of his assistant. Amber
was clearly up for it and history did have a way of repeating itself in
Hollywood, hence all the remakes. So I was on my own this time. What
was the best approach? Should I take Amber to lunch? Should I wait
until next week when Scott was in New York again? I instinctively
reached for the phone to call Luke for some emotional support and
moral guidance, but as quickly as the desire hit me, the reality hit me
harder. Luke wasn't waiting on the other end of the phone willing to listen to my silly assistant dramas anymore. He was probably having the
time of his life dating women who looked like Heidi Klum, spoke seven
languages, and played Chopin on the piano.

I took a deep breath and tried to remember how happy I was to be
independent and not the appendage of a rich and powerful man. I was
absolutely thrilled. Being single was exciting with a surprise around

every corner. I could do whatever I wanted in the evenings now. I didn't have to pick up his socks, which he somehow could never manage to get into the laundry basket. I was certainly more focused on my career than I had been in ages. And I could have uncomplicated one-afternoon stands like the one Jason and I had shared the other day. Life was brimming with possibility. So I picked up the phone and dialed Jason's cell phone instead. He'd gone to USC. He must have taken a class in how to outsmart a devious rodent.

"Hi, Jason, it's me." There was a long pause on the other end of the line. "It's Lizzie!" I said a bit mortified to have taken my place in his life so for granted. Yes, we'd had sex, but I knew better than to think that actually meant anything in this town, even to one of my best friends.

"Oh, hi, sweetheart. I was just thinking about you," he said.

I sighed with relief. Maybe I wasn't being presumptuous, after all.

"Were you really?" I asked in my best surprised, God-yes-I'd-almost-forgotten-we'd-slept-together voice.

"Sure was, baby. I need a suit or a tux for the Golden Globes, and since you're the producer, I thought you could find a stylist for me."

"A stylist?" I probably shouldn't have sounded so horrified, but it just popped out before I could rein in my tongue. How was I supposed to lust after a guy who wanted his cufflinks to match his underwear? The next step was having his balls waxed.

"Yeah . . . Is that a problem?" Jason asked in a tone that reminded me just how fragile his ego was. I back-tracked as quickly and delicately as possible.

"No. No problem at all, Jase. Of course you need a stylist. I just"—I was desperately trying to dig myself out of the hole—"totally forgot that you were going to the Globes." Actually, I hadn't forgotten at all. Quite the opposite. *Sex Addicts in Love* was the talk of The Agency. The talk of the town, even, and everyone at work was treating me with a bizarre mixture of deference and irritation as word spread that I was the producer. With the increased marketing spend and awards push, even box-office receipts were picking up, and it looked in danger of making money, too. Even though none of it was earmarked to me. I was actually getting the occasional excited phone call from college friends back home saying they'd seen my name on the big screen.

"Listen, Lizzie, you know I'm really sorry not to have a ticket for you," Jason said feebly. "But since I was nominated as best director and not for best picture, they only gave me the one extra ticket. And you know I would have totally taken you as my date if we'd been, you know, together at the time. But I already asked my mom and she's so excited."

Jason was really a sweetheart, after all. I gave myself a mental smack on the hand. It was unfair of me to pass judgment just because the guy wanted a professional to dress him for one of the biggest nights of his life. He obviously just wanted to look good for his mommy.

"And between you and me, I do think it's kind of good for my image to take her, don't you? Remember when Ben Affleck and Matt Damon took their moms? The press lapped it up." Why did everyone in Hollywood always have to have an ulterior motive? I wondered. Apart from Luke, of course. I breathed a silent sigh.

"Jase, you're not wrong. Unless you can persuade Julia Roberts or Lindsay Lohan to walk you down the red carpet, your mom is probably the best person to take. Anyway, she deserves it. She's had to put up with you for thirty years," I said.

Jason laughed appreciatively.

"You okay, babes? You sound kind of blue," he said with the perfect amount of worry and genuine interest. Somehow Jason's concern was all I needed to feel the burden lift ever so slightly from my shoulders.

"I'll survive," I said. "Can we get together soon and discuss that new movie idea we were talking about the other day? I'd love to sink my teeth into another project."

"Sure thing," Jason promised. "Just as soon as I'm done being feted." He laughed.

Los Angeles could be a lonely place and since my breakup with Luke I'd been feeling it acutely. I had made the classic error of moving in with my boyfriend and then not having the energy or the inclination to keep up with newfound friends. It was just so much easier to drift around together in our own little bubble and forget that the rest of the world existed. I'd only been living in LA for a year when we'd moved in together, so I'd slotted neatly into his network of friends and acquaintances. But now that it was over, I didn't somehow feel comfortable calling his friends. They'd all been lovely, but I didn't really know them well enough to ring them up on a Saturday and say "Hey want to go catch a matinee?" So it was nice to have Jason back in my life as a friend or a lover. To be honest, it didn't make much of a difference to me which it was. Though it was fun to fantasize about a life together, at the moment, I was just happy to have someone to talk to every night before I went to sleep.

I quickly looked around to make sure Amber hadn't slithered back in while I wasn't looking. I whispered into the phone to Jason, "Listen. Amber, Scott's Second Assistant, usurped my position while I was away, and now she's trying to get me fired. What should I do?"

"Baby, you should quit!" he said easily.

Quit? Was he on acid? I'd just spent all the money I'd saved in Thailand on a deposit and first and last months' rent for a much-too-expensive little one-bedroom bungalow in Venice.

"That's not an option," I said categorically.

"Why? You can move into the Bluebird house with me. I put a bid in, by the way. You know even if nothing happens between us, I love having you around."

Though this was a very sweet and generous offer, it made me want to *scream*. A mere eighteen months ago, Jason had been debating the merits of a soy latte versus a skinny latte as he tried not to dirty his brown apron at the Coffee Bean. I was consumed with pure old-fashioned jealousy as he tossed around the idea of a five-million-dollar house while I struggled to pay fifteen hundred dollars a month in rent. How could he forget so quickly how important even my little unimportant job was to me? I tamed the green-eyed monster and forged ahead.

"Jason, I need my job. And an apartment. I made that mistake once, you know? No more moving in with anyone. Anyway, I love living alone. Or at least I will once I move. So, any ideas?"

"I know, I know. You're an independent woman. I promise never to offer you a free ride again. But you know if you did move in, you could pay me in services if that made you feel any better."

I started to laugh as Amber walked in. I noticed she was carrying three Barney's bags.

"Okay. Great. I'll give Scott the message." I quickly hung up on Jason as I didn't want to give Amber any added ammunition.

"Talking to your friends again on company time, Lizzie?" Amber said with a smile. I was immediately seized with guilt. God I hated her.

"Actually, Amber, it was a work call. Daniel Rosen has been calling Jason Blum trying to poach him from The Agency." I lied through my teeth. "And of course Scott is very interested in anything I can do to help him keep clients." That shut Amber up for once. She just stroked her new purse and shoved her shopping bags under her desk.

"Nice purse, by the way," I added. "Amazing what you can get for fourteen hundred dollars these days, isn't it?" I recalled the days of old, before I knew about Lara and Scott's affair. Lara would appear with fantastically expensive designer purses and dresses all the time. I knew how much that little Chloe beauty she was fingering was worth. I quickly glanced at Scott's schedule in terror. Could I be that blind twice? Amber wasn't having an affair with Scott, was she? I saw with tremendous relief that Scott was lunching with Katherine Watson today. And I'd confirmed with her assistant myself, so I knew for certain he wasn't the plastic. Anyway, Lara had quite smartly insisted on taking over the management of their credit cards and bank accounts in order to keep some control over their life. What she of course didn't know was that as soon as Scott agreed to this arrangement, he'd opened up a separate bank account that he kept nicely padded for his private needs.

But even if Scott wasn't the culprit, I'd obviously hit a nerve, because Amber's eyes narrowed and all the sweet pretense dropped away. She stepped dangerously close to my desk. I actually felt a moment of real fear as she stuck her freckly face as near to mine as possible. I could smell her minty breath, and the only thought that kept running through my head was what smell the mints must be covering. And I strongly suspected that it wasn't garlic.

"Mind your own business, Lizzie. Or you'll live to regret it," she said, and then smiled sweetly, brushing a piece of hair off my face. "You look so pretty with your hair off your face, Lizzie," she said loudly. Then backed off and casually shoved her bags farther under her desk.

It was only when I looked up that I noticed the reason for the sudden, schizophrenic shift in her personality. Scott and Katherine were headed toward our desks.

"Hi, ladies," Katherine said amiably, then turned her full attention to Amber as I handed Scott his call sheet.

"Amber, are you joining Michael and me at the gallery opening tomorrow night? I'd love to get your opinion on one of the oils I'm interested in."

"Definitely, Katherine," Amber preened. "I looked at the pictures online and I see he studied at The Slade. I have some friends who went there. I've asked one of them to check his prices in London for you."

Katherine looked thrilled. "Great. We can go together straight from here tomorrow night."

"I can't wait," Amber said with a relaxed, casual smile as Katherine walked away. Then she turned her brown laser beams on Scott, and dumped me in it royally.

"Oh, Scott. I noticed it wasn't on your call sheet, but Jason Blum called for you. Lizzie says he's thinking of leaving The Agency. Apparently he's been talking to Daniel Rosen."

Scott's eyes lit up. Battle-ready. There was nothing he loved more than a fight. Especially with Daniel Rosen. Since the takeover they'd pretended to be buddy-buddy, but everyone knew that was just a façade, especially when male pride was at stake.

"Lizzie, why didn't you put this on my call sheet?" he said accusatorially. "You've really got to get it together. Amber, I need to see the copy of the contract we signed with Jason last year when he dumped Daniel."

"Right away, Scott. And I'll have Lizzie grab you a coffee."

"That would be great. Thanks." He disappeared into his office without even looking back. I just sat there dumbly staring at Amber with an open mouth.

"Would you mind grabbing me a soy chai latte while you're at the Coffee Bean?" she said with a dictatorial tone in her voice. I stood up in a rage. How did this girl manage to best me at every turn? I wanted to cry I was so furious.

"It would be my pleasure, Amber. If it has a faint whiff of urine when it arrives, just ignore it. Occasionally their soy tastes a little off." Then I grabbed some petty cash and stormed out of the office.

I was pathetic. All I could muster up was the old pee-in-her-coffee line. I had to do better than that or I wouldn't have a hope in hell of sur-viving the next few months. And I knew it would take me at least that long to find a film project, let alone one I was being paid for. I stepped out into the rain and realized I'd forgotten my raincoat. I made a mad dash across the street and flew in the door trying unsuccessfully to dodge the raindrops. The combination of my new flats, my speed, and the slippery linoleum floor proved a disaster. I went flying headfirst into the Coffee Bean like a bowling ball, plowing all the unsuspecting cof-fee-clutching pins out of the way. I slid to a stop right at the feet of some very expensive stiletto boots and a tiny little miniskirt.

"Lizzie!" the boots screeched with genuine pleasure. Someone snick-ered, probably at my red leopard granny underpants that I realized were on display for all customers to see. But I was focusing on the screech. I still had occasional nightmares about that voice. I looked up slowly and there smiling down at me was Emerald Everhart.

She hauled me up off the floor with incredible dexterity for a tooth-pick on stilts. Then she threw her arms around me in the most gener-ous embrace. And to my shock and surprise, I squeezed her back with true emotion. Though Thailand had been a roller coaster, ultimately, in her own twisted way, Emerald had been one of the most loyal people I'd ever worked for. And her smiling face was a welcome sight on a rainy, Amber-hating afternoon.

"Lizzie. I was going to call you, but I wasn't sure if you wanted to hear from me."

I looked around suspiciously for lurking paparazzi. Let's just say I'd learned from past experience. I spotted a suspicious-looking guy in a raincoat in the corner. I lowered my voice and leaned in. "Em, that guy in the corner could be press. So keep it down."

Emerald rolled her eyes at me in exasperation. "Lizzie, he's got a dog with him."

I glanced down at the suspicious man's feet and saw the most enor-mous pooch. "It's really hard to chase stars down the street or jump on a motorcycle with your Newfoundland in tow," Emerald said, laughing. "Unless he is planning to hop on the dog's back and ride after me."

"Point taken, missy, but you've scarred me for life," I said as I steered her toward a secluded table in the corner. Emerald looked momentarily guilty, but then smiled like a madonna.

"I'm on the straight and narrow now, Lizzie. No drinks. No drugs. No sex. It's actually kind of fun. I had no idea what a brilliant excuse being clean was. When I don't want to do something, I just blame it on AA. And my sponsor is even more famous than me." She dropped her voice to the usual indiscreet stage whisper. "Kate!" she said excitedly. I was appropriately impressed.

"Are you coming to see Scott? I didn't see it in his schedule," I said, truly curious as to what Scott had up his sleeve for her comeback.

"Yeah. I have an appointment. I confirmed it with that English girl. I don't know her, but I don't like her already. There's just something so distasteful about that fake British accent. I could do a better one than that."

"It's real," I said. Annoyed that I felt the need to set the record straight for Amber.

"She may be from England, Lizzie, but that cut glass thing is so affected. Trust me." Emerald was teaching her grandmother to suck eggs here.

"So what are you coming to see Scott about?" I asked, changing the subject. I wanted to forget about Amber for at least fifteen minutes.

"Well, he's got this really interesting proposition."

"Go on," I said, intrigued.

Emerald leaned in close to me with an excited look on her face, her teen skin glowing and her pretty eyes filled with a vitality I hadn't seen before. "Well, you know that I can't even get arrested in this town at the moment, right?" she said without rancor. I looked at her blankly not wanting to make her feel bad. Scott had been doing his best to get Emerald work, but the stripping photos were still flying around the Internet and nobody wanted to hire the sullied teen dream. But her banishment wouldn't last long. Soon someone would take pity on her and cast her in a brilliant indie flick that would go to Sundance and win all sorts of awards, I was convinced of it. She'd fly back into public consciousness having moved from girl to woman and every director in town would want to work with her, seeing her little indiscretion as a sign of hidden depths. But for now she had to wait it out. Hence the AA, I imagined; at least it was something to do besides shop.

"You'll find something, Emerald. You're such a talented actress. Those photos just need a little bit of time to blow over," I said.

Emerald nodded in agreement.

"Well, Scott does actually have something for me." And this time she really *did* whisper. "A proposal."

"What kind of proposal?" I asked, worried that my unscrupulous boss might be offering her some seedy deal.

"A marriage proposal!"

"Scott proposed?" I said, completely confused now. Emerald smacked my arm.

"No. Silly. He's married. A certain actor that he represents wants a wife. I'll give you a few hints. He's one of the biggest action heroes in the business, he's in his forties, he has his own production company, he's cute, and—"

"No!" I said as the lightbulb illuminated my sleepy brain. "Why would he need to go to such lengths to get a wife? And why you?"

"Well, he's seen my photos, of course, and apparently we met once, but I don't remember. My partying days, you know," she said with a casual wave. "And he saw me in *Innocence* and was blown away by my performance. So, he asked Scott to arrange something."

"So he's in love with you and wants to marry you? Em, isn't that a little creepy?" I grimaced.

"I don't think he's in love with me, silly. But he thinks a wife will improve his image, and Scott said a white wedding will certainly improve mine. And check this out. He'll pay me two million dollars just to show up at the wedding, fifteen million if we stay married for five years, and thirty million if we make it to our tenth anniversary. Now that's incentive not to get divorced, huh?" She grinned. I had never heard something so completely twisted in my life. And Emerald seemed to be seriously considering it.

"But Emerald, there's something wrong there. Why does he need to buy a wife? He's one of the biggest stars in Hollywood. It doesn't add up."

"There is a little hitch." She sighed. "I have to join his church."

"His church?" I repeated.

"Well, it's not really a church, more of a cult. But it's a religion. It's called HOGD."

"There's a religion called HOGD?"

"It stands for . . ." Emerald opened her notebook and read from the pages, "'The Hermetic Order of the Golden Dawn.'"

"I've never heard of it. It doesn't have anything to do with Manson does it?"

"No. It's a cult you'd approve of. It's for smart people. Educated people. Scott said it's been around for hundreds of years. Everyone who joins seems to have huge careers. And it's a nice name isn't it? Golden Dawn? So why not? And the best part is, it's a secret!"

"You mean a secret society?"

"Exactly. So don't tell anyone. But I have to get initiated if we get married. If I sign the contract, I'll start going to classes right away. So I want Valentino to design my wedding dress. Will you come to the fittings with me? Oh please, Lizzie?"

"Emerald, are you sure you want to do this?" I asked seriously. "You don't need the money and you're so young. Why get married to someone you don't love?"

When I said this Emerald literally guffawed. "Lizzie, you're so naïve for a girl your age. That's why I love you so much. Just think about it for a second. One in three marriages ends in divorce and in Hollywood it's more like three in three. So why not have an arranged marriage with realistic goals and expectations instead of going into something blind and deluded and coming out heartbroken and jaded?"

I hated it when Emerald managed to turn the most ludicrous idea into a sensible or may I even say, wise, approach to life.

"But what about sex?" I said, cringing at the thought.

"I don't have to sleep with him if I don't want to. It's in the contract. But it also stipulates that if either one of us gets caught screwing around, the deal is null and void. But I think I'd really *like* to sleep with him. I had a poster of him hanging inside my closet door since he did *Spy Mission* in ninety-five. And apparently he's already bought me the most incredible Fred Leighton yellow diamond. It's romantic, isn't it?"

Well, "romantic" wasn't what sprung to *my* mind. But maybe a little stability was exactly what Emerald needed. She had no family to speak of. Since her mother's tell-all had come out, she'd pretty much disowned her entire family. And if the rumors were to be believed, her fiancé was a pretty decent guy. I thought about her new approach to relationships and I realized I might benefit from taking a page from her book. Not the arranged marriage to a movie star page but the more practical approach to romance page. If I were brutally honest with myself, I'd have to admit that I hadn't quite been feeling the enthusiasm I'd hoped to feel about my budding relationship with Jason. The sex had been fantastic, don't get me wrong, but our everyday interaction just seemed so pedestrian. So familiar. Which obviously came from being such good friends with nothing left to discover about each other. So everything was nice and safe. The usual insecurity of a new relationship didn't exist. Hence the fire felt a little bit more like a spark. But listening to Emerald I realized that nice and cozy in Hollywood was the exception, not the norm, and I should try to appreciate it. What I had with Jason was special. I just had to get used to a different kind of special.

"So, Emerald, do you ever find that the first time you sleep with a guy it's great, but you maybe don't fall in love?" I quizzed my new and unlikely relationship guru. Emerald drifted into deep contemplation, as a guru should, then shook her head violently.

"Nope. I always fall in love when I have sex. I just get over it when I come." She sucked her raspberry Tazo.

"I see." I nodded while trying desperately to wipe the look of mortification off my face. But as my blush faded I realized I was secretly pleased that some things never did change. Emerald still had the unerring ability to shock me into yesterday.

Seventeen

Hollywood has always been a cage . . .
a cage to catch our dreams.

—John Huston

I took a deep breath and inhaled the cool, slightly salty air. The sun was glinting off the Pacific and I felt warmed from head to toe. It was only eight in the morning, but I'd been out of the guesthouse for an hour already. Scott had called and woken me up bright and early so that I could retrace his morning run with a pedometer. There were certainly some disadvantages in living a few hundred yards from your boss. He was training for a charity triathalon and had become obsessed by his speeds and distances. This morning he'd taken a new route by accident. And instead of getting in his car to retrace his steps himself, he'd spent half an hour on the phone explaining his route so that I could walk it to let him know the exact distance. I actually would have told him to fuck off, but I'd already offered to take Lachlan on a godmother outing so I figured that getting a little exercise with the jogging stroller wasn't a bad thing.

Lately Lachlan and I had been spending Saturday mornings in each other's company. Saturday was Scott and Lara's one day a week without Fernanda, their Mexican nanny. This was on purpose because Lara felt if she didn't schedule some Lachlan/Scott quality time, Scott might just stick his head into the nursery one day and realize Lachlan had gotten married and that he'd missed the wedding. But after a few weeks, Lara realized that if she didn't schedule some Scott/Lara quality time, she'd pop her head into his study one day and find he'd married someone else. So I had taken over Saturday mornings, and I loved it. My maternal cravings were satisfied in one weekly dose, and Lara and Scott both spent all of Saturday with enormous grins on their faces.

Lara was starting to see that though she'd had a child, she couldn't forget her other child, Scott. So she'd been shifting more of the responsibility of Lachlan's everyday care onto Fernanda and stepping out with Scott more frequently. Not to say that they were bad parents. Both Lara and Scott had just slipped into the classic overprivileged parent model. Lachlan was fed a fully organic diet, attended all the best music lessons, and had the best sign language teacher money could buy. And no, he wasn't deaf, but Lara read that teaching infants sign language allowed them a method by which to communicate before they learned to speak. A practice made risible by *Meet the Fockers,* but that only seemed to encourage Hollywood in its latest child-development crush.

"Perro!" Lachlan squealed with delight as a man jogged by with his schnauzer. The other by-product of Lara and Scott's renaissance was that Lachlan's first words were in Spanish. Lara tried to assuage her guilt by saying how many people longed to be bilingual. I hated to tell her that her son wasn't bilingual, just Mexican.

I bounced Lachlan's stroller down the steps and crossed the road, heading toward the beach. We both loved to lie in the warm sand and roll around together until we were both completely covered in the stuff. So there I was rolling around in the sand laughing like a lunatic with a one-year-old when Jake Hudson walked up. He had perfect timing— always managing to catch me at the worst moment.

"Lizzie, congratulations! That is quite something!" he said glancing down at the sand-covered Lachlan. I was trying to pick shells and sand out of my hair when Lachlan decided that if I wasn't going to roll in it, he'd throw it at me instead.

"Oh, he's not mine. I'm just borrowing him," I explained. Jake looked confused and then looked again at Lachlan.

"It actually didn't occur to me that you might have a kid. I know you're not that together. The congratulations are for your nomination."

"What nomination?" I said, truly perplexed. I wracked my brains. Had I entered some contest unwittingly? Amber had probably sent my application to *Survivor* in order to get everyone to laugh at me on national television. Jake was shaking his head in disbelief, and I was getting more uncomfortable by the second. At that moment Lachlan decided he didn't like Jake and started to scream his head off.

"Your Oscar nomination!" Jake snarled impatiently. But Lachlan was screaming so loudly I was sure I'd misunderstood Jake.

"My what?" I yelled over Lachlan.

"Lizzie, you've been nominated for an Oscar," he said, as if to an idiot. I started to laugh. Jake was such a joker.

"Lizzie," Jake said patiently as he sat down in the sand next to me. "*Sex Addicts in Love* has been nominated for an Oscar in the best-picture category. Since you're executive producer, that means that you, Elizabeth Miller, have been nominated for an Oscar." I blinked a few times unable to comprehend what Jake had just said. I watched his lips continue to move but there was an odd rushing sound in my head. An Oscar? There was just no way that I could be nominated for an Academy Award. Then suddenly everything went black.

I opened my eyes to Lachlan's laughing as he shoved sand down my shirt and Jake's pouring a cup of cold, salty water on my face. I blinked up at Jake Hudson and had a flashback to the first time I'd met him. "What happened?" I said, dazed. "I think the sun must be too strong. Or maybe I haven't eaten enough."

"I looked around for a hockey puck, but I think you passed out spontaneously this time," he said.

"Did you say I was nominated for an Oscar?" I repeated dumbly. Jake started to laugh.

"Yes. Did you really not know? The nominations were released at seven this morning."

"I've been out of the house since six-thirty and my cell phone died," I said as I scrambled in my bag for my pointless cell.

"Welcome to the big time, baby." Jake laughed and gave me a pat. A girl in a thong bikini walked by and Jake's eyes followed her cheeks as they swayed down the beach.

"Lizzie, feel free to call me anytime. You know, if you need some advice on how things work or anything like that. But I've got to run. I've just seen lunch." He winked as he nodded his head toward the thong bikini, chucked Lachlan under the chin, and jogged off after the perfect behind.

I picked Lachlan up and swung him around in a circle, suddenly unable to stop giggling. It was just too weird to be true. I was an Oscar nominee? I'd never imagined in my wildest dreams that befriending Jason two years ago in the Coffee Bean would lead to an invitation to the Academy Awards. Actually, not just an invitation but a nomination, with my very own seat and ticket. I was going on my own merit, not as anyone's date. It was too good to be true. I needed someone to confirm this information. It did cross my mind that maybe I'd just imagined the entire thing. Was it possible that I had drifted off for a second as I lay in the sand? I looked down the beach to see if I could see Jake, but there was no sign. It was just too much to take in. I unceremoniously dumped Lachlan in his stroller and then sprinted as fast as possible back to the Wagners' house.

I was barely breathing by the time I arrived at their front door. I was sublimely unfit. Though, like most of the world, I'd planned to turn over a new leaf for the new year, I had yet to really institute it. And I certainly regretted it now. I tried to ring the doorbell but was hyperventilating so badly I had to just bend over and catch my breath. Luckily Lachlan hadn't lost *his* breath.

"Mama! *Casa!*" he yelled.

The door flew open and Lara bounded out and wrapped me in the most enormous embrace.

"Lizzie, you've been nominated for an Oscar! I can't believe it." She grabbed Lachlan out of his stroller and the three of us bounced up and down on her doorstep in total euphoria.

"Is it really true?" I asked, having just managed to regain a bit of my breath.

"Of course it's true. *Sex Addicts in Love* has been nominated for almost every category. They're predicting it's going to sweep the board," she said. I stopped jumping and was frozen to the spot as a chill ran through my entire body. I was just coming to grips with the idea of a nomination. It hadn't occurred to me it could win.

"Are you okay?" Lara said as she watched all the blood drain from my face. I leaned against her heavily, feeling faint again.

"Lara, I don't deserve this," I said in terror. "I didn't earn this, and now something is going to go terribly wrong. I know it. Someone in my family is going to get sick or I'm going to get killed in a drive-by shooting." I looked around nervously at the quiet Santa Monica street.

"Don't be ridiculous," Lara said as she looked around nervously as well and quickly pulled Lachlan and me into the house. "You deserved that credit. Jason promised it to you when you agreed to help him. That script would never have seen the light of day if it weren't for you."

Lara plopped the baby on the floor and eased me down onto her plush velvet sofa. Then she walked to the cabinet and pressed a hidden button. The wall magically opened and there was an entire temperature-controlled secret wine cellar. She disappeared into the cavernous space and returned with a bottle of champagne. She showed it to me proudly.

"Dom Pérignon work for you?" she asked with a smile. I looked at the bottle with apprehension. Lara sat down next to me and took my hands in hers. "Listen to me, Lizzie. If it hadn't been for you, that film would never have been nominated for anything because it wouldn't have been made. Do you know how many times Jason Blum asked me, and every other person at The Agency, to read that script of his? A million. He'd been trying for two years to get someone to look at it with no luck until you came along. You know what? If I remember correctly, I think one of the agents had actually given it to one of our readers the year before and the reader had passed. You read it yourself and then actually followed up. You did something about it. That's what a producer does. She puts unlikely people together."

"But I wasn't even on set when they made it."

"And neither are half the producers in Hollywood. You did the hard part, my love. You found the director and the material a home. And if Jason Blum hadn't screwed you out of your credit in the first place you wouldn't be having a moment of guilt for your good fortune. Why is it that men feel entitled and women feel guilty?" Lara said contemplatively. "You know, I suffered from the same fate. But not today! Today we are entitled and empowered and inspired." And with that Lara popped the cork off the bottle of champagne. It hit the ceiling with gusto and then skittered across the old stone floor where Lachlan could chew on it happily.

The sound was obviously like the scent of a truffle to a French pig because Scott appeared out of nowhere.

"What, a celebration that I'm not invited to? Get your ass over here, Lizzie," he said. I walked toward Scott, dragging my feet like an embar-

rassed teenager. Lara was my best friend in LA and it made my relationship with Scott really confusing sometimes. But Scott didn't seem
to notice or care as he gave me a big old hug. "Way to go, Lizzie. Makes
the office look good. Now just make sure Jason extends his contract
with us and I'll give you a monster bonus."

He let go of me and grabbed one of the two glasses of champagne off
the coffee table. Lara looked at him disapprovingly as I studied the
lovely paint effect on the ceiling.

"Come on, baby. Just relax. It's only a glass. And it's for a good cause.
One little sip won't kill me." Lara shook her head in warning, but Scott
just smiled and chugged the entire glass. She took a deep breath and
walked to the cabinet and got a third glass. But determinedly refused to
refill his glass when he held it out toward her.

I looked down and noticed Lachlan clutching the champagne cork in
his fat little hands. Then in one smooth movement, he shoved the entire thing into his mouth. I quickly bent down and extracted the cork
from his jaws and he let out the most unholy of screams. I held it up for
Lara and Scott to see.

"Like father like son," Scott said proudly.

Lara turned a lighter shade of puce for a brief moment. I dived in
and changed the subject.

"So are you two around to celebrate tonight?"

"Are you kidding! Of course we are!" Lara said warmly.

"How about dinner at Nobu and then you ladies can accompany me
to my poker game at Leo's? It's always good luck to have a bit of poker
pussy on hand," Scott said with a devilish smile.

"Scott, you are foul!" Lara said, trying very hard to hide her laughter.
Scott pulled her into his lap and we all clinked glasses.

"Hey, Lizzie, why don't you bring Jason along tonight?" He said it like
a suggestion but I'd never heard a clearer order.

When I'd finally recharged my cell phone there were about seven
hundred messages from every person I'd ever met in my life. The first
call was from Jason, screaming in total delirium. Then my mother and
father, my sister, my entire group of high school friends, a boyfriend
from college whom I hadn't spoken to since he'd dumped me, and a
bunch of people from The Agency. Mingled in with those messages

were another ten or so calls from Jason demanding to know my where-abouts, and a variety of people I'd never heard of in my life. When the last message played I felt oddly disappointed, and I knew exactly why. There was no call from Luke.

I guess I shouldn't have been too surprised. The last contact we'd had was about the untimely death of his cat at the hands of my fishnets. But I'd really thought that this enormous event in my life would be the excuse he needed to call me. But then he was Luke and he didn't really need an excuse. If he wanted to call me he would. It was abundantly clear that he hadn't forgiven me for my childish behavior. And more than likely, he probably never wanted to speak to me again in his life. I had to bite my lip to stop the overwhelming feeling of self-pity that was taking over like the invasion of the body snatchers. I willed my thoughts away from Luke and focused on the positive.

I dialed Jason's cell phone and we had a mutual moment of pure joy and self-congratulation. Well I congratulated him and he congratulated me. A lot of "No you're brilliant!" "No you are." "No really, you are." It felt really nice to be part of a team. No matter what the future held for us romantically, Jason was my friend, and we were sharing one of the most amazing moments in both of our lives. And that brought us closer than sex ever could. I told him about Scott and Lara's invitation, and Ja-son thought it sounded like the perfect celebration. He'd been taking secret poker lessons and he was really looking forward to tossing his chips in with the big boys. He was certain that he was on a winning streak and he was positive he'd be able to buy himself a Ferrari tonight if he played his cards right. I was even promised a fur coat if he got lucky. In the heady excitement of the moment, I accepted his generous offer, totally banishing from my thoughts my family membership to PETA that my sister had just given all of us for Christmas.

We had a fantastic drunken dinner with the sake and crazy lychee martinis flowing like water. And for once, for good or for bad, Lara ig-nored the fact that Scott was probably breaking all twelve steps in one fell swoop. It was the first time I had seen Lara really enjoy herself since she'd had the baby. She was carefree and fun. Scott looked at her so adoringly that it made Jason and I hold hands under the table. We even tried to duck out of the poker party with whispered plans of checking into a suite at Shutters. But Lara wasn't having any of it. She'd heard about Scott's poker parties for ages and had never actually been invited. So there was no way she was going to miss this evening for love or money. And Jason and I were necessary for moral support.

As we walked in the door of the eco-friendly canyon spread, I longed instead for a big king-sized bed and a nice, fluffy, white robe. The drinks and excitement of the day had left me absolutely exhausted. I could barely string a sentence together and Jason wasn't doing much better. There were a few other girls milling around looking a bit drunk and bored. At least for once I was wearing the right thing. It had taken me hours to get dressed. I'd never been invited into the inner circle of the Hollywood elite before, and I'd needed to look casual yet cool. It was a look that every girl in LA seemed to be able to achieve with minimal effort but one that I was completely incapable of pulling off. Ever. It was only made worse by my mother's reminder that this was just the beginning. Now that I was an Oscar nominee, I'd probably be expected to show up at a variety of parties, luncheons, and interviews perfectly dressed and groomed at all times. I was raised in Maryland. Now that meant you either wore Levis or Banana Republic on special occasions. And though I now bought all the right labels, on sale of course, I never had the requisite hauteur to carry them off. So tonight, in emulation of the style of the upper echelons who were too cool to care, I managed to do don't-give-a-fuck chic brilliantly.

We were all greeted by a friendly, ever so scruffy Leo who introduced us to the girls. The boys were in the den settling in, he informed us. "Ben just showed up," Leo said with a slightly apologetic tone. "Jason, I know you're new to the game, so remember no one needs to get macho here. If you fold early, we'll think you're the smartest guy in the business," he said. Jason laughed uncomfortably as Lara leaned in and whispered in my ear.

"Apparently Ben is some huge poker champion. Bets like a half-million a hand." Jason overheard this and I could see his hand shake ever so slightly as he rubbed his eyes trying to wipe away the alcoholic haze.

I felt really sorry for Jason as I watched him be led away by Scott and

Leo like a lamb to the slaughter. Success had hit him like an oncoming train. And though he was invited to the parties and welcomed into the fold with open arms, he was still a bit out of his depth. He was making money now, but he hadn't yet had the chance to stockpile it like these guys had. To them half a million was a week's work. To Jason it was still his father's salary for ten years.

"Lara, do you think Jason will be okay?" I asked as we heard laughter and smelled the fragrant whiff of the best Cubans money could buy.

"Lizzie, he's a big boy. And you never know, he is on a winning streak. Now, let's keep this buzz going or I'll probably pass out," she said. I couldn't have agreed more. Leo had pointed to a bar outside, so Lara and I cruised out to the pool.

The entire environment was pretty low-key. We made ourselves strong vodkas and then sat down with a few modelly looking girls who were smoking pot on a swinging sofa.

"So, what do you guys do?" I asked stupidly. I reminded myself to think up a new introductory line. It had just become habit as it was always the first thing anyone ever asked you in Los Angeles. In the early days it had disgusted me, and there I was falling into the same trap. And in this particular case, the answer couldn't have been more obvious.

"I'm at UCLA studying biochemistry," the girl who looked like a prettier version of Helena Christiansen said with a friendly smile. That would teach me for succumbing to stereotypes.

"Let me guess," I said jokingly to the blonde. "You're studying rocket science?" Lara and I laughed at my dumb joke. Feeling superior in our age and, unfortunately, size.

"No. Genetic engineering, actually. What do you two do?" the blond asked sweetly without the slightest trace of much-deserved sarcasm. Lara and I looked at each other and took enormous swigs from our vodkas.

"She was just nominated for an Oscar and I just had a baby," Lara blurted out, placing much more emphasis on the first half of the sentence.

"Congratulations!" they both said with genuine enthusiasm.

I was about to launch into the story, starting to really enjoy recanting my miraculous Oscar nomination, when the genetic engineer pushed on.

"I'm so jealous. I'm dying for a baby. Lucky you," she said to Lara, who fell in love instantly. Poor Lara was so used to being blatantly ignored when she revealed that she was a stay-at-home mom, that she didn't quite know how to respond to this Grace Kelly look-a-like's warm response. "It's such a big decision to bring a life into this world. The most important thing you can ever do. I've just started dating this great guy. And he's such a family man. I mean, we've only been going out for a few weeks, but we're already discussing kids." Lara and I exchanged a look.

"Well, if you ask me, he'd be the luckiest guy in the world if he married you," I said. And I meant it. She was perfect.

"I promise you. I'd be the lucky one. Luke is a rarity in this town," she said.

My heart stopped.

"Luke Lloyd?" I choked out. Already knowing the answer. Lara spontaneously grabbed my hand.

"You know him?" she asked openly. "He's incredible. So down to earth. The only flaw I can see so far is this poker habit of his." She laughed as I struggled to breathe. "But then I guess even the most perfect diamond has to have a flaw, right?"

"Luke's here?" I managed to squeak.

"Well, I hope he's still here, since we did come together. So how do you guys know Luke?" She smiled, her perfect skin glowing in the moonlight.

"He's my . . . he was my . . ." I couldn't finish my sentence, and there was a slightly awkward pause.

"He's a friend of my husband," Lara jumped in smoothly.

"You don't play the piano by chance? Chopin?" I couldn't help but ask.

Grace Kelly broke into a big smile.

"How did you know? He's my favorite. Are you in the mood for some music? You're absolutely right this party does need some livening up."

She ran off to find the piano just as Luke walked out with a glass of white wine in his hand. I hadn't seen him since that morning in bed, and it was as if I'd been kicked in the stomach. I watched from a distance as he put his hand on the girl's long graceful arm and whispered something in her ear. She took the glass of wine and kissed him playfully on the lips. My heart was in my throat. I wanted to scream or cry or find a sharp object and drive it into her perfect heart. Then he looked up and our eyes locked. His hand dropped from her arm and I may have been imagining it but it looked like he took a physical step back from her. He said something and she nodded and disappeared into the house.

Luke walked in our direction and Lara grabbed the brunette by the hand.

"Let's go find some snacks in the kitchen for the boys. I'm sure all that gambling is going to make them ravenous." She pulled the brunette to standing. "Hi, Luke," she said with a nod, then walked off toward the kitchen. I could hear some Chopin tinkling away in the background as Luke sat down across from me.

"I hear congratulations are in order," he said without much emotion.

"Yup. I guess so," I said, trying to sound light and breezy.

"I wanted to call you and say it earlier today, but I was so angry with you after our last conversation, that I deleted your cell number from my phone." He laughed at himself and shook his head. I looked at him and desperately wanted to melt into his arms. "So I couldn't."

"That'll teach you," I said pathetically. "I don't blame you for not ever wanting to speak to me again, actually."

"It was a moment of madness. I know you didn't kill Charles on purpose and well . . . I can understand why you did the Emanuelle thing. Really immature, but understandable."

"I guess that's me. Immature. Unlike Grace Kelly at the piano," I said. I couldn't help myself, but Luke graciously ignored me.

"Lizzie. I'm really happy for you. I mean it. And if you ever need anything, I'm always just a phone call away. Okay?" he said. "Unless you've deleted me, that is." I was too terrified to look into his eyes to see if he was offering me his eternal friendship or something a bit more interesting. So I focused on my chipping nail polish and waited for him to elaborate on his statement.

But before he could continue, a proprietary arm slid around my shoulder.

"Lizzie babes. I need you to come and be my good luck charm. I've just lost my first hand," Jason said possessively. And to make his point crystal clear he gave me a lingering kiss on the neck. I glanced up nervously at Luke and caught a flash of recognition and then slight annoyance in his eyes. This was all the ammunition I needed to behave like the immature girl I was trying desperately not to be.

"Okay, baby. Luke and I were just about to come in, anyway," I said as I turned around and planted a lingering kiss right on Jason's lips.

"We sure were," Luke said in a clipped tone as he stood up, just as the genetic engineer reappeared. She took his hand and he slipped his arm around her reedlike waist. "Grace, have you met Jason Blum and my friend Lizzie Miller?"

I picked up my vodka and took a gulp to calm my nerves.

"Lizzie thinks you'd be a very lucky man to marry me," Grace said playfully. I inhaled sharply and the drink went down my windpipe. I started to cough and splutter, turning an unattractive shade of red.

"Are you okay?" Jason said as he slapped me hard on the back.

"I know the Heimlich manoeuve," Grace said. Of course she did.

EIGHTEEN

Hollywood is a place where a
man can get stabbed in the back
while climbing a ladder.

—William Faulkner

Award season was heating up and Universal had, to my astonishment,
started to include me in a few interviews to promote *Sex Addicts in
Love*. Jason had mentioned to one of the publicity girls that we were
dating and they decided to use it as an angle to sell the film. They put
Jason and me in a room together and had us talk to whomever wanted
to listen about how we'd met at the coffee shop and what I'd done to get
the script into the right hands. And then how after the film had finished, we'd fallen in love. That was pushing it, but neither of us bothered to contradict them as we were buying into the fantasy as much as
everyone else was. We both easily ignored the middle part where Jason
had totally screwed me over and then put me on as producer only after
he thought the film was going to be a total flop. But who cared about
the truth? We were in Hollywood after all. Maybe it was because Jason
and I were such good friends or perhaps it was because we were sleeping together, but we just bounced off each other in the most organic
way. I thought I'd be terrified, but it was actually a lot of fun.

I was still flying high when I screeched at great speeds into the garage
at The Agency. I wound my way down into the depth of parking hell and
jumped out of my car while it was practically still moving. With all the
excitement I'd been a bit distracted at the office lately. But thanks to
the nomination and all the attention I was getting, Amber had backed
off slightly. It seemed that all of her evil scheming had ended up working in my favor. She had gone to such lengths to exclude me from the

goings-on at the office that I found it remarkably easy now to spend most of my time these days playing Su Doku and fantasizing with friends about what famous designers might lend me a dress for the awards ceremony. Amber was now in absolute control and she was quickly learning that it wasn't all it was cracked up to be. The bonus was that she was so busy she didn't have a spare moment to torment me. Whenever something needed to be done now, I just turned to Amber and said that I had no idea how to do it and I was sure she did it better, anyway. And no task she could think up seemed to bother me, I was so ebullient. I was even thrilled to do the coffee run, as it gave me some time to do notes on Jason's latest script and potentially my next producing gig.

The elevator doors opened on the ground floor of the garage and I waved at the Josés as a handsome young actor joined me in the car. I was struggling to figure out if he was that sexy English actor from *Match Point* when a hand flew into the elevator and pushed the closing doors open. It was tall, skinny José. He looked at me gravely and a feeling of dread filled the tiny space.

"Lizzie. *Borra con el codo lo que escribe con la mano,*" he said urgently.

"Your hand doesn't know . . . Oh José, you know my Spanish sucks and you know I know your English is better than mine. What does it mean?"

"The left hand doesn't know what the right hand is doing," the cute actor with the double-barreled name, which I could never remember, said with a rakish smile.

"Thanks," I said, and then turned back to José. "Okay, now that I understand the words, do you mind telling me what it means?"

"*Con paciencia y con maña, un elefante se comio una araña,*" José said even more urgently.

"Little strokes fell big oaks," blue eyes translated again. I really wasn't liking the sound of this.

"José, are you trying to tell me that something bad is going to happen to me?" I said, looking around. Just then Katherine Watson arrived behind José and stepped past him and into the elevator. I saw José nod and then disappear into the parking garage.

"Morning, Katherine," I said, trying to mask my concern. She nodded at me. Did I see a pitying look in her eyes or was I just imagining it? The Josés had never been wrong before. Maybe I should just get off the elevator now and go home. I could call in sick, but for how long? I was already doing minimal work at the moment, not showing up at all seemed to be taking it a little bit too far.

And though I was an Oscar nominee, it made absolutely no difference to my empty bank account. I was spending money at the moment like it was going out of style. I'm sure my credit card company thought I had a chunk of the grosses at the rate I was charging, but unfortunately that wasn't the case. I certainly wasn't complaining. It just seemed that everyone in town thought I was minted after my nomination and somehow it was just easier to behave like I was. So whenever something arrived with the Washington Mutual logo on it—my bank— or a familiar random PO box—my credit card—I stuffed it into a drawer to deal with later. They were stacking up, and I knew that one day soon I'd have to deal or I'd end up in debtors' prison.

So on the ride up to the top floor, I experienced a bit of a reality check. Nothing bad was allowed to happen to me for a couple of months. I needed my health, my job, and my sanity in order to get my finances in order. Once I was solvent again and had paid and recycled the bills, come what may. I decided to make a renewed effort to get along with Amber and try and be as helpful and indispensable as possible. Katherine and I stepped off the elevator at the same time and she put a hand on my arm.

"Elizabeth. Don't lose heart, okay?" she said enigmatically. Then she smiled and walked off. I stopped in my tracks. Okay, something was going very wrong and I was totally unprepared. I didn't want to go any farther. I could see Amber's empty desk in the distance next to mine. I glanced at my watch. It was nine-fifty-five. Amber was usually always here before me and why was Scott's door closed? Scott was never in before eleven.

I walked slowly to my desk and noticed a Coffee Bean cup sitting on Amber's desk and her coat. I felt the cup, still hot. Then I tiptoed to Scott's door. I heard voices and jumped back guiltily when the door suddenly flew open. Amber walked out looking all morose and tearful.

"Elizabeth, can you come in here and shut the door behind you, please?" Scott said. As I passed Amber I was sure she flashed me a quick but deadly grin.

"Sure, Scott," I said as I walked into his office and shut the door quietly behind me.

I sat down opposite him and tried to get a good look in his eyes but he just kept looking around me at the floor, the wall, the computer.

"So, Lizzie. I've been meaning to talk to you about this for months, but I guess I just hoped it would go away." Scott glanced at me for a brief second and the look he gave me made my heart stop. The problem was that we'd muddled that fine line between boss and friend. And now we were about to pay the price.

"Scott, if you mean the missing papers? I can explain, you know. I burned them. I know it's stupid, but I was addicted to Su Doku so instead of actually filing them I put them in the trash and lit them on fire."

I breathed a big sigh of relief having finally revealed my big secret. Scott of all people had to understand, no matter what Lara said. It was lazy and I probably deserved to be fired, but he would never fire me over something that unimportant. That's why I loved Scott. He hated to be the bad guy. But when he started to laugh, I knew things were much more dire than I'd suspected. It wasn't a jolly "aren't you a silly, hopeless case?" laugh. It was more of a bitter, hard "you're shit on my shoe" laugh.

"You see, Lizzie. If that were the problem I wouldn't have to fire my wife's best friend and the godmother of my son." Scott said something else but the only thing I heard was the word "fire" reverberating through my head.

"Fire?" I repeated. Scott became immediately defensive and jumped up from his desk and started to pace.

"I mean, Jesus Christ, Lizzie. If you have money problems you could have just come and talked to me," he said passionately. How on earth did Scott know about my money problems?

"Well, Scott," I started slowly, "I thought that my silly financial affairs would bore you. I mean, I spent a bit too much on those Christian Louboutins, but I don't think it would really count as a problem. Yes, the Crème de la Mer set me back, but the way I look at it is that it's a whole lot cheaper than a facelift in twenty years." I laughed lightly.

"Lizzie, cut the shit!" Scott barked. I blinked back shocked tears. "How could you blackmail our clients, Lizzie? Sell photos to the press? It's just so fucking low and sleazy. Do you know I've been on the phone with three different stars convincing them not to press charges? Though I should probably let them. A little time in jail might straighten out that drug problem of yours."

"What?" I said stupidly. I was just too confused to even defend myself. Scott walked to the window and stared out at the street.

"You better fucking have a serious coke habit, Lizzie, or otherwise you're just the most reprehensible scum of the earth I've ever met in my life."

"Scott. I haven't blackmailed anyone. I have no idea what you're talking about. Who said I did? Amber? Well let me tell you, she's been out to get me from day one. It's like living in a constant game of dodgeball. But I have never blackmailed anybody. Call the police. Have people press charges. Because at least then I could defend myself, for Christ's sake. Then they'd at least have to come forward and show some evidence instead of just hurling nasty invisible arrows." I was in a fury. Finally I was standing up for myself; it's just a shame I hadn't done it with Amber several months ago.

Scott picked something off his desk and threw it in my lap.

"You want evidence, Lizzie? Well, there's all the proof I need. Explain that. But you know you can't. You got caught," he said. I picked up the paper. It was a copy of my bank statement.

"It's my bank statement. But that's not my balance," I said, totally confused by the twenty-thousand-dollar total sum.

"Now, Lizzie, you're going to have to do better than that," he said.

There was a knock at the door and Katherine Watson walked in. Amber was hovering at the door, listening.

"Scott, I swear to you, I have no idea where the money came from. Someone else must have made that deposit." I looked to Katherine for support. She had just said something nice in the elevator. But she just looked at me with a punishing gaze.

"Then when this mystery money appeared in your account, Lizzie, why didn't you mention it to anyone or call the bank? Instead, you seemed to go on a shopping spree," Scott said. It looked so bad and everything I said seemed to get me into deeper and deeper trouble. This was incredibly serious.

"I haven't looked at my bank balance in months. I knew I was overdrawn. Someone put that money in my account to frame me, Scott," I pleaded.

"Yeah, Lizzie, they went to all these efforts to blackmail someone and then they frame you. Why? Because you flirted with their boyfriend? Doesn't add up."

"Occam's Razor," Katherine said calmly. "The simplest explanation is the best one," she said. I looked at her for a second.

"The money that was paid into your account will be withdrawn today. We found the negatives taped to the bottom of your chair so that won't be a problem." Scott pressed on.

"You found what negatives?" I said dumbly.

"The negatives you were blackmailing John with. Of him cheating on his wife? The ones we'd already bought off a scumbag paparazzo and kept under lock and key in this office. Don't play dumb now. Please. We all remember your fancy degree from Georgetown. I should have guessed this is what they taught you in Washington."

I saw Amber laugh but she stopped immediately when Katherine swung her head around and caught her eye.

"Elizabeth. We'd like you to leave the building immediately. Do not take anything from this office. Someone will pack your personal effects after making sure you haven't stolen any other piece of Agency property," Katherine said quickly.

"I can explain this. I don't know how, but it's all not true. I would never blackmail anybody. Come on, Scott, you know me?" I begged.

"Do I, Lizzie? I thought so," he said sadly. "I thought you were family, but that's the strange thing about this town. You make a family out of people you don't really know very well. I'll need you out of the guest-house by the time I get back from Sundance. I don't want you around my son and wife."

I almost fell to the floor at this last blow. I couldn't prove my innocence, so the only thing there was to do was retreat in apparent disgrace. I stood up, unable to look at either of them, and walked to my desk past Amber with my head hung low. I felt so ashamed yet I hadn't done anything. But I knew that Amber had already told everyone in the office that I was guilty and they all probably believed it. I could just imagine all the other assistants gleefully eating popcorn as they watched the fantastic rise and fall of Lizzie Miller. My apparent total lack of moral values was probably reassuring to them. It made them feel that the pinnacle of success in this town, the Oscar nomination, was still sacred. It confirmed their hopes and suspicions that the only way an assistant could have been nominated for an Oscar was through foul play.

The case against me was so foolproof I almost believed it myself. It occurred to me as I grabbed my coat and purse that maybe I was Sybil and had seven different personalities. What if Lizzie just didn't remember my alter ego's bad deeds? As one of The Agency's security guards searched my handbag and pockets as if I were a criminal, it occurred to me how absolutely fucking nuts this was.

I walked from the hallowed portals of The Agency in disgrace. I didn't want to talk to anyone or even make eye contact on the way out. I took the elevator straight to the basement, too embarrassed to even see the Josés. I hoped in my heart of hearts that they'd be the lone pair who believed my innocence. They had tried to warn me, after all. But for the moment I couldn't handle their disappointment if this wasn't the case. I drove out of the basement into the light. Maybe it was the rapid dilation of my pupils but more likely the fatal blow that had been dealt in Scott's office: I started to cry. I had to pull over or risk the entire thing looking like a suicide attempt confirming my guilt.

I sat in my car and looked out the window at the grass growing along the curbside. A fresh, warm spring breeze blew in the window and it occurred to me that Katherine wasn't wrong. "The simplest explanation is the best one." I had been set up. And I knew that Amber had orchestrated my demise. I wasn't going to take this lying down. It was just a matter of time before I proved my innocence. I just had to go home, get over the shock, and mount my defense.

I dialed Lara's number and she picked up instantly. "Sweetie. I just heard and ripped Scott a new asshole. I told him he'd have to fucking move out before you did. I know that English bitch set you up, and we're going to prove it if I have to hire Anthony Pellicano from prison. Okay? Are you all right?"

"I don't know." I sniffed pathetically into the phone, so thankful to have this brilliantly strong woman as my ally. I needed all the support I could get at the moment. But where was I going to go? No matter what

Lara said, I couldn't stay with her. I didn't want to cause trouble in her marriage. It was a daily challenge already. "Listen, Lara. If you don't mind, I'll stay until Scott gets back, but then I'll go stay with Jason until we figure this out, okay?"

I heard a slight sigh of relief but she protested like the good friend that she was.

After I hung up the phone, I got back on the road and marveled with horror at my life. The current highs and lows were almost too much to handle. I thought about what would have happened if I'd never left D.C. I breathed a sigh of relief, thinking about home and the safety and predictability that life used to provide. I thought of my parents and how destroyed they'd be at the mere hint that their daughter was involved in something as sordid as this. But at least I knew the story was safe from the press. No matter how much Amber or another assistant would want to leak it, they knew better. This level of scandal was negative publicity a place like The Agency didn't need. And then John's affair and the photos would be out of the bag and the entire thing would do them a lot more damage than it did me. As I merged into the oncoming traffic, I promised myself that if I managed to jump this hurdle I would seek out a simpler life. No more creating drama where none existed. I didn't need to. There seemed to be plenty enough in everyday life.

NINETEEN

Hollywood is like being nowhere
and talking to nobody about nothing.

—Michelangelo Antonioni

In the run up to the Oscars, I had more party invites than I'd received in my entire life, but none of the events were as high in entertainment value as the one I attended at Nathalie Cook's apartment with the fifteen-million-dollar divorcées in Malibu. Since the day Luke was seen to publicly cheat on me, I'd become an honorary divorcée in the eyes of Nathalie and the other ladies who crunched (both settlement figures and their midriffs) in her building. And even though I'd avoided the blandishments of their book clubs and never once forwarded one of her *International Fine Woman Day—please send this to ten beautiful, intelligent, fabulous women of your acquaintance* e-mails, I must say that when the piece of card arrived requesting the pleasure of my company at

Mojitos To End Third-World Debt

I was sorely tempted. Not simply because it was impossible to resist an offer to rid the world of economic evils by sipping alcohol, but also because I really wanted to know who did the best "baby hair" in town, and Nathalie et al. were guaranteed to know.

Since I'd been informed by Lara that the secret to eternal beauty was to return to the hair color you were born with, I'd become horrified by my brassy highlights and could hardly exist another day without going back to my roots. I'd even got my mom to scan me a picture of me aged six months in a bid for accuracy. Though with only three hairs on my head it was hard to tell whether I ought to opt for caramel or vanilla. And as I literally only had a few weeks left until the big night itself, when I was to show up at the Kodak Theatre and hold my own against Nicole Kidman, I really needed to get on with all that looking-good stuff.

I had six dresses hanging in my room that friends who had friends who were young designers had lent to me, but to be honest, they were all pretty weird. One of them I couldn't work out which was the arm-hole and which was the neck, and got stuck in it when I tried it on; another was made from recycled yogurt cartons—and much as I endeavor to save the planet on a daily basis, to the point of pulling the plug out of my kettle when I go to sleep—I couldn't imagine Grace Kelly compromising her timeless chic for fear of wantonly squandering a meter of velvet. So I figured that sometime in the next few days I was going to call Talitha and ask her to help me out with borrowing something from a more established designer. Like Coco Chanel, say, who'd been dead longer than the time it took a yogurt carton to rot.

In the meantime, though, I was going to enjoy the cachet that this Oscar nomination had bestowed on me, and Nathalie's was a good place to start. Lara was my partner-in-crime in all this as Jason always seemed to be taking care of the business side of things. "Sweetheart, I'll go to the press junket, you just think about your skirt."

For some reason men didn't seem to know the difference between a dress and a skirt, but that was fine; what wasn't so fine was that Jason seemed to have forgotten how in the early days of the movie he was only interested in my opinion, my notes, and my determination to get the script read by as many agents and financiers as possible. He'd have gladly pushed me out of the door stark naked if he had to. But now he seemed a little too willing to relegate me to arm-candy status. "Honey, if we win best movie and you *have* to come up onstage, that's great, just look pretty and let me make the speech, okay? I mean, I know that it's unlikely, but if we do win you might go into shock and start speaking up there."

"You didn't mind me speaking when we were taking it to IEG," I said, reminding him of a very tough meeting with a very exacting film finance company when he'd played the silent auteur in his fraying college sweater and I'd talked numbers with the formidable CEO.

"Baby, that was a long time ago," he said as if to a five-year-old. "Just let me handle it, okay?"

"Sure," I said. I guessed it was his movie, after all. But still it made me a little uneasy and I didn't tell Lara because I knew she'd blow a gasket and never shut up about how much I'd earned my credit as producer and how Jason would be equally recompensed for his passion when it came to the Best Director nomination. And financially. So I smiled and focused on my hair instead.

Lara and I arrived at the party and were hit with a strange sense of déjà vu. "It doesn't seem two minutes since we were here that night for that weird vaginal deodorant party and you found out about Luke's cheating, does it?" Lara said as we pulled into a parking spot.

"Are you kidding? It seems like forever ago," I said with relief, though during the past few weeks my mind had been flickering like cheap strip-lighting back to Luke. Now that Jason had turned into Misogynist of the Year with a nomination in the Most Selective Memory category, I couldn't help but remember how supportive Luke had always been of what I did. Even if I'd made vaginal deodorants for a living like Nathalie, he'd have been proud of my achievements, I imagined.

"Elizabeth, Lara, come in!" Nathalie greeted us at the door with her usual manic bounce. "You're both looking great! Congratulations, sister!" she said to me. "Do you know what you're going to wear?" she yelled as she led us to the sitting room. See, what chance had poor Jason of thinking that women gave a shit about anything other than a skirt if a woman with an MA in Oriental studies who spoke Mandarin could think of nothing else?

"Not yet," I confessed, "but I do need to ask you about my hair." Fuck it, I decided, if Harvey Weinstein looked as cute as Gwyneth Paltrow when he collected one of his numerous Academy Awards, he'd be even more powerful than ever, right? So as long as I did a good job, I could worry about my hair, too.

"Ask away, but let me get you a Mojito first; remember, it's for a good cause," she said as she tripped over to the kitchen where a host of very handsome gay men were mincing over the mint and exchanging barbs about the amount of sugar in the perfect Mojito.

The thing is that that night Lara and I never actually got our Mojito. We stood in the room for a couple of minutes waiting for Nathalie to return, admiring the remodeling of her apartment—which was now in the style of the bathroom of the Hôtel de la Mirande in Avignon, France, apparently, but it still looked great—when we spotted Amber on the balcony, deep in conversation with somebody more powerful than herself, so we turned the other way and began discussing "the floor," which was black-and-white harlequin, and doubtless indistinguishable from its French counterpart.

"Who let her in?" Lara spat.

"Only one person who would," I said as we looked in the art deco mirror in front of us and surveyed the room behind us. "And there she is, Katherine Watson," I said. "God, that's annoying."

"No it's not. You're at the top of the heap looking down on them now," Lara reminded me. "You've got what everyone in this room would give their left tit for."

"What?" I said as I watched Amber walk toward the kitchen on her cell phone, probably hoping everyone would think that she was something way more important than an assistant.

"You've made it, Lizzie, whether you win on the night or not, you've done it."

"No, but it's not as if I've been in the business twenty-five years and made a hundred great movies," I said sheepishly.

"This is Hollywood, you're as big as your last movie, so go over there and capitalize," Lara said firmly, taking my elbow and spinning me around. "Come on, let's go."

But no sooner had I got it into my head that I had every much of a right to circulate at this party along with the woman who'd fired me and the witch who'd orchestrated the firing, than I was reminded of what I'd left behind at The Agency.

"Look what the cat dragged in," Amber said, as Lara and I collided with her on our way to hunt down our stray Mojitos. She was looking much less plain than she used to; she'd taken to wearing expensive, architectural, high-design clothes that cleverly seemed to offset her symmetrical face and made her look, dare I say it, stylish and very affluent.

"Wow, somebody's been buying lots of Jil Sander for her," Lara said as she too clocked Amber's attire as she made her way toward us in a satin shirt and black skirt. "I wonder who she's fucking?"

"Amber," I said, and stopped in my tracks. She put her phone down on the counter and picked up a drink without missing a beat. "How are you sleeping at night? I hear the guilt becomes harder to bear with time."

"Guilt, are you joking?" she scoffed. "I'm loving every minute behind your desk, and in a couple of weeks I've got an interview at Paramount for a development executive position."

"Great, well maybe you'll be working on Lizzie's next movie," Lara said with a snide grin. "Or haven't you decided whether you're going to take the deal at Paramount yet, Lizzie?" Lara turned to me.

"Well, let's just say it's between Universal and Warner Brothers at this stage." I shrugged. "Though if Paramount comes through with some great offices and a golf cart, then, who knows."

"Guess you wouldn't want to go to Paramount in case you ran into Luke Lloyd," Amber said with all the ease of a pro tennis player serving an ace. "I hear he's only dating the most beautiful women in town these days. It wouldn't exactly help rebuild your shattered ego after that humiliating dumping, would it?"

"Oh, that was a long time ago." I managed a smile, even though I felt as if I'd just received a body blow. "Before Jason."

"Oh yeah, Jason Blum. Well I guess he has a few weeks left of anonymity before he hits the big time and realizes he's saddled with a loser. But by then he'll have 'people' to get rid of you, so it won't matter. He won't have to dump you to your face. But then I suppose you're used to that, aren't you?"

"Oh well, nice running into you, Amber. I hope whoever's husband you're fucking finds out really soon," Lara said as we walked away, leaving Amber as speechless as I'd ever seen her.

"Do you really think she's having an affair with a married man?" I asked Lara as we followed a waitress with a tray of cocktails onto the balcony.

"I *know* she is," Lara replied. "She's wearing expensive but unsexy clothes. A man never likes his mistress to look cheap or available so he'd have bought those for her. She looks 'kept' but off the market. She has very discreet but insanely expensive little diamonds in her ears and she's lost her puppy fat so obviously spends all her weekend at the gym. Which means her married man probably has a family, too. Remember, I know these things. I was a mistress once."

"That's genius." I laughed as we watched Amber tuck her hair primly behind her ear and look riveted by Nathalie's conversation. "And she did look completely thrown when you mentioned the married man."

"Thank God those days are gone," Lara said. "So this party's kind of boring. Shall we make a break for Souplantation and get an 'all you can eat'?"

"Sounds great," I said, and abandoned the idea of the cocktail I was reaching for.

We were heading for the door, trying not to let our hostess see that we were making a break for the border, when Lara remembered she'd left her cardigan on the balcony.

"Wait, I'll just be a minute," she said and fought her way back through the Mojito-sipping millionairesses. I was standing in the doorway to the kitchen and fiddling with my purse so I wouldn't be engaged in conversation with some woman about the merits of the birthing pools at Cedars Sinai, when I heard one of the caterers shout out, "Hey, ladies, someone's cell's going off in my face!" He was clearly having a stressful moment because he picked up the phone and held it aloft. But nobody came forward. A few of the women looked up from their Mojitos in an affronted fashion—how dare staff interrupt their inane banter? But he persisted as the phone rang again. "Okay, it's 555-723-5698. Who's phone is it?" he called out. Clearly feeling a little premenstrual.

"Oh, that's my husband." I saw Katherine Watson look slightly embarrassed as she waved her hand in the air and stepped forward to reclaim her phone. "Sorry about that, guys."

"No problem," the caterer said as he handed over the offending item and spun around to deal with the more serious business of canapés.

"Oh, hang on a minute," Katherine said as she looked at the phone. "It's not actually my phone." For a second she seemed puzzled. Then Amber appeared out of the bathroom.

"Oh, is that my phone? I must have left it on the counter." She didn't seem to notice that a curious hush had fallen over the party as everyone half-watched Katherine wrestle with some unidentified conundrum. "Sorry, I was in the bathroom. Was it ringing?"

"Yeah." Katherine scowled and kept holding the phone, still staring at it as if she were expecting it to tell her something. "Amber?"

"Yes?" Amber now looked equally curious. In fact, the only person who looked as if she knew exactly what was going on was Lara, whose face had suddenly lit up with anticipation.

"Why was my husband calling you?"

"Your husband?"

"Michael. He just called on your phone." Katherine stared hard at Amber, but she remained inscrutable.

"Maybe he was trying to get a hold of you?" Amber shrugged and made as if to return to her cocktail chatter. Katherine pulled her phone out of her purse.

"He didn't call me," she said, looking at her slick black cell phone as if she were computing the facts very quickly.

"Oh I'm sure there's a perfectly good reason." Amber started to fluff her lines slightly and waved her hand around too much, as if trying to dust away invisible evidence.

"Let's find out, shall we?" Katherine looked at the phone and pressed the unfamiliar buttons. "Let's call him and see what he wants."

"Okay," Amber said in a casual way that reeked of insincerity and panic. "I'll call him back." She put her hand out to take the phone from Katherine's grasp, but Katherine held on tight.

"I'll call," Katherine said calmly, though standing as close as I was I noticed that her hand shook as she pressed the Call button and put the phone to her ear. The entire room had stopped what it was doing and was now blatantly engaged in the drama that was unfolding.

Though I'm certain that, as the last actor to have appeared on this particular stage, I was relieved, not only that I wasn't the center of attention this time, but also that whatever sordid tale was unfurling before us, Amber was looking very unlikely to come out of it smelling of roses. An embalmed silence enveloped the room, and from where I stood I could hear the ringing tone.

"Hi, sweetheart, you done yet?" A man's voice was unwittingly broadcast through the receiver.

"Michael?"

"Amber?" The man's voice could be heard even more clearly than before now, as everyone held their collective breath.

"Actually, Michael, it's Katherine," Katherine informed her husband, then continued coolly. "Did you want Amber?"

"I . . . er . . . I . . ."

"I thought so," Katherine said and snapped the phone shut. Then she handed it back to Amber.

"We were discussing your birthday present," Amber said with all the conviction of an accomplished pathological liar. "It was going to be a surprise."

"Oh, it *was*," Katherine replied. And you had to admire her composure. The only sign of agitation she displayed was brushing her hair off her face with a hint the obsessive compulsive. Otherwise she didn't miss a beat.

"How long have you been sleeping with my husband?" Katherine asked with no emotion. Amber didn't flinch.

"I told you, we were planning your birthday present."

"Where did you first meet?" Katherine persisted, and it was all the women in the room could do not to lean too far forward and fall off their proverbial seats.

Finally it appeared as if Amber had met her match, and if any of us had underestimated Katherine Watson and mistaken her sweetness and fairness for lack of mettle, we had our minds altered swiftly. The look in her eyes was one of ferocious determination, her will was like steel. And Amber, despite being Mussolini manqué, didn't come close to being a worthy opponent of a girl from New Jersey who'd paid her own way through Harvard and survived years as the pretty protégée of one of Hollywood's greatest agents and most legendary shits.

"We've been having an affair for a year," Amber said, and actually raised her chin in a defiant manner. "And you can't fire me for it."

"I know. But I will find something to fire you for." She smiled.

"It wouldn't be very good publicity for The Agency when I sue," Amber said, still with the same shameless sneer on her face.

"No, but it would be so much fun." Katherine smiled. Then she turned to Nathalie. "I'm so sorry, but I'm going to leave now. I have to go home and scream at my husband. Great party."

"Oh, it was my pleasure," Nathalie said and gave Katherine a kiss on the cheek. It was definitely an impressive display of coolness under fire, but then I suppose that was the least one would expect from women who regularly underwent nostril-hair waxing.

As Katherine walked by Amber, she hesitated a moment, and then reached out both hands and tore the diamonds out of her ears. "Oh, and I'm sure you'll understand if I have these back, but they're my children's college education. And before you think of suing for them back—they were bought with my money because my lazy bastard husband hasn't done a day's work in five years." And with that Katherine made her way to the door without looking back. Amber just stood there with bleeding ears and a faraway expression on her face.

"So what do you think's going to happen to her now?" I asked Lara as we sat in the lounge at the Chateau and celebrated the preposterously satisfying exposure of my nemesis with a round of cocktails. We'd decided to change venue from Souplantation when it became apparent that tomato-and-rice soup with a side salad was never going to cut it as a victory supper.

"Amber?" Lara asked.

I nodded.

"Well I guess they'll find out about the blackmail eventually. Then she'll get arrested, get a trial date, and find herself a gazillionaire to pay her legal fees, then dump him when she's acquitted. She'll be the head of an agency or studio within three years."

"Seriously?" I said as our cocktails arrived looking good enough to dive into after a night of deferred alcohol. "I thought she'd at least get deported."

"You're so naïve sometimes, Lizzie." Lara shook her head and we raised our glasses. "Here's to Mr. Katherine Watson." We clinked and sipped. "No, sadly, she'll probably just find her career's accelerated because she'll become a minor celebrity for wearing great clothes to her trial. Then she'll be invited to even more parties than you and every company in town will want to hire her because she's ruthless and famous and famous for being ruthless."

"Fuck, this place is twisted." I shook my head.

"I know, but her downfall's going to be so much fun to watch." Lara grinned. "But you know you'll never get rid of Amber. She'll be snapping at your heels for the rest of your life in Hollywood."

"Well, best just enjoy it while I can, then, and make sure that when I give evidence at her trial it makes her sound as boring as possible."

"Exactly," Lara said, as we finally tasted our first Mojito of the night, though it was saving nobody's lives but our own.

TWENTY

In Hollywood, brides keep the
bouquets and throw away the groom.

—Groucho Marx

This was supposed to be one of the most exciting days of my life. I was invited to the hottest ticket in town and yet I could barely muster up enough enthusiasm to get in the shower. I had always thought that the Oscars were a big deal or that Elton John's birthday party was the pinnacle of invites, but I was wrong. Nothing seemed to compare to the amount of hype surrounding the wedding of Emerald Everhart to Jizzy James. The difference was that both those parties were events that your above average punter could get into with the right connections but this wedding was for a select group of three hundred only. And no amount of begging, borrowing, or stealing was going to get you an invite at the last minute. And I knew right from the horse's mouth that it was all being done as a publicity stunt, so I was damn certain the guest list wouldn't be overloaded with Jizzy's great aunts from Texas or Em's hairdressing cousins from Missouri.

A wedding invitation had arrived in the mail a month ago and I'd kept it for my scrapbook. Not because it was a celebrity wedding, but because it was the most beautiful thing I'd ever seen in my life. The paper weighed as much as a small child and was the most magical shade of green that made you dream of fairies and secret gardens. The names of the bride and groom were spelled out in tiny pressed flowers and they were even scented with something that smelled like a combination of moss and night-blooming jasmine. But no matter how many times I looked at it, I couldn't find the location of the wedding. I searched the eighteen envelopes within the envelope for a missing bit, but nothing was there. Poor Emerald. She'd gone to all this effort and obviously hadn't caught the printer's mistake.

I wandered over to the main house to discuss the disaster with Lara, and she just laughed at me. Apparently leaving the location blank was the only way to show you mattered in the world. It was intentional in order to throw off the paparazzi. Scott had told Lara that Emerald and Jizzy's publicists were planning four different mock weddings for the same day in different locations around the globe. They were casting a group of Emerald look-alikes and using mannequins as guests. I was impressed with Emerald's efforts at privacy until Lara explained that they'd sold the story to *Vanity Fair* and were getting the costs of their multimillion-dollar wedding covered, but the deal was contingent upon no pictures sneaking out in the press.

When a courier in an armed vehicle arrived the day before the wedding, I had an absolutely terrifying moment thinking the police had come to arrest me. Lara and I had spent the last few days since I'd been fired sitting on the guesthouse floor going through all my bills, receipts, schedules, and notes looking for something that would prove that I hadn't tried to blackmail anyone. But the result of all our efforts had the opposite outcome. The closer we studied it, the more guilty I appeared. Due to the award nomination, I had been spending like I'd just married Donald Trump. I was even moving into a bungalow in Venice next month that I could barely afford, and to make matters worse, I'd paid them first, last, and security in *cash*—my per diem, of course, but to avoid the taxman, the production had given it to me under the table. Lara and I were at a loss. She had sweetly offered to pay for a detective to follow Amber, and I was seriously thinking about taking her up on the offer. I would pay her back no matter how long it took, but I couldn't think of any other way to clear my name. It occurred to me that if I ever saw Katherine Watson again, I could ask her if she wanted to go halfsies. I bet she was longing to see Amber go down more than I was. I hadn't even told Jason yet, because he'd called from a press junket in New York and was so excited about everything that I didn't want to freak him out. And to be honest, I was ashamed to even repeat the accusations.

As I lay in bed and looked out the window I decided that today I was going to have a good time. As far as I was aware no one knew the sordid details of my departure from The Agency yet, so I might as well go and have one last hurrah, wining and dining with the rich and famous before I had to go into hiding and leave the country. And after the scare the day before with the invitation delivery, I was certain that my life had been cut short by a good five years. I'd actually grabbed my passport and wallet and was hiding in the bathroom when the armed guards had knocked at the guesthouse door. Luckily Lara and Scott were invited to the wedding, too, so the guards had left my directions and final invite in Lara's care. But for some not-that-mysterious reason, my invitation was missing the plus-guest line. I had been invited solo, even though I had told Emerald I was dating Jason. I was sure I'd be on call at some point in the day.

The shower lifted my spirits a tiny bit, but they plummeted back down again as I took out the red dress and sexy Louboutin shoes that had been part of my demise. I wanted to take them back to Barneys, but I knew if I did I'd have an anxiety attack trying to get dressed for the wedding. And my life was anxiety-provoking enough at the moment. As I put the dress on, I felt like Scarlet O'Hara in that scene where Rhett makes her go and face the wolves at the party alone in that red and black dress. Though she's innocent, of course. Somehow this memory gave me strength and I made an extra effort when I put on my makeup and slid into my shoes. I could survive this thing. I knew I could. I was innocent and the truth would come out in time. The only problem was, how much time did I have?

We'd all arrived at the requested location on the top of Malibu Canyon, but instead of being ushered into a tent and given a cocktail and canapé we were hurried into a fleet of waiting helicopters. They'd staggered our arrival times so that no one would be kept waiting, and I was in the first batch. The ride gave me a new perspective on life. But it wasn't the coastline or all the tiny little houses that made me alight from that helicopter feeling like a new woman. It was who was on board that did that. I was the first one to climb in, and as I made myself comfortable in the back I looked up to see Katherine Watson. My face went hot with shame but instead of looking the other way and giving me the cold shoulder, she walked purposefully in my direction. I wanted off the helicopter but everyone was pouring in the door and to try and get off now would make a total scene. So I just turned my gaze away and looked out the window. I knew this had been a bad idea. I shouldn't have come.

Katherine took the seat next to me. She didn't say anything and neither did I as the excited guests chattered away and said hello to the secret circle of the rich and famous that I definitely wasn't part of. I counted the seconds wondering why she felt the need to take the one seat next to me when there had been an entire empty helicopter to sit in. But as the propellers started to whirr and the noise increased to a cacophony, Katherine tapped me on the leg to get my attention. I turned to her, braced for the assault.

"Elizabeth, I'm so sorry," Katherine said as quietly as possible. She looked around to make sure that no one else was listening. "I know you didn't blackmail anybody and so does Scott." Was I hearing her correctly? "I wanted to come to you sooner, but I couldn't until I got the fingerprints back from the lab. Amber was smart enough to wear gloves when handling the negatives but forgot to wipe the Scotch tape she used to stick the negatives to your chair."

"But why are you whispering?" I said loudly, wanting to announce it to the world.

"I know this is a lot to ask, Elizabeth, but we need to keep this under wraps just for a couple of more days. The Scotch tape, though it exonerates you in our eyes, isn't the proof we need to really get Amber. And I can't even begin to tell you how much I want to do that," she said with a rueful grin.

I looked at Katherine and knew she meant every word. Amber had ruined my life temporarily. The damage she'd done was thankfully now fixable. But she'd struck a mortal blow to Katherine. Amber had destroyed her family. Her kids would now be a product of divorce and her faith in human nature would never be the same again. And the worst part was that Katherine had invited her into her house as a friend.

I nodded my head slowly. "So Scott knows the truth, right?"

"Yes. He never wanted to believe it in the first place but Amber was so insidious. She even had me convinced. She's been planning it for months. The police are still involved. They think she's blackmailing more clients than we've been informed of, which is why your firing had to be so real. I suspected then that something was going on. But Amber has to be certain that you've been blamed so she can feel secure to operate again. It'll just be a matter of time. And in the meantime, you will be paid your full salary and I will make sure The Agency compensates you for your pain and suffering."

"Listen, Katherine, I don't want to be compensated. My salary would be nice until I get my job back, but besides that I just want my name cleared."

"I understand that. . . . You know, I used to think I was a good judge of character." Katherine sighed and closed her eyes for a brief, painful moment.

I breathed a huge sigh of relief, feeling a tremendous burden lift from my shoulders. I wanted to jump up and down and celebrate. I wanted to call Lara, who was on the next shift of helicopters, but felt I couldn't be too celebratory in front of Katherine and I was sure Scott had already told her. I just had to manage to keep it all quiet for a bit longer. I truly wanted to see Amber go down and go down hard. No little slap on the wrist would do for that conniving cow.

"Katherine," I said somberly. "Can I ask you a favor?"

"Anything, Lizzie."

"Can you get her deported?" I asked.

Katherine started to laugh. "I think I could manage that. I do run one of the most powerful agencies in Hollywood. There's not much that we can't do if it's necessary." She winked at me as the helicopter descended and the pilot spoke into our headphones.

"Hello, guests, welcome to Catalina. This is your final destination today. I do hope you enjoyed the ride, and send my best to the happy couple." I looked down at my red dress and my red-soled shoes and smiled for the first time in days.

Katherine and I stepped off the helicopter but went our separate ways. She apologized profusely before we landed as she said she would have loved to have a good old newly single girl time, but she didn't want our coziness filtering back to Amber somehow. And I agreed. Now that I knew my innocence was in the bag, I didn't care if no one talked to me all night.

But I didn't get a chance to feel lonely. I literally had just walked into the cocktail area and been handed a glass of vintage champagne when a woman with a headset hurried up to me.

"Elizabeth Miller, can you come with me?" she said officiously.

"Look," I said defensively, "I'm invited and I haven't blackmailed anybody, okay? I have proof." The woman looked at me strangely and then at my glass of champagne.

"I'm sorry, Miss Miller. It's just that Emerald asked me to bring you to her the second you arrived. I should have made myself clear. Would you come with me, please?" she asked pleadingly. I blushed, embarrassed at behaving like such a paranoid freak. Obviously the last few days had taken their toll. I smiled and followed the stressed-out wedding planner. I couldn't help but recall a similar situation the first time I'd met Emerald at the airport. I wondered what trouble she'd gotten herself into now. I felt truly flattered, though, that she had obviously called upon me to fix it.

I stepped into the suite and struggled to see anything through the gloom. All the curtains were drawn and the lights were out. The wedding planner quickly shut the door behind me. I took a step forward and heard a crunching sound. As my eyes adjusted to the low-level lighting, I looked down and realized I was walking on the remnants of various vases. There were white roses covering the floor. There had obviously been a serious meltdown. I heard sniffling in a corner.

"Em? It's Lizzie. Can I come in?"

"I've been waiting for you. What took you so long?" she said accusatorily. I decided to ignore this as I'd always heard how stressed out brides got on their wedding day.

Instead, I followed her voice, as I'd done so many times before, and picked my way around the broken vases. I finally saw her silhouette seated at a dressing table in front of an enormous mirror.

"Can I open the curtains, sweetie?" I asked gently.

"I guess so." She sniffed pathetically. "I just don't want anyone taking my picture at the moment. But I guess it's probably safe as the perimeter is surrounded with armed guards. Jizzy's taken this whole privacy thing a bit too far if you ask me. Something about his silly Hermetic Order of the Golden Dawn," she said with annoyance. "Do you know this place had to be blessed at sunrise and sunset every day for a week before the wedding?"

"It's certainly a romantic location for the ceremony," I said, trying to inject some positivity into the situation.

"He didn't pick Catalina because it was romantic, Lizzie; he picked it because the airspace is restricted due to some military base in the area. He thinks he's starring in his own personal action movie. I had to have it put in my contract that he's not allowed to keep guns in our house."

So there was trouble in paradise already. I walked to the window and opened the heavy curtain, letting the light pour into the gloomy room. I gasped as the warm afternoon sun landed on Emerald's face. She was the most beautiful creature I'd ever seen in my life. She looked like a fairy-tale bride. Her hair was pulled gently back from her face and her green eyes shone through the antique lace veil. Her dress was the thickest, most luxurious satin in a subtle champagne color with the most detailed embroidery imaginable. Valentino had outdone himself. I had expected to see her looking like a Christmas tree dripping in diamonds. But she was tastefully adorned with an antique diamond, pearl, and emerald necklace. The green in the stone picked up a bit of green in the dress's embroidery that then brought your focus back to her eyes. The only imperfection was the tear-stained cheeks and slightly smudged mascara.

"Oh, Emerald, you look so stunning," I said and meant every word. I couldn't even dream of looking like that on my wedding day. There were just some summits that us mere mortals would never be able to reach. Luke's face flashed into my head.

"Really?" she said, lighting up for a second. I pulled up a chair across from her and lifted her veil from her face. I handed her a Kleenex to wipe her nose.

"Really," I said, as I glanced at the clock. We really needed to get moving if we were going to avoid a scandal. "So, what's going on? When I came with you to that dress fitting a couple of weeks ago, you said you were actually in love with Jizzy. You know it's normal for couples to fight."

"There's nothing normal about Jizzy. Let me tell you," Emerald said. Well, that wasn't a great surprise. He'd purchased a wife through his agent. Certainly wasn't a traditional form of courting that *I* was aware of.

"But I thought that's what you liked about him?" I said.

"Even 'unique' has its limits," Emerald replied vaguely. I got the impression that she really wanted to tell me something but was holding back. She looked around the room.

"Emerald, is there someone else in the room?"

"Not that I know of, but those HOGD people are everywhere. I have to drink blessed water or I won't be pure enough to kiss my husband." Poor Emerald certainly seemed in over her head.

"Well, at least we know Jizzy isn't a fool. He picked you, right?"

Emerald could hold it in no longer. She leaned in so close that her lips touched my ear. It was in such a low whisper I could barely make it out. "He's no fool, Lizzie. He's a fairy." She pulled back to see the impact her words had on me. Obviously it had the desired effect, as she seemed pleased for the first time since I'd entered the room.

"No," I spluttered incredulously. It just wasn't possible. Jizzy James had been the über-male icon for the last twenty years. Every girl I knew had dreamed about being ravaged by him at one point or another. But I guess we could all just keep dreaming. It all suddenly made sense now. Why I hadn't put two and two together in the first place was the real mystery.

"I'm a beard, Lizzie. Just a beard," Emerald said with perfectly pitched melodrama.

"A beautiful beard," I assured her, knowing of no other approach but flattery at this late date. Good old Emerald started to laugh. Then she threw caution to the wind and spoke openly.

"I know it's silly to be upset. I just wish someone would have told me. It wouldn't have mattered, but at least I wouldn't have been so shocked when his fucking boyfriend burst into our bedroom and tried to scratch my eyes out this morning."

"So did you two . . . you know? Do it?" I whispered, now totally puzzled.

"No. Not yet. We've only fooled around a bit. Kissed, you know, the basics. He said we should wait until our wedding night. And I stupidly thought that was because he was so old-fashioned and traditional."

"And we thought it was all about secret sects but really it was just about secret sex," I joked. That one seemed to go right over Emerald's head. She just looked at me blankly and I decided to keep the humor to a minimum.

"Or no sex, in my case. I just don't know what to do now. Tell me what to do, Lizzie?" she pleaded.

I took a deep breath. My instinct was to tell Emerald to pick up that ninety-foot train and swim to the mainland if she had to. But that was what I'd do, and we were very different people. Anyway, her dress weighed fifty pounds, so suggesting an ocean swim wasn't the best of ideas. As I seemed to be this girl's only adviser, I had to try and approach the situation like an adult. Which was obviously a struggle for me at the best of times.

"Em. You know there are two different ways to look at this situation. Option A." I sounded like my father. "If you decide to do a runner, I'm with you all the way. I'll help you paddle back to LA in a canoe if need be. So there's always that option." Emerald nodded gratefully, but I knew I had to press on with Option B. "Or, you can look at the situation in a different light." She waited patiently for me to flip the switch. "You were never marrying Jizzy for love in the first place, right?" I pressed on. Emerald nodded. "So just take your head back to where you originally started. It was a marriage of convenience and good for both of your careers." I could see Emerald struggling to get on this bandwagon. "And to be honest, his homosexuality is really a blessing in disguise. Gay men make much better friends, most of them have a superior fashion sense, and . . ."

"And I bet he could teach me how to give the best blow job on the planet," she jumped in excitedly. Well that thought was slightly left of field but whatever worked for Emerald. I continued.

"Maybe. But even better, he probably won't give two hoots who you sleep with as long as you're discreet." If I didn't have Emerald at hello, I certainly had her now.

She jumped from her chair with remarkable ease considering the weight of her dress and wrapped me in one of her now infamous breastie hugs.

"Oh, Lizzie, you crack me up. Who says 'hoot' anymore? But you're so right! I can't believe I've fallen into the best situation in the world and I couldn't even see it. I get all the respect of being a married lady with none of the downsides. I mean, if we wanted a baby, I bet Jizzy would even pay for a surrogate mother to carry it so I don't get fat. It's great, right?" She squealed. Luckily she didn't wait for a response because, to be honest, the entire thing was almost too horrific to comprehend. And now in some small way I was culpable.

Emerald turned toward the mirror and excitedly started to bark orders. "Lizzie, can you call my makeup and hair back in, please, and let Belinda, the wedding planner, know that it's a go. Also tell her to let Jizzy know that we're on again." She stopped in her tracks as something caught her eye. She turned around and grabbed my right wrist. I was wearing the bracelet she had given me in Thailand. "You didn't sell the bracelet?" she said with tears in her eyes.

"Of course I didn't sell it. It was a gift from you. I wouldn't do that," I said completely shocked by Emerald's emotion.

"You really are my friend, Lizzie. Aren't you?" she said more as a statement to herself than a question. I just nodded in agreement. Then the doors flew open and her entire entourage flooded into the room.

"Darling, your makeup is a disaster," a woman with enormous hair said. "It'll take me an eternity to fix. Quick. Quick. Where's my case?" she demanded.

"Look, her dress is wrinkled," an annoyed little Italian man said, and so on and so on.

I quietly snuck from the room and walked outside determined to get back to the party and admire all the fabulous guests. After all the drama of the day, I was dying for a glass of champagne and some caviar. Then when I was old and wrinkly as a Sharpe I could tell my grandkids how I'd been at Emerald Everhart's wedding to Jizzy James. But before I could enter the tent, Scott spotted me and motioned with his head for me to follow. I did as I was told, as ever, and we walked to a cliff overlooking the sea a bit away from the party.

He looked around like he was in an episode of Sherlock Holmes and then handed me something. I took it warily. We hadn't spoken since he'd eviscerated me in his office. And to be honest, I wasn't sure I could forgive Scott for not believing in me. Everyone else, fine. But Scott was supposed to be my friend. "I'm not sure I should accept mysterious parcels from people anymore, Scott. I may just get accused of crimes I didn't commit," I said like a spurned lover. I glared at Scott determined to hate him, but he looked so guilty I forgave him instantly. But that didn't mean some groveling wasn't required.

"Lizzie. I'm really sorry. I am. You have to understand that I'd been defending you for months and then the bank-account thing just tipped me over the edge. I felt betrayed. And to be honest, I thought I was protecting my family." The tears I had been biting back for days finally overwhelmed me. I started to sob and Scott looked absolutely horrified. Lara, who had obviously been watching the situation from afar, rushed over. She punched Scott painfully hard in the arm.

"What are you doing now, you asshole?" she hissed. "Haven't you done enough damage already?"

I tried to explain but the sobs were just coming at such a rapid rate that I couldn't get a word out. Lara put her arm protectively around my shoulder. Scott looked like a naughty boy.

"I was apologizing and I bought her a present. I swear. I feel like shit, Lara. I do," he said desperately. Lara looked at him suspiciously as my gulping sobs started to subside.

"Drink some champagne, my love. It'll make you feel better. I heard all about the planned sting operation. You should sue them, Lizzie." She punched Scott again as I took a big swig from a beautiful crystal flute. "I told you you were being an ass. You deserve to be sued," she said.

I handed back the wrapped box to Scott and took a deep breath. "Thanks, Scott, and I accept your apology, but I don't need gifts. Just the apology will do."

"Lizzie, please just open it. It's nothing silly or extravagant. Just kind of sentimental, I guess."

Lara raised an eyebrow. "Well that would be a first," she said.

I wiped away the tears on the back of my hand and opened the blue Tiffany box. Inside was a gold charm bracelet. I pulled it out curiously and examined it. There were three little diamond letters on it.

"What are these?" I asked, puzzled. There were two Ls and an S. Last time I'd checked they weren't my initials.

"One L is for Lachlan, one for Lara, and S, well, that's for me. I understand if you want to take the S off and that's okay, but I got it to remind you that you always have a family here in LA," Scott said shyly. Lara and I looked at each other in absolute shock and my tears started afresh.

"Oh God. Don't cry again. I can't handle crying women. How many times do I have to tell you that?" He rolled his eyes heavenward. Lara threw her arms around him and gave him a big kiss.

"Thanks, Scott. That means the world to me." I sniffled as I put the charm bracelet on my bare left wrist.

"Cool, babe. Glad to hear we're kosher. Now will you be back at the office once we chop the head off the rattlesnake who's there now?" He was all business again.

Oddly this very question had been weighing on my mind for a while now. And I hadn't realized I'd made a decision until just that second.

"No, Scott. I think it's time I moved on," I said firmly. The words were out of my mouth before I really knew what I was saying. I had never been great at steering my own destiny, but I suddenly realized that it was time.

"Not a surprise, Lizzie-o. You're wasted at my desk. Anyway, I don't think I could handle walking by your Oscar every day on the way into my office. I hate to feel inadequate. But if you ever need anything, I'm always here for you." He touched the S on my bracelet, grabbed Lara's hand, and walked back toward the party. Lara gave me a wink and a wave as I followed a few discreet steps behind.

It was then that I decided that I was going to exact a very necessary pound of flesh from my erstwhile boss.

"Scott!" I called out. "Can I borrow you for just one second?"

"Huh?" Scott turned around and Lara nodded, pushing him toward me.

"Go on, Scott. Lizzie wants you," Lara said.

"Better be quick, baby. Unlike you, I have work to do." Scott put his arm around my shoulder and I wondered whether it was right to ruin our new affection with what I wanted to say. But when I looked at Lara, it was a risk I knew I'd have to take.

"Scott. Will you do one thing for me?" I asked quietly, so as not to be overheard.

"Maybe." Scott was smart enough not to put his name on anything he didn't know inside-out and back-to-front. "What is it?" he asked suspiciously, removing his arm slowly from around my shoulder.

"It's the women." I took a deep breath. This wasn't easy.

"The women?"

"The affairs, Scott. The panting ladies with no panties whom you secrete away in your office and we never can find but we all know they're there because we can hear them moaning." There, I'd said it.

"The affairs?" Scott said, with an unreadable expression on his face.

"I'm loyal, Scott, but when I'm not there to protect you and turn the volume up on my Ipod, I'm sure some other assistant will let the cat out of the bag and Lara will find out. So if you don't stop I'm going to have to tell her. And she really doesn't deserve that." I looked at my feet. Then, getting no reply from Scott, I slowly raised my head to see his face.

To my surprise, he was smiling. Beaming. Broadly. Then, in a move that caused my heart to momentarily stop beating, he called out,

"Hey, Lara, you gotta come listen to this, honey!" And Lara turned around and headed back to us.

"Lizzie thinks I'm having affairs." He let forth a peel of laughter.

"She does?" Lara squinted her eyes and looked lividly from me to Scott. Not sure whom to hate the most.

"But I'm not." Scott scooped us both into a big hug, "It's hentai, ladies. It's Japanese cartoon porn. It's the coolest, sexiest thing you've ever seen, well, I've ever seen—apart from you, honey." He squeezed Lara's ass at this point. "And I have to confess that I'm totally and utterly fucking addicted to it."

"Hen what?" I asked, completely puzzled.

"Hentai." He laughed. "Hen fucking Tai." And so I guess that was that, then. Life was even better than I had thought it was five minutes ago.

As we all took our seats for the ceremony, my head was spinning with the thrill of possibility. I was about to start a new chapter of my life. I looked at the two bracelets, one on each wrist, and I felt like the luckiest girl in the world. I had family in LA, after all. And that family wasn't nearly as dysfunctional as I'd first thought.

TWENTY-ONE

I can't talk about Hollywood. It was a horror to me when I was there and it's a horror to look back on. I can't imagine how I did it. When I got away from it I couldn't even refer to the place by name. "Out there" I called it.

—Dorothy Parker

I sat nervously at the Coffee Bean, clutching my cell phone, waiting for the call. Today was the day that Amber Bingham-Fox was going down. And for some reason I was incredibly nervous. I'd put on my most re-spectable black Banana Republic suit and the strand of pearls I'd been given for my eighteenth birthday. I know it was dramatic, but I wanted to look the image of the wronged woman. And I must have achieved it because I swear people were looking at me pityingly. They probably thought I was on my way to a funeral. I could only wish.

The phone vibrated and I jumped out of my skin. I looked at it and saw that it was Jason calling. I answered it quickly.

"Hi, Jason. I'm waiting in your alma mater for the Amber phone call," I told him.

"Do they have a picture of me on the wall yet?" he asked seriously.

"Yeah. An enormous one the size of the window."

"Really?" he asked excitedly.

"No, you idiot."

"Oh. Are you coming over tonight?"

"Sure. I can't wait to see you. Once this is all over, I'll be able to relax."

"Cool. Can you pick up a copy of *Belle de jour* on your way?" he asked.

Call waiting bleeped into my phone and I could see it was The Agency.

"Jason, that's them. Got to go."

"Have fun, babes. Give her hell," Jason said supportively.

I switched the call over to Scott.

"Okay, I'll be right there," I said as I stood up, banging my knees clumsily against the table. I suddenly felt sick. I realized as I walked across the street that I was actually scared of Amber. I wouldn't put it past her to run at me with her fancy silver letter opener and try to gouge out my heart.

As I walked into The Agency's famous atrium, I felt oddly disconnected from my body. I waved to the security guard, who had obviously been informed of the impending bust because he gave me a respectful nod then walked me to the elevator. Scott and Katherine had given me the choice to either confront Amber first, say my piece after the police arrived, or stay at home and hear the details later from Scott. At first, I'd decided on the last option. I just wanted to forget the entire thing had ever happened. As long as I knew Amber was going to get her just desserts, I didn't feel any need to witness it. But when I'd finally filled my parents in on the details, they had felt that it was vital that I confront her at The Agency in front of everyone. Only then would my name be properly cleared through the whisper-down-the-lane method that Amber had used so well to her advantage. Unfortunately I knew they were right, as parents so often are, and for once I listened to their words of wisdom. I would face Amber at The Agency and then the police would come and arrest her. They were already in the building somewhere, and no doubt they'd be watching the scene.

As the elevator door opened, I took a deep breath and walked with purpose to Amber's desk. A new assistant was sitting at what used to be my desk. She looked at me blankly and I quickly realized that this wasn't because she didn't recognize me but because Amber had wanted to make sure there was no competition so she had chosen the dumbest girl she could find. If only I had been so crafty.

"I'm here to see Amber," I said to little Miss Vacant.

"Oh. Good," she said, then studied the call sheet intently. I waited there for a few minutes until it struck me that she wasn't in the process of producing Amber for me.

"Can you get her, please?" I asked patiently.

"Oh. You want me to get her?"

"Yes," I said as slowly as possible.

"She's right there." The new girl pointed to the opening doors of the elevator.

Amber and I locked eyes as she walked toward me. She had a smug, gloating look on her face. I was already thrilled to be here.

"Elizabeth," she said loudly so everyone could hear. "You know you're not supposed to be in the building. It's not me really. It's Scott. If he sees you, I could get fired."

"I'm not going anywhere, Amber," I said as I sat down in her chair and put my feet up on her desk. Amber was totally taken aback. She didn't know if I'd become unhinged or what was going on. I was personally relishing the moment.

"Lizzie," she said more menacingly than before as she picked up Miss Vacant's phone. "I'm calling Security."

"That's a great idea, Amber. Because you're going to need them to escort you out of the building," I said. Amber just laughed arrogantly in my face.

"I don't think so, Lizzie." She walked over to me and literally shoved my feet off the desk with one forceful sweep of her arm. It knocked me slightly off balance and I fell backward in her office chair. I was trying to at least get off the floor, but she moved her face as close to mine as possible and held me and the chair down purposefully on the ground. I blinked in astonishment at her agility and my total lack of coordination.

"You're so pathetic, Lizzie. Did you ever really think you were a match for me?"

Never in my life have I ever done anything remotely violent. I am a pacifist. My family are all pacifists. Catfights are in my opinion the lowest of the low and give women a bad name. But suddenly I was filled with an all-consuming rage. This woman had almost ruined my life. She was the incarnate of evil and there she was with her face an inch away from mine. My fist literally acted on its own accord and it came out of nowhere, landing a right cross smack on her average little cheekbone. She recoiled in shocked horror as I said a quick, silent thank you to the boxing instructor at Crunch. I scrambled off the floor in a big hurry to protect myself in case she decided to retaliate.

"You hit me!" she screamed.

"You framed me. You blackmailing black-hearted bitch!" I yelled back. This seemed to get everyone in the building's attention. People started to flood in from various random corridors. There hadn't been this much excitement since the hostile takeover. But I can tell you from first-hand experience that this was much more hostile than the takeover.

"Security!" she screamed. "Police! I want her arrested for assault!" The two detectives emerged from Scott's office.

"You called?" the woman officer said, dangling her cuffs. Amber was slightly confused as to where they came from, but she was in such a rage she didn't bother to think.

"Yes. Arrest that girl for assault and blackmail. We all know what low-life scum you are," she said to me. "I don't care, Scott, I'm not keeping it a secret anymore. I'm pressing charges!" she howled.

Scott gave a nod to the police and the woman officer walked up to us. Amber looked thrilled, but when the policewoman snapped the cuffs on her wrist, she blinked in confusion.

"You have the right to remain silent. Anything you say can and will be used against you—"

"Get off me!" Amber ordered in her imperious British accent. But the policewoman, who had obviously been made a bit of a fool by Amber's web of lies, wasn't loosening her grip.

"I demand to be released right this instant. Scott, come on, this is Lizzie spinning her web of lies."

"Amber. You're caught," I said with glee. "Everyone knows. They have your fingerprints. They found the payphone you used to place the blackmail calls. It would have been smarter to use one a bit farther away from your house," I said with relish.

"Oh, and Amber," Scott said, with his usual laid-back tone, "We've convinced three clients to press charges. I have one word for you: Jail." He turned around and dusted off his hands. "Everyone get back to work. The show is over," Scott said as he closed his office door.

Amber just stood there in shock. The policewoman gave her a tug and started to lead her from the building. They got to the elevator and as the doors opened there stood Katherine Watson. Katherine was possibly the coolest woman I'd ever met. She just looked at Amber, looked at the police, and gave Amber a little wink. Then walked past her and into Scott's office. I breathed a big sigh of relief, and as the elevator doors closed, I heard the pop of a champagne cork from Scott's office. I smiled as I walked in to join the celebration.

"Honey, it's me!" I called out as I cautiously pushed open Jason's front door. Although he'd given me a key, I still never felt the way I had when I let myself into Luke's. Jason's house just wasn't somewhere I felt comfortable hanging out, and I knew in the back of my mind that it was never going to be home. That wasn't because Jason had terrible taste in rugs, either, it was just that I didn't have the same hormonal nesting instinct with him. The way I had felt about Luke had made me want to wear an apron, bake cakes, and sit on the porch and drink beer with him in the evenings. Which may just have been because he was Southern and that twang brought out the old-fashioned girl in me. But I figured that really it was because my relationship with Jason had nearly always involved business. We had fun, but it was usually when we'd had an amazing interview or were deeply absorbed in a conversation about Visconti. Otherwise we just had sex as some peculiar force of habit. It was comfortable. But it completely lacked the sense of excitement and romance I'd had with other men in my life. Nevertheless, as I walked through Jason's front door, I tried to push this thought to the back of my mind. We hadn't seen seen each other in a week and I had so much to fill him in on. I was still slightly buzzed from the champagne celebration and I couldn't wait to tell him all about Amber and gloat.

"Hey, Lizzie! Come see this!" Jason called out. I followed his voice and made my way to his bedroom, where he was looking up at the largest plasma screen I'd ever seen.

"Is that forty-two inches?" I asked.

"No, darling, it's bigger. It's fifty-four." He grinned as he sat crosslegged on the bed and flicked between channels. "Don't you love it?"

"Yeah," I said as I dropped down onto the bed and gazed up at the screen. "Isn't it a bit intrusive in your bedroom, though? Shouldn't it be in a screening room?"

"No, it's perfect in the bedroom. Can't think of anything I'd rather do in bed than watch movies," he said as he flicked to a DVD of *Sex Addicts in Love*.

"Not even *you know what?*" I said as I kicked off my shoes and sidled up to him, putting my hand on his thigh in a suggestive way, but not going straight for the crotch in case he really wasn't in the mood.

"Maybe after the movie," he suggested as he put his hand over mine and maneuvered it to his chest in a friendly manner. "I read a review today that compared some of the camera angles in *Sex Addicts* to *Belle de jour* so I want to check it out. I mean, I can't see it myself, but I guess I could have been unconsciously influenced, y'know?" he said as he kissed the top of my head and then lay back happily on his pillow.

"It's really good to see you. I've had such a crazy week," I said, shrugging off the clear rejection because really I was probably as un-in-the-mood as Jason was for getting hot and heavy. Anyway, I was still flying high from my victory and nothing was going to get me down.

"Really? Great. Well you can tell me about it later," he said and sort of patted me as his eyes remained glued to his own camera angles.

"Amber was so pathetic," I persisted. "Did I tell you she was having an affair with Katherine Watson's husband as well as blackmailing people? They offered me my job back. Not that I want to be reinstated, but it's good to know I'm in the clear. But I think I want to start a production company of my own. I have no idea how I'll survive until then. Maybe I'll learn how to bartend to make ends meet."

"Honey?" Jason said, not unkindly, "do you think we can talk about this after the movie?"

"Sure," I said and shuffled out of his embrace and into the kitchen.

As I stood in Jason's kitchen, it became clearer and clearer to me that being here was a mistake. Being in Jason's life like this was just wrong. We were great friends and we had been ever since that first day we'd met in the Coffee Bean. Pretending that we could be anything more was nonsense really. Even if I didn't have Luke in my life, at least I owed myself the space to find someone else. I wasn't Emerald Everhart; I expected more from love and marriage. I went to the fridge and poured myself a glass of milk. Then I sat down at his kitchen table and began a Su Doku on the back of the newspaper. I hadn't done one since

I'd been fired; for obvious reasons, it had left a nasty taste in my mouth. But I couldn't resist this one. I chewed my pen and lost myself in the numbers.

Ten minutes later I was deep into my puzzle when Jason's landline began to ring. I expected him to pick up in his bedroom but clearly he was too busy getting off on the similarity between his shots and Buñuel's. Jason's machine clicked in.

"Hi, this is Jason. Please leave a message. *Beep.*"

"Jason, hi, it's me." A woman's most try-hard sexy voice filled the silent kitchen. From down the hall I could hear the movie playing. Jason clearly couldn't hear the message. *"Listen, the thing is, I'd love to come to the Oscars with you. I just wasn't sure if I was going to be away filming, but I have a few days off. So I guess it's a date. Call me."*

I put down my pen and thought hard about where the next number nine would go in my Su Doku. I could have sworn that I recognized the woman's voice but had no idea where from. She was obviously an actress, because I could hear her pout all the way down the line. But curiously I wasn't too concerned about what should have mattered the most—the fact that I had clearly been usurped as Jason's Oscar date. I just kept on with my Su Doku and wondered whether I should call my dad in D.C. and ask him to be my date now. When Jason finally wandered into the kitchen half an hour later, he rubbed his eyes and yawned, "Should we get takeout or something? I could call Matsuhisa."

"I've finished your cookies," I said and pointed to the empty package. "So I'm not really that hungry anymore. But I'll have some yellowtail if you're ordering."

"Okay." Jason went to the phone and hunted in a drawer for a menu.

"Oh, by the way, someone left a message," I said and glanced up at him.

"Thanks." Jason reached over and pressed the Play button.

"Jason, hi, it's me. Listen, the thing is, I'd love to come to the Oscars with you. I just wasn't sure if I was going to be away filming, but I have a few days off. So I guess it's a date. Call me," she said again. And I knew that I recognized the voice but still couldn't place it.

"So I guess I should find myself another date? Right?" I asked as Jason looked down at the machine incredulously. As if it had bitten him on the ankle.

"I er . . ."

"Who is she?" I asked, not really even caring, just curious to see if I knew her.

"She's nobody." He ran his hand through his hair and looked defeated.

"You asked nobody to be your date to the Oscars? Well, if you don't mind me saying so, that's pretty dumb. It's going to be the biggest night of your life."

"I just thought that it might be good for my profile if I had an actress as a date, you know? The power couple thing."

"Oh, so she *is* an actress." I nodded sanguinely.

"Lizzie, don't be mad. You care as much about my career as I do, right?" He looked imploringly at me.

"Well no, actually, I don't. Because if I cared as much as you, I'd be certifiable. But I kind of understand. Why be with the homely producer-girl-who-got-lucky when you can be with . . . ?" I quizzed.

"Carmen Cash," Jason said reluctantly.

"Carmen Cash?" I squealed. "You did not!"

"She's sweet," Jason said defensively.

Something to remember: You can always tell when a man's sleeping with a woman because, provided he's not a total butthole, he will defend her honor, even if it gets him into trouble. Lara taught me this. Apparently she once caught Scott out when he was having an affair with a girl from his gym who customized jean jackets with studs. She said, "I can't believe you're sleeping with that fat, blond airhead." And immediately Scott replied, "She's not fat." QED.

"She wears a ring on her thumb." I gasped.

"Does she?" Jason looked as if he was casting his mind back to a bygone hotel room. Though clearly her thumb ring was not the most memorable part of their night together.

"She also has breasts like unripe cantaloupes." I grimaced, casting my own mind back to Thailand where Carmen had spent the majority of her days perched on the counter of the craft services van in a miniskirt without any panties on. She really had a knack for putting people off their food. Men and women alike, but, I guessed, for very different reasons.

"I know," Jason said as his eyes lost the ability to focus.

"Okay, well, that's fine by me. But maybe if you want to do the whole 'power couple at the Academy Awards' thing you should call The Agency and ask if one of their finer actresses is available for the night. How about Scarlett?" I suggested.

"I already asked her," he said quickly.

"Okay." I tried not to sound bitter but I guess as the woman who'd considered herself to be his girlfriend for the last two months I did have a right to a small hissy fit. "Kirstin Dunst? She's bright but not out of your league."

"I checked. She has a fiancé." Poor Jason, I almost felt sorry for him. Not.

"Nicole Kidman?" I asked, my voice laced with irony. I mean Jason had won a Golden Globe but his movie had only taken in fourteen million. He wasn't exactly Scorsese.

"That's a great idea. Is she repped by Katherine?" he demanded excitedly, then suddenly became downcast again. "But what should I do about Carmen? I can't let her down."

"No, that'd be a really terrible thing to do," I said sarcastically. But Jason was too wrapped up in his dating life to notice that he'd done just that to me. I guess I wasn't an actress, so I didn't count.

"Jason, I think I'm going to head home. It's been a long day," I said as I folded up the newspaper and smuggled it into my purse so that I could finish my puzzle later. Jason poured himself a glass of wine from the fridge and pondered the limitless options of the young director on the ascendant.

"You're not going to stay?" He looked as if I'd popped his bubble when I picked up my shawl.

"Jason, you know I love you, but . . ." I said as I hitched my purse onto my shoulder.

"Whoa there, we're doing 'love' already?" He took a step backward and defended himself with his wineglass.

"As a friend, you idiot," I clarified. "The thing is I love you like a friend but there's no way that you and I are ever going to work out."

"There isn't?" He seemed genuinely surprised at this assertion. I decided to break it to him gently.

"You're a total slut and you love movies more than human beings."

"No!" he protested in outrage.

"Yes," I said as I leaned in and kissed him on the cheek. "I want a man who's going to be faithful to me and who would rather look at my breasts than Catherine Deneuve's."

"Well, darling, in that case, your prince may never come," Jason earnestly informed me.

"That's a chance I'm willing to take." I smiled.

"You mean we're not having sex tonight?" He looked forlorn.

I shook my head. "We're not having sex ever again."

"Is it something I've done?"

"No, Jason. It's not you. It's me." I giggled. I'd always wanted to say that but had never had the pleasure of dumping anyone before. And as breakups went this had to be one of the most enjoyable for both parties. I was on a roll.

"I hear Carmen does this thing with her thighs, they're supposed to be rock-hard." I headed toward the door. "If you ask her nicely she might show you."

"Christ, I know. It's fucking amazing." Jason's eyes watered at the memory.

"Thanks for not lying to me." I waved and opened the door onto the balmy LA night. "See you at the junket tomorrow?"

"Sure," Jason said, then called after me, "If I find any of your panties, can I keep them?"

"Sure," I shrugged. "And if I find any of yours can I sell them on eBay when you win your Oscar?"

"Be my guest," Jason said proudly, probably before rushing to his bedroom and putting a couple of pairs of his boxer shorts into a jiffy bag for future generations of movie fans to cherish.

TWENTY-TWO

Hollywood is a place where
people from Iowa mistake
each other for a star.

—Woody Allen

The week before the Oscars, a strange sort of malaise settles over Los Angeles. Before the pandemonium of the ceremony itself hits, there's a period of desperation beyond compare. It's known as Oscar Fever. And no matter how important, how cool, or how indifferent a person appears to be to the whole Hollywood circus for the rest of the year—they find themselves sucked into a swirling vortex of hope, shamelessness, and humiliation during that week.

Thankfully I'd never really given too much of a damn about the Academy Awards before my own nomination. When I lived in D.C. I'd hear about who won and who lost on my car radio on my way to work. I also had a vague recollection of some of the sillier Oscar frocks—Celine Dion's backless tuxedo, Björk's swan costume, and Lara Tin Foil's ballerina dress all left me bemused. But that was before I arrived in Hollywood and exchanged the sound of one hand clapping for the local mantra of choice: "All publicity is good publicity." Then I understood why people would willingly embarrass themselves in front of an audience of millions. For the entire week the town was governed by three simple rules:

If you're not invited—lie your way in.
If you get in—get noticed.
If you don't get noticed—make a total ass of yourself until you do.

I have to say that even as an assistant at a talent agency I'd never really succumbed to Oscar Fever. Mainly because I was just too far down the ladder to even be able to see over the fence into the pen where the people-who-live-in-hope-of-an-invite were. I was about as likely to be invited to an Oscar event as a mailman in Michigan might be. Hell, my first year in LA Lara had to beg some friends of hers in Silver Lake to let me come to their Oscar party. You'd have thought that Steve McQueen would be making a guest appearance, their door policy was so tight. But when I got there it was just a bunch of wannabes whose big talk couldn't disguise the fact that everything they knew about the entertainment industry could be learned from the *National Enquirer* and their red carpet commentary on everyone from Angelina Jolie to Billy Zane was so damning they made Joan Rivers sound like Shirley Temple.

Last year I got it right. If you aren't nominated, spare yourself the depression of feeling like a total loser in a town where clearly you're no one if you're not a nominee and don't circulate. Because there is no in-between strata—the wannabes of Silver Lake are nobodys; but the TV presenters are wasting their Harry Winston–borrowed sparkle and Badgley Mischka gowns, too, because they're just common bystanders as well; even the winners of two years ago start to look like has-beens when Oscar Fever strikes—not unlike yesterday's slightly curling, unappealing sandwiches left out after the celebratory Women In Film lunch.

Best on Oscar night to forget you have anything to do with the industry, put on an old pair of pajamas, grab a blanket, and get bulimic with the carrot sticks. . . . I know, it should be Ben & Jerry's, but to be honest watching those women when you have a pint of ice cream inside you is such a one-way street to self-loathing that you might just welcome a "relationship with food" with open arms and then head straight for the bathroom. Best stick to carrots and pretzels, trust me.

Only this year I couldn't hide my light or my unwaxed legs beneath any bushels or blankets, I had a date at the Kodak Theatre and it would have been un-American of me to spend fewer than seventeen hours getting dressed for the big night. I had to abandon myself to the Zen of the Oscars with a pure heart. By the way, the Zen of the Oscars is evident everywhere you look. It was as if Zac had been coaching the whole town on the subject. Because during Oscar Week the present is all that matters. Last year counts for nothing. Next year's nominees are probably as yet undiscovered or waiting to be rediscovered, not even making it to the top of their agent's call sheet. The power of now is all that counts.

Each year there is a slight variation on the parties that one has to be invited to in order to be socially viable. This year, I heard from Jason so it was undoubtedly meticulously researched with no margin for error, it was Barry Diller's lunch party on Oscar Saturday; Daniel Rosen's house party on Saturday night; and the *Vanity Fair* party on Sunday as ever. That was the queen, king, ace of parties, and if you weren't holding the royal flush then you might as well wrap yourself in bandages, carry a bell and rock up to the Ivy and declare yourself unclean before your peers, like the social leper you are.

Of course it was already Friday night and somehow my invitations to this hallowed trinity of events still hadn't turned up in the mail and I was becoming increasingly concerned. But like a nasty outbreak of blisters on an intimate part of your body, you don't exactly want to advertize the fact that you've been overlooked. Until the eleventh hour that is, when you realize that it won't actually matter if you share your dilemma with a close, trusted friend because by this time tomorrow the whole town will know your sordid secret anyway.

"Jason," I whispered as we sat with our heads under foil at the Frédéric Fekkai Oscar suite on Saturday morning (yes, this was a free cut and highlights and of course I was excited but I was trying to blend in so couldn't nail my excitement to the mast quite as eagerly as I wanted to in public), "I'm not sure what I'm doing tonight."

"Well, you're coming to Barry's party, aren't you?" he said as he sipped his complimentary chamomile tea. Apparently he'd been in pretox all week for his big night. I had tried to cut out alcohol and adhere to the old faithful Brussels sprouts diet, but after just one day of boiling water in saucepans and a kitchen that smelled like a Victorian sewer, I'd given up and headed for Pinks on Melrose for a celebratory chili dog and fries. This was, after all, supposed to be the time of my life; I wasn't going to blight it by spending my days running to the bathroom instead of

taking advantage of all the fabulous free massages, haircuts, and mani-
cures that were being doled out to nominees.

"I haven't been invited," I said, moving my head tightly into his, so
that our foils rustled together.

"Of course you have, honey. Your invitations are at my house."

"They are?" I nearly leaped out of my seat with joy. I hadn't acknowl-
edged even to myself how miserable I'd been by my Oscar ostracism. If
I couldn't get arrested when I was nominated for best producer, then
there was no hope for me.

"I'll call Carmen and ask her to bring them with her. She's coming in
for an Indian head massage at eleven."

But unfortunately all was not quite so simple. Primarily because Jason was dating an unscrupulous egomaniac with a sense of entitlement
that usually only accompanies heiresses to billion-dollar fortunes not a
former model-turned-actress whose only talent seemed to be to make
her skirt mysteriously disappear every time she sat down.

"Here are the invitations." Carmen handed me a couple of battered
bits of card as she made a beeline for Frédéric and crushed her chest
against him when they air kissed. I looked at my coveted treasure with a
sigh of relief, until I realized that the ace in my pack was in fact missing.

"Jason, she's forgotten my *Vanity Fair* one," I said as I ironed out the
abused invites.

"It's probably in her bag." Jason shrugged. "Carmen honey, c'm here
a minute."

"Coming!" Carmen kissed a little more ass with the manicurist and
makeup artist to ensure her goody bag later and then returned to her
walking, talking, breathing Academy Award ticket, aka Jason.

"Carmen, have you got my *Vanity Fair* invitation?" I smiled, trying to
look past her numinous bosom as all six feet of her zaftig frame towered
over me.

"Oh no, I gave that to a friend," she said as she moved in close to the
mirror to scrutinize a nonexistent pore on her nearly as nonexistent
nose. My head twitched involuntarily and I wanted to say something
but I didn't have the capability, I was so stunned.

"Oh, come on, baby, you didn't really, did you?" Jason said as he pondered which of the male nail polishes he'd be wearing tomorrow night. It wasn't quite the alpha-male anger I needed from him at this juncture in my weekend.

"You did what?" I couldn't help myself.

"She really wanted to come. She's never been before." Carmen turned and addressed not me, but Jason, with a sweet pout. She was clearly a smart girl.

"Oh shit, Lizzie. I'm so sorry," Jason said, then handed the manicurist the most masculine nail polish he could lay hands on. Obviously a guy has to have good looking nails if he's going to be manhandling Oscar. However it did make me very glad that we weren't still having sex, especially when topped off with a head of Malibu male lowlights and an inability to stand up for me, I felt positively repelled.

"Sorry isn't good enough." I shook my head. "That was my ticket and I want it back."

"Not possible." Carmen shook her already perfect mane over her shoulder as she settled into the chair on the far side of Jason. "She's already had a dress made for her by Galliano on the grounds that she's going to be there. Otherwise it would have cost her twenty-five thousand dollars." Which strangely didn't make me any more compelled to donate my ticket to Carmen's friend. Especially as I was going to be wearing an admittedly lovely, but uncouture, sample gown by Chanel that Talitha had found in the press cupboard at work, which had small sweat patches under the arms. And which I had to give back by noon on Monday.

"Jason," I barked, by way of an order.

"What can I say, Lizzie? I'm sorry."

"I'll be your plus one," I demanded.

"Also not possible." Carmen informed me. "My sister has Jason's plus one."

"Oh and don't tell me. She's already had her dress hand-appliqued by Christian Dior himself."

"Don't be stupid. He's dead," she said, then turned to the hairdresser who was ready to give her a massage. "I like it very firm." She giggled. At which point I knew that I had lost Jason's support. He was barely able to conceal his burgeoning delight at his horny girlfriend, even beneath an oversized, parachute silk hairdresser's robe. So I took my new highlights and goody bag of minisprays and shampoos that should have delighted me and instead made me want to swing them around and thwack Carmen on the head and stomped to my car.

By the time I arrived back at Lara's, I had resigned myself to going to Elton John's post-Oscar party instead.

"I don't see what all the fuss about the *Vanity Fair* party is, anyway," I lied to Lara over lunch. "One party's going to be just the same as another. And Elton might even sing that song, 'Daniel you're a sta-ah-ah-ah-r, and you fell from the sky.' I love that song."

"You can't give up that easily," Lara fumed. "That pussy-for-rent cannot just give your invitation away. I'll get Scott to call Graydon."

"Don't be silly. The world and his hamster will be calling Graydon, and he's probably at Barry Diller's lunch as we speak. He won't be poring over the guest list with a pencil ready to add me to it."

"Okay, but I swear to God we'll get you into that party. I'm not going on my own with Scott. That'd be no fun at all. What's the point of Gwyneth's postpregnancy boobs if we don't get to check them out together?" Lara asked incredulously.

Naturally both Lara and Scott were invited to every fannybumper on the face of God's earth. They were even going to Daniel Rosen's party at his house tonight, despite the fact that only a year ago Scott had launched a hostile takeover of The Agency and ousted Daniel from his post as president. Daniel was now head of a major new agency and so could afford to be magnanimous—he was still two positions above Scott on the *Entertainment Weekly* Power 100. So he was officially the bigger man.

"Let's break into their house tonight and steal their invitation," Lara said.

"I'm going to Daniel's party. I can't." I shrugged.

"Are you kidding, that'll be over by nine-thirty. Everyone needs their beauty sleep. Why don't we just leave early and swing by? You still have a key, don't you?"

"Yes, but I couldn't. Anyway, it has Jason's name on the invite," I protested.

"That's okay. We'll take theirs and hold it hostage until they give yours back," Lara plotted.

"I'm not sure that I want to go that badly," I admitted. "I mean, how much fun can it be?"

"How? Much? Fun? Can? It? Be?" Lara was incredulous. "Listen Lizzie, you know me. I don't rat's ass about celebrities and all that and since I got fat I don't even care about clothes that much, but you know what?" She gawped at me.

"No?"

"This will be the most extraordinary night of your life." She sighed happily. "Have you ever seen more than two movie stars under one roof ?"

"Only at premieres," I said.

"When they had the same goal—to sell tickets to their movie. This is so different, you can't begin to imagine."

"Really?" I was surprised, I'd never seen Lara so impassioned before, certainly not about a party.

"It's a freak show." Lara laughed with a glint in her eye. "Can you imagine Catherine Zeta-Jones's face when Pammy Anderson squeezes Michael Douglas's knee? Can you imagine Angelina checking out Jen just to make sure she's not prettier than her? Scarlett Johansson and Lindsay Lohan, who hate each other, running into each other in the bathroom?"

"No." I shook my head. I had thought of the Oscars as a pop-up edition of *People,* just glossy stars in 3-D—not living, breathing, dysfunctioning human beings intermingling.

"Everyone has slept with someone in the room and they're all pathologically insecure egomaniacs who are the pivotal point of their own universes until they get into a room with people who earn more money and have less Botox than themselves. Then they don't know what to do. It's so much fun."

"It sounds dangerous," I said, though I was still unconvinced that I should commit a felony in order to be admitted to the circus. Couldn't I just read all that in Defamer, I wondered. "But not as dangerous as putting Carmen Cash's ticket to the party in jeopardy. She'll break my neck with her knees in a nonerotic way."

"I'll do it then," Lara said. "You can drop me off after the party. I'll run in, grab it, and we'll call later and tell them the terms of the ransom."

"Lara!" I protested, but I knew it was to no avail. The most I could hope for now was for Lara to get so hammered at the party that she wouldn't remember her name, let alone her ingenious plan. "I really don't mind not going, honestly, I don't care if everyone thinks I'm a loser 'cause I'm not invited. Anyway, you only want me to go so that you have someone to play with when Scott's wiping his clients' tears when they don't win."

"Nothing wrong with that." Lara sniffed. "So let's go have some lunch and start getting ready for tonight. Where does Jason leave his invites? On the mantel? On a bulletin board?"

"Hmmm, let's think," I replied as I furrowed my brow and pretended not to remember.

Lara had no intention of abandoning her plan, though. She even packed a pair of fold-up shoes called Lola's in her purse so that she could slip them on in the car and race at breakneck speed into Jason's house for the robbery.

"I think you're just getting a sick thrill out of this," I scolded as we nestled luxuriously in the back of a chauffeur-driven Bentley on the way to Daniel's house in Coldwater Canyon. Scott was welded to his cell on the other side of the car, staring out the window. "You don't have enough excitement in your life, that's your problem. You need to get back into your novel writing. Then you'll be more fulfilled."

"You don't know what excitement is, otherwise you wouldn't miss this party for the world." She snapped back. "Anyway, I'm having lunch with a book agent on Monday who loves my first three chapters. So there."

The truth was I think we were both quite nervous about the whole weekend. Lara was anxious that her black couture dress, for all its cunning draping and darts, wouldn't conceal her postbirth girth, and I couldn't even begin to fathom that this time tomorrow evening my petrified face was going to be flashed onto millions of television screens worldwide.

"Lara, what if my looks aren't telegenic? What if my parents and all the family in D.C. are crowded into the ballroom of the Hilton, see me on the big screen, and mistake me for Charlize Theron in the *Monster* sequel?" I grimaced.

"Millions?" Scott had slyly ended his call and was now eavesdropping on my paranoia.

"Yes, millions," I reiterated with a quiver in my voice. God, the fear of that alone was enough to break me out in hives.

"Try a billion," Scott said and snapped his phone shut.

"Don't exaggerate, agent!" I spat.

"I'm not." He laughed cruelly. "Close to a billion people worldwide watch the Oscars. And Charlize is dead in the sequel."

"I know. That was my point," I hissed. I had to open the window for some air.

"Don't worry," Scott blithely informed me as he dialed another number. "Nobody's going to be looking at you."

"It's true," I said. "Unless I fall on my face and find myself hermetically attached to Will Smith's lips, nobody will notice me. Blink and I'll be gone." And you could tell I wasn't an actor in sheep's clothing because the idea of being anonymous made me feel much happier than I had felt a minute ago.

Daniel's party was the zenith of decadence. The last time I'd been here I'd been organizing the festivities and I'd ended up nearly naked in the pool with the strippers and wearing a borrowed diamond necklace. Tonight I was going to make an effort to stay dry, unless I was presented with an unlooked-for opportunity to push Carmen Cash into the deep end with a piece of garden furniture tied to her ankle, in which case I'd be happy to take a momentary dunk myself.

The Bentley let us out and we walked down the rose-petal-strewn garden path, lined with Persian lanterns, and entered the house. Whereas last time it had been a jungle-themed party, tonight the place had been transformed into an Eastern paradise. Pomegranate and mint martinis greeted us, and Daniel mingled in pajama pants and slippers.

"Jesus, for once I'm not the most underdressed guy in the room." Scott went over and slapped Daniel on the back. They hugged, their chests colliding in an unspoken competition to see who'd been doing more crunches at five A.M. with his trainer. Who was the harder man.

"Scott." Daniel turned around and looked at the Judas who had been responsible for having him escorted by security guards from the building a year ago, and, apparently without a trace of rancor, said, "So glad you could make it, so glad you've put the substance abuse behind you, and isn't this the lady responsible for your cleaning up?" He waved Lara over. "Have you met Ridley Scott?"

Bravo, Daniel, I thought, as he managed to wreak revenge on Scott in three fell swoops:

1. This guy's a drug addict.
2. He's got a fat wife.
3. He needs *me* to introduce him to the major players in town.

Daniel was definitely back.

Lara and I left Scott and went on our own excited-teenager tour of the room. We tried every canapé on the way, smiling at people we didn't know with duck pancakes filling our cheeks, and we played "who would we swap lives with" until we decided that we didn't want to be anyone except ourselves because then we'd have to talk to people about their last movie and the marketplace and we didn't know much about either of those things. So we circulated and gaped at every major powerbroker in town until I suddenly found myself face-to-face with Jason and the chairman of a studio whom I'd been sat next to at the Pre-Oscar Women In Film lunch last month.

"Elspeth, good to see you," I said as I dropped a minihamburger that I was about to scoff into a potted fig tree so I didn't have to worry about ketchup lips. She was actually nice except for the fact that she was head of a studio, had three children, and managed to do two hours of yoga every morning. The last part made *The Crucible* spring to mind a little too readily.

"So, Lizzie, do you have another project lined up?" she asked.

"I honestly don't know," I said, because funnily enough since I'd left The Agency I hadn't had a moment to dwell on the fact that I was unemployed, and possibly unemployable. I'd had two sets of highlights, about eighty lunches, I'd been shopping in Saks at three in the afternoon, and I'd finally visited the dentist to have my cavity filled. I just hadn't gotten around to thinking "what next?" despite dreaming of everything from marrying Adrien Brody, whom I was planning to meet at the Oscars, to becoming a florist, because I loved the fresh, green smell of a flower shop and they were advertising a position at Moe's Flowers on Melrose, which was my favorite place in the whole town.

"You have another project, don't you?" Jason grinned, thinking he was doing me a favor. "It's just still under wraps, right?" I took it that he meant his new movie, which we'd vowed not to mention to anyone under any circumstances as it was eminently stealable.

"Not really," I told them. "I'm thinking of changing career direction, actually."

"Really?" Now Elspeth looked interested and Jason nervous. He was doubtless hoping that I wasn't going to tell her about the range of panties that I'd been meaning to design when we were together. "Were you thinking about taking an executive role?" She leaned forward and because Jason looked so pathetically afraid and I felt sorry for him—even if he was a manicured pussy who couldn't stand up to Carmen, I loved him—I lied.

I nodded. "I'm thinking about it."

"Inter-esting," Elspeth said. "Well, you clearly have great taste. I mean *Sex Addicts in Love* is a wonderful movie. Is that the sort of material you usually like?"

"Thank you. I guess so," I said, taking a rare compliment in front of Jason, who was generously encouraging me with his smile. "I actually always wanted to make *Crime and Punishment,* but maybe updated, as a noir thriller."

"I like your thinking," Elspeth said, then she spotted Bill Clinton across the room.

"If you'll excuse me I have to go say hello to an old friend, but it was good to see you again, Lizzie." She shook my hand warmly and looked intently at my face, as if she were memorizing me so she could sketch me later. "Oh, and Jason, very good to see you, too. Good luck tomorrow night, both of you."

"Elspeth's nice," I said as I watched Clinton greet her with a flirtatious kiss. "And lucky."

"You have a crush on Clinton?" he asked with a grimace.

"What sane woman doesn't?" I sighed.

"So Elspeth was asking me a bunch of questions about you before you got here," Jason informed me.

"Really? Why?" I was puzzled. "Maybe she wanted a threesome with me and Bill," I concluded.

"Jesus, Lizzie, that is so inappropriate." Jason was horrified.

"Oh and Carmen's bush making public appearances all by itself isn't inappropriate?" I said as I spied lover-girl, whose skirt seemed to have ridden dangerously far up her thighs, on the other side of the room chatting with a television executive. "Did you choose her crotchless, hot pink panties, Jase?"

"You shouldn't be looking," Jason snapped, suddenly unable to tear his eyes away from the distinctly unprivate view. "So, did you get a ticket for tomorrow night?" he asked warily.

"Not yet," I replied guiltily. I wondered whether I ought to tell him what Lara was planning to do, so that he could avert the whole catastrophe by being home and rendering the burglary impossible. But at that minute I overheard a couple next to us and suddenly felt more convinced of the moral rectitude of Lara's plan,

"I have the ten P.M. *Vanity Fair* slot tomorrow, what about you?" a woman proudly asked a fellow guest.

"I'm a nine-thirty," the guy replied in a self-satisfied way. She deflated. Lara was right, everyone was going. Maybe I was missing out after all.

"Jason?" I asked my coproducer, who appeared to have torn his eyes away from Carmen's cutebox and was now looking rather puppyishly at another girl in the corner of the room. "What time was our . . . sorry, I mean what time is *your* slot at the *Vanity Fair* party?" I enquired politely.

"I think we were eight-thirty," he said. "Hey, do you see that girl over there?"

"Is that the best time to be invited?" I persisted. "Like once-in-a-lifetime best slot?"

"I guess it's the earliest slot, and they only come along to nominees and superstars, yeah," he said distractedly. The *Vanity Fair* party, you see, happens in half-hour increments, with the hottest half-hour being the earliest, right after the ceremony, when everyone arrives with their Academy Award fresh off the lectern and barely warm from being fondled yet. Hell, even Graydon Carter's mother probably had to wait for a ten-thirty slot at the earliest.

"That's Paige," Jason said, transfixed.

"Who?" I asked.

"My old girlfriend." Jason was now holding my arm, so I glanced over at the attractive blonde in the corner. "She lives in Africa."

"Maybe she won't want her invite to the *Vanity Fair* party, then." I ventured. Oh God, were these the first symptoms of Oscar Fever? I checked my ego for signs of inflation.

"She's not in the business," Jason stammered, flushed with color. "She works with wild animals."

"What, like Scott Wagner?"

"Like lions," he replied, then he drifted over to the other side of the room, leaving me wondering what Carmen would do when she found Jason talking to an ex-girlfriend who managed to look pretty without fillers. Maybe I'd get to use Jason's *Vanity Fair* ticket tomorrow night, after all, if he was going to be in the hospital with broken bones, I thought optimistically.

"So, it's nine o'clock. Are you almost ready to go?" Lara arrived at my side, as if she'd been standing in the shadows like a traitor behind a pillar in ancient Rome, just waiting for Jason to go.

"The thing is, Lara, I really do want to go to the party, but isn't there another way?" I pleaded. "Jason has Armed Response."

"You have a key, you knucklehead." Lara poked her elbow into my rib playfully. I scowled.

"I love Jason. I can't steal his ticket. It's his big night." I looked over and saw him chatting excitedly with the lion girl on the other side of the room. She didn't look his usual type, nothing about her was fake apart from her leopard-print scarf, and she didn't look as if she could pole dance if her life depended on it, which was a big break with tradition for Jason.

"Sorry, honey, he let it happen to you," Lara said unequivocally. "One more drink and then we're out of here."

"Okay," I agreed reluctantly. Carmen was now rubbing the thigh of a pudgy man in the corner and I had to admit that my hatred of injustice was pretty hard to quash, it was clear that she was just using Jason for his ticket. I was darned if she was going to get her hands on mine as well when I wasn't even getting sex out of it.

As I took my last-martini-before-certain-arrest from a nearby waiter, I found myself suddenly on the periphery of a group of people, one of whom was an old client of The Agency. She spotted me at once.

"Elizabeth, right?" she asked.

"Hi, Jessica." I smiled.

The group of four people surrounding her looked curious for a moment, she was after all a Hollywood doyenne, until she added, "Elizabeth was my agent's assistant." Then all their interest beat a hasty retreat. I smiled politely and was about to try to make my escape when it seemed I'd arrived in the middle of a story. And a tragic one at that.

"I was just saying that I'm feeling terrible today." Jessica, who was more renowned as a star with a constellation of husbands than as a great actress, was clearly channeling Laurence Olivier tonight, because the emotion was almost heartfelt. "Last night I got a phone call at midnight telling me that my oldest, dearest friend, Patrick, had died of a heart attack."

"Poor you." The man beside her touched her arm.

"No warning, just dropped dead." She choked back a tear.

"Was he in the business?" someone else asked.

"He was a director." Jessica sniffled.

"I'm sorry," I said. And while the group all looked mournful, I made my excuses and ran toward the cloakroom, where Lara was gathering her coat.

"Ready?" she asked as she dropped a couple of dollar bills into the cloakroom attendant's dish.

"Wait, we don't have to go." I almost skidded across the floor and stopped a few inches from her face.

"What do you mean? You're not going to tell me how much you love Jason again, are you? Because this isn't about Jason, it's now about that strumpet Carmen in there who just asked me when my next baby is due," Lara sneered.

"No, no. I have a great idea," I said.

"Yes?" Lara tried in vain to make her coat buttons meet their buttonholes.

"Jessica has a friend who died last night of a heart attack," I said, as if this was all the information that Lara would need.

"Yes?" She squinted at me.

"I thought that the dead guy might have been invited to the *Vanity Fair* party, and if he was, then maybe we can ask Jessica if I could have his ticket," I blurted out without taking a breath.

"You what?" Lara was looking at me as if I was mad.

"Well, he's dead. I'm sure he wouldn't want his ticket to go to waste," I said, my shoulders suddenly sinking. It had seemed like a good idea a minute ago; Jessica liked me, she'd have been sympathetic to my plight if I'd told her. But then again maybe not.

I delved into my bag instead and rifled through it to find my cloak-room ticket. It was only when Lara dashed off to say good-bye to Scott that I sensed that I wasn't alone. That someone was standing close behind me. I turned around and saw Luke Lloyd standing with his arms folded, resting against the wall, watching me intently, looking painfully beautiful. I scrolled back over the last thirty seconds in my mind. He hadn't heard me talking about taking the dead man's ticket had he? Please God. *I will never again even contemplate profiting from another's misfortune.* Luke smiled and raised his eyebrow knowingly.

"If you want to go to the party that badly, I'd be happy to take you."

TWENTY-THREE

You can take all the sincerity in Hollywood, place it in the navel of a firefly and still have enough room for three caraway seeds and a producer's heart.

—Fred Allen

It had taken all my powers of persuasion, not to mention a modicum of emotional blackmail, to persuade Luke that he should be my date for the Award Ceremony.

"It's the least I can do," I told him on the phone the next morning, as I had my toenails buffed, for free, in the Beauty Boudoir at the Chateau Marmont. "You're taking me to the *Vanity Fair* party, so I'll take you to the awards."

"Don't worry, I'll just meet you at Morton's afterward," Luke said in a measured voice. I wondered if I'd overstepped the mark. He had, after all, merely saved me from the jaws of potentially one of the worst cases of Oscar Fever that Hollywood might ever have seen. It wasn't as if he'd asked me on a date, I had to keep reminding myself.

"Sure. I understand," I said, backing off. "I just wanted to reciprocate the favor." Did that sound impartial enough, I wondered?

"It's not that I don't want to come, just that, well . . ." Luke was struggling to remain diplomatic.

"You have a girlfriend?" I asked, almost kicking the pedicurist in the teeth, I was so cross that the question had slipped out of my mouth.

"It's possibly the most boring ceremony on earth," Luke informed me.

"No!" I was incredulous. My pedicurist was mutinous.

"Darling, I'm afraid so." Luke sounded instantly guilty for popping my bubble. "But hey, I mean, you're nominated. It's never going to be boring if you're nominated."

"I know." I sighed as quietly as possible. "I just thought that you might want to share the night with me because it's . . . well, it's my big night. . . . But then why would you? I mean, it's really kind of you to take me to the party but . . . it's not as if I'm a part of your life or anything anymore, is it?" I added, with no desire to manipulate. It was the plain truth. And I don't think I'd told Luke the truth in a while. The pedicurist forgave me and added an extra topcoat because I was so pitiful.

"I wouldn't miss it for the world," Luke finally conceded.

"I don't want you to be bored," I protested, hiding my elation.

"I'll be fascinated from start to finish," Luke promised sweetly. "I'll even stay awake for foreign makeup artist and best Russian animation."

I wanted to say, "I love you," but instead I said, "Thank you."

Of course I was a long way off from being certain that anything was going to happen between Luke and me. Clearly he'd forgiven me for my vile lies about Emanuelle and clearly he wasn't married to her, or even going out with her anymore. But that didn't mean that he wasn't dating up a storm with a hundred other women like Amazing Grace. And most significantly, it didn't mean that he wanted me to be his girlfriend ever again, even if he lived to be 148. But no matter how tenuous our date was, and how likely it was to be based solely on goodwill to all nominees, just like the free salt scrub I was about to receive, I was still excited, and suddenly longing to look my best tonight, not for the billion viewers but for Luke Lloyd.

When Luke arrived at the door of the guesthouse that afternoon I looked quite *Sunset Boulevard*. Someone named Kevin had put so much makeup on me in the Beauty Boudoir that I might as well have been wearing a burka, the real me was so obscured from view. Kevin had instructed me that three inches of foundation was obligatory if I didn't want to look washed-out under the lights. When I opened my door it was all I could hope that Luke didn't think I was washed-up.

"Lizzie." He kissed me politely on the cheek and stood back for the full effect. "You look . . . lovely."

"Do you have a flashlight?" I asked as I smoothed the satin of my dress self-consciously over my hips.

"No. Why?" He was still, understandably, a bit cautious of me. I had, after all, murdered his cat and vomited a diamond on his doorstep.

"Well, you need one to see how I'm supposed to look, I think," I explained. "Apparently it'll all make sense under tungsten lamps."

"Can't wait." He laughed. "So have you lived here since . . . ?"

"Since we broke up?" I filled in the blank. "Yeah. Lara and Scott have been great, but it's a little small." I flung my arm out to illustrate my point and bashed my hand on the wardrobe door.

"I'm surprised you didn't get a place of your own," Luke said, doubtless taking in the fact that I ate all my meals with Lara and the baby and every time I wanted to so much as buy a newspaper I had to walk through their house.

"It's a bit retarded, I admit, but I do have a deposit on a place by the beach, it's just not ready yet," I said as I fixed the clasp on my purse and took a final look at what was supposed to be me, but in fact seemed to be someone else, in the mirror.

"Are you still in the same place?" I asked Luke as he smiled appreciatively at me.

"I'm in a very different place, actually." He winked. "And for the record, you look amazing."

"Really?" I was genuinely surprised. It had been such a long time since a man noticed the way I looked. Jason certainly had only ever noticed the way other women looked.

"Yes." Luke nodded. "And I'm proud to be accompanying a real-life Oscar nominee to the party."

"Oh God, I am, aren't I?" I realized for the four thousandth time, but was still unable to take in the fact. I took Luke's arm as I navigated the cracks in the garden path.

"I'd sell my soul to Beelzebub for a nomination," Luke said as he slowed down to my tortoise-in-a-tight-dress-and-five-inch-heels pace.

"You've never been nominated?" I asked. "That's so weird cause it feels as if you should have been. I mean you're so important and influential and . . ."

"We're not going to start that again, are we?" Luke grimaced mischievously as we walked through the house. There was no sign of Lara or Scott so I assumed that Lara was putting Lachlan down for a nap and Scott was blow-drying his hair before they went off to watch the ceremony at a party at George's house.

"Wow, I'd almost forgotten how sore I used to feel about how people never took notice of me when you were around. Maybe I'll get my own back tonight." I nudged him as I gracelessly got into the waiting limo. Luke had driven over in his station wagon and the car I ordered a month ago was waiting outside, which made me feel more princesslike than I'd ever felt in my life.

"Ah, that's why you wanted me to come? In fact, is that why you got yourself nominated? Because revenge is a dish best served cold and you wanted me to come along and suffer the way you suffered when we were together?" He laughed as he climbed in beside me.

I looked at Luke when he said this and felt an unidentifiable sensation in my stomach. This man and I used to "be together." We used to share the same bed and cook dinner for each other and go to the market together and I used to put his dirty laundry in the washing machine and we used to argue and share secrets. And now I didn't know him. I had gone from knowing what he did almost every hour of every day to not knowing whether he'd been to the moon and back in the last six months. I felt decidedly nauseous. I think because I knew immediately that I still loved him.

Even though I thought that Luke and I had left plenty of time to get to the Kodak Theatre and it was a Sunday evening, I hadn't anticipated just how many people were heading to the Academy Awards. As we drove along Highland, we suddenly found ourselves bumper-to-bumper in a limo jam. So in an attempt to pass the time without discussing "our relationship," and a bid to stave off the fear that we actually might miss the entire ceremony due to traffic, we reached into the underwhelming Oscar box in the back of our car and found some warm champagne to pass the time.

"You're not allowed to get drunk, though," Luke informed me as he filled my plastic champagne flute to the very brim.

"Why not?" I took a sip and the bubbles made my eyes water.

"Just the small matter of a speech if you win."

"I'm not going to win." I laughed. "Anyway, it's Jason's movie and Jason's speech. I don't get to say anything."

"If you win and don't say a word your parents are going to disown you. And so will I," he said firmly.

"Thanks, now you've just added a whole new level of fear to my day. Not only might I trip on my dress or go into a trance and get up and collect the award for Best Actor by mistake, but now I have to speak in front of a billion people. Honestly, why do people actually want to win awards?" I asked, genuinely perplexed.

"Just say thank you to the Academy and thank you to the team," Luke said. "As long as you don't go into the list of dead relatives and grade-school teachers, you'll be fine."

"Thank you to the Academy and thank you to the team?" I asked dubiously. Then, after some hard thought, I said, "No, it's too long. I'll never remember it."

Half an hour later, after polishing off the better part of a bottle of champagne, we finally drew up outside the theater.

"Identification please, miss," the heat-packing security guard who opened our car door demanded before we'd even emerged into the afternoon sunshine. Luke and I handed over our IDs and stepped out of the car. So much for a smooth vehicular exit, a stroll down the red carpet amid the flashbulbs of the paparazzi. In fact we barely got to walk on anything other than sidewalk. The red carpet was reserved for the stars and TV presenters of all denominations and hair color and we were constantly ushered out of the way of people we hadn't heard of since the John Hughes movies of our childhood; the so-called paparazzi flashbulbs were in fact simply fake flashes of light to make the whole thing look more glamorous to TV viewers, because only a very select few photographers were granted entrance to the inner sanctum for security reasons. Then, when we finally reached the door of the theater without seeing a single star or being adored by a single fan, we were subjected to metal detectors, sniffer dogs, and body searches. After which we were plunged into the dark cavity of the theater foyer, away from flashbulbs, stars, and any other form of light.

Luke and I had been planning to meet up with Jason and Carmen in the foyer but as we circulated we became so overwhelmed by the sheer volume of famous faces that we started to feel as if we were just wandering around Madame Tussauds wax museum on a rainy New York Saturday afternoon.

"Shall we just go in and take our seats?" I asked Luke as we passed Robin Williams for the eighteenth time and the security guards probably put out an APB to watch out for "those two people who nobody has a clue who they are."

"We're going to be sitting down for three hours as it is," Luke said skeptically.

Thankfully, we didn't have to make that decision because the next moment we ran into Jason.

"Hey guys," he said. "How are you doing? Not too nervous, huh, Lizzie?" I was surprised that Jason wasn't his usual nervous, monosyllabic self, in fact, seeing him was just the boost I was looking for. I suddenly felt that compared to him I had nothing to be worried about. Best case scenario, I wasn't going to have to make three acceptance speeches tonight and worst case scenario, I wasn't going to be nominated three times and win nothing. Either way, I was in the money. Also, no matter what happened, he was my partner in crime and we were in this together.

"A little," I replied, looking around to see where Carmen was. Perhaps giving Russell and the boys a warm-up lap dance on the stage before proceedings began, I guessed. "I'm glad you're here."

"Me too, honey." Jason hugged me warmly, "Oh, and by the way, this is Paige," he said as the cute blond from the other night appeared and smiled at us.

"Nice to meet you, Paige." I shook her hand and could tell by Jason's smile that she was good news. But before we could get to chat with her, an announcement came over the loudspeaker that we were to begin to take our seats in the auditorium.

As we all got caught up in the melee, I managed to ask Jason a few discreet questions.

"What happened to Carmen?" I whispered as we entered the auditorium and saw the distinctly unspectacular stage, certainly the Oscars was a well-lit event because in real life it all looked depressingly shabby.

"She met Bob Evans at Daniel's party last night and she's coming as his date."

"Of course she is." I laughed. Carmen was perfect for Bob Evans, she'd have the time of her life, and he'd get his ticket's worth out of her in every sense of the word. Plus, I guessed that when she wasn't stealing your boyfriend or your party invitations, she might even be construed as a hot up-and-comer with a certain joie de vivre.

"And so you and Paige . . . ?" I tried to be discreet.

"I haven't seen her for five years," he said. "We used to date in high school and then she went to study zoology. I run into her every so often cause she works as a consultant on these great wildlife documentaries. But we haven't both been single at the same time, ever."

"That's amazing," I said, though of course Jason wasn't strictly single, ever. There were always at least three dates with other girls pending, even when I'd been his girlfriend. But that was a technicality.

"So, do you have your speeches prepared?" I asked as we headed for a woman with a guest list whose job it was to point us to our seats.

"Oh sure, I've had them prepared since I was seven," Jason said confidently. "And I cut the bottom of my new shoes with a key so that when I go up onstage to collect them, I don't slip."

"Good to be prepared." I laughed as he gave the woman our names and Luke and Paige looked on and chatted with each other.

Our seats were surprisingly far back, leading me to conclude that we definitely hadn't won anything because how on earth were we to get to the stage from there? For sure our rival nominees were closer to the lectern, and certain success. At which point I decided to relax a little and take a sip from the hip flask that my father had sent to me as a congratulations present and instructed me to fill with "nothing younger than a thirty-year-old scotch."

"Oh my God, that's us," I said as I noticed that my seat and Jason's had large pieces of paper on the backs of them, not only with our names but also with our photographs.

"Cool," said Jason, who for once was being so much more relaxed than me. Obviously Paige had a good effect on him.

"Oh," I said as we got closer and rejoined ranks with Luke and Paige, "It's not me."

"Oh," said Paige.

"Oh," said Jason.

"Ooops," said Luke. It was in fact a picture of a woman of about sixty with blond hair and a lipless smile but with my name printed out underneath.

"I always knew it was too good to be true." I laughed. "I wasn't nominated after all, was I? She's some veteran producer and I got the care package from Universal by mistake 'cause there are two of us listed on IMDb."

"Oh well," said Luke as we moved our bits of cardboard and took our seats, "anything for a free drink."

"Exactly. Not to mention some very expensive minishampoos, the loan of a pretty dress, and a free haircut," I said as we sat down. Wanting to add "a chance to win over my ex-boyfriend again" but deciding instead that discretion was definitely the better part of not making a total ass of myself.

The purpose of the big pieces of card apparently was so that the cameras knew where Jason and I were sitting so that when our nominations were announced they could flash us onto all those TV screens from Connecticut to China, so seat-switching with someone prettier than oneself, in order that everyone you were in high school with thinks you morphed from an ugly duckling to a swan wasn't advisable, either, in case they saw your card and busted you.

Luke, sensing that the reality of the billion viewers was beginning to dawn on me, took my hand—sadly more like a father than a lover, but right now the needle on my adrenaline-o-meter was right in the red so this was probably all I could handle. The auditorium was filling up at a rapid rate now and there was a mounting excitement in the room. The front rows were laden with the AAA list and last-minute sound checks were being carried out onstage. The cast and crew of *Sex Addicts in Love,* who now felt like family because we'd all hung out together so much in the last month, were starting to take their seats around us, and a party atmosphere began to take hold.

"Lizzie," I heard a familiar voice squeak behind me, "Howyadoing?" I didn't need to turn around to know that it was Emerald. I got up from my seat and crushed Jason to greet her.

"Emerald!" I cried. I was delighted to see another friendly face. In fact, two friendly faces—Jizzy was standing beside her and looking very happy. Or was that just the glow of spiritual satisfaction, I wondered, as I noticed his glazed expression beneath his cowboy hat. "You're looking amazing," I told her truthfully. And she was. Admittedly there was something of the fifties housewife about her, with an Alice band in her hair, a shiny-apple glow in her cheeks, and a dress that my mother might wear to visit her bank manager, but the overall result was so stunning that if one didn't know she was in the advanced stages of religious conversion she would definitely be purveying the hottest and latest look of the night.

"You too." She hugged me warmly as Jizzy stared dreamily in the direction of Tom Cruise a few rows in front of us.

"Well, marriage is definitely agreeing with you," I remarked,

"I know, it's great." She turned around to check that Jizzy couldn't overhear. "I'm meeting Colin Farrell in the bathroom during Best Foreign Film," she confided. "I can't wait."

"Oh!" I said in surprise as I noticed her high, almost-Victorian neckline.

"You're wondering about the Amish virgin look, right?" She laughed when I nodded.

"Actually, I was."

"The boys think it's so hot. I get laid way more in these clothes than I ever used to. And being married is such a turn-on for other guys. I tell you, I get more action than . . . well, than my action-hero husband."

"Great!" I laughed as a be-clipboarded man approached with a stern expression. "You guys better run to your seats. But I'll see you soon."

"We'll have tea after church one day." She winked wickedly, then took her husband's arm as they made their way to their seats in the front row before the lights in the auditorium dimmed.

Yet despite the amusement of running into Emerald and seeing the cast and crew and having Jason with a date I might actually like to be friends with, in the main, Luke had been right. The ceremony was at least six years long and less stimulating, I imagined, than one of Emerald's new church services. In fact, the most exciting moment was watching Emerald get up halfway through, wink to Colin Farrell, then emerge from the bathroom twenty minutes later with two mother-of-pearl buttons missing and beard burn. But then I guess beard burn is what you get if you marry a gay man.

The rest of the ceremony was punctuated by the short nap I got during the costume and makeup awards and then the sadness of watching the roll call of greats who'd died in the last year. I always find this bit pretty sobering, even at home when I'm painting my toenails and only half paying attention—seeing these extraordinary people, some of whom you assumed had died years ago and many you hadn't even noticed had died—flash up on the screen in their carefree heyday. But that sentiment is made all the more meaningful when it's shown before a group of people who often believe that they function in an industry that can somehow cheat the inevitable things in life—poverty, reality, old age—who then start to realize that death just might be waiting in the wings.

After what felt like the four millionth time I'd put my hands together to clap that evening, it almost came as a shock when the ceremony began to wrap up. Suddenly it felt as if there was a race to get all the good bits into the remaining half hour of the evening. Jason, sadly but not surprisingly, had missed out on the Best Original Screenplay award earlier on, but we'd still all whooped with delight when his face was shown on the television broadcast. But now they had to fit the big nuggets into the end of the show. Best Director and then Best Motion Picture. Of course, I suddenly decided that I was bursting to go to the bathroom only seconds before Best Director was due to be announced, but when I told Jason that I might run off quickly he gave me such a look of terror that I knew I was just going to have to cross my legs.

"I need you Lizzie," he said, crushing my fingers until the tips were white. "You're the only one who understands. Fuck, why did I ever make a movie? This is too much stress; it feels like my hair is going white at the roots."

"You made it so that you can be the youngest director ever nominated," I said in such a tone as to remind him that he was the biggest idiot ever nominated, too, if he had to ask that question. "Oh, and because the studio might give you a million-dollar bonus if you break a hundred million dollars."

"It's true," he said, as a huge smile washed over his face. "But you're still not allowed to pee until it's over."

"Okay," I grudgingly agreed, with fear in my heart as to how long the line for the Ladies was going to be when the ceremony was over. One thing I had learned in my time in Hollywood—celebrities use the bathroom way more than lesser mortals—though their motivations are often different—snorting, vomiting, and vanity being more popular than peeing among their ranks, I imagined, which really only made the line even longer in my experience.

When the nominations were announced for Best Director, Jason turned an unearthly shade of green. This, I discovered, was why Kevin the makeup fascist had insisted on the scaffolding of foundation that helped me look normal no matter what I was feeling. I wondered if they had put a

PLEASE DO NOT ADJUST YOUR SETS

notice on television screens worldwide when Jason's peculiarly colored face flashed up. He grinned the grin of Skeletor as the names were read out and kept his teeth firmly clenched when it was announced that he wasn't the most talented director on the planet, after all.

"Oh well, it's been a fun ride," he finally said through a frozen jaw as the winning director made his epic-length speech.

"It's not over," I reminded him. "You've got to grin and bear it one more time."

"I think my teeth might break." He sighed. I don't even think he was disappointed, he was just on some insane adrenaline roller coaster that he still wasn't allowed to get off, and he was simply very spun out.

"Okay, here we go." Luke leaned over and took my hand as Jon Stewart announced the last award of the evening, and the biggest of them all, Best Motion Picture. And it all happened so quickly and was so surreal that I didn't even hear *Sex Addicts in Love* called out. I just stared blindly ahead at the stage. I also didn't hear when Dustin Hoffman pulled the piece of paper out of the envelope and read out our names, "Jason Blum and Elizabeth Miller."

I did, though, feel a tug on my hand as Jason tried to pull me to my feet. In fact, it was only when Luke leaned over, kissed me on the cheek, and quite firmly said, "Darling, you gotta get up and collect your award." He stood up and helped me to my feet as the audience drowned out any thoughts I might be having, so I just focused on what Luke was saying to me and tried to follow instructions. "Now walk up there as slowly as you like and don't forget to enjoy yourself."

When I watched the footage later I looked like the most miserable person ever to receive an Oscar in the history of the Academy Awards. Now I knew why Halle and Gwyneth shed tears—it was a truly harrowing experience. In those torturous moments absolutely nothing went through my mind apart from putting one foot in front of the other, not getting my dress caught under my shoes, and not falling on my ass as I made my way across the highly polished stage floor. I forgot to kiss Dustin Hoffman or even to thank him as Jason and I found ourselves staring at tier upon tier of people who'd never heard of us but who were clapping madly nonetheless, and waiting for words of brilliance, or even simply English, from us. We stood and stared ahead, Jason clutched his Oscar as if it was a stick of dynamite and an army of thousands was advancing with spears in our direction. He had no clue what to do with it and no clue what to say. I simply hid behind Jason.

Thankfully, Jason found his voice before he threw the Oscar into the audience and ducked.

"I-I-I-I can't believe this." Jason held his award aloft. "I gotta say, well, thank you, and well, I've known what I was going to say when I got up here since I was seven years old, but now I have no idea what it was. Apart from thank you. To the Academy, to my parents, to Elizabeth Miller, the most loyal producing partner I could wish for." Jason put his arm around me and I could feel his entire body shaking. "To the cast and crew of my movie, to Universal Studios, to my agents Katherine Watson and Scott Wagner, the tutors at UCLA, in fact to everyone who was ever nice to me. Thank you. I love you. More than you'll ever know." Jason somehow managed to say all this on one lungful of air and then collapsed as sweat poured down his face.

Which left me with possibly the most split-second decision of my entire life—the Hamlet of decisions again. I chose To Speak.

"To win this precious award was beyond our wildest dreams when we began working on *Sex Addicts in Love,* but we always hoped it would find the appreciation it deserved, and for you all to have enjoyed this movie is the highest accolade we ever wished for." I heard my voice but it came from some distant galaxy. Then I clutched my Oscar to my chest and waited a full three seconds to hear the applause before Jason and I looked at Dustin Hoffman as if he were wielding Laurence Olivier's drill from *Marathon Man* and fled the stage.

It had all happened in about two and a half minutes flat. I had gone from being Lizzie Miller, erstwhile First Assistant at The Agency to Academy Award–Winning Producer Elizabeth Miller. I barely knew myself. I had no concept of the implications that this prize might have on my life from here on in. All I knew was that I needed to use the bathroom. Badly.

TWENTY-FOUR

Strip away the phoney tinsel of
Hollywood and you find the
real tinsel underneath.

—Oscar Levant

The *Vanity Fair* party was a blur. We'd briefly dropped by the Governor's
Ball and refueled and passed around our little gold men as if they were
newborn babies, but the pressure to be anywhere other than the party
you were at was intense. No sooner had we laid hands on a drink than
we were ushered by our overenthusiastic NBF publicists who told us
that to miss the eight-thirty slot at Morton's was professional suicide and
the traffic on Melrose was now so backed up that we'd be lucky to make
it there before Labor Day. So we took their advice and spent yet another
half hour of the "most memorable night of our lives" sitting in the back
of a car resisting the urge to just get out and walk.

When we eventually arrived at the hallowed party, I managed to find
Lara in the crowd, by judicious use of cell phone, and with different
celebrities as our pole stars, we made contact.

"Okay, I'm to the right of Elizabeth Hurley and south of the super
skinny one from *Desperate Housewives*!" I yelled into my phone.

"Where's that in relation to Jennifer Aniston?" Lara inquired.

"I have no clue, but, do you see Oprah?" I asked, waving at Luke who
was chatting nearby to some business acquaintances he ran into. He
smiled back at me and rolled his eyes in mock horror at being trapped.
"You must be able to see Oprah." I groaned. "She's talking to Debra
Winger."

"Okay, I see her," Lara said. "But you're not there."

"Yes I am. Here, right next to Debra."

"So not," Lara complained. "God, she looks fatter than she did in *Alien*."

"No you idiot. That was Sigourney Weaver!" I shouted so loud that Oprah turned around. "I'm here, by the buffet."

"Oh, well why didn't you just say?" Lara said, appearing at my side two and a half seconds later and helping herself to a barbecued shrimp. "You knew I wouldn't be far from the food."

But despite Lara and I having more fun than was decent for two women over sixteen, by midnight we were running out of steam. We'd seen every celebrity, even staying for the later slots of the party so we could check out the really great D-list stars who were always the most interesting anyway because they were the ones you had hung in your locker at school; the ones your parents would be most excited to hear about; and the ones most likely to smile at you and chat if you told them how much you loved X movie or Y TV show that they'd been in.

We'd also tried every single cocktail on the menu, we'd done as many things as it was publicly decent to do with an Oscar statuette— including using it as a back-scratcher and a Liberty torch—Lara had managed to lose Scott, and I had managed to avoid dancing with Bob the Producer, whom I'd made the mistake of going on a date with when I first arrived in town. Back then he had spiked my drink in a bid to have sex with me and videotape it. Bob's tape collection was more prolific even than Rob Lowe's back in the eighties. He'd even had special labels printed up with his own Bob logo. When he sidled up to me earlier and offered me a fizzy Mojito, I had grabbed Lara's hand and escaped to the dance floor. In short, we'd exhausted the party and ourselves by the time our carriage was due to turn into a pumpkin. But we really weren't ready to admit that it was time to go home.

Luke came up behind me and touched my arm. "Honey, I'm going to head off." I was leaning back staring at the remains of the party, with tissue paper peeling off the pillar behind me and blisters on my feet, my bedraggled hair sticking to my tired lipgloss.

"Already?" I turned to him.

"It's pretty late," he said gently. I must have looked as if I was about to burst into tears because he quickly added, "If you like I can drop you off at Patrick's party. This one's done but I'm sure his is just starting.

And there's a swimming pool. I think it's traditional to swim in your party dress if you win an Oscar, right?"

"Is it?" I cheered up immediately. Hurray! There was life after *Vanity Fair*.

"That's what I heard," Luke assured me.

"Great. Well, I'd love a ride in that case." I perked up. "I've just got to find Lara to say good-bye," I said, scouring the balding party for my friend.

"Oh, she left with Scott a while ago," Luke told me as we headed toward the door, where Jason was helping Paige into her jacket.

"But if it's any consolation, she didn't look too happy about leaving. I think I heard the word 'divorce' mentioned."

"Hmmm." I pondered. "Then maybe I'll let her off the hook for not saying good-bye. Hey, Jason?" I said as we approached him.

"Good-night, sweetie," he said, raising his Oscar in lieu of a wave. (Use number 583 for an Academy Award.) "Congratulations, my coproducer." He hugged me.

"Are you going to Luke's friend Patrick's party?" I asked, certain that I had at least one person who would jump into the pool with me at dawn, even if it wasn't Lara or Luke.

"Oh, we're going home. We're going to celebrate in private." Jason kissed me on the cheek. "We've got a lot of catching up to do."

"Well," I said, trying to hide my disappointment like an Oscar winner, "it was lovely to meet you, Paige," I said and gave her a kiss goodnight, too. "Maybe see you soon?"

"Definitely," Jason assured me as he and Paige headed out and jumped into the back of a waiting limo and began to kiss like teenagers. As it happened that was the last limo we saw all night.

Luke and I had been standing outside Morton's for twenty minutes, at the back of a line many-drunk-people long, when we decided that unless we wanted to watch the sun come up here, we were going to have to walk.

"We can't walk back to Lara and Scott's," I told him as I looked down reluctantly at my shoes. "It's miles."

"We could go to mine and I could give you a lift—" Luke began, then remembered—"but my car's at your place."

"Hmmm," I thought. "Well, I guess you could give me a piggyback to yours and then we could call a taxi."

"Sure." He smiled gamely. "Hop on board."

"Okay." I removed my heels, transferred them to my hand, and held on tight to Oscar.

"One two three hup." Luke bent down and I attached myself to his back like an ancient, battered barnacle. Minutes later we were walking away from the party along Melrose, as the people in the limo line broke into a round of applause. It was much sweeter music to my ears even than the Oscar cheers had been. I was on Luke Lloyd's back and he was carrying me home.

Oh well, a girl can dream. Two blocks later he was groaning so much that I stopped using my statuette as a riding crop. "Okay, you can let me off if you're too much of a wimp," I said as he ground to a grateful halt.

"I'm sorry." He huffed as I slid to the floor.

"You know I'm going to get a complex about my weight and it'll be all your fault," I teased him as he shook out his numb arms.

"It's not you, it's the Oscar," he said.

"It's not you, it's me." I laughed. "Wasn't that what you said when we broke up?"

"I did not!" Luke sounded incredulous as we walked side by side along the deserted street, with only the occasional car speeding by. "I would never have been so lame."

"You were," I informed him.

"Well, I guess I was lame enough to break up with you, so anything's possible," he said, shaking his head in disbelief.

"Do you think it was lame, really?" I stopped in my tracks.

"Come on, Elizabeth Miller, we're not having this conversation now. Or here. We're going home. We've still got two miles to go."

"Why not?" I protested. "Just tell me one thing. Do you really think you made a mistake?"

"Go." He laughed as he smacked me on the backside. "Move."

"Spoilsport," I complained as we strode along at an ungodly pace up the hill to Lookout Mountain.

Finally Luke and I arrived back at his house, our aching feet forgotten in all the laughing and talking we'd done and spying in people's houses and wondering which we'd most like to live in.

"Oh no, your porch." I winced as I flashed back to the last night I'd been there. "Did you ever find that diamond?"

"No," Luke said forlornly as he put the key in the lock.

"I bet Mrs. Mendes found it." I sniffed. "Has she been dressing better lately? Showing up for work in a Porsche?"

"You're so mean to Mrs. Mendes." He laughed.

"I bet she told you about the time she found me and Jason in bed together."

"Well . . ." He shrugged as we piled through the front door into the familiar room, the smell of beeswax and detergent mingling with the magnolia blossom outside on his veranda. I almost swooned I breathed in so deeply. "She did mention that you had been less than faithful to me."

"No? But you know I wasn't, don't you? You know that I had all my clothes on and wouldn't have wanted Jason if he'd . . . well, even if he'd been you." I rushed to get through the sentence.

"Well, that's a compliment . . . I think." Luke laughed to dismiss the subject. "Of course I know it wasn't what it seemed. Though I have to say when you and Blum became an item later, it crossed my mind," he said.

But before I could scream I looked at him and saw that he was grinning evilly. He just knew that I wasn't interested in Jason when I was with him. In fact, I wasn't really interested in Jason when I was with Jason.

"Now what can I get you to drink?" He walked over to his drinks table and studied the bottles carefully.

"Not champagne," I stipulated. "Anything but champagne."

"Okay, tequila it is." He reached for a couple of shot glasses, then wandered into the kitchen to find a lemon while I sat on the edge of his familiar moss green armchair and examined my feet.

"I'm turning on the pool lights in case you want to get traditional!" he shouted from the back of the house somewhere.

"Great!" I yelled. I guess he wasn't calling me a taxi just yet, then.

While Luke pottered around the poolside, I reached into my purse and checked my cell phone. I had twenty-eight missed calls.

"Shit." I groaned. I had of course called my parents and sister from the bathroom at Morton's as soon as I'd arrived. I'd then been passed on to my grandmother, three cousins, and a grade-school teacher I'd forgotten existed but who was very sweet in her congratulations and delighted because, well, "based on your drawings we were never sure that you weren't going to end up a social misfit," she told me. I thanked her and told her that's exactly what a producer was and how smart of her to notice all those years ago. My parents, of course, were in tears and my grandmother kept asking what Rita Hayworth was like. They were all coming to visit me and Oscar in a couple of weeks, so I didn't feel too bad that they hadn't been able to make it here for the ceremony owing to granny's new hip.

I scrolled through the text messages, saving most of them for later, apart from the one from Cingular Wireless telling me that I was over my monthly spending limit; that one I deleted recklessly. Then I picked up the voice mail. Lots of party sounds and incomprehensible shrieking; I guessed these were from Alexa, my old neighbor, Talitha, and assorted other friends. But among those was a remarkably sober-sounding one, with no party interference in the background. I had to play it twice before I heard it. At which point Luke walked back into the room.

"What are you looking so serious for?" he said as he set down two shot glasses, a saucer of salt, and some lemon slices on the coffee table,

"I'm not sure," I said, staring at my phone. "Will you listen to this and tell me what it says? I think my brain's so overstimulated it's stopped functioning."

"I'm listening." Luke perched on the edge of the table opposite me as I switched my cell to speakerphone.

"Hello, Elizabeth, this is Elspeth Cowan. I just wanted to congratulate you on tonight's success. Your speech was wonderful. I also wanted to be the first person to offer you a job." Luke looked at me and raised one eyebrow. "I'd like to make a formal offer on Monday, but in the meantime I'd be delighted if you'd consider accepting the post of president of production with the studio."

I turned the cell off and Luke looked at me in faint disbelief.

"That was Elspeth Cowan," he said, as if I hadn't a clue who she was. "CEO of the studio."

"I know," I said, with similar skepticism.

"She wants you to be president."

"I know."

"That's . . ." Luke struggled to find the word.

"Unbelievable?" I still couldn't connect with my brain. Somewhere along the way tonight I'd been short-circuited.

"It calls for a celebration," Luke said, but similarly without a hint of celebration in his voice. We were both confounded.

"I know." I reached over and doused the back of my hand in salt before closing my eyes and pouring the tequila down my throat. It burned. Luke followed suit.

"So you'll be running a studio. You'll be the prexy."

"I'll be the prexy," I repeated.

"Luke?" I asked as I bit my lip in concentration.

"Yes?" He frowned.

"That's pretty weird, isn't it?"

"It is, yes." Luke admitted.

It was several minutes before Luke and I managed to shake off the reverie of contemplation that we'd been plunged into by Elspeth's message. When we finally lifted our heads from our prayerful poses and looked at each other it was still with a sense of unreality. I had been fired from my job as First Assistant, even if it had been erroneous, and when my job was offered back to me, I'd turned it down. I had coexecutive-produced a movie, which meant that I had found agents and talked numbers and budgets and all that jazz before Jason had stitched me up when he finally made his deal with the studio. And then I had been reinstated. But that didn't mean that I could run a studio. I had been a political intern in D.C. for about five minutes.

"I guess you won an Academy Award," Luke said by way of explanation.

"I did," I said and cast my eyes over at Oscar who had his own place on the sofa.

"Shall we go for a swim?" Luke asked as he poured us a couple more tequilas.

"I guess we should," I said, and Luke and I downed our tequilas, and I felt the fire race down my throat again. Then we looked at each other and high-fived.

"Race you!" I shouted as I hitched up my dress, grabbed Oscar, and pushed Luke out of the way as I dashed toward the swimming pool.

"Hey!" he yelled, coming up behind me fast. "Not fair."

The next thing I knew we were in the deep end of his pool and my satin, floor-length dress, which I had to return by noon tomorrow, was trailing like a mermaid's tail through the water. Oscar was watching from the side. Luke had stripped down to his shorts and was splashing beside me.

"Luke, I'm going to be the prexy of the studio!" I screamed over the sound of water.

"Congratulations, baby!" Luke shouted, then ducked under the surface and swam underneath me. I tried to escape but the next thing I knew he was right beside me, breathless and brushing his sodden hair off his face.

"I'm really happy for you," he said as he took me by the hand and swam a little closer to the side of the pool.

"Thanks." I grabbed on to the side of the pool with one hand.

"Do you think this means, now that you're more successful than I am, that you might be able to come to dinner with me sometime?"

"Dinner?" I said, a slow smile breaking over my lips.

"Or lunch? If you think dinner's a little . . . you know . . . ?"

"Forward?"

"Exactly," he said.

"I'd love to have lunch with you," I said as I took my hand off the side of the pool and put it around the back of his neck. My feet weren't touching the bottom and my dress was heavy in the water, so I had to cling to him a little more than I'd anticipated to stay afloat.

"Great," Luke said as he looked me in the eye for a second too long and then leaned in to kiss me. "I've got myself a date with the prexy."

"I'll put it in my diary." I kissed him back this time. "But you have to promise me one thing?"

"What's that?" Luke asked as he absentmindedly wiped some drops of water off my cheek.

"That you're not even going to *think* about sleeping your way to the top, Luke Lloyd." I laughed as he held me up in the water and began to kiss my neck, with Oscar looking on.

"I promise," Luke said. "Anything to make the prexy happy."